Elizabeth Garner was born in C London, where she works as a script editor. This is her first novel.

'An evocative and haunting tale of obsession' *Bookseller*

'Imaginatively told' *Big Issue in the North*

'An enchanting relationships novel about love questioned and love lost' *Publishing News*

# NIGHTDANCING

## ELIZABETH GARNER

review

First published in 2003
by REVIEW

An imprint of Headline Book Publishing

First published in paperback in 2004

10 9 8 7 6 5 4 3 2 1

British Library Cataloguing in Publication Data
is available from the British Library

ISBN 0 7553 0252 4

Typeset in Adobe Caslon by Avon Dataset Ltd, Bidford-on-Avon, Warwickshire
Design © Griselda Greaves

Papers and cover board used by Headline are natural, recyclable products
made from wood grown in sustainable forests. The manufacturing processes
conform to the environmental regulations of the country of origin.

Printed and bound in Great Britain by
Clays Ltd, St Ives plc

Headline Book Publishing
A division of Hodder Headline
338 Euston Road
London NW1 3BH

www.reviewbooks.co.uk
www.hodderheadline.com

*For Neil and Steve*

# ACKNOWLEDGEMENTS

Writing is a long and lonely process, and my heartfelt thanks go out to the people who have been there throughout: Anne Batz, Sam Heath, Alix Heywood, Duncan Noltingk, Ken Anderson, Jam Heywood, Joe Garner, Gilbert Greaves. Your gentle support and good humour was invaluable.

Thanks also to all those who opened up their homes to give me space and time to write. Without you, this book would not exist: Ben Haggarty and Waz, John and Rachael Mitchinson, Liz Heywood, Chris and Linda Davis, Graeme and Anna Williams.

Thank you to my agents, Sarah Ballard and Simon Trewin, for their constant faith and enthusiasm. Thank you to Mary-Anne Harrington, for meticulous editing, and astounding patience.

Thank you to the teachers who showed me what words could do: Lesley Ashworth, Peter Holmes and Helen Cooper.

And, of course, thanks to my parents, for never discouraging me from making things up.

# 1

This story has a history of false starts.

I never could tell good stories, not like her. In the early days, when she was eager to tell me everything about her past, she would tease me for my lack of stories. 'Tell me something about yourself!' she would demand, lying across the bed with her head in my lap, laughing up at me, blowing smoke in my eyes. 'Man of mystery, I know nothing about you.'

I told her I wouldn't know where to begin.

'So begin at the beginning.'

I didn't feel brave enough to tell her that she was my new beginning, that that was the whole point. And what she took for mystery was just me lying there, tongue-tied with wonder.

So if I began my story there it would never leave that room. I would say, 'In the beginning a woman walked into my life, set my heart racing and somehow stopped time. She kept the outside world at bay with her laughter, and she courted me in the dark corner of a bar with her wild smile and wicked eyes.

She pulled me out of that darkness, and after years of feeling stranded or lost at sea, all I knew was that I was being offered a safe haven and something was beginning.'

I'd never before had such a sure sense of my life beginning again as I did the night I met her. I was twenty-two years old. Before then any new beginnings had been clearly mapped out before me, through my school years, through the regimented hours of university. I thought I knew what to expect, and I expected very little from life then.

But that night changed everything and forced me to focus. There was something about her that demanded attention and made the rest of the world stop and fall away as she took my hand and we walked out of that bar and back to my room. She would not let go of my hand all the way home, even pulling the keys out of my pocket for me, saying, 'I'm not going to let go, so don't even think of asking.'

Then, once inside my grey little room, there was nothing more that needed to be said or done or thought of. Not for hours, or maybe it was days because even time fell away from us and faded into the background. When we caught hold of time again it was the end of the weekend and then it was me who was terrified to let her go, holding back stupid tears at the sight of her getting dressed.

She held me and kissed me. 'What are you so afraid of?' she said. 'This is just the beginning.'

Since that new start, time has never quite been the same. It runs backwards, trips me up with memories. Like a scratched record it skips and sticks, repeating and repeating scenes that I would rather not revisit.

In some ways this is her story, all those tales I could never tell her when she asked me. Then in other ways it is mine. A brutal attempt to stop my own history skipping rings around me, to place events in order and make time play out in a straight line again.

So, I think she would start our story in the same place: 'In the beginning there was just the two of us and the rest of the world didn't matter and no one knew and no one could find us.' Although she would say it differently, partly to tease and partly to teach. She would say something like, 'In the beginning there was a lonely boy who had never seen beauty and never known love. He was caught in a strange enchantment where he was invisible to the rest of the world. When he spoke no one ever heard his voice; when he walked into a room, no one could see him, although more sensitive folk would feel a cold wind blowing past them and wonder where it came from. After years of never hearing the kind words of another soul, the boy grew colder still and his heart froze over. But one day a beautiful princess, lost in a foreign land, found him sitting alone in the corner of a dark room. At first she thought he was just a statue, sitting there so still and silent, but when she put her hand on his, something in his pulse quickened, and slowly but surely with her tender kisses and kind words she taught his heart how to beat again . . .'

Yes, I think that's how she would begin it. She loved to retell our life together, turning it into the stuff of myths and legends.

After that first meeting, we played out our romance in the grim streets of my northern university town. I never settled in the

3

north, with its cold winds, grey skies and unfamiliar people. I'd been born and bred in London, and for the first time my accent made a difference and I felt an outsider. The university choice, as I remember, was the result of another petulant argument with my mother and, on a whim, I put the length of the country between us. It seemed the easiest and most obvious defence. It probably was. Either way, I got my just deserts: three miserable years of bad weather and bad company.

Then one weekend she came up to visit a friend. They had gone for a drink in the bar, and she found me in the corner. She said later that I looked like I had been rooted to the spot, and that she thought I must have been sitting there for ever and ever, waiting and hoping for the moment that she would come to claim me. The last three years suddenly seemed like time well spent, just sitting, waiting for that moment.

After I finished my degree we stayed in the north, desperate for a summer that never came. Every morning she woke and wished for sunshine, but always pulled back the curtains to find rain. And the dismal days weighed heavy upon her; I became claustrophobic, she got restless. It didn't suit either of us. I forced the change: 'I want to go back to London, and I want you to come with me.'

A quick decision easily made. She was staring out of the window, breathing on the glass, drawing pictures in the steam. I put my arms round her. 'Let me take you to London. Come and live with me properly –'

'– and be your love?' She smiled, drew a heart in the fog on the window, and pulled me closer. 'Are you sure?'

'Never been surer of anything in my life.'

And I hadn't.

We packed our bags in a couple of hours, got on to a train, and raced our way back down south.

Although, truth be told, that wasn't a proper beginning. Our first couple of months in London were just as grey and claustrophobic in their own way as the time we spent stranded up north. The only difference was that it was a claustrophobia I knew all too well. We went back to my mother's home in north London. An ugly modern house with bad associations and walls that were too thin. We only meant to stay for a week, but got stuck for a couple of months. Full of plans, but forever in limbo, I felt like a child again.

It proved harder than I had first thought to find somewhere that might do her justice, and to put our plans into practice. The city was too vast. We spread out the tube map in front of us: the different lines that linked up, then split away from each other were a labyrinth to her untrained eye. She said it was a true depiction of the city – all so knotted up and messy and turned in on itself.

The urban sprawl of London shocked her. My mother lived off the Holloway Road, and I could understand how the crowds could seem intimidating. She said that all the troubles of the world had taken on human form and were running riot on every street corner, and she would not risk venturing out of the front door. Instead she would spend her afternoons in my mother's back garden, soaking up the sunshine left over from the end of the summer, smoking spliffs, poring over street maps, tube maps, only able to cope with the city in two dimensions. Even then, the scale of the place was a shock.

'It's like a different world,' she said, wide-eyed with wonder and fear. 'It's like you've taken me into a different world.' I laughed and told her it'd be fine, she'd find her London legs in no time.

She said she wasn't sure that was what she wanted. 'But I do know I want you,' she said.

She had come into the city to be with me. It was quite a sacrifice.

She had grown up in a village where the fields rippled with corn and, from what I could gather, the sun always smiled down and it was possible, if you had a fine day and strong determination, to walk to the sea. She had photographs of herself striding through the long reeds, her hair caught up in a scarf, a cigarette in one hand and a can in the other, grinning back at the camera. Confident in her teenage years.

She was gentler when I met her, so it never occurred to me that I might be asking something that was too hard, for her to tear herself away from a place she loved so much. It was a conflict that I could not understand. For me, anything outside London was a disappointment. I always found wide open spaces difficult. I needed parks with borders I could see. Fences and edges made things clearer. I was most comfortable walking through cluttered chaotic streets.

The city was a touchstone, a place I knew, and on my return I found myself walking those north London streets of my childhood with an unshakeable grin. The urban backdrop gave me a better context for our love. I returned to teenage haunts, passed my old school, passed pubs and playgrounds, and laughed away the shadows of painful memories. I was no longer a lonely boy. I was loved and I could love back. That was what mattered. I could see nothing else.

So, my first admission: I didn't really know what I was doing, this playing at being an adult. But she had only to put her hand in mine and I felt like I knew it all. I told her we would build a home together. Was I selfish? I didn't think so at the time. I thought it was what she wanted. She said she would travel to the ends of the earth to be with me. I used to tease her, tell her I would run away in the night just to test her, just to see if she would come looking.

She said that if she woke in the middle of the night and indeed found me gone, she would cry a river of tears for me, and follow that river wherever it might lead her. She said she would wear out iron shoes as she climbed over glass mountains to find me, she would wander the whole wide world, just to hear news of my fate, until the clothes on her back were nothing but rags and tatters. She said that if she could not find me then she would go to the cold, cold waters at the edge of the world and beg the ferrymen to carry her over into the land of the dead. She said she would walk through fields of ash and bones to seek me out and bring me home. I laughed at her absurd tales and told her that sometimes I wished I could believe in the fantastic things she said, that I could see the world as she did, full of charm and magic. She threw one of her favourite fairytale phrases back at me.

'Be careful what you wish for,' she said. 'It might come true.'

*

'And what about you?' she said. 'What would you do for me?'

Stoned challenges whispered in my mother's garden.

I could only ever tell her the truth. 'I'll love you for ever and never leave you.'

'Oh, will you? Well, that's hardly original, is it?'

But I meant every word.

During those limbo days, the tube map was a map of loyalties, a battleplan to be tested. She would trace a coloured line round and round with her slender fingers, giggling up at me, and say, 'Look, they're every colour of the rainbow. One colour for every mood. I don't like the black bit we're in now. Promise me we won't stay anywhere on this bad black line. We have to live somewhere here,' she said, pointing out the curves and corners of the District Line. 'We should live here, somewhere right here on this very green line.'

To an extent, I saw her point of view. It was black and difficult staying in my mother's house.

We were placed in separate rooms, with the familiar justification 'Not under my roof.' The more nights I slept in my teenage room, the more I felt as if I was shrinking to fit it. I became adolescent around her, stammering and blushing at her touch. It wasn't a good arrangement. We would wait until my mother was asleep and take turns to corridor-creep the dangerous steps between our rooms. I preferred it when she came to me. I would lie awake straining for the sound of my door opening and watch her slipping quickly round the shaft of light. I can't explain how strange it was to have her there, in a room crammed full of reminders from another time – reminders of the shadow of a person I was before we met. She laughed at my trembling hands, thinking I was scared of discovery. 'Don't be such a mummy's boy,' she would say. 'Let her hear us. I don't care.'

But we weren't so daring. We would break apart before dawn. I would snatch a few hours' sleep, pressed up against the wall that divided us, trying to catch her heartbeat through the plywood.

Squashed together in that small house, we were hemmed in by the listening walls. If my mother's jealousies seem unreasonable, it's only fair to say that they were part of a wider picture. Part of an entirely different desertion.

My father had been a shadowy figure all my life, appearing on cue for birthdays, all generosity and laughter for a couple of hours before he slipped away. When I was young my mother romanticised him, saying he was an amazing man, an explorer of foreign lands, and all the presents he brought back for me proved this theory. But by my teenage years my mother could only refer to him as a selfish careless bastard. My father the property developer, with his love for warmer climates and younger women.

Whatever dreams he was chasing, my mother couldn't keep up. The visits stopped, and there were no more exotic gifts waiting for me on birthday mornings. My mother told me he had some sickness of the mind that made him forget us completely, that he had used up all his love for us and was never coming back. For months and months afterwards, I was haunted by nightmares where I would be for ever wandering through strange lands in search of my father. I would stumble into Aztec ruins, I would scale the highest peaks, I would swim savage oceans, calling for him to come home.

I was sixteen when he died of a heart attack. He left my mother nothing, but I inherited a small fortune. He stipulated I should use it to make myself a man, to get some independence. But I was scared what kind of man I might become: if I took that money and followed in his footsteps, would I be condemned to live out my life on foreign shores and never make it back home? I saved the money, and carried on living the same safe life I always had. Until I met her, and saw I had a future I could invest in.

So, with her by my side, I took my father's legacy seriously, and set out to find us a home. At first I wouldn't listen to her ridiculous demands. I was the voice of reason, forcing her onto tubes, taking her to the wealthy world of west London, pushing our way through markets on Portobello Road in pursuit of what had always been my dream houses: those large white mansions with front doors that dwarf you, porches with huge pillars that could almost be made of marble. I wanted to give her a rich man's abode, a home she could be proud of. A style my father loved to emulate in foreign lands. As a child, I fell in love with glossy magazine photographs my mother had kept. My eternally young father, standing in front of a huge white house, with the blue sky above him and the great sea behind.

But even with all that money, we couldn't come close to such aspirations. We could only afford damp basement flats with

postage-stamp-sized gardens. In any case, I had grossly mis-
judged her taste – she hated every property we saw, she said it
felt like I was trying to force her to live underground. She said
once that she could feel the weight of the rest of the building
pressing down on top of her, crushing her. And even more she
hated the people: they all seemed so polished and proud.

It was part of what I loved about her, the way she wore her
emotions like a second skin, and I would never have forced her
into a place that made her unhappy.

So I abandoned my dreams and instead took her east, past
the Square Mile and out into the busy streets of Whitechapel
and Bethnal Green. I explained the different territories of
London to her: the way that the river cuts the city in two,
creating a stand-off between north and south Londoners.
Although when she asked what the different places meant, I
couldn't really tell her. I told her how the west was rich and the
east was poor: that was how it had always been – class and
social history dictated value beyond reason and sense. And
when we arrived in the east, the estate agent proved my theory:
here we could buy a house with a huge garden, we could live
within walking distance of canals and she could spend her days
serenading the swans, teaching them to eat from her hand.

But she hated this side of London just the same, although
for different reasons. She said it was a half-blasted terrain, that
the modern houses we were offered lacked any history. She said
that living there would be living on a wounded landscape: the
mismatched architecture and open parks served only to remind
her of all the bombs that had fallen. And to her the green
spaces, with their trimmed hedges and their ordered flowerbeds,

were a statement of submission, nature tamed and tidied. I could have bought her a mansion there, but she would not have stayed.

We argued about it on the tube on the way back. I told her she was being ridiculous, it didn't matter all that much where we happened to end up. We were looking for a home and the home would be whatever we made it.

She didn't agree. She said we had to be sure we had very good foundations. She said it was a matter of instinct and that I should trust hers – she would know when we found the house that was meant for us.

We spent the evening negotiating, sitting in the garden with the tube map spread between us again. It was a map I barely recognised, with so many areas crossed out in her black marker-pen strokes. The only line that really stood out now was the District Line, the mischievous branch that divides at Earl's Court and pushes through Putney, Southfields, right down to Wimbledon. It curls off on the lower left-hand side of the page, like a green sapling shoot.

I was still reluctant to cross the river. But she was insistent: 'Please, let's try this very green line. I'm sure this is where we should be.'

By then her hatred of the London I knew was beginning to frighten me. What if my love wasn't strong enough to compensate for all the ugliness and the noise? In addition, I was pulled apart by my mother's silent judgements. I recognised it was no bad thing to put the length and breadth of London between what I had come to think of as my two families. I listened carefully to what she was asking of me, negotiated the loan of my mother's car and we drew up a plan of escape.

I had never navigated across London before, and it was a difficult drive. We left the bustle of north London behind us, pubs and steel-shuttered shops jostling for pavement space. She couldn't stop laughing as we raced down the Holloway Road, she kept on telling me that we were breaking free. Every time we stopped at traffic lights she would cover me with kisses, telling me to have courage, we were off on an adventure, off to find our right and proper place. I tried to take cunning short-cuts along side-streets, but was thrown by the one-way systems and instead emerged on to Bishopsgate. The tower blocks rose up all around, reflecting the grey day. We got caught in a predictable gridlock, cars snarling on all sides. As the traffic shifted gradually, reflections flowed into each other. Warped by the architecture we were the abdomen of an elongated creature that slid its lazy way around the sides of the ring of steel.

She didn't like it at all. 'What the fuck is the point of all this?' she said. 'How can people live like this?'

I took her over London Bridge, to give her the whole panorama, pointed out Tower Bridge and all the other landmarks, trying to share some of the history of this city that I loved. We were suspended, for a second, above the water. She wasn't impressed.

'That's not a river. It's a brown creeping disease.'

I followed the signposts that led us further and further south. We navigated our way past the Elephant and Castle, past Clapham and Wandsworth until Wimbledon Common opened up before us like a blessing.

We caught tantalising glimpses of tall trees standing proud above the fences. She wound down the window and leaned out dangerously. The streets were wide and the air was clean and there seemed to be just that little bit more sky. The sun came out and shone in our honour. And her hair, caught in that light, was soft-winnowing and golden. Her broad-beaming smile lit up her entire face. In this open part of London, she was suddenly back to her old self, full of laughter and promises.

'Let's stay here tonight,' I said. 'Let's never go back.'

We found a bed and breakfast and booked a room for the week. My first investment. There and then. I could be as spontaneous as her, given encouragement, and she did always encourage me.

A room of our own. A taste of what was to come.

# 2

She insisted that we explore the common.

It was growing dark as we made our way through the undergrowth that separated the wood from the road and I was easily scared of isolated places at night. 'Is this wise?' I asked her. 'We could get lost.'

Nothing ventured, nothing gained, she replied, and ran on. The silver birch trees caught the colours of the sunset as the light changed. Damp leaves, still sodden with the rain of the last few days, clung to her but she kicked them away. I ran after her. She was swinging herself round the trunks, like an overexcited child. I hadn't seen her so happy for weeks. I realised that this was only the beginning: there was something about her that only closeness to nature could draw out, the childwildness of her that came racing out in wide open spaces. Another thing I soon learnt to love.

'Let's catch our ghosts!' she said, and taught me a game from her childhood, where we had to chase each other through the woods and stand on each other's shadows. If your shadow was caught you had to stand stock still and count to ten. The victor would hide and the game would begin again. This was her natural habitat and she was cunning. She caught me many times and, while I was frozen, would fling dead leaves into my face and run back out into the gathering gloom. Her 'Catch me if you can!' echoed from every direction.

Then she told me that we had to escape the forest before nightfall or we might never make it out at all.

We ran through the woods hand in hand, screaming and laughing together. Half scaring each other, pretending we could hear footsteps and breathing behind us, our shadows lengthening in our wake, cross-hatched by the patterns cast by the silver birch trees.

We emerged suddenly into a triangle of land near Wimbledon village. The headlights of passing cars were a shock, cutting through the dark, illuminating our smudged, smirking faces.

The pub signs at the side of the road welcomed us in. 'The Hand in Hand,' she identified. 'That's us, love.'

We spent the whole evening drinking, sheltered in a wooden alcove, oblivious to the sudden September rain, which had come back with a vengeance. We planned our future in linear terms. She sat with her *A to Z* in one hand and a pint in the other. As the night progressed she marked the map to show me what she would and would not have. The more she drank, the more ruthless she became. The page became a black mass of concentric circles, spiralling patterns that looped around the green of the common dominating the double page. The only streets we were allowed to live on were those that let us see the common or the park. And as she drank she told me how this was now our place, this green land at the end of the green line: this was the way it was going to be. She decreed that we would never go back to north London, apart from with bags and boxes to separate ourselves for ever from my mother, and to embark on the next stage of our story, the beginning of the wonderful life we deserved.

She drew up a two-dimensional plan of action.

I made promises I hoped I could keep.

She was full of confidence when we visited the estate agent the next morning. I could see he was trying not to laugh when she presented him with her map, but she stared him down and gave her orders in that calm determined way of hers: 'Somewhere in these streets, please. It's your job, after all.' Her previous experiences across London had made her even more certain than before: 'Our house is out there, and I'll know it when I see it.'

The estate agent tried to fob us off to begin with, but soon learnt otherwise. The first viewing was of a suburban bungalow on one of the estates that hid round the back of the common: all gravelled driveways and twitching net curtains. We might just as well have been staying with my mother.

Then there was a time when he took us to see a tiny cottage that was also hemmed in by modern estates. A tiny red-brick building, it looked abandoned and unhappy in the middle of the new developments. There was no natural light, and too many ripe, undefinable smells. The estate agent, who couldn't have been much older than me, and was probably equally susceptible to her charms, stammered apologies as she told him clearly and politely that when she said she wanted a house with a history, she didn't necessarily mean one that someone had recently died in and would he sort it out, please, and stop taking the piss and wasting our time.

She had this way about her that made her difficult to lie to. Her forthright manner made the whole process easier. She would march in and ask him if he had done his job yet and, if not, why not? We had a couple of frustrating weeks when there was nothing to do and nothing to see. She drew up the survival tactics for those days, a quick walk through the common, wondering at the fast-changing colour of the leaves, and then down to the pub for the afternoon.

'Hand in hand to the Hand in Hand!' she would declare.

I suggested that it would be healthier if we explored the area instead of just skirting round the edges of the common and heading straight to the pub. But she disagreed. 'Let's not explore too much until we're sure that we can stay.'

Places mattered very much to her.

She used to say that places were like people: every one had a different character and different agenda, and that it was best not to get too involved until you were sure it was right.

I challenged this argument with our intimate history but she just laughed and said, 'With you I always knew. That was the whole point.'

Then, one afternoon, the estate agent greeted us with a broad grin and a firm handshake: 'A most unexpected piece of luck. A wonderful opportunity for the first-time buyer.' It was the top flat of an old Victorian mansion and the landlord wanted a quick sale. Initially, she wasn't impressed to find that the house faced a busy road, with another street between us and the common.

But I told her that this was inevitable: there would always be roads forming rings around us wherever we went. This was a city. There would always be other houses blocking our view.

It was a proud townhouse that had clearly seen better days. A house with a history, she said. A house from another time. The strong stone walls formed a grim façade for the outside world. She said it was like a frowning face, like a fierce old man trying to keep a secret. A man with many eyes, a man who has seen it all.

I could see what she meant. The large sash windows were like hooded eyes, glaring down at us, dirty and disapproving.

Since it had been divided up into flats most of the building was deserted. I liked it instantly. I liked the silence. I liked the hollow echo of the steep stairs. I liked the way that many of the doors we passed were boarded up. I didn't mind the damp or the stale air, the peeling wallpaper and stains from another time.

And I could tell that this was exactly what she wanted: she skipped her way through the vast rooms that were opened up for us, she flung her arms around my neck and said, 'This one or nowhere at all, my young man.'

A frightening ultimatum.

I handed over the deposit on the very same day. We celebrated in the Hand in Hand, which would soon be our local. She was showering me with kisses all night, insisting on buying me all the drinks she could think of in her enthusiasm; I had to stop her bankrupting us completely. She told me she would make it beautiful, more beautiful than I could imagine, a shelter against the world, she said, 'Just you and me, my young man, just you and me and the rest of the world can go to hell.'

'I will make our house into a world of treasure,' she said. 'We will live like a king and queen and we will want for nothing. We will have only the softest silk sheets for our bed, and we will eat off silver plates, and drink the finest wines from golden goblets. We shall always be happy and never grow old.'

The way she said these things, it was as if she meant every word. Then, within minutes, it was something else. She was curious about all those boarded-up doors and hidden chambers. Like me, she loved the fact that there was this whole empty house beneath us, full of mysteries and silence. 'There could be anything behind there,' she said, nuzzling into me as we curled up in bed together, almost too drunk-clumsy to make love. Almost, but not quite.

'Yes, there could,' I said, playing along with her. 'There could be trolls.'

'Yes, absolutely, of course there could. There might be boggarts and beasties.'

'And gremlins?'

'Well, possibly, there might.'

Hardly original, but at least I was trying.

The next morning papers were signed, money was spent. Within the following week the keys were ours. We had found our place.

\*

On the first day it was just a chaos of half-opened boxes strewn throughout the three rooms. She made me carry her over the threshold, laughing as I spun her round, swinging her off my back and down on to the floorboards. 'Here we are then, living in sin,' she declared.

My mother's phrase. I liked hearing it coming from her lips.

She pulled me down beside her saying, 'Come on, let's exorcise the flat, chase out the old ghosts.'

It didn't take her long to place things in order and make it our own. There was our bedroom, with its big window that stretched half the length of the eaves, and an old-fashioned window-seat that filled in the alcove. She loved to perch up there with a cup of coffee, drying her hair in the sunlight with one hand, the other dangling out of the window, letting the smoke from her first cigarette of the day weave its way out into the morning.

Those mornings were hard. Our new home came at a heavy price. All my father's money was suddenly gone. And now there were many bills to pay, all in my name. It was time for me to go out and work.

'Time for me to grow up,' I said to her, one night, as we sat squashed together in the alcove, her legs stretched out and resting on my shoulders. The room below us was a war zone of scattered objects and dirty clothes, flung like discarded skins into every corner. We were watching the winds shaking the trees, rippling over the common, stripping the branches of their burnished autumn leaves. I always used to love this time of year – the only time when certain streets in London could look plausibly as if they were paved with gold. I could never really connect it with the thought of things dying.

'Please don't,' she said. 'I don't want you to.'

She behaved as if I was doing it to spite her.

'I have to go, love. I have to get myself a job so we can stay here.'

'It's not fair.'

'I know.'

'We shouldn't be apart.'

'I know.'

'So why are we even discussing it?'

'Because we have to.'

Afterwards, she told me that she was only joking, she knew I had to go, it just made her sad, that was all. At the time, I thought she was being stupid and naïve, and it made me angry, this tendency of hers to want the best of both worlds. We talked vaguely about her going out to work, but neither of us found that a viable option. Her wayward youth had left her with precious few qualifications and her options were limited. I couldn't bear the thought of her shut away in some high-street shop, or waiting on tables, returning exhausted and washed out by the city. And, truth be told, even in those early days I didn't want her to have a life separate from mine. She was my safe haven, and it was important to me that she remained so, untainted by any other contact. At the time, she loved me all the more for it, telling me that she was so lucky I looked after her so well. Back then, she never accused me of being jealous or of keeping her shut away from the world. Back then, she believed me when I told her that all I wanted was to keep her safe and well.

Besides, I knew my strengths. Again, those three difficult years up north suddenly seemed like an investment. My mathematics made me eminently employable. I got myself a job in the City, working alongside traders and investors. I secured a salary that would keep us over and above the style we were accustomed to. I found I was worth more than I could ever have imagined. Quietly proud of my achievements, I told her we would want for nothing.

'My clever man,' she said, when I broke the news after only three days' searching. 'My clever man, too clever for his own good.'

But the reality of the situation was difficult to adjust to. Sometimes, in those first workday mornings, I couldn't bear to catch her eye. I would dress with my face to the wall. If I had looked at her I wouldn't have been able to leave the room. It was hard not to be hypnotised by her, caught by every movement. I found myself mesmerised by the curling patterns of her smoke rings, snaking their way through the sunlight. I moved her damp hair aside, kissed the nape of her neck, slid a hand down her back and left home.

It was a shock, no exaggeration to say that I went into another world.

Those early days of work were my vertigo days. I suddenly had a different, dizzying view of the City. My office was on the twelfth floor of a tower block. I didn't have a good sense of timing and I was always a few minutes late, always delaying the inevitable departure from our bed. The digital clock that dominated the downstairs reception winked at me as I strode through the sliding doors. A sly wink at 9:05, cruelly reminding me of all the hours I had to fill before I could be by her side.

My office was all open-plan and bright lighting. Identical desks for everyone. Familiarity by surname only for the first few weeks. The tall windows gave a spectacular view of the City. From our suspended perspective I saw towers cluttering the horizon, as if strips had been torn from the sky leaving dark scars behind. It was such a contrast to the haven of Wimbledon: I found it hard to believe that she was out there somewhere, beyond the ever-expanding mass of grey buildings and people.

My vertigo days. I had a pathological fear of falling from grace, of being exposed as ignorant, a fraud, and not worthy of any of this good new life I had found. Everything seemed unfamiliar and fragile then; I was sure it couldn't last.

It reminded me of when I first met her. During the first month or so, while our relationship was still being played out in snatched weekends, when I was still startled to wake up and find her beside me, it was almost too much to comprehend. I couldn't believe I was so lucky. I sometimes found it hard to be close to her, had to look at her from a distance, hold her at arm's length to get any sense of perspective. Needing to touch, but terrified of falling. Every part of her was unknown territory.

# 3

All the difficulties of work were compounded by the demands of the journey. I had to put the whole of London between us and each day lost precious hours travelling back and forth. And the closer I got to the Square Mile, the harder it became. At each stop more and more men, just like me, would pile into the carriage, all similarly suited, all folding and unfolding their newspapers in unison. It felt like every day I was being faced with future versions of myself. There was a vision of me in ten years' time, with a cocky smile and smart tailoring, holding forth with confidence to a bemused junior colleague. There was me on the board of directors, greying and fiftysomething, sweating under the bright lights of the tube carriage, with the flushed face of advancing alcoholism. I wondered if she would still love me by then, when so many years had passed between us. I didn't talk to her about these things, but she could read my many moods well and knew I found the enforced separation hard. Every morning she would tell me to smile, be brave, and not to worry about her, that she was perfectly happy and would make me a home I'd be proud to come back to. And she did, she transformed that abandoned flat into the happiest home I had ever known.

I loved our bedroom best of all. It was a simple, small attic room, with a large wardrobe built into the wall opposite the bed. Stacked in a corner, covered with stickers and dents from a previous time, was her old, much-loved stereo. In that room it was always her music: she sensed my mood when that was important, or she imposed hers upon me when she did not feel like words.

When she knew that I didn't want to leave, she would put on some old, old soul, which would get me to work with a spring in my step and a smile on my face, just thinking of her dancing around the room, pulling me to her and buttoning my shirt, pushing me out of the door and throwing my shoes after me, then opening the window and leaning out, turning up the volume so that I could still hear it on the street three storeys below. She would wave and blow me kisses and I would know that we were in love.

That's how it was. Our bedroom was always full of light and laughter. To begin with, it was a world within a world, the heart of the house. When we were still struggling with our unpacking, and the rest of the flat was a bombsite, we would retreat to the bedroom and shut the door and pretend that none of it was out there, that we had nowhere else to be but sheltered in our bed, together. She told me that we were the sole survivors of this world of chaos. 'It's like we were the only ones who escaped the flood,' she said. When I told her I didn't know what she meant she laughed at me for my lack of imagination, and told me one of her stories.

She said that a long time ago, but not so long ago as you might think, there was a traveller. And this traveller roamed the world we live in, gathering trades and many riches. He would settle in a city only long enough to learn the skills he could take from it. So in one place he learnt the crafts of stone and steel, how to build strong walls and good houses. In another, he learnt the arts of painting and poetry. In yet another he saw how barren fields could be irrigated and planted to bear fine fruits and produce. He met wise men, who taught him to predict the weather; he met cunning men, who showed him how to find his own future in the patterns of the stars.

When he was a young man, the pursuit of knowledge for its own sake was enough. He made a book of records, full of facts and figures and grand theories, and guarded his wisdom like precious treasure. As a young man, he was in love with his own company, the freedom of the road at his heels and the open sky above. But as he grew older, he felt that the world was growing too wide, there were too many distances for him to cover. All places looked the same to him. He would camp every evening by the roadside and his nights would be troubled by quiet domestic dreams where he had a home, with a roof above his head, and a fire in the hearth, and space for some company.

After one nagging dream too many he awoke, and decided that, from that day on, he would fight against his wandering nature and try a different life. He walked to the nearest town, and there he settled. He found a house on the outskirts. It was nothing more than a windblown shack, with broken windows and a roof reduced to rafters, open to the sky. It belonged to a farmer, who had used it to house his cattle. Now it was even too tumbledown for the animals and he sold it gladly to the tattered traveller for a bottle of whisky and a handful of tales about the lands he had roamed across and the wonders he had seen.

The traveller had been many years upon this earth, and it stands to reason that he had wandered into other worlds, and other places, than the ones that we now know. One of the dangers of this delineated world, where we play out our lives within the same few square miles, is that we remain unaware of those other lands, which are often much nearer than we think, gateways hidden in the shadows of rocks, at the bottom of a clear lake, or at the back of a mirror. Where he had been I cannot tell you; all I know were the skills he had returned with. Within a week, the house had a new thatched roof, sturdy walls, and a garden full of produce, all of nature teeming in a patch of land that, for as long as the farmer could remember, had only been dust.

There is something rooted deep in human nature that makes us suspect strangers. And when these strangers have riches and blessings, it makes it all the worse. So it was with the traveller. He would take his surplus produce to market every week, but no one would sample it. Folk said that such fine foods must surely be poison to the soul, if not the body; they said the traveller had too much magic about him and that he was not a man to be trusted.

Over the months, the traveller used all his knowledge to try to charm the cityfolk. One week he brought hand-woven silks, so fine that in certain lights they seemed invisible, and the women of the town could not help but wander over to touch. But when touching led to talking, the men became angry and upturned the traveller's stall; they trampled over his soft cloth with their heavy boots, accusing him of trying to tempt their women away. So the next week he fashioned metal and took it to market: fine bridles; strong chains, complex locks and the keys to fit them. But the men turned over his stall again, accusing him of using magic rather than true craftsmanship to ply an honest trade. And it's true, his metals were stronger and brighter than anything that that town had ever known.

After a year of such rude treatment, the traveller decided he would take no more. He retreated to his house, bolted the door against outsiders and would have nothing more to do with the cruel ways of jealous men. But, still, his hearth was lonely with only him beside it. Even his house, it seemed, was too large and too empty.

So, using all the skills he carried in his hands, the wise traveller set out to make himself a wife. He brought back supple willow twigs from the forest, and wove them together to form a skeleton. He found fresh saplings, which he stretched between to make muscles and sinews. He dug pale clay from the side of the riverbank and gave the wooden girl soft white skin. He spun golden threads of fine silk for her hair, and her eyes were forget-me-nots plucked from the forest floor. He cut his finger and gave her ruby-red lips, painted with his own blood. He made more silks and satins and sewed them together to make beautiful dresses, fit for a princess. His wild stick-woman was made with all of his arts combined. And he loved her with all his heart.

And what greater power is there in this whole wide world than the power of love? We should never forget what love can do. The traveller kissed his stick-princess on her still-wet lips, and her whole nature changed. A heart began to beat beneath those wooden ribs. A warmth came to her pale skin, and blood rushed to her cheeks; her blue eyes began to twinkle, that ruby red mouth formed into a smile, and that smile turned to laughter, the sweetest laughter the traveller had ever heard. And his hitherto lonely house was suddenly alive with love.

The traveller had learnt enough over the year to know that he should keep his new-found joy a secret. He kept his door bolted against intruders, and he and his woman spent simple days together, tending their garden by day, their fireside by evening and their bed by night. The traveller found love and lost his restlessness, and his small self-created world held nothing but joy.

But no paradise can go undiscovered for ever. One evening, the traveller and his wife were sitting by the fireside when there came a knock at the door. Before he could answer, his wife was springing up from her seat, drawing back the bolts, welcoming the stranger. It was none other than the farmer, on his way home from the inn with a bellyful of beer and a taste for company. He was welcomed in and given a place by the fire, some fine whisky and tall tales. But at the end of the night, the traveller and his wife begged the farmer to keep their love a secret.

And the farmer kept his promise, like the honest man he was. Soon he became a welcome guest at the house, often appearing at the door with a bottle of whisky and a mind for stories. Every time he left them, he repeated his vow: he would not tell a soul.

But secrets do not need to be spoken to be discovered. The farmer's wife was a shrewd and jealous woman. She minded that her husband was often absent from their home in the evening; she minded even more that his eyes were full of laughter these days, that his step was lighter and he would not tell her why.

So she did what any cunning wife would do: she bided her time and she watched and she waited. She followed him to the inn, and saw him drink just one glass of ale, but take a bottle with him for the journey home. She followed him down the road out of the city, and stayed behind him as he took the dark lane that led to the traveller's house. She watched with wonder as the most beautiful woman she had ever seen opened the door to her husband, kissed his cheek and led him inside.

The next morning the traveller was woken by shouts and screams and the sound of an army of men beating down their door. But the door was strong and sturdy, and would not give way. The whole city had gathered on their doorstep. The women were shrieking and wailing, saying that the traveller must have taken some woman hostage, that they had come to take the poor girl to safety. They called the traveller a devil and demanded justice.

The wild stick-princess heard their protests from the safety of their bedroom, and laughed at the absurdity of it all. She flung open the window and called down to them, saying she was in love and she was happy and they should all be happy for her, and go home. But her words only caused more trouble. Because the minute the men of the city saw her beauty, they could not look away. Their hearts overflowed with love. The women recognised the change in their husbands' eyes and were consumed with jealousy. 'She must be a witch,' they whispered to each other. 'As like attracts like, this strange woman must surely be full of hidden wiles and unnatural arts.'

And jealousy spreads like a disease. The men whose eyes had been full of love in the morning had nothing but hatred in the evening. They hated the woman they could not touch. Under their wives' instructions, the men went out into the forest and brought back swift-kindling sticks. They built a pyre around the small house, and stood guard.

As the evening sun bled across the sky, the men and women took torches and flung them on to the dry wood. And from their tall bedroom window, the traveller and his wife wept to see it.

'The fire will come and it will catch us,' she said to her husband. 'I will burn brightly and quickly and be nothing but ash and clay.'

The traveller kissed his wife gently and led her to the bed. And they both wept as they made love for the last time. But as their salt tears and their sweat mingled and ran down the silken sheets, something began to change. The tears multiplied as they fell, and soon there was a stream of water running across the floor. The water flowed beneath their bed, and the light wood lifted and rocked, like a ship upon the ocean. And they both laughed to see it. The traveller opened his window, and the multiplied tears ran in a waterfall down the wall of the house, and quenched the fire beneath.

The traveller and his wife made love all night long. And neither of them could stop their tears coming, but they were tears of joy by now, full of joy at their love, which could save them from all the jealousies of mankind. Their bed, still swimming on a tide of tears, rocked them to sleep in the silent dawn. They never gave another thought to the world outside their window.

Some say it was the traveller's magic that could turn tears into an ocean, but I believe that the breaking heart of a woman is strong enough to bring about the strangest of miracles. When the traveller and his wife finally drew back the curtains to greet the new day, they looked down upon a drowned world. Waves were lapping at the window-ledge, and as far as the eye could see, there was a sea of tears. And bobbing sickly on the surface of the water were the bodies of the jealous cityfolk: here a bloated henwife, there a drowned soldier, his fine red cloak floating along in his wake. There, sadly, the corpse of the farmer, drifting by.

The traveller and his wife watched at the window for many days and many nights as the ocean gradually subsided and the bodies were taken away by the retreating tide. And when the waters finally vanished, what a land was left behind. The solid stone wall of their garden had been washed clean away. The boundaries of the traveller's lands stretched as far as the eye could see, and all was full of life. Animals were feeding from his strange fruits, which had only thrived in the flood. The forest, so long drowned, was now green and rich and full of birdsong. The traveller and his wife had made a whole new world, forged out of love and tears and magic.

So it was for the rest of their days. They lived in that house like a king and queen. And they were never troubled again by curious intruders or jealous women.

She told me that that was how our home would be, an enclave of love left over from another world. She said that we would live a quietly charmed life together, and nothing would ever break us. I didn't doubt it for a second.

She loved her plants and her flowers. She used to say that a house was not a home without them. If she had to leave her country idyll behind, she would re-create it the best she could. The first arrival was the big ivy plant, which she placed on the window-seat. 'Something good and green for our room,' she said.

'It's just a weed,' I said.

'Depends how you look at it.'

At first it was just a spindly shrub, but after a month of her attention it was bursting into life. Like anything and everything with which she came into contact, it flourished. She tried to tame it: she wanted it to grow all over the seat so that she would have a cushion of greenery.

In the spare room she built me a study. A proper room for a proper working man, she said.

She was so good with her hands. It was a birthday present. She knew exactly what I wanted. The room had an identical layout to our bedroom. She adapted the window-seat into a desk. She converted the wardrobe into a bookcase and unpacked my books in alphabetical order. She always laughed at my need for order, but also pandered to it, allowing me my belief that everything has its right and proper place.

When I came home, exhausted, she sat me down on the sofa in our still chaotic living room. She put a glass of champagne into my hand and gave me a parcel to unwrap. It was a picture: a charcoal sketch of an old gnarled tree. A piece of work from her teenage years, a tree she used to walk past on her way home from school, back in the village of constant sunlight and adventures. She had always thought that it looked like a man reaching up to the sky. She said she had always hoped that she would meet a man like that, who stood strong and tall against the horizon and looked up towards the heavens. I should go and hang it in my new room.

The polished floorboards felt smooth and cool underneath my bare feet.

I cried. It was the first time I had ever cried in front of her. She was the kindest person I had ever known.

'Do you really like it?'

I told her that yes, yes, I loved it, that I couldn't believe how much she cared. She took my hand and she moved the lamp off the broad desk. She perched on the edge and I reached behind her and pulled the blinds together so that no one could see her when she leant so slowly back.

I realise that I am writing about the order of rooms in the same order as she created them. I am still a mimic, still trying to follow in her footsteps, looking for clues, trying to trace the truth of our story through every little detail. That's another thing she taught me – it's often the little things that matter most. While I was out working, she would be making things for the flat. As often as not, I could spend a whole evening with her and not notice the changes she had wrought. She would get frustrated with my lack of observation, telling me that I should pay more attention. It became a game between us, always something new for me to notice every night – a set of candlesticks for our evening meal, perhaps, the light curtains she made to shut out any peeping Toms. The bright covers for our bed.

The kitchen and living room were one large open room, with high ceilings and huge windows that gave us a good view of the edges of the common.

She steamed away the ragged wallpaper, and painted the walls a gentle white, and from then on that room drew the light into it. She covered the walls with her paintings and photographs: they were glimpses of a younger version of herself, peeping out from cornfields or perched in trees. I featured in some of them, grinning from ear to ear because she was there.

I never lost that habit. I could grin my way through work because I knew she was waiting. I didn't mind when autumn gave way to a cold, bitter winter, unlike my colleagues who complained of seasonal depression. I would watch the sunset through the smog, watch the grey snow fall on all sides of our building, and was comforted by the thought of the warm nights ahead.

That winter we cheated time again and again, stretching out the days despite the darkening hours, spending weekends cocooned in bed, watching the snow stroke the windows, falling on to what seemed another world outside.

When the snow came to the common it settled there for days. The willow trees were encased with ice, the frail branches chiming with stalactites. The softness suited us. One evening, fortified by whisky, she persuaded me to sneak out with her to make angels in the snow. The common by night was a frightening no man's land. The black sky was broken up by the silver-birch trees, slender tapers rising from the deep drifts. From a distance it looked as if the night had slammed itself down like a portcullis, barring our way. But hand in hand we found a secluded spot and lay down. A quick flurry of arms and legs and we left ghostly couplings in the snow. A heavy frost came and, if you knew where to look, you could see impressions of angels for days. Everything she touched, and everywhere she went, was imbued with magic. We created a secret world of treasure out on the common, in the safety of our flat, and in the privacy of our bed.

I would leave in the dark and return in the dark. The street-lamps that lined the roads from the tube to our house were beacons that guided me back to her, a sure and certain chain of light. Forty-two of them altogether. I used to set myself markers. Juggling numbers, timing my footsteps by the distance between the lights, drawing up fractions, calculating the exact time and movement expended until I would be with her. When I came in she would place wine in my hand and food on my plate. That was winter. The days were short and the nights were long. It felt like we were hibernating.

\*

After that soft stasis of winter, the changes of the following springtime came as a shock. I saw it coming. One Saturday, a fierce thunderstorm was followed by bright sunshine and a rainbow suddenly streamed across our window. She leapt out of bed, pointing where it arched down towards the common. 'It's a sign!' she said. 'It's a sign we must follow – we might find ourselves some gold.'

I ran after her as she flitted between the trees. We lost sight of the rainbow, but her winding route took us back to the place where we had lain in the snow. Now that dip in the land was scattered with snowdrops, and she told me it was a good omen: our angels had turned into flowers. It had to be the sign of something new beginning.

Sure enough, a few days later, our home was also blossoming. I came back to find the living room like a haphazard jungle, strewn with plant pots, ferns unfurling, spider plants and small dragon trees beckoning in the sunlight. And that was just the start of her transformations. At the end of the hallway, there was a locked door. She insisted that we keep it so, although we had been up there when we had first seen the flat. The stairs were steep, but not too steep, and led us up on to the wide roof with its tall chimney behind us, and a good broad patio stretching in front. There was a fence to one side that reached our shoulders. She was on tiptoe, trying to peep over, but there was no sign of life, no neighbours. Perfect. The far side looked out over the common and there were wrought-iron railings to keep us from falling. She leant over, the wind whipping her hair back into her face. The sky was wild with tumbling clouds. I could barely hear her above the roar of the elements. She shouted that this place had to be ours, another ultimatum: if I bought it for her, she would make me a hanging garden of delights. But she wouldn't let us go back up there until the good weather came. She said that it would always be summer up there.

And when the good weather did come we transformed the rooftop in one night. I came home to a strange greeting, opening the door to find a pot of primroses with a Post-it note stolen from my desk stuck on it, declaring 'FOLLOW ME!' Behind them were geraniums, a small rosebush, ferns, some buds just poking through the earth, with the promise of unknown blossoms. I followed the trail through the house, up the stairs and out on to the roof. And there she was, barefoot, in her dungarees, her hair tied back, her sunglasses on, grinning. 'Get changed,' she said, 'and help me with the garden. The clocks have changed and summer's coming.'

I went into the bedroom only to find the way blocked by a bale of Astroturf.

'I thought we needed a lawn,' she said. 'Come on!'

We hauled it up the stairs and it covered half the patio, right up to the newly painted fence, still damp to the touch. There was a bold swipe of silvery blue along the bottom. Then, along the top two-thirds, a deep, deep midnight colour, covered with fragments of a mirror. She delighted in telling me how she had smashed one of her old mirrors, and spent hours gluing the broken pieces on to the board. Always superstitious, I told her that she was tempting fate: wasn't that inviting seven long years of bad luck into the house? It was hardly an auspicious beginning. But she laughed and told me that we had so much luck in our lives, nothing could harm us. 'I wanted to make the sea at night,' she explained. 'I wanted something to remind me.' Under her instruction, I placed two huge ferns at either side of the board, to complete the illusion.

She clapped her hands with delight and laughed to see it. She told me how, as a child, nothing could drag her away from the sea. How she used to run along tidemarks and call up to the gulls that wheeled around her. The great white birds seemed massive to her then, and she used to screech up at them, trying to learn their language, pleading with them to pick her up in their strong claws and fly her away to unknown lands across the water. Or she would sit in the shadows among the tidemarks and sing to the sea, trying to call dolphins or seals or stranger creatures out of the water. She would put messages in bottles and float them out across the waves, hoping that the fairy folk who lived in the cities under the sea would read them and come up to the surface world to play.

'Do you miss it?' I asked.

'Not as much as I would have missed you, if we'd never met.'

The night was cold, but she insisted we should christen our rooftop garden. So we piled on jumpers and coats and drank ourselves warm as the sun died. And as the light faded, and the twinkling mirrors caught the candlelight, I saw, as always, there was magic in her craftsmanship. There was the sea at night, after all, rippling away at the edges of our rooftop.

We lay back on the prickly plastic grass, gazing up at the stars, faint but still outshining the orange pallor of the street-lamps.

'We should wish on them,' I said. It was an old tradition.

'There's nothing more I could wish for,' she replied, as she folded herself around me.

# 4

Spring quickly gathered momentum and the days grew lighter and our mornings were ushered in by birdsong rather than the traffic's roar. I would leave her stepping out into the pool of sunlight that fell on our bedroom floor. The way she reflected the light back into the room, I sometimes thought she must be made of ivory and gold.

But, looking back, she was more like the plants she tended: she grew with the sunlight, becoming stronger, more vibrant. I would come home to find her playing loud music and dancing round the room like a dervish. 'Come and dance with me! It helps them grow!'

Our living room overflowed with greenery, and she would soothe me to sleep by telling me tales of the garden that would blossom upstairs. It would be a paradise up there, a second Eden where no one could find us and no one could see.

I loved the home she made, and the way she thrived on every new creation. But as the days grew longer I also found myself becoming restless. We had not been outside Wimbledon since we moved. She often said that that was what she loved about the place: it still felt like a village, and she couldn't believe that the press and rush of the rest of London really existed anymore. In many ways she was still just a mischievous little girl, and, looking back, I'm sure that was part of why I loved her so. She delighted in her own irresponsibility, and forced me to care for her. In the early days, I loved the fact that she made me grow up, and abandon my previous role of the sullen, stunted son. The only thing that irritated me, and it sounds petty now, was her refusal to acknowledge the city properly. She took the same attitude as a naïve child playing hide-and-seek, covering her eyes and thinking that if she could not see the rest of the world then it couldn't really be there.

But the city was out there and I wanted to show her everything. I wanted to walk through crowds with her on my arm. I wanted to take her on a boat up the river. I wanted to see her against a backdrop I knew: I wanted to lose her among the pigeons in Trafalgar Square; I wanted to take her to the Tower of London and, playing with her imaginative side, show her the armour of knights who had died for love, tell her everything I knew about that tall tower and its history of imprisonment – I thought that these were things she might like to see. I wanted to navigate her though the busy streets and bring her home wiser, able to put our love in a wider context.

These things were important to me: I wanted her to understand where I had come from. Because when I was growing up I didn't have the luxury of wide fields and seaside adventures.

My freedom, gained through heated arguments, was charted in terms of tube lines and zones. My early teenage years were spent negotiating the three stops down the line that would take me to Camden Town. I shuffled through markets, intrigued by the colourful people but feeling awkward. I settled in the bookshops.

In the comfort and safety of our flat, it was hard to connect that old incarnation of myself with the luck and love of the present.

She put her fingers on my lips to stop me speaking. 'Why would you want to go back there?' she asked, laughing down the years at my past self. 'There is nothing but this,' she said, as she leant over and above me. 'And I don't want to be anywhere else apart from here, with you.'

I was easily placated, took her compliments as intended. I soon accepted that my world, for the immediate future, would be split in two. Half the time, living a lover's life, sheltered in our flat, the other half caught up in the bustle and noise of the office. The chorus of telephones and the babble of all those voices made it hard, to begin with, for me to think straight. I would struggle all day, having abstract battles with my mathematics. In the early days, she would tease me with more fairytale parallels, telling me that I must have made a deal with Mammon himself, that I was condemned to an eternity of money-counting, that our happy home had cost me my soul, that I had paid a high price to be with her. I laughed back, and kept my resentments well hidden. It was very like her to turn what was different in our lives into some great joke.

It would have been much easier if I had agreed with her but, actually, I was pleasantly surprised by my working world. Once that initial panic subsided, I soon found my bearings. The office housed hundreds, but we were divided and subdivided into teams. I worked alongside the charismatic James and the painfully shy Simon, sitting in the middle, striking a balance, I'd like to think. It was an unconventional arrangement: usually whole departments are sectioned away together. I should have been placed among the ranks of other mathematicians who applied abstract equations to the reality of the money markets. But we were an experimental alliance: our progressive boss Mr Collins had decided to try a different way of working – training us up through collaboration rather than isolation. We were given a projected itinerary to follow for the year. We were entrusted with a specific selection of shares, and a precise budget. We were given targets to reach by the end of every month, and in a year's time we were expected to have expanded our portfolio by 50 per cent. Mr Collins told us that it was our task to make money from money, and if we could pull it off then we were destined for a great future. Mr Collins told us to have belief in ourselves: we had been hand-picked for our academic strengths. We were a team of geniuses. We would go far.

(She teased me about it when I came home that first night. She said she should watch out: if I really was a genius I might just figure her out. I told her that she had nothing to worry about, she was an insoluble problem that was sure to carry on into infinity.)

Genius may have been an exaggeration, but we certainly had

our strengths. Simon was the computer programmer. He devised the networks and programs that made the money flow. He found conversation difficult, and only seemed really happy when he was programming, but I sympathised with him, and for the first couple of weeks, I really did try to draw him out of his shell. I asked him about his degree, but didn't understand his answers. When I asked him about his home life, he blushed and said nothing.

As the weeks passed, I grew fond of Simon's eccentricities. His overt awkwardness made it easier for me to settle in: however nervous and removed I might have seemed, I was nowhere near as bad as him. But also that was only my opinion. Simon operated on a different plane from us. I think when Simon dreamt, he must have dreamt in computer code, so finely tuned were his skills of programming and innovation. Simon didn't really seem to see any distinction between man and machine, and interacted similarly with both. He would give us basic commands in simple sentences, always infuriated by how long it took me to adapt to his latest upgraded program. To Simon, the human body itself was a desperately underused commodity. Or, rather, the human brain – Simon had hardly any physical presence at all. When there was a lull in work, Simon would tell us how little of our brain capacity the average human being uses, then busy himself with memory exercises, or intelligence tests, in the hope of reprogramming himself to a higher level.

James, in contrast, was everything Simon was not. Confident, good-looking, never at a loss for words. The same age as me, but with a wealth of experience behind him. Well educated, well dressed, and with a confidence that can only come from never being denied anything in his life. He had spent his summer after university travelling the world. He intended to invest the next five years in making millions, then spend the rest of his years living a life of luxury. His plan was to buy a yacht and sail the high seas. And if ever a man was going to achieve such a life then without a doubt it was James. He attracted money and good luck, and he did it with such charm and ease that it was impossible to dislike him. Eventually, unexpectedly, we became good friends, and by the end of the summer, I really believed that James was the only person in this world on whom I could rely. But that mismatched alliance belongs to a much later part of the story.

James worked with the shares. Not for him the frenzied pit of the trading floor: he found it all a little undignified and was not ready to will himself a premature nervous breakdown. 'You've got to make the work work for you,' he advised me, very early on. 'You've got to make sure you're living the life you want – no one's going to do that for you.' So instead he was the personal contact for nervous investors. He kept track of funds, took educated risks and, during the entire time I knew him, there was always more profit than loss by the end of the day. He had a magic touch with money. He would take long lunches and come back richer still. The smart secretaries would linger by his desk, perching on corners.

As for me, I did the maths. I worked in derivatives. A complex word for a simple procedure: I dealt with the possible outcomes of investment; I took share prices and predicted their rise and fall, then programmed them into formulaic patterns.

As the technical linchpin between Simon and James, I put my numbers into columns and they fell into ratios of possible achievement. My speciality was risk limitation – in laymen's term, making sure that investors took the safest options. I always felt like a con artist when I delivered my reports: I was providing guarantees, and plucking money out of thin air. But James told me I was a fucking magician, and, after a while, I believed him. Together, the three of us were the Bright Boys, a term coined by the ever-cheerful Mr Collins, who would occasionally stop by our desks and tell us that we were a credit to the firm.

And that was how it was – my time split neatly between two self-created worlds. As weeks and months passed, I gained confidence in both: I juggled numbers and made safe predictions, gained an authority I had never had before. I mapped her soft skin with my cautious fingers, and even after so many months together, every night was an exploration.

Of course, occasionally I confused my two worlds. I would return home and try to tell her about my success, millions made with instinctive predictions. I wanted her to be proud of this side of me, to understand that I could make her rich and happy; that, given time, we would be able to live whatever life she desired. But she wasn't interested. She just laughed at my workday self, saying, 'As if I care. What could possibly make you think that I care?'

She would pull me out of my suit and remind me that this daytime life was only ever a means to an end: I shouldn't forget where I belonged. 'There's more to this world than facts and numbers,' she said.

But I quietly kept hold of my love of numbers, and calculated all my unexpected assets, a windfall of love, luck and learning that had come cascading into my life. I counted hours; counted lamp-posts; counted the rise and fall of her breathing. Balancing my emotions like equations, surprised and pleased with the outcome.

# 5

Then came the first night that it was difficult to sleep beside her.

She always slept with her face towards the window and her back to me. I loved the shape of her. I would strain my eyes, trying to make out the silhouette: the hills and valleys of the side of her body; the pattern of the shadows caught by her shoulder-blades; the Braille message of her spine. She drifted off to sleep as I watched. I was just reaching out for her, just gently moving her hair to one side so I could press against her back when the wild rumpus began next door.

They came stamping across the floorboards and our walls shook as they dumped down the boxes.

It was past midnight. I caught snatches of conversation.

'Good to be back!'

'Smells like a shit-hole.'

'But good to be back.'

The old place had an old smell and they had to open the

windows to let in the air. There were crashes and curses as cupboards were opened and the contents came clattering down.

It was a rude invasion.

I got out of bed and spent a good hour pacing the living room, summoning up the courage to go next door and challenge these unknown intruders.

I didn't want them there. I didn't want anyone near us. This was our home and they had no right to break into it. I wanted to hammer on the wall and shout back at them as they opened their beers and roared their laughter and congratulated each other on their timely return. I wanted to storm into their space, and demand to know who the hell they thought they were.

But I lacked the courage. I went back to bed, and muttered my curses and insults to the pillow. I slept fitfully, praying for the morning to come quietly. It didn't. At the time I was angry that she slept through it, contrary to all natural laws. I wanted conversation, for us to collude together in how we would drive out the invaders.

Now I feel thankful for every hour I had, watching her sleeping.

I woke early in the morning, blinking myself awake, seeing how the sun made its path across her body, turning her white skin golden in that early morning light. She was still sleeping, but even in sleep she was responding to the warmth of the new day. She was stretching out into the pool of sunlight that gathered in the centre of the bed, and smiling. I noticed a bright red line on her skin, marking her cheekbone: it looked like she had scratched herself in her sleep. But that was impossible, her nails were all broken. She had complained the night before as she had rearranged the plant pots on our rooftop yet again, so that she could set up a picnic table and feed me a banquet underneath the stars. She had snapped them to pieces, but it had been worth it just to surprise me.

As I stroked her hair I saw it was full of little thistles, green and purple flecks, caught up in her curls. And as she stretched herself into the sun, I noticed that her arms were scratched. Her pale skin bruised easily and it always hurt me to see it. She was much more fragile than she thought. But at the time, I thought no more of it. It's only in retrospect that these things matter so much – that her marked skin and the flowers in her hair are suddenly pulled into sharp focus. With hindsight it's easy to look for patterns before the patterns began and forge links and suspicions before they were made. Perhaps the flowers were only flowers from the common, and the scratch just a scratch made while sleeping.

She was still half asleep as I got ready for work. And for a change it was me flinging clothes at her and telling her to get out of bed. On my way out, I turned up the music until the walls were shaking. I didn't want our new neighbours to waste the day, not with summer just round the corner.

Work was also difficult that day. It was one of the first warm days of the year and everyone resented being shut inside. The air-conditioning was faulty and we had interchangeable doses of baking heat and freezing cold. My numbers were rebelling, refusing to give me the same total twice. At the back of my mind, I could still hear the voices from last night. Two strong male voices, just on the other side of the wall, laughing.

The air outside was so thick that the street below rippled like a mirage – as if the City was just a figment of our addled imaginations. James was in his element, nose pressed up against the window like a child in a sweet shop, ogling all the newly revealed flesh. He didn't even try to include Simon (to appreciate great tits you really did need to have some sense of the three-dimensional world, apparently) but he was pulling me away from my desk, saying, 'Come and look at the legs on this one, wouldn't you just love to . . . And this one, doesn't she look the type . . .'

In the end, it was too much and I turned and snapped at him, telling him to shut the fuck up, we had work to do.

James just laughed in my face. 'All right, Bender Boy, I get the message,' he said, and reluctantly came back to his desk.

The nickname stuck for the rest of the day, used at every opportunity.

'Oi, Bender, these are last week's figures. For fuck's sake.'

'Oi, Bender, can you not even add up straight today?'

And so on, until even Simon was laughing. I was very glad to leave.

But I'm no saint. Just because I refused to play along with James's games doesn't mean that I didn't listen. By the end of the afternoon I was weighed down by my desire for her.

When I emerged at Wimbledon the sun was still shining, the streets were in bloom and the walk back from the tube station was a joy. I always loved the first day of sunshine in London, walking home through crowds of workers, caught out by their own winter attire, and the unexpected warmth. Everyone smiling.

She was sitting on the top of the wall as I turned the corner, waiting. 'Hello, lover!' she called out. 'I thought I'd surprise you.' She grabbed my briefcase, and threw it over the wall. 'I've found a short-cut,' she said. 'It's much better.'

We skirted the edges of the common, little muddy tracks that wove their way through the bushes. A short-cut that was easier for her – she was agile and smaller, and could duck under branches and not worry about the swipe of the brambles. I picked my way through the undergrowth and shared her wonder at the treasures of the common.

Wild flowers clumped by the side of the path. Everything was green, glorious and full of promise. It was the end of that slow creep from January to April, when every day could bring sunshine or snowfall, or both. Now the whole common was bursting with the imminent summer, the whole landscape straining with the force of a well-kept secret hidden under-ground for months.

She said that the common had turned itself over and was baring its belly to the warmth of the first sun, showing its true colours at last. She said it was all for us, that we were lords of the land, and from our rooftop garden we would watch as the common became greener and richer and wilder as the nights grew longer.

'Nearly home,' she said, as we squeezed through a gap in the railings, and then more surprises.

The flat was filled with the smells of her cooking. We were going to meet the neighbours, a special treat. There was a cake, made in their honour, and the rest of a pack of beer. She had been talking to them before she went out. They had been making such a racket all day long, hammering and sawing, and music playing at full volume, and laughter, so much laughter. She wondered who these strange men might be, and what arts and crafts they had brought with them. Where had they come from? What could they be building next door? She had hammered on the walls and called out to them, shouting, 'Who are you? What are you doing in there?' They had shouted back, delighted: they had had no idea they had neighbours, they'd never had neighbours before. They invited us round to get pissed.

I was tetchy and defensive after a stifling day of lewd remarks. I was tired, and I didn't like the idea of her calling to unknown men through the walls. 'You'll give them ideas. And how do you think it makes me feel?'

'Don't be so stupid,' she said, on the verge of tears. 'It's all in your mind.'

I told her that I simply wasn't in the mood, I hadn't slept well.

The men next door hammered into the argument. 'OI! NEIGHBOURS! ARE YOU THERE?'

She giggled and said, 'Told you they were friendly. My green-eyed jealous man.' She ran into our bedroom and thumped on the wall. 'HE DIDN'T SLEEP MUCH LAST NIGHT. HE'S TOO TIRED.'

They laughed, too close for comfort.

I shouted back, 'WHAT ABOUT TOMORROW?'

'ALL RIGHT, MATE, SEE YOU THEN.'

My show of hospitality meant that I was quickly forgiven.

'After all,' she said, as she pulled me down on to crisp, clean sheets, 'there's plenty of time. We've got months ahead of us. They're here for the summer.'

They were considerate that evening, and I felt bad that I had not been more sociable. They kept the music down, and giggled as they tiptoed around. Even so, I resented them. Back then, they had been faceless strangers, listening to her moving through the flat while I was away. It felt like my boundless world had shrunk and her excitement about these 'new friends for the new season' didn't help a bit. I silenced her words with kisses, all the while forming wild plans about the best way to keep these new neighbours at a distance. I had a brief rush of vertigo as I looked down at the expanse of months that might follow, unravelling with uncertainties and unwelcome changes.

My sadness and unease must have hovered over me all night long. When I woke I had leaden limbs. I was sleepy and disoriented, with a heaviness in my heart to match the heaviness of my body. I felt bound to the bed by my own sorrow.

But she was full of energy, covering me with a whirlwind of kisses, laughing away my tears, saying no wonder I was sad, I had to work on a day like this. She stepped out of bed and into the sunlight, ivory and gold again. She pulled me into the shower with her and tickled me with the water until I woke. She was trying every trick to keep me there, saying, 'They won't miss you as much as I will. Stay, stay and play in the sunshine. Come back to bed, come back to bed, they'll never find you. Come back to bed – I'll throw the sheets over us and they will become an invisible cloak and we'll hide from everyone and everything. Come back to bed.'

I was tempted, but I couldn't, and I turned sharp with her, telling her she didn't make it easy, she wasn't helping. She kissed me some more and told me sometimes she didn't want to help. 'Come back to bed,' she said, 'or you'll be sorry.' Teasing again, she danced around me as I dressed, unbuttoning my shirt, hiding my shoes and socks. I quickly shut the door behind me, before she could pull me back in. I ran down the stairs, racing against time, with a smile on my face, but still a heavy heart. I thought about the unknown men next door and hoped her mischievous mood wouldn't tempt her to go visiting before I returned.

From the street below I could see her waving from the window, still laughing, leaning out over the ivy plant. Her hair streamed out, like spun gold in the sunlight, and I lurched with a sudden sickness, as if my heart was being pulled out of my chest. And time stuck, for a second. She was frozen as she leant across the ivy to blow me kisses upon kisses. That image of her in the sunlight was an echo of something. The three storeys of the grey walls of the house stretched far up above, and she was impossible to reach. 'Come back to bed! Don't try my patience!' she shouted, laughing down the wind at me. 'Come back to bed! You don't know what you're missing.'

I did know, but I forced myself away, turning back towards my daytime life.

I took my sadness and my quietness into work with me, and huddled down at my desk, trying to be as invisible as I could. Impossible, within that open office. James did a comedy double take as he sat down beside me, then flashed a grin of collusion. 'You look in a right state. Big night last night?'

'Something like that.'

He told me to keep my head down, look as if I was busy.

Drink some water. I played along, and didn't take offence at James declaring I was a lightweight and a disgrace to the cause.

Even Simon had his say: 'Alcohol actually destroys brain cells, on average ten per unit.'

'Thanks, Simon,' I muttered. 'That's exactly what I wanted to hear this morning.'

James just laughed at me again and said it would all get easier.

But it didn't. I sat with my list of figures and began to copy and collate, catching names and numbers in the nets of my spreadsheets. Millions gathered in my margins, and I thought about the life that such money might bring me. I saw myself returning home, my pockets heavy with cash, and telling her that whatever she wanted, whatever we needed to make our life complete, could be hers, she had only to ask. And I saw the floor of the flat awash with tides of crisp fresh banknotes, which we would throw at each other like confetti, and we would be laughing together, in the knowledge that we would be rich for ever more and never have to be separated again.

'Make yourself a man,' my father had said, in the note that came with my inheritance. I thought about the investment I had made, and how the riches in my life were now less tangible. I thought how a home is much more than just bricks and mortar and firm foundations.

At the time, my mother had mocked my legacy. 'Typical!' she sneered. 'He never did learn that money cannot buy you love.'

And on the tail end of that memory, something else was gathering force. Something black and brooding, left over from the night before. I concentrated on my work, placing and ordering, but there was the undeniable feeling of something creeping up behind me.

I shivered in my seat.

'Steady, now,' said James.

I had seen her crouched on the window-sill in the moonlight. She had glanced over her shoulder to see that I was still sleeping.

'Steady yourself, mate,' said James, 'you're shaking.'

I was. I couldn't even hold my papers. James went to get me some water. I sat at my desk, suddenly stranded and small and the full weight of the previous night's bad dream came crashing down around me.

I had dreamt that I woke in the night. I had woken into a room that was and was not the room I knew. The walls were bathed in an eerie silver light, which threw grey shadows into the corners and made everything look sick and strange. And in my dream, I could not move. A slight breeze played across the ivy, rustling in the night. The ivy and moonlight worked together to cast long shadows across the ceiling, creeping nearer and nearer to the bed. I was paralysed and it took all my effort to turn my gaze away from the shifting shapes. She was kneeling up on the window-seat, crouching over the ivy plant, crooning and whispering to it, as if she was breathing life into the very leaves.

Her song was a wordless murmur, which echoed all around. As she sang the ivy grew, longer and longer, curling in towards itself. And the black shadows it cast out danced to the music, and grew above my head. From my limited perspective, bed-bound and frightened, those dancing shadows formed a net or a cage to contain me.

Then suddenly they were gone. She had thrown the coiled ivy out of the window, lowered herself down it and disappeared. I could move again. I pushed myself out of bed and stumbled over to the window to see. The ivy had become a rope, trailing down the side of the house. Charmed by her quick fingers, it had become something more than ivy, cold and scaly to touch.

I leant out to get a better view. But just then black clouds passed over the moon and there was nothing below. The ivy that was not ivy led into a deep wide well of darkness, and I was afraid. It was very far to fall. But there was something out there, beyond the window, tugging at me. Echoes of her song came drifting across the air, coaxing, calling. I held on to the lintel, my body yearning towards that dark and dangerous place outside. Wake up, wake up, Jesus, please wake up, I was screaming at myself in the deserted room. Don't jump, don't go, don't fall, save yourself, wake up.

'Drink this,' said James, handing me some water and a black coffee.

'Don't fall,' I muttered, pushing back the bad dream.

'What?'

'Nothing.'

'Get a grip, man, for Christ's sake.'

Get a grip. Hold on. Don't fall.

I steadied my hand on the desk. I forced myself back to the present reality. The nightmare retreated. I focused on the clocks that hung on the far wall, at the other side of the office. They told us the time in all the different parts of the world. American time. Japanese time. Different towns that gathered or lost hours during the course of my day. I thought back to my degree, and recalled abstract theories about the relativity of time and place. I found it strangely comforting. I drank my coffee, set to work on my spreadsheet and put the strange night behind me.

# 6

By the end of the day all my numbers were set sure and firm in the right and proper places. More trades were done and our success could be pared down to satisfactory figures. The money flowed and Mr Collins was proud. Money cannot buy you happiness, but it gives you ballast and keeps you earthbound. Finally the clock that mattered moved its hands round to the right alignment and it was five p.m. and the day was over.

James and I shut down our computers. 'Hair of the dog?' he suggested.

Not for me, I just wanted to get home. 'Another time,' I said.

He winked at me. 'Keep up the good work,' he said, not without irony.

On my way to the tube I stopped off to pick up a bottle of champagne, in honour of our intended night with the neighbours, a gesture I knew she'd approve of. It was her favourite drink, and what was I working for if not to cater for her expensive tastes? I would propose a toast to the summer nights, which was just the kind of thing she liked me to do, and the neighbours would be instantly impressed with my generosity. The new neighbours, those unknown men, separated from us only by a wall. I had spent the whole afternoon trying to push them to the back of my mind, but their loud voices and their laughter kept intruding. I was more eager than ever to get home. If we had to meet them, she and I would do it together, a united front. I know my jealousies seem petty, but these things mattered.

As I pushed myself on to the tube, I took an unexpected comfort in the press of the people. The packed carriage hurtled its way home, and the journey beat away the remnants of my bad dream. By the time I reached Wimbledon I could see things as they really were: I was just a victim of my paranoia. I had a charmed life: what was it in me that would undermine it with nightmares? I refused to dwell any longer on that cold ivy, and those creeping shadows. I shrugged them away, they meant nothing at all. As soon as I laughed at the dreams, they dissolved around me, and were lost on the summer winds.

My mind had played such tricks on me since I was a child. I would wake in floods of tears, and never know why. My mother tried to be sympathetic, but really it infuriated her: she would tell me not to wallow, not to play for sympathy. She would wash my face and pack me off to school, saying that it was all for my own good. I could never tell her how terrified I was and would walk to school always looking over my shoulder, with this unshakeable sense that something was coming up behind me.

On one of those mornings, when I was still at primary school, I closed my eyes for the morning prayers and shook the assembly hall with my screams. Suddenly I was back in my bedroom again: it was the middle of the night and I couldn't move. I felt something crawling over the foot of my bed, and there, sitting on my shins, was a scaly black creature with skin as tough as leather, tiny red eyes, and claws that shone razor-white in the moonlight. It grinned at me and bared its steely grey teeth, hissing and spitting into the dark. And then crawling out behind it was another, and another: these cackling creatures were swarming up from underneath my bed. I tried to shake them off, but they were scampering over the covers, pulling the sheets up over my head so that I couldn't make a sound.

When the screams came, I could not stop them. My mother was called and I was taken home and sent to bed but could not sleep for days in case the creatures came back. When I finally confided in her, my mother made me crawl underneath the bed with a torch, and I cried but she would not let me out until I admitted that there was nothing down there at all.

'Don't be such a baby,' she said. 'Big boys aren't afraid of the dark.'

When the creatures came back from time to time, I never told a soul. I learnt to keep my screams tight inside and muttered my mother's curt advice. 'Don't be such a silly little boy. Dreams are only dreams.'

As I approached our street I saw my lurch of fear at work as just a momentary lapse into childhood habits. I was different from that lost little boy. Now I had a girl who loved me and a home of my own. And together we would meet the neighbours, who would no doubt be full of envy for all that we had.

As it happened, by the time I got home she had already met them. I opened the front door and the hallway was resonating with music. She had left the locked door open, and the stairs were acting as an amplifier for the whole building. There was music up on the roof and the sound of three voices.

And my heart sank when I heard it: her wild laughter mixing with strong male voices. I realised things would never be quite the same again. Two unknown elements had been introduced into our life.

Later, very much later, this resentment of change will be the cause of great arguments between us. She will say that I am rude and unwelcoming and never think about what she needs. She will say that I am possessive and mean, that I am heartless and cold and would be happier if she was made of stone, just a marble statue that I could keep behind glass so that no one could touch her. I will overreact, rail against her melodrama, tell her that real love is harder and stranger than her stupid stories with their simple, happy endings. I will be unable to tell her that I was at my best when it was just the two of us, and in the company of others we aren't as strong as we should be. But at the moment that is still far enough away in the future; at this point in the story we aren't anything like those kinds of people. So for the moment I just shouted up the stairs to her, 'Love, I'm home!'

But she didn't hear; the music was too loud.

When I ran up to the rooftop she was by the fence, standing on tiptoe, leaning over, talking to the men on the other side.

They were looking down at her, resting their forearms on the top of her picture.

She ran to me, threw her arms round me and kissed me and said that she had been hoping that I'd be home soon because she didn't want to get too drunk without me. She had told them all about me, Phil and Richard. It took me a week to tell them apart. They were old, old friends, and had similar voices and habits, short haircuts, and identical handshakes. Phil and Richard, old friends who came back to the city for the warm months, they explained, to open up the house and delight in summertime London before leaving in the autumn, chasing the good weather around the globe.

Instantly charming, they were stumbling over each other to be the first to greet me, saying, 'Pleased to meet you, mate, come on over.'

They gave her a lift over the fence and I scrambled after, landing clumsily on their patio.

They had ivy growing all over the walls of their garden and it was creeping across the flags. There were many soiled cushions scattered in the centre and bowls of food and candles and cans of beer.

'Perfect,' she said. 'You're both just perfect.'

That first evening didn't last long.

She was like a little child, and couldn't be kept still. Their living room, adjacent to our bedroom, was a world of treasure for her. They had renovated the house, ten years ago, when they first came to the city, when they were in their early twenties. When they heard our tales of recent arrival they delighted in the nostalgia. They told us we'd stay for life now, that this house never let people go, and after a Wimbledon summer we'd never be tempted by anywhere else in London. I was surprised to learn of the age difference between us: there was certainly nothing in their manner to suggest that they might be older and wiser.

When they had moved in, the first thing they had done was smash down walls to let the light in. They had hung sheets from the high ceilings, experimenting with all the different ways they might divide the room. In the end they couldn't bear to lose much. They made separate bedrooms, two tiny boxes sectioned off from the main room, little more than the dimensions of a double bed. Each room had a window that ran from floor to ceiling, framing a view of the common.

She loved it. 'Couldn't we do this?' she asked.

I saw her point. They had totally reinvented the space, making our hitherto perfect home seem cramped and confined. Their stairwell was not boxed off into a narrow little corridor. With long, sweeping wrought-iron banisters, their stairs spiralled down into the centre of their huge living room. Instead of our battered brick chimneypiece they had skylights. They said that some nights they just sat in their room downstairs and watched the stars grow dim and the dawn break across their ceiling. They had long red curtains that draped down like a circus tent, easy to draw closed to hide the sky when it was stormy and dark.

'Oh, don't worry, love,' I said, 'we'll do things like this and then some. Just a matter of time and money. And we've got plenty of both.' I was crudely staking a claim, arrogant on so many levels it's embarrassing to recall.

She made straight for their record collection. She pulled out old favourites and wouldn't go home until they were all played out. This was how I liked to see her – my wilful, laughing girl.

'You're a lucky man,' they said to me, grinning and handing me glasses of wine. 'You're a lucky man, I can see why you need your early nights.' I let them tease me and held her close. But she was reluctant to sit still: the more she drank the more boisterous she became, tugging at my arm.

'Old music for a new summer,' she said.

She lurched over to the record-player to prove her point. I stood beside her and steadied her, telling her to watch out, to be careful not to scratch. She rested her head against my chest, reaching one arm around my neck so that she could pull me down to kiss her.

'My man with the steady hand,' she said.

The boys sniggered from the candlelight behind us saying, 'A lucky man,' over and over again. Lucky man.

I didn't like it: it felt like an intrusion, their running commentary on our relationship.

'He's a lucky man, but does he deserve it?'

'Well, I doubt that very much, Phil, I really do.'

And she was laughing along, not quite in collusion, but she was certainly encouraging them. And just for a second I had a brief flashback to the time before I met her, when all I could do was sit in lonely corners of bars and watch the women I wanted being approached by my peers, who always knew exactly what to say and never went home alone. That night the boys reminded me of where I had come from, and I didn't like it. It felt like everything was being upset and everything was changing. If this was the new beginning she had predicted, I wasn't sure I wanted it.

'Shall we call it a night, love?' I asked her, as she slumped down beside me. She was having none of it; the night was young. She lay down and put her head in my lap, but insisted that she wasn't sleeping. So it was now up to me to make conversation with the boys, which I suddenly found impossibly hard, without her to prompt me. I couldn't find the right words. I was never any good at small-talk, I only had a limited register: I talked in numbers at work, and at home we talked a private language that I wasn't prepared to share.

Actually, in all honesty, I don't think we did talk that much before the neighbours came. I'd like to say that we did – that we knew each other inside out, that we had a real meeting of minds, that we argued politics and religion late into the night, that every morning we re-established our love for each other with an apposite turn of phrase that might bind us together more closely than ever before. I'd like to remember us having a wealth of words to match our movements together – that love was something we could say, define between us in a common language. Maybe we did, on some days. It's not what I remember. What has stayed with me are her stories, and even those, warped by my clumsy retelling, don't capture what they should.

So that night when Richard was just being his usual overbearing self, bombarding me with questions, I was reticent and must have seemed cold to him. I adopted language that belonged to the office, kept him at a distance from the two of us, preferring to baffle him with false enthusiasm about my working world. I painted a rosy picture of male camaraderie, reinvented the boredom of my regimented time with thrilling stories about the joy of gambling with other people's money. I even offered him advice about investments, telling him how the City was a wealth of opportunity for boys like us. A strange performance. Not me at all. Or perhaps very like a part of me, but not any part I was proud of.

His flatmate Phil was more drunk, more argumentative, telling me I was wasting my time, gesturing flamboyantly as he sank further down into his bed of cushions. This, I grew to learn, was his favourite pose. Semi-reclined in the darkness, he would contribute to the conversation in short, single, abusive syllables and Richard would nod sagely as he lit another cigarette.

'Too right, Phil . . . absolutely. It is a waste.' Winking at me as he passed me another beer.

'Yes, Phil, I agree completely that our new neighbour is a wanker. He needs our help.'

'No, I'm fine as I am, thanks,' I replied, gesturing down at her, asleep in *my* lap, after all. I knew I had the unspoken advantage.

As the last of the candles was spluttering out, they were both on their feet again to help me carry her home, insistent that we shouldn't wake her, she looked so peaceful. In her sleep, she drew her arms tighter round my neck and it was easy to lift her. Richard held open doors as I carried her through to our bedroom. 'No hard feelings, mate,' he whispered, as he tiptoed out into the corridor. 'You know we're only joking.'

I smiled back as expected, but privately thought about all those true words that are spoken in jest.

I was glad to reach the end of the day. I fell into bed beside her, a tight-knit tangle of limbs. Although exhausted, I was reluctant to go straight to sleep. I thought about the ways that other true words are spoken, about how your own fears can come whispering to you through your dreams.

I woke suddenly in the middle of the night. I was sitting bolt upright, and shouting, 'Don't jump. Don't!'

And she was shaking me, saying, 'Wake up, wake up, it's all right, I'm here, don't worry, no one's jumping.' Her voice was like liquid silver and lulled me back to sleep before I was even awake, and if there was anything dark and lurking in the corners of our room, it hid in the shadows, undisturbed.

When my alarm rang I woke sharply, almost leaping out of bed, before nausea took hold and I fell back on to the pillows.

'Are you all right, love?' she asked, leaning over me. 'What's wrong?'

Sudden tears came. All I could tell her was that I'd had a bad dream.

'What was it?'

But I was reluctant to say, as if whispering it to her might make it begin to happen, make it all come true, in broad daylight.

'Tell me . . .' she said.

But it was hard to begin. I had woken, again, in an empty bed. Again, shadows of the leaves played above my head, and I could not move. Again, she was perched up on the window-sill, silhouetted against a cloudless sky, playing with her ivy. She sang to the plant in a soft voice, and it moved around her with more intimacy than before, tendrils lingering on her arms. The ivy poured itself out into the night. The stars danced above her, even the heavens themselves were calling her outside. She caught hold of the rope, swung herself out of the window and vanished.

'Don't. Don't jump!' I shouted, as I pushed myself out of bed and ran to the window. The ivy was a strong chain of silver leaves, sneaking, snaking its way out into a void of blackness. The minute I touched it, I felt a tug deep in my chest again, as if those long green fingers of the ivy had crept under my skin, into my veins, and were pulling and pulling at my very heart strings, coaxing me outside.

Then with the clarity that sometimes comes with nightmares, that false pause they give you before they gather their true momentum, I saw that this was only a dream, but that dreams come to us for a reason. I saw that this was all in my mind. I had given myself the most difficult boundary to cross: a steep fall with no visible ground beneath. But perhaps this came as a challenge to my fears. If I fell, my vertigo could be cured. I paused on the very edge of the window-ledge, and weighed up the odds. Behind me there was the warmth and comfort of the home I knew. In front, there was the ivy, drawing me into an unfamiliar darkness. But it was a darkness that she had already gone into. I took hold of the rope, and jumped.

I fell down the side of the house but the ground caught me. I landed on a soft cushion of ivy that had grown over everything I knew. It had thickened as it fell and poured itself over the lawn like a silver sea. Where there had once been neat borders and manicured flowerbeds, there was now a reflective green blanket of leaves. It made a path to follow, stretching across where there had once been a street and leading me into a forest.

This was not a forest I knew, not the familiar land of the common. There were no silver birches catching the moonlight. These trees were closely packed and stood stern like sentinels, daring me to pass between them. They were broad and dark and stretched up for ever above my head, unlike any trees I had seen before. Far above me large black leaves rattled, like the clacking of tongues.

I took courage from tales she told me. *Be bold, be bold, but not too bold*, I whispered to myself as I slipped through the first two trees, stroking the bark for luck. A strange sensation: those old black trunks felt as soft and supple as skin.

Once inside, the woods thinned out. The canopy of leaves did not close out the sky and the light of the moon spilled out all about me, illuminating the wild beauty. Wrapped around the trees the ivy looked like stencilled patterns, etched in silver. Beyond the rustling of the leaves above, there was another sound – the echo of her laughter, calling to me through the night.

I started to run, with unnatural speed, still being coaxed along by that trail of ivy, which wove a slippery path through the forest. And as I ran, I left my earlier caution far behind. I was laughing, with a voice I didn't recognise. I ran from shade to moonlight, to shade again, dappling myself with silver. I raced with my own ghost, watching it lengthen behind me, stepping into the shapes cast by the tree-trunks and letting my shadow be swallowed by the sway of the branches.

Suddenly I stumbled into a small clearing.

The moonlight showed me the clear choices ahead:

Stretched before me in the middle of the forest were two paths. There was nothing to distinguish them, no indication which I should take. The faint sound of her laughter, nothing more than a whisper, echoed from both. Not sure which would lead me to her, I stood undecided, looking for clues.

I saw that the forest, courting my childish side, had tricked me into feeling safe. But now the child in me began to see these wild woods as a dangerous place with dark corners. The whole landscape was static. None of the branches beckoned or pointed to show me which path to take. The ivy trail had dwindled away and I was left alone.

The minute I began to fear this world, my anxiety seeped out into the dream. The rustling leaves sounded like whispers: *But not too bold, not too bold.*

I knew that I had to make a choice, and that it mattered. I had to be quick and determined. I ran towards the right-hand path, then hesitated, ran towards the left, then turned back on myself again. I was turning in circles in that central clearing, not trusting the forest, doubting myself, doubting everything I could see, painfully aware that I was losing her somewhere up ahead. And then, then . . . the dream fragments. I was left with that sickening memory of myself, twisting and turning, trapped by my own indecision.

'What happened?' she said. 'Tell me.'

I couldn't, I was too ashamed of my dream, which had laid out my secret fears so they were as easy to read as her fairytales.

But some of it slipped out, despite myself.

'Was it a very bad dream?' she asked. 'Tell me. Tell me, it'll make it go away.'

'You left me and I couldn't find you.'

She kissed me to stop me saying any more. 'As if!' she whispered. 'As if I could ever leave you.'

'Not even when I test your patience?'

She laughed to hear that I had taken her teasing words of yesterday even remotely seriously. 'You know me,' she said. 'You know I don't mean half the stupid things I say.'

She told me that I always had mad dreams when I drank too much, that she'd lost count of the times I had woken her with my restlessness. 'My poor troubled man,' she said. 'I'll never leave you.'

She fed me coffee, sympathetic but still laughing, telling me I'd need a training programme for the summer: we'd challenge the boys to drinking games every night and in a couple of weeks all the bad dreams would be beaten into submission.

# 7

Her prediction came swiftly true. The summer rolled gently in. Days ran parallel, always the same patterns, with a few fairly predictable variations. Every evening, the sunshine lasted longer, and our rooftop patio became the garden of delights she had promised. The boys were self-styled hedonists. Their role in life, it seemed, was to intoxicate and entertain. They did it with a charm and an ease that were hard to resist. I soon lost the awkwardness that had kept me so reticent that first night we met. The boys were kind and welcoming, and even in my most protective moments, I could not resent them. They brought a lightness and laughter to our world. I could have learnt a lot from them.

Although they were a confident double act, the boys were very different individuals. Phil was taller and more silent, while Richard had a mischievous smile and a greater capacity for beer. Often it was just the two of us who stayed up talking late into the night, our companions passed out amid the detritus of cans and candles.

Richard soon became a good friend to me. Despite the difference in age, and the different lives we had led, there were reassuring similarities: Richard had a thoughtful quietness about him, as if he also found life a puzzle at times and was still looking for a key to decode it all. We would pick that puzzle apart together in those snatched hours on the rooftop, although inevitably in the morning neither of us could quite remember the exact solution to all the woes of the world.

But I would be lying if I said I wasn't jealous of what the boys had. Everything came that little bit easier to them. They had no harrowing journey into the City: they both worked from home, and had jobs that interested and amused them, rather than draining their energy and leaving them bored and listless.

Phil was a craftsman. Their rooftop was his workshop. Occasionally, in the early morning, I would go up on to the patio to have my cup of coffee before I braved the tube. I would lean over the railings and gaze at the common, all green and rich in the morning light. I would fix it all in my mind, noting the position of the trees, the patterns of the shadows on the grass. A survival trick – when work seemed too loud and claustrophobic, I would look out of my office window and remember this other view. It became a game. Blessed with a photographic memory, I could demolish the ugly skyline with the blink of an eye and project the never-ending common up there instead.

One morning I heard the sound of sawing coming from the

other side and peeped over to see Phil, surrounded by chunks of wood and twisted branches, laid out before him in deliberate patterns.

'All right, mate? Betcha can't guess what this is going to be.'

I had absolutely no idea.

'This is my ticket to a quality weekend. Wait and see.'

A few days later he came round to show us the finished article – a beautiful set of boxes, which fitted together, still keeping the shape of the original wood. 'Sold to some gullible tart over and above the asking price,' he said proudly. 'Let's go to the pub.'

I was impressed, tried to hide my envy as I told him how talented he was, that he made me feel clumsy, that I was never any good with my hands.

'That's not what I heard,' he replied, and she laughed along with him.

'Come to the pub with us,' she demanded, pulling me out of the door.

Richard was equally talented in his own way. He designed computer games. I remember the first time he showed me his work – I returned to find the three of them crowded round his computer, Richard hunched over his psychedelic screen. 'Look at this,' he said.

I watched as colourful backgrounds ran past at an alarming rate. The whole game was constructed like a bad horror movie, shot from a shaky protagonist's point of view. He led me down tunnels where monsters warped out of the walls and came chasing after. Black shadows with teeth. The kind of shadows that lurk under your bed and come creeping over the covers in the middle of the night.

'Very impressive,' I said. 'They're terrifying.'

'Who'd've thought I could make a career from my acid flashbacks?' laughed Richard, as he made some minor adjustments and closed down for the night.

'Shall we go to the pub?' she asked. 'Let's get out into the fresh air. I've had enough of these monsters.'

The more I saw of those boys, the more I enjoyed their company. They were worlds apart from the people I encountered at work, living by the exact opposite of the values I had to accept. If they had money, or thought about it, it certainly didn't show. They lived simply and they lived well. They were also very different from the world I grew up in, where appearance was everything and it was always important to watch your manners. With their irreverent ways, they could make her smile her broad wicked grin without touching her, a skill I sometimes envied. But for all their bravado they also had hidden sensitivities. They were kind and considerate and did everything they could not to make me jealous.

It's difficult not to dwell on the changes the boys brought to our life. Part of me just wants to stop her story here. Keep this collage that I have built, glimpses of our shared days and nights. The memories and the phrases twist around me with the ingenuity of a kaleidoscope, fractured scenes difficult to pin down. But I have to remind myself that, much as I might be tempted, this story is not being written for the boys. In the end, it must be a broader testament and move beyond them – out into more difficult places.

\*

That April and beyond was unexpectedly warm. It felt like the boys had brought the good weather with them, along with everything else. We would have raucous Saturday nights when we would invade their flat in the early evening, and she would often cook for them, saying it was the least she could do. Phil would keep her company in the kitchen while Richard would challenge me with his latest games prototypes. I was all fingers and thumbs, often succumbing to instant death in the dark corridors. I lost my lives easily. He later told me that I was his benchmark: if I ever managed to complete a level, he knew he had a lot more work to do. A benchmark of the lowest common denominator.

At the time this division of company seemed quite natural. Phil was a schemer and an artist, like her. During that summer they often worked together during the days. He would carve simple things and she would paint them for him. She made beautiful designs, wreaths of flowers decorating the edges of bowls; candlesticks painted with constellations; simple boxes adorned with fairytale creatures – dragons, angels, wizards and fools. Phil could double his prices and they still sold well in the boutiques of Wimbledon village. He tried to pay her for the work, but she insisted it was a labour of love. I told her she should be more practical: they could make a tidy profit if they went into business together. I could even afford to help get them started. But she didn't want to.

'The boys have given us so much,' she said. 'I don't want to spoil it.'

There was no doubt that she and Phil worked well together.

Their meals were also artistic statements, perfectly crafted and presented. We held banquets in the tented room and proposed toasts between, during and after courses. 'To us!' she would cry, and we would clink our glasses in agreement.

'And all who sail in us!' Phil would retort from the other end of the table.

I was so proud of this colourful lifestyle I had found. She would tease me as we lay in bed, playfully poking my full belly. 'Look at you.' She laughed. 'You look like the cat who's got the cream.'

At the time, that's exactly how I felt. Contented, settled and secure – no discernible vertigo at all.

On Sunday afternoons we would have our leisurely strolls. These are the times with the boys that I remember most clearly – perhaps because of our comparative sobriety. We learnt our way around the common with them. They took us down hidden tracks and we pushed our way through bushes and brambles. Then we would dare each other to run screaming across the golf course with no consideration for the games in play, racing each other up to the windmill. Phil always led the way, crying, 'Upwards and onwards,' commanding us to be brave and bold and go further in. We left noisy roads behind and she was in her element, running ahead to be with Phil while Richard and I took a slower pace, stepping gingerly over puddles. She would run back and grab me in one of her wild bear-hugs just as I was negotiating slippery paths, jumping on my back mischievously, nearly pushing me into the mud with the weight of her love. 'I love this!' she would shout. 'This is just like being back at home!'

I bit my tongue, stopped myself telling her that I'd thought this was her home, here in this place that we had created together. I thought that had been the whole point.

And Phil was a funny one. Out on the common, he was a little removed from us. Always scanning the ground for twigs and bits of rubbish he might be able to transform, he would break off in the middle of a conversation and run ahead when something caught his eye. She called him the magpie craftsman, not without affection.

Phil chose his specimens with care. He searched for flawed pieces – gnarled chunks of wood, trees that had twisted in on themselves under the slow pressure of the years. He would run his hands over them gently, saying, with quiet empathy, 'Would you look at that? Nature can be fucking cruel.'

These Sunday rambles established our territory.

All our rituals gathered momentum. We learnt short-cuts and street-names. With the boys' introductions we were accepted as local characters. The four of us would walk into the Hand in Hand and our drinks would be lined up on the bar in seconds. My earlier desire to show her the best of London seemed pointless when compared with the quality of life we had found on our doorstep.

Sometimes the boys would have visitors and, for me, this was hard. I felt awkward, and didn't quite fit. In this kind of company she was more confident than me, inquisitive about these people who had just come to the city for the weekend, were often passing through on their way to more exotic locations, off to travel the world, to work in foreign cities, launching exhibitions, or blagging a place on some exclusive theatre tour. She was intrigued. I found it difficult. The minute I confessed to my profession, something shut down in those people. I could see the assumptions gathering behind the awkward silences. But she was aware of the tensions and did understand. She would always come back to my side when I was quiet and uncomfortable, the smell of alcohol and cigarettes on her breath as she leant over and kissed me, whispering in my ear that I had nothing to worry about. She wasn't about to run away and join the circus.

People came and people went, stayed for a few days and then were gone. I can't remember their names. I never really listened to those tales from times past. Apart from one. There was a girl with short blonde hair, whom Richard held close to him one night, all through the evening, and would not let go. Her name was Charlotte.

The minute she arrived, Phil was more agitated than we had ever seen him. He was mobile, despite his intoxication, pacing the kitchen and casting suspicious glances over to Richard and Charlotte, who were curled up on the sofa like young lovers, intensely focused upon each other. Just looking at the way he sat with her, how his nervous fingers hovered inches away from her face, I felt a sudden affinity at this glimpse of a younger Richard, and had compassion for him as he fell in love with his past all over again.

We took Phil back to our flat and he filled us in on the history, with drunken outrage. He explained that Charlotte and Richard had met the first year the boys came to London. She had been working in the Hand in Hand at the time, and

Richard had wooed her with a drunken resolve. He had spent every other night propping up the bar until way past closing time, insisting with slurring sincerity that it had to be love. Would she lock him in the pub with her? There were things he needed to say. Would she come home with him? He was so sure they were meant to be together and they shouldn't waste any more time. Phil sat and watched this all unfold from an alcove and worried from a distance for the sanity of his friend.

Then one night Charlotte did come home with Richard. Phil had to walk on ahead, through the dark of the common alone. And then Charlotte spent a couple of months with them, in their still derelict home. Phil saw little of Richard in those months, just shadows behind sheets. Phil spent all his time working on the structure of the house, building the walls of their bedrooms, separating their space, making it private so that he wouldn't have to see and hear things that he didn't want to know. Phil explained how Charlotte upset the balance between them and nothing was special any more. In the end, Charlotte proved to be fickle, unfaithful, or maybe just too young. Richard walked into the Hand in Hand one night to find her ensconced in one of the alcoves with another man, giving him kisses that Richard thought were his alone. Richard lost his love and found his anger, upturned tables and threw pints over them both. Charlotte came back to the flat but Phil would not let her in. He told Richard, resolutely, that it was all for his own good. 'No one does that to my mates,' Phil said, falling into old patterns of defensiveness that had been dormant for ten years. 'No one does that to my mates, and they certainly don't do it twice.'

I thought she would be sympathetic, and subscribe to the romance of love regained. But she shared Phil's attitude to the turn of events. 'Who the fuck does she think she is?' she said. 'Silly cow, coming back and spoiling everything.'

It was a relief to see her react defensively: I always presumed it was just me who felt things in this way.

Phil was ready to go back and confront Charlotte, but I wouldn't let him. 'People change,' I said, with false authority. Instead we fed him whisky until he was happily supine, and left him on the sofa.

The next day Richard called me from Wimbledon station and asked me to meet him in the pub. Not the Hand in Hand this time but the less intimate Fox and Hounds, in the centre of the village. He wouldn't talk much to begin with, and I hadn't seen this side of Richard before, closed around his pint. But after a while it all came out, his confidential whispers competing with the arcade machines.

'The problem with Phil is . . .' he said cautiously. I wasn't sure that I wanted to know. I wasn't sure I was ready to have my sense of the perfect friendship suddenly undermined.

But apparently the problem with Phil was that he didn't believe in love. Not at all. He thought it indulgent, childish, something you grow out of – like believing in fairies or Father Christmas. That was just his nature: Phil was a pragmatist and that pragmatism coloured everything. Right from the start, he didn't have any patience with her stories. Often at the end of the evening, at Richard's request, she would tell one of her tales of enchanted princesses and Phil would disrupt it and refuse to play along.

'In the beginning there was a princess whose evil stepmother had trapped her in a tower all her little life. The tower had a tiny window at the top from which she could see nothing but clouds and blue sky. This was all the princess saw of the world outside and didn't even know there was a land waiting for her below, and knew nothing of the men who walked upon it. Then on the night of her sixteenth birthday—'

'She built a fucking ladder,' Phil interrupted. 'She shimmied out of the fucking window, got a shag and joined the fucking human race. The end. Who wants a beer?'

Phil told her that she was addicted to her stories, that like any kind of junkie she couldn't live without them. He told her that they were only words, only childish, stupid words with no meaning or sense. She argued back: she said that words were never just words; words made things happen, words could build cities and change lives.

Phil said the only kind of cities she could ever build would be castles in the air, that she should learn to speak sense, join us in the real world.

She protested, but in the boys' company she soon learnt to leave her stories behind. She didn't really need them: we were too busy living our own.

In the light of Richard's confessions, Phil's bolshieness made a lot more sense. He couldn't stand her fairytale words because they showed him another point of view: they opened up another world, where love was the strongest weapon and the sweetest spell. Richard told me how Phil didn't believe in love because it might alter everything. Richard had borne witness to it time and time again. All the times that Phil had been offered love, and refused to see it. There was always an excuse: one girl was obviously just looking for a bit of rough; another was too young and didn't know her own mind; another too old and too serious, and the last thing Phil wanted was children. All good excuses, but all untrue. The reality was simpler: the last thing that Phil wanted was love. And, of course, this just made women all the more desperate to convert him.

Richard's theory was that Phil drank and smoked himself into a coma every night, not really for entertainment but more as a desperate attempt to keep his feelings at bay. Phil never wanted to remember anything about their nights of adventure, and the encounters he might or might not have had. It meant that he could live in an eternal present, and never be caught out by his past or the temptations of anyone who might promise him love and company for the future. It was strange to hear Richard so angry, as if Phil's behaviour was a betrayal.

It was stranger still to hear the other side of the story, the side that I could empathise with. Ten years ago Richard had wanted to give Charlotte everything, would have been happy to stay in Wimbledon all his life, needed nothing else but to walk to the pub every night and watch her work and take her home. Richard then saw Phil as an intrusion and didn't know how to reconcile the different parts of his life. So when Charlotte left, it at least solved something.

And now that she had returned, it was too much, too late. She had thought that their first love might still be there, now that she was ready to come back and live the life he had offered her all those years ago. But all Richard could think about were the many other lovers and other histories that now stood between them, his adventures abroad, which just demonstrated all the differences and distances that had developed across time. And although there was some happiness in falling back into bed together and rediscovering old tricks, it didn't match the emptiness and the echoes of the lost years. So he had sent her away on the morning train, preferring the indecision of the future to the mistakes of the past. 'There's no point in going back,' said Richard. 'What's done is done.'

Richard's sincerity surprised me, and I also felt flattered. It marked a sea change in our relationship: we were now allies intent on romance, although it was months before we talked like that again.

Later, as we walked home across the common, locked away in our own thoughts, Richard's story began to frighten me. I had rarely felt the age difference between us before, but I saw it suddenly then: for the first time I questioned the love I had found. It terrified me to think that the home and fortress we had built together might not stand the test of time, that our love might grow old before we did and that I might find myself, in ten years, stranded again. Or, even worse, revisited and finding I had no love left.

I said nothing of this to Richard: it would have seemed unsympathetic. But that night, and for many nights afterwards, I guarded her jealously, and separated our time a little more from the boys. I romanced her anew, like the early days, with flowers and gifts and flattering words. Truth be told, I don't think she quite knew how to take it. 'If I didn't know better, I'd think you were having an affair,' she said, laughing over the latest bunch of roses. 'Maybe you are – maybe you're shagging your secretary and now you're over-compensating.'

I knew she didn't mean it, but told her she shouldn't even joke about such things.

Then, soon, it was the weekend again, and we fell back into our old communal patterns of intoxication by night and exploration by day. Phil and Richard were as thick as thieves once more; it felt like nothing had changed at all. It only took a few nights for me to forget that women might be fickle and love might wane. It all seemed so unlikely then.

So that's how we whiled away our springtime days and nights. It would be easy, now, to say that it wasn't like that at all, that our life wasn't ever that blessed. But I won't succumb to the cynicism of hindsight. I trust my memory, and my memory tells me that's just how it was. The boys were our supporting cast, bringing out the best in both of us.

Friendships were built around easy, sociable rituals: repetition with variations. To some, this definition of love might seem mundane, not a grand emotion at all but a collection of habits and predictable routines. For me it was quite the opposite. I was for ever amazed at the wonder I found in our normal life together. A simple evening meal suddenly became charmed, as I fell in love with her all over again just because of the movement of her hand as it closed around a wineglass. She drunkenly made little sculptures out of the twisted wire casing of champagne corks. I sifted through the detritus in the morning and slipped them into my pocket as lucky charms, which made the long working days easier to bear.

# 8

So we had learnt to share ourselves with other people.

Not that I found the sharing easy. I didn't distrust her and I didn't resent the boys themselves, but I resented the differences between us. Phil roamed the common and, with a sleight of hand, turned driftwood into treasure. Richard ventured into the City maybe twice a month, collected ridiculously large cheques and returned untainted.

He surprised me at work one lunchtime. He was brought into the office by James. I hadn't told James about the arrival of the boys, and of all the changes they had brought with them. Phil and Richard belonged to a different world, and it was important to me to keep that private. I knew he would have disapproved of their lifestyle, their lack of proper jobs, and I didn't want to have that kind of discussion with him. I could cope with all these conflicting values in my life only if I wasn't forced to look at them too closely. Besides, I didn't want to give James ammunition for taking the piss. If he had known, I doubt he would have let an hour go by without taunting me about those men and my girl, basking on a rooftop all day long, saying that I was a fool to trust her, that in his experience all women could be persuaded, given the right kind of encouragement.

James attracted the attention of the whole office, shouting, 'Oi! Bender! Your boyfriend's here.' I blushed with embarrassment but Richard negotiated his way through the maze of desks, unfazed.

'Time for lunch?'

I couldn't. I was a curt, different self. 'No. Sorry. Got a big deal going through.'

'Right. Later, then.'

He couldn't leave quickly enough.

It was even awkward that evening. I hadn't liked Richard seeing me in that environment.

I came home to find them slumped together on a pile of cushions, very merry and very drunk.

'I don't know how you can stand that place, mate,' said Richard.

'Ah, but he loves it, really,' she said, laughing at me. 'You'd be surprised, he loves his fucking money.'

'Well, rather you than me, mate.'

I was surprised by the aggression of my response: 'Actually, Rich, if I had my way, rather you than me also. Much rather you stuck in that fucking office, and much rather me pissing the day away.'

There was an awkward silence. Then she laughed and broke the tension, saying neither he nor Phil would last five minutes in the City: they would bankrupt the world within seconds.

They were only being mean because they were so envious of my superior skills; jealous of my Midas touch.

I knew it wasn't true. There was precious little about my life that they could possibly be jealous of, apart from the obvious – her.

I suddenly saw myself from their point of view, from the perspective of boys who were, of course, not boys at all, but men who had grown into a life that they had shaped for themselves. They knew their own nature, worked with their talents, pursued their pleasures without remorse, and never let their work take them away from the things they loved.

I saw how I must seem to them, returning every night suited and booted and miserable, playing at being a grown-up, the kind of grown-up they must secretly have despised, playing with other people's money and making false promises about the future.

A few weeks previously, one drunken night, I had confided in Richard about the other paths I might have taken, if I'd only had the courage. Before I retreated into the world of numbers I had dreamt of being an explorer, finding new continents and strange lands across the sea. As a very young boy I would build tents and dens in my mother's back garden, constructing fantastic castles from poles and sheets and upturned flowerpots. I would fly a flag from base camp and hunt for savages in the overgrown flowerbeds. I must have been less than eight years old when I confided in my mother about this secret ambition, telling her I wanted to be like Daddy, to build cities and have streets named after me all over the world.

Very gently, firmly, my mother showed me page after page of

my father's battered atlas, the cities that he had worked in ringed with red marker-pen. And she told me very calmly that all the world had been charted and discovered by now, and all of it was going straight to hell. There were no cities of gold out there, no maidens to be rescued, and no buried treasure left unpillaged. All these exotic lands were unsafe and full of hidden dangers. By the end of the evening I understood that I had been born too late: the age of adventures was over, and it was better for me to stay at home.

The next morning the garden was only a garden, all too familiar. I lost the knack of den-building and never really turned my hand to anything practical again. My ambitions for my future shrank back into the clear confines of London. Although I always kept hold of that atlas, a last link to a life I could have had.

Richard laughed at my confessions, and told me I still had time to change: we could leave the next day if we wanted, just the four of us. I surely had enough money and we could travel the world and send my mother postcards to taunt her, the silly unimaginative bitch.

I confessed that I had become a creature trapped by my own habits, that my boywildness had turned in on itself, and now I was afraid of unknown places and suspicious of new people.

'It's never too late to change,' said Richard. 'I was a right little wanker when I was your age, and now look at me.'

'Yeah, and now you're just an irritating old wanker with less fucking hair!' shouted Phil, from the end of the patio.

We drank to growing older and wiser – and balder – together.

'And, anyway,' said Richard, 'if you'd pissed off and become the next Columbus you'd never have met us, would you?'

'Or her,' I said, gesturing into the dark at the far end of the patio as the love of my life swayed drunkenly against the fence.

'And then you'd never have got laid!' shouted Phil, supine in the shadows.

The boys. It makes me smile even now to write about them. I had never known friendship like that before. I was part of a close-knit group, not an outsider, watching with envy and not understanding.

Time played pleasant tricks back then – all the best parts of my life kept on repeating themselves. Every evening held a comforting sense of *déjà vu*.

I loved to return to find the three of them up on the rooftop: Richard raucous and swearing, flicking beer at my suit, Phil joining in half-heartedly, horizontal among the plant pots, and her sitting between them, her bikini top on and a sarong wrapped around her waist, laughing and reaching up for my hand.

So it was a typical night when I came back and found them in that predictable alignment, with Richard holding forth. The tiles of the patio were warm. The Astroturf had a sticky feel beneath my feet.

'The bloody grass is melting!' I said.

She kissed me, whispering, 'Don't tell Phil. He won't be able to take it.'

Richard patted the patch beside him and told me that it was not melting there just yet. I should catch the last bit of the sunshine. Relax.

'He's got something to show you,' she said.

Richard was in his element, his bloodshot eyes twinkling with laughter. 'Yes, I have. It's the best invention to date. Look at this beauty.'

I squinted up into the sunlight where he was pointing. Sure enough, there was a thick line of rope stretching above me, linked to a precarious pulley resting on the top of our dividing fence.

'What does it do?'

'What doesn't it do?' Richard shouted. Even Phil was sitting up, grinning, awaiting my reaction.

'It's a machine of genius!' He gave the rope an almighty tug, and a steel bucket came jolting up over the top of the fence. 'Mind your heads!'

It swept down over the partition and an express delivery of champagne on ice came skidding to my feet. We drank a lot of champagne during those months. It became another game: each of us took turns to try to come up with something to celebrate. Hers were always the best, unequivocal: 'Us! What other excuse do you need?'

This bottle was in honour of 'Great Ideas': I took it for granted that we figured among them. She ran downstairs for the glasses.

Richard was irrepressible. Apparently this was just the beginning. With different weights and different containers we could easily transport all sorts of things.

I asked if he could make a stretcher so that we could airlift Phil off our patio with minimum disruption. I didn't mean anything by it.

But Phil was taking us dead seriously and started quoting weights and strengths and the full works. 'It would be brilliant. Can you imagine a better way to travel? You two could just yank the rope at the end of an evening and send us over.' Then Richard got all animated and started banging on the fence, testing its strength. That's what made her come running back upstairs.

'This is the answer,' he was saying. 'What we want to do is make ourselves a nice doorway here. Just cut a hole in the centre, right here,' and he scratched the paintwork.

Phil was in absolute agreement. 'Let's do it now, save us the walk.'

They were only joking, but she was furious, suddenly screaming at the three of us. 'How dare you? Who the hell do you two think you are?'

She flew at Phil with that unexpected fury of hers and pushed him away from the fence.

'You think our house is your home too? You think you can just knock down the walls when you fancy it?'

Phil sobered up in a second. He tried to touch her, he was sorry and he'd never meant a word, but she shrugged him off, scowling.

The boys made their quick exit. They had never seen her like this before, never witnessed that fierce, explosive side of her.

'And you didn't say a thing!' she practically spat in my face, and threw the bucket back over the fence. 'They were ready to cut straight through my painting, spoil everything. You know how much it means to me and you didn't say a thing. You're such a fucking coward.'

There were things I could have said, for sure. I could have

taken her side, I could have told the boys that, despite everything they had given us, their time, their humour, their good company, they shouldn't presume so much. I could have said to them that they had to respect her boundaries, these invisible, irrational boundaries that she would create on impulse, then dismantle a few hours later, with no explanation. But then, for all their compassion, they didn't love her like I did. There was no reason for them to understand.

Or I could have taken their side. Especially Richard's: he looked as if something he had been sure of had been ripped away from him; as if he had suddenly lost all his lives. Phil was more reserved, shuffling down the stairs, looking possibly a little disdainful, as if she was behaving like a spoilt little girl. Which, indeed, she was.

So instead I did what I always do in those situations where I feel pulled in two directions at once. I did nothing and said nothing. I watched the boys leave and I went downstairs to talk to her, but she was prickly and kept her distance. She put on music too loud for conversation, and used it as a barrier between us. While she drunk-stumbled at the other end of the living room I made our dinner, telling her she had to soak up the alcohol, she'd regret it in the morning otherwise. She was drunk, but her sulky expression made her seem even more like a petulant child.

It was difficult to touch her for the rest of that evening. She was agitated and wouldn't sit still. We heard no noise at all from next door.

I told her what she wanted to hear, how much I loved her garden, how I knew what it meant to her, that the boys were just taking the piss and of course I would hate it if anyone damaged it. After many such platitudes she said, 'All right. Let's put an end to a horrible evening and just go to bed.'

So we went to bed and she let me hold her, but the muscles in her back tensed up against me. 'I know you think I'm mean,' she said.

There was a hardness in her voice. I tried to make it go away, to soothe and settle her, to undo all the knots she had gathered up inside. I rubbed the curve of her spine until she could stretch herself out again.

She said that it must always be our place. She said that places are like people, that you must always protect what you love about them and never take anything for granted.

I thought about how much I loved the boys' presence in our lives, and told her we would go round tomorrow and make amends and there would be no harm done.

'Not tomorrow,' she said, and pulled my hand close to her chest as she drifted off to sleep. 'Soon, but not tomorrow,' she said. 'Tomorrow we'll have our own quiet day, just you and I, my poor neglected man.'

Inevitably, troubled days bring troubled nights. I should have seen it coming. But at the time it felt like those fragmented dreams belonged to a different life. We had a whole brave new world unfolding on our rooftop, spilling over into the flat next door. Our evenings held so many entertainments there was no need for me to dream up adventures to keep me on my toes. I should have known that the minute our new home was shaken, the wild wood would come rushing back.

It returned with a vengeance. The nightmare came so quickly and so clearly, it felt like I was waking rather than falling into a deep, sudden sleep. I opened my eyes to find the room bathed in moonlight again, giving a crystal clear illumination, cutting through the dark. That light transformed her into an ethereal beauty, poised on the window-sill with a white sarong wrapped around her waist. She might have been made of marble, her face so still and concentrated as she played with the plant, twisting and turning it into a rope once more. But marble lacks her quicksilver movement. She flowed with the ivy, out of the window, out into the night.

I was still carrying the tension and shock of that unexpected argument and I didn't want this. I kept on telling myself to get up, wake up. If only I could wake up I would be back in the safety of my real room, with her sound asleep beside me, rather than faced with empty acres of space between me and the window, the white sheets turned into a silver sea between where I lay and the world she had run to.

But no matter how hard I wished for it, I could not wake. That moonlight was too strong: it caught and held me in this dream world; it showed me the land below my window with such clarity that it was impossible not to believe in it. There was the rope of ivy, boldly rooted to the lawn. There were the dark woods, spreading out for ever, merging with the edges of the night. And there was a fragment of her, just the semaphore flash of her sarong as she ran into the forest. I knew I had to go after her, call her back, back to our home, where she belonged. Instinctively, I knew we should not be divided both in the daytime and at night. The ivy pulled me out of the window and I had to follow.

The minute I ran into the woods, I became swift-footed again, and couldn't stop myself laughing as I ran through the maze of trees, and all the anxiety of the daytime was left behind. The clarity of the moonlight added details: I could see hidden colours playing across the surface of the leaves, deep greens and dark purples giving those black leaves a raven beauty. In the patches of moonlight that fell at my feet I saw that the forest floor was a carpet of ferns and flowers. Bluebells and daisies vied for space with snowdrops and forget-me-nots, in delicate patchwork patterns. An out-of-season springtime wood, a clustering beauty. I trod lightly, reluctant to trample, and they sprang back, uninjured by my footsteps. I felt lighter than air, as if I could do no damage, and the new-found child in me loved that lightness.

I was close behind her, but no matter how fast I ran, I could not get any nearer. There was an energy in her movement, like her familiar dancing energy, but something more, magnified by this place. She flowed through the forest, as if she was a part of it – and there was always the same distance between us.

So when I got to the clearing for the second time I had lost her somewhere up ahead. Her laughter echoed from both pathways. Yet again, I was faced with an impossible choice. The sharp moonlight mocked my indecision. The clearing was a pool of white light. The dark openings of the two pathways stared back at me, like a challenge.

I refused to be afraid this time. And with that refusal came a moment of understanding. This was a dream and only a dream, just a maze of my own thoughts. Any clues I needed, I myself could provide. If I willed this landscape to help me, it would do so. If I wanted it enough, surely I could forge my way through and find her.

I stepped out into the clearing, into the silent, concentrated moonlight. Time stopped again for a second, and nothing moved. Every edge of every leaf, every wrinkle-rippled tree-trunk stood out sharp and clear. It was like being trapped in a hall of mirrors, identical images on all sides. Impossible to make any choices, impossible to move at all. But the moonlight shifted again, and seemed to pour itself intensely into one corner. There I saw something stuck on the bushes by the side of the left-hand path. It was just a tiny scrap of her sarong, glowing brilliant white among the greenery – a marker to show me the way.

Suddenly the tempo of the dream changed again. There was nothing to be afraid of. I left those uncertain paths behind me, and the way ahead was obvious. Everything was a game. I was following a trail that could only lead to her. I ran quickly down the path, which led deeper and deeper into the trees. The undergrowth was thicker here, and there were no flowers breaking up the dark sheen of the winding wood. Branches hung low, with ivy caught between them, and I had to push my way through. Changed terrain, this part of the forest was wilder, and more tangled, but still beautiful in its untamed ways. And the winding routes through the trees didn't faze me: every time the path forked, a piece of white cloth was caught on the brambles as though to guide me. The forest raced by on all sides as I ran.

Then I turned a sharp corner, and suddenly the path split in several directions. On every side, there were black openings in the line of trees. The moonlight trickled through the canopy, hinting at the paths beyond. The sway of the leaves played with the echo and it seemed that the trees were speaking with her voice, saying, *Catch me if you can, if you can, catch me.*

I was turning in circles again, like in the previous dream, desperately looking for the next marker. But there was nothing, just the gaping dark mouths of the pathways, surrounding me. And then I saw that this might not be a game after all, but a subtle trap. She had scattered scraps of her sarong through the forest only to lead me astray so that I would be swallowed by the wrong opening. No sooner did I think that than the moon waned, the light retracted, and all was darkness. I couldn't even see my own hand, held inches in front of me.

The creak of the branches and the sway of the leaves were amplified in the dark, and it sounded as if the whole forest was stretching itself around me. I thought I could hear scampering footsteps up ahead, but without the light to guide me, I could no longer be sure it was her. Suddenly I needed to be home again. I willed myself to wake, I stood stock still in the middle of the forest, closed my eyes and refused to believe it was there.

I opened my eyes, and there still was nothing but blackness ahead. My fears poured themselves into the darkness, and I could not move. It felt as if I had reached the end of the world, that I was standing at the edge of some great precipice, and if I took another step I would fall down into a deep, dark well of unknown space, and be lost, for ever falling through that blackness. And yet I still had a little strength, it seemed: I dreamt some subtle help for myself. It was the strangest thing.

Ahead of me all was still pitch-black dark, but in the woods behind me, the moonlight still shone clearly on one of the paths, showing me the safe route I had taken, marking out the trail I should follow to return. The contrast made the velvet-dark night all the more terrifying. And even if I'd had the courage to challenge the blackness and step forward, that silver light drew me into it with a force far stronger than my own will. I had no choice but to abandon her to the night ahead, and follow the snaking line of moonlight, as it led me all through the forest, all the way back home.

The stars were dancing along the line of our rooftop. I focused on the wall in front, made myself look at the solid bricks and the creeping foliage. The climb was a struggle: I am not naturally agile, and that ivy was good for departure, but tricky upon return. I made slow progress, counting the bricks in the wall as I inched my way upwards. The ivy coiled up against me, and I kept losing my grip and my footing, slip-sliding back, having to catch myself, never looking down at the land below.

The minute I was back in our room a swift heaviness of sleep within sleep came upon me, dragging me back to the bed. I would not let it take me. Earlier I had wanted the dream to be over; now I wanted to choose the ending. I wanted to see her return. I sat up on the window-ledge and waited. From this vantage-point I could see the whole forest rippling below – a soporific trick, it was hypnotic to watch.

Sure enough, she soon came running out of the forest, a flash of silver in the deep dark night, the moonlight playing over her skin and catching what was left of her sarong, ripped up to her thighs, reduced to rags and tatters. I leapt away from the window, and hid under the covers. I could hear that ivy rope striking against the side of the building as she climbed up. The plant beat a soft rhythm against the stone, which carried me back into a deeper sleep.

We were both very quiet the next morning.

She looked pale and sickening when she woke, as if all her energy had drained away while she was sleeping. And this is a side of her that hurts, even now, to put into words. But it's part of our story, the other side of the coin. She had turned round to face me in her sleep and I woke up to the unfamiliar sensation of her clenched fists pressing into my chest, her knees drawn up to her chin, her shins against my stomach. Her body was curled into a tight question mark.

She used to say that on the bad days it was like all the colour had left the world, and everywhere she walked she cast black shadows. Shadows that would catch anyone who came too close.

She couldn't bear to face the sunlight. There was no music that morning and I had to tiptoe around her. This time I kept my bad dream close to my chest and said nothing. She had said once that words were never nonsense: words made things happen, words could build cities and change lives. In the current circumstances, I wouldn't risk articulating the fears of the night.

It was horrible to leave her, but she wouldn't let me stay. 'You'll only make it worse,' she said.

I was used to being shut out when she was like this but it didn't do either of us any good.

I came back after a day wasted by worrying. I had sat at work, staring out of my window, unable to see anything but that twisted shape of her, compacted by the weight of her own distress.

A few days before, I had scanned an old photograph of her into my computer, which flashed up before me as a screensaver if I sat idle for too long. At the time, I had told James that it was concrete proof I was in no way a bender boy. He told me that he wouldn't believe a word of it until he had three-dimensional evidence. But, really, it was nothing to do with him. It was another cunning survival tactic, like the remembered landscape of the common that I liked to project on to the office blocks. That day I spent as much time as I could on paperwork, scribbling numbers in margins, reassured by the image of her flickering on my screen, smiling down at me. A fixed picture: there was no chance that her features might contract at any moment into a fierce frown.

James noticed, and kept leaning over and flicking my mouse so that my screensaver disappeared, leaving my spreadsheets glaring down at me instead. He laughed when I finally lashed out, smacked away his hand and told him to stop pissing about. 'Jesus, mate,' he said, 'I'm only messing. You have got it bad, haven't you?'

On my return I opened the door very quietly, just in case she was sleeping. Everything was as I had left it. I walked through to the bedroom, and there she was. Sitting with her back against the wall, her knees still drawn up to her chin. 'Be very quiet!' she hissed.

I wanted to stroke her arms and take her hand, watch her

slowly relax as I kissed her, moving her knees away from her face. I wanted to make her smile again as I unfolded her out of herself.

She just sat there, as if she was holding herself down. I told her that it was all going to be fine, it was just a hangover or a headache or something and she'd be over it by tomorrow morning. 'We all have bad days,' I said.

That might sound like false comfort, but they were actually very old words of reconciliation. Tried and tested sentences that would normally get through. A set formula for turning bad days into better ones.

She looked at me with utter disdain. 'Listen!' she said.

The traffic below, beyond our window, was a distant hum. There was nothing distinct. 'What? What am I supposed to hear? There's nothing.'

'That's it! There's nothing. The boys are always back before you. Always, and now they've gone and I did it.' She started to cry. 'I did it,' she said. 'They've left, and soon I will do something so wrong that you will leave too.'

I didn't believe her. I had to go round to see for myself. I knocked on the door, but there was no answer. I hollered and yelled, 'Richard! Phil! It's the Peace Corps!' Trying to make a joke out of a situation that blatantly wasn't funny. I ran up to the patio, which was still scattered with the wreckage of the night before, unwelcome reminders. I tripped over bottles and cans. No wonder such a petty argument had erupted, there was evidence of a whole day's carnage up there. Standing on tiptoe, peeping over the fence, it was obvious that she was right. The door on to their rooftop was closed, and the curtains were drawn across the skylights. They had clearly deserted.

I went back into the bedroom and held her, and she cried and cried in my arms, saying over and over again that she was wicked and mean, she always drove people away and one day soon I would leave too.

I told her she didn't know what she was talking about. I held her and told her I would never leave her. How could I? I promised she could be as mean as she liked and still I would not go. She turned her face to the wall and pulled the bedclothes up tight around her neck. I sat there, stroking her skin through the sheets until she had sobbed herself to sleep.

I lay beside her, outstaring the tall doors of the wardrobe. I listened to the sound of her breathing, which, even in sleep, carried echoes of her side-shaking sobs. Guilt and fear crept through the silent house. I felt like a careless child, as if I had accidentally broken something I had never even realised was precious.

# 9

We didn't speak much over the next few days.

She got out of bed with me the following morning but was still shaken and vulnerable. She pushed open the curtains, but she wasn't really looking out on to the day ahead. She wouldn't put any music on. It didn't feel right. 'When the boys come back,' she said. 'We'll have music all the time when the boys come back.'

I remember those mornings for their silence. We trod cautiously around each other: the flat felt full of unmanageable gaps and spaces. I was shocked at how small and displaced I felt in this home that, before the boys arrived, had been more than enough for both of us. But now that they had gone, the rooms felt too large and too quiet. And she was so sad and sorry, unable to look me in the eye. I would come back in the evening after a long day at work, needing her to be full of energy and comforting words but instead finding her curled tightly in on herself and silent, still waiting for any sound from the other side of the wall. I could tell that she had spent the whole day sitting there, still as stone.

'Tell me a story, love,' I would ask, with false brightness. But she would have nothing to say. I would talk nervously about work, but my sentences would falter, unfinished. On those nights, it was just too hard to say anything at all. She was finding it difficult to sleep and, of course, I couldn't sleep for worrying about her. Those were nervous vigils, starting at every creaking floorboard, willing it to be the return of the boys, but in my heart knowing it was just the usual noises that the old house made as it settled itself in the night.

To combat the silence, we took turns to read to each other. I would read her my books from work to send her to sleep and to keep me up to speed. Business jargon and strings of numbers to keep me in my place. Then, after a few hours, she would wake and read to me, from a pile of glossy magazines that she kept by the bed. Light reading for heavy days. If I dreamt at all those nights they were brief nightmares of female fantasy and sexual paranoia, the bland platitudes of agony aunts lulling me to sleep.

And during those days work was very difficult. I couldn't focus. Quite literally, I couldn't see the numbers on my screen as clearly as before. I was carrying a dark cloud of worry with me wherever I went. It settled on my shoulders throughout the working day and wouldn't shift. It gave me tunnel vision, all black and blurred around the edges. Always the same sad heavy worries: where had the boys gone? Would they be back that night? In her shame, would she go off to find them and would

I come home to an empty house? With such uncertainties at play, I couldn't connect with my life at the office. It was hard to see the point of this world of wealth and numbers.

James tolerated my miscalculations on the first day after their departure. But the next day, when my mistakes were multiplying, he turned on me abruptly. 'What the fuck is wrong with you? This is basic stuff.'

I felt ashamed. I couldn't tell him what I was really think-ing, that there was no point in investing time and energy in predictions of any kind when – as the boys' desertion had proved – nothing could be taken for granted. 'I'm sorry, mate,' I mumbled. 'I'm not sleeping very well at the moment.'

'Well, sort it out. You're fucking us all up.'

James, for all his bravado, was a professional and wouldn't tolerate any weakness in the system.

Even Simon had his say. 'Do you know that the human brain has a biological need for eight hours' sleep a night?'

'Does it really?'

'Yes, and for every hour you miss, your IQ actually drops by ten points.'

'That's fascinating, Simon, but hardly what I want to hear right now.'

I painstakingly double-checked all my figures, reined in the chaos, but felt none of my usual pride in a job well done, took no joy in the money we were making.

No, my mind wasn't on work at all. I thought that I had learnt how to segment my life into different time zones and prioritise accordingly. But take away the constants and all those boundaries came crashing down. When the boys had been gone for two days, I couldn't help listening to the whisperings of my deepest fears: what if they didn't come back at all? If her fierceness had frightened them away for good? If so, it was just as much my fault as hers.

It was my fault for withholding information, for not preparing the boys for this part of her nature. I had allowed them to believe in the perfection of our relationship, and let them think that she was always free and generous and easy to love. Just as much a deception as the fact that at the start of this story I kept her darker days hidden. But in both instances I did it for a good reason – it's the beauty of her that matters and, just as I had my time, so everyone should be given a chance to see it pure and uncorrupted, at least at the start, not to know her always as a difficult girl.

I had been too embarrassed to go round that night and explain to them that this was a part of her that only came out rarely, that I didn't really believe she had meant it, it was so out of keeping with the rest of her, that vicious, defensive side. In the days before we had our home, with my mother, or even further back at university, it had always been clear to me that I had to take her side. It was us against the world. But this time it had been different. I should have realised. I should have acted as an interpreter between our two households, explained to the boys that when she had said that, what she had actually meant was . . . and then the fantasy failed me. How would I have played it? Would I have been able to laugh about it with them, to lapse into a softer version of the male banter that I was learning at work? To have talked about mood swings, to have shared a beer and asked them to help me lighten the burden. I could never have spoken of her like that: it would have spoilt the illusion of our life together. Even now, I think it would have been a lie. She was always more of a blessing than a burden. That was the whole point.

On the third day of desertion I persuaded her to come up to the rooftop with me for an early breakfast. The sun was warming the day through already. The patio was still scattered with the remains of our last night up there, the rope-pulley system sagging sadly above. She tugged it half-heartedly, like a broken bell-pull. All the right signals, but still no response. I suggested that it might be best to tidy it all away; it didn't suit her to live in squalor. She should make the house into something the boys would want to come back to, and then they'd be sure to return.

I spent that day at work hunched over my numbers, not talking. James tried to prise the truth out of me. 'What's up, mate?' he said, cockily. 'Trouble in paradise?'

'Something like that.'

'Ah, she'll get over it, they always do.'

I didn't want to talk about it, didn't want to tell him she wasn't like other girls: she didn't just get over things quite so easily.

But, actually, James was right. That evening I came back to a flat filled with music and laughter again. Suddenly everything was fine.

There was Richard, crouching by my stereo, spliff in mouth, battling with the complexities of the CD player. Phil was sprawled out along the length of our couch, 'City boy!' he roared, as I came through the door. The CD was sticking and the same three notes kept repeating. Richard gave it a thump and it stopped altogether. They seemed embarrassed by the silence, but she came out of our bedroom smiling and saying, 'It's all right, he doesn't mind. He's as pleased as I am.'

And I was, but part of me wanted to shout at her, ask her why she hadn't phoned me the minute they had returned, why she had let me be worried and unhappy for any longer than was necessary. Instead I shook Phil's hand and smiled. Richard gave me an unexpected bear-hug. I had to force myself to let go. The boys were back.

Then came their awkward confessions. They'd both seen that we might need some space so they had left London for a few days and it had been brilliant. I stopped them mid-sentence, telling them how good it was to have them back, no hard feelings. A convenient lie: I didn't trust myself to show any signs of irritation with them, to hint that I was quietly furious at their carelessness, that they had just upped and left with no explanation. A more rational part of me knew that my anger was unreasonable. How could they have known, after all, the effect of their actions?

But I didn't want her to hear their countryside tales. Not that I was really worried: they had gone up to the hills, back up north. After we escaped our grey beginnings, she said she'd never go up north again; there had been nothing worthwhile up there for her, apart from me. Even so, I talked over their anecdotes, interrupting and distracting them at every turn. Even then, I didn't want to tempt fate.

'So, you're back for a while now, are you?' I said, feigning indifference.

'Yeah, it'll do,' replied Phil. 'Miss us, did you?'

'Of course I did,' she said. 'I was so bored. There was nothing to do.'

'And it's good to be back,' said Richard. He said they had never meant to take the piss. He promised that we'd both be consulted on any plans for structural alterations to our property. There'd be no more rude intrusions, and, to prove a point, they made ready to leave.

Seeing them standing by our door, looking sheepish and stoned, I didn't want them to go. I didn't want things to change; I wanted our old habits back. I was afraid of the long stretches of silence that the two of us had endured in their absence. 'Don't go just yet,' I said. 'Let's make a night of it, we've nothing planned.'

Phil's relief was evident in his broad smile. 'All right,' he said. 'We'll have a good night.'

They left to get supplies and we were to meet them on the roof at nine – we were straight back into a routine we could all trust. We had a couple of hours to spare, and she was all smiles and bold energy as she pulled me to bed. Suddenly it was fine to touch her again. Overcome by all the changes of the day, carried along by the force of our quickened heartbeats, I told her how this was another fresh start, a second chance.

She laughed down at me when I tried to speak. 'Every day together is a fresh start, love,' she whispered. Her hair tickled my skin. 'Every day is an adventure.' She bit her lip and put her fingers in my mouth so that we wouldn't embarrass the boys next door.

Afterwards, we couldn't help but smile at the sounds on the other side of the wall. Undoubtedly the house was alive again.

'Those boys were blessed with a good life,' she said, half dreaming.

I laughed at her, telling her that these things come with time and practice and educated choices.

But no. According to her, they had been blessed at birth by gentle guardian angels who had bestowed enough adventures upon them to last a lifetime.

I told her that if that was the case then my good angel must have been sadly absent. She told me not to be so stupid: hadn't we managed to find each other remarkably soon in our lives? What was that, if not a blessing?

We drifted off to sleep in each other's arms, and it was simply so easy to believe in this new interpretation of our love.

I woke to see her standing at the foot of the bed, her arms full of fresh flowers. Of course. She always said that a house is not a home without them and these were to welcome the boys back.

'Get up, get up,' she was saying, 'it's nearly time.'

The excitement in her voice. She threw clothes at me, I dressed, we went up to the roof hand in hand.

There, by the side of the fence, was a pile of bricks forming makeshift steps. She had done it this morning, because after I left she realised that I had been right. Something had to be done to bring them back. Ever the home-maker, she had built the steps so that we could go over and see the boys when they returned. They had a similar rudimentary rockery on their side of the fence. No sooner had she placed the last one down than they had come running out on to the rooftop, thinking they had athletic burglars. She explained that she had done it for them, to make sure there was never too tall a fence between our two houses. Phil was delighted and promised to cement them down on both sides. I swung my legs over and jumped down, holding up my hand for her as she followed, the flowers balanced in the crook of her arm. She said that she wanted to decorate their place for them and then all would be equal. A slightly theatrical peace-offering.

The three of us sat on the cushions and watched her at work. She held the flowers close: the pollen had brushed off on to the skin of her chest and arms. Making her way round the borders of their garden, she wove flowers among the ivy, gently turning them so that the heads were twisted out to face us, all the time moving unconsciously to the faint music rising up from their living room. The boys' candles illuminated the colours and cast shadows all around. Very different shadows from those I'd encountered in my dream, but still a reminder, as if by her actions she was trying to coax it out. I half expected the ivy to reach up towards her, to pluck the flowers out of her arms. Time slowed down and slipped into dream time, and every detail of her touch on the ivy was crystal clear. I couldn't hear if she was humming to herself while she worked. We didn't say anything: it would have broken the spell. None of us dared move. It was as if she had forgotten we were there. We watched quietly as the fence gradually became overgrown.

She walked over to us, put her arms round me and broke the silence.

'You must do this twice a week,' she said to them earnestly. 'Isn't it worth it?'

Another ritual was established between us. For the rest of our shared summer I would come home and find them up there, her patiently trying to show them the trick of bending stems without snapping them, Richard with pollen all down his shirt, Phil shedding petals, determined that he wouldn't be defeated.

It almost hurt me to have the boys see that side of her, so graceful, so beautiful in her private moments. But then it was broken, and she was running downstairs with Phil to choose the music. Richard moved closer and, in drunken whispers, asked if I thought it was all going to be all right now. I told him I was sure it would be. Nothing had changed.

We sat quietly for a while.

'I don't envy you,' Richard said.

I thought he was joking, but he looked concerned.

'It can't be easy,' he said.

I didn't know what he meant.

He said he couldn't imagine it was easy for me being with her. You were never sure what she was thinking. It was an invitation for information, a reminder of our alliance in the Fox and Hounds.

But I wouldn't admit any weakness, so instead became stupidly defensive and said that I thought I knew her a little better than he did, that sometimes we were so in tune that it was difficult to remember to speak. I told him about the early times when we would spend days in silence, just touching, no need for conversation. Then, after days without language, we would open our mouths at the same time and begin our first sentence with the same words.

'We all have that, of course,' said Richard, smiling. 'We've all had days like that – God help us at our age if we haven't.'

'No, I think we've got something a little bit different from all the rest.'

Richard gave me a wry smile. 'That's what everyone thinks, the first time,' he said.

A small silence passed, broken only by the laughter as Phil argued with her over her choice of records, somewhere down below. Something in me shifted and just for a second I saw an alternative future to the one she had promised me. Maybe we wouldn't grow old together, after all. I saw myself briefly, waking up alone, in a strange bed, in an unfamiliar room, calling out for her. No sooner glimpsed than it was gone.

I persisted, maybe a little too enthusiastically, painting a pretty picture of our life together, telling him about our early days in Wimbledon, in the pub, her absolute certainty that we deserved a good home together. I told him about all the light she had brought into my life, how I now really genuinely saw my life severed in two: before and after times. I told him how I just knew that time was now on our side, how I could see the months unfolding and gathering momentum, how I looked forward to the time when I realised I had had her with me for longer than all those formative years I had spent alone. I told him how everything she did seemed charmed, and that if he wasn't jealous he wasn't a real man.

'Fair enough,' said Richard. 'But you wouldn't be the first to be fooled.'

'So you think I'm kidding myself?'

Then Richard laughed and tried to lighten the mood, saying, no, of course not, of course he was just jealous: I was the guy who'd got the girl after all. 'But she is tricky,' he said. 'She doesn't give you any clues. Most women at least help you along with a hint or two. Then some women leave you clues strewn around all over the place and you're still too fucking stupid to see them.'

'What's that supposed to mean?'

'Well, here's one for free. When they tell you you've got nothing to worry about, start worrying.'

I laughed nervously. I didn't like the way this conversation was headed. I told Richard that he was just a cynical old bastard and he shouldn't project so much.

'You're probably right,' he replied. 'But just so you know, when they start asking you to trust them . . . don't.'

I wasn't quite sure what I should say. A renegade part of me wanted to give him some clues of my own and see what he might make of them. Part of me was tempted to tell him about my dreams of the wild forest, to ask him what he thought all the winding ivy and the dark trees might mean. But there was always an element of risk with Richard. You had to catch him in the right mood: he might understand everything and give you all the answers you needed or he might just laugh in your face and torment you for the rest of the evening. I stayed silent that night – I wouldn't have been able to take it.

Instead I went downstairs and teased her as she struggled with a tangle of speaker wires and extension cords. 'Not so agile now, are you, drunken love?' I said.

She hugged me, all excitement and warmth still, telling me that we were in for a long night. While the boys fussed with their bits of machinery, she vaulted over the fence again, that now familiar fluid movement of hers. Standing tiptoe on her precarious steps, she handed me more bottles of wine, raided from our kitchen.

It was a perfect summer's evening.

The sky was clear and the stars stretched in an arc above us, giving the night depth and distance. 'Almost like a country sky,' she said.

Phil laughed at her. 'Bollocks,' he said. 'It's nothing like. We saw shooting stars in the hills. When was the last time you saw a shooting star?'

'Did you know...' she said, pausing for dramatic effect. 'Did you know that shooting stars are actually fallen angels?'

'Fuck off! No, they're not.' Phil reacted in character, delighting in playing along with her.

'Yes, they are, shooting stars are fallen angels who are—'

'I'm not listening.'

'Fallen angels who are coming down to earth to tempt us.'

'No, they aren't. They're bits of rock, quite often from the moon, that are pulled into the earth's orbit and catch fire.'

'It's the same thing.'

'In what possible fucking way is that the same thing?'

And so on and so forth until everyone was laughing.

By the end of the evening I had fallen in love with her all over again, this time for her wild mischievous words, and the way her blue eyes flashed bright when she was teasing. The black days were behind us, and it was like she was making up for lost time. I wish I had recognised what we could have done with the time ahead.

I wish I had turned round and told her that we could go anywhere she wanted, up to the hills with the boys, if she so desired, or down to her home village – anywhere. Or that maybe, just maybe, she might be able to reawaken the child adventurer in me and we could travel to strange new lands together. To go on a hunt for fallen angels and follow them wherever they led us. Told her that wherever we ended up, it would make no difference to me: she was my compass and my only lodestone.

But I didn't even mention it.

As the evening drew to a close Richard was almost an embarrassment, all slurred apologies. He thought he had overstepped the mark again, he hadn't meant anything by it. Of course, looking at her tonight, it was obvious. His first suspicions had been right. I was a lucky man.

She was giggling down at us saying, 'Lucky? Too right. And he doesn't even know it.'

'Oh, but I do,' I replied, and grabbed the hand she held out for me, lurching against the fence, trying to find my footing on the wobbly steps.

But then she wanted to go under rather than over that night: she wanted to walk through the boys' rooms again now that they were back. The music from their roof echoed through the hallway as we negotiated the staircase. Then, holding her to me, I led her very slowly, half dancing, half leaning on each other, all the way home. Cocooned in our bedroom, I watched her reaching up to undo her dress, moving slightly, still dancing to the music that could be heard from the other side of the wall. The boys were back, the weekend was just starting, she was laughing as she nestled herself into me. The summer had regained its familiar alcoholic haze. Everything was back in its right and proper place.

And this was proved by the following day: an old-style Saturday wasted on our rooftop. The garden was overflowing with all the different blossom, everything celebrating the strong sunshine and the boys' welcome return. We took up our positions on cushions and fell into our usual banter, and smoked and drank our way through the day. And in the evening we had another fine banquet full of affirmations.

She always used to laugh at my Sunday morning lie-ins, telling me I was wasting the best part of the weekend in sleep. She used to say it was like sharing a bed with a corpse, that nothing would move me. Often I would wake to find that she had cooked me a full breakfast, and then I would be plied with coffee while she would tell me all her tried and tested techniques for rude awakenings that had failed to rouse me from my slumbers. I would play along with her, encouraging her dirty words and then, laughing, carry her back to bed where we would waste more hours before we declared the day open.

So initially when I woke and found that she wasn't lying beside me I wasn't worried. I tiptoed into the kitchen, hoping to catch her by surprise. But there was no sign of her, and none of the tell-tale aromas of breakfast. That wasn't right. I ran back into the bedroom, to be greeted by the wide open window, and I panicked.

I rushed across the hallway and hammered down the boys' door. Richard answered, his hair sticking up in a shock, rubbing sleep from his eyes. I was incoherent, my words stumbling over each other. I can't remember what I said. Something about her having left in the night.

Richard fed me coffee. But he didn't look all that concerned. He was trying to calm me, but also smiling, saying, 'Take it easy, mate, I'm sure it's not what you think.'

I couldn't stop and was telling him that he didn't know the half of it. I started to deconstruct the story of our domestic bliss. I told him that we might well seem the ideal couple, but appearances could be deceptive. I told him that sometimes I wasn't sure I could keep her. I told him that occasionally, when it was just the two of us in a room, when we were talking, or even worse when we were in bed, I got the feeling that she was not really focusing on me at all. Sometimes I caught her gazing beyond me, over my shoulder, off into the middle distance, as if she was looking at something coming up behind me. I didn't like it. I'd never liked it. I insisted to Richard, now nearly sobbing, that it really was very possible that she could have gone for good.

He was laughing at me, but clearly worried at the same time, saying, 'Jesus, calm down, it's really not what you think.'

He showed me the note that Phil had left, telling him that he had gone out to the common with her, that we were to meet them at the windmill at two o'clock and await further instructions.

'Simple explanation,' said Richard. 'It's a treasure hunt.'

He told me how when they first moved, Phil would go

roaming over the common for hours on end. Although you would never believe it from his confident wombling gait, Phil had an awful sense of direction and he used to have to leave himself signs so that he would be able to make his way back. Like an amateur Scout, he would leave broken twigs and bits of string to mark his path. Richard used to follow behind, moving his markers, until Phil found himself being navigated, against his will, down to the open triangle of land by the pubs, where we had first emerged all those months ago. And Richard would be sitting out on the lawn with a pint waiting for him, triumphant in his orienteering.

A few years back Phil had resurrected the ritual for a midsummer party. Friends gathered at the windmill at midday and each was given a separate set of clues. Without the aid of an *A to Z* they had to decipher Phil's riddles, collect a specified item from the common and reconvene at the pub. A motley crew emerged hours later, with stray branches and handfuls of weeds. They all went back to the flat and Phil used their finds to create one of his more abstract sculptures. Richard dug out the photos, and there was Phil, looking muddy and proud beside a dubious construction decorated with twisted bits of beer cans, labelled 'Underground Overground'.

'Trust me,' said Richard. 'It'll be another treasure hunt. Nothing to worry about. It's a sign of affection.'

Richard insisted I should stay for breakfast, saying that I wasn't safe to be left alone. I laughed along with him, but at the back of my mind I was thinking about the games she played. I thought about the treasure hunts she had conducted around our house, when we first moved, when she would tease me for being unobservant; I remembered the trail of flowers that she had made to lead me up to the roof garden, when spring came. I thought of the way she almost always went off scavenging with Phil now whenever the four of us went out walking on the common.

If Phil didn't believe in love then maybe, just maybe, he could take it by mistake and not even realise. Maybe that's what those dreams were saying: that I should watch her when she went out into the woods, and worry when she ran ahead of me.

But then again, this might also have been a charitable gesture on her part, going out with Phil to construct a game that would knit our two households back together. Pooling all their skills to show that there really were no hard feelings. This theory was verified when I went home to change. There, stuck on the bathroom mirror, I found a note saying she had gone off to make mischief in the woods with Phil, that I was to meet them at the windmill and that she loved me very much.

Richard and I walked out together. I made him promise not to tell a soul, not even Phil, about my early-morning panic. I tried to laugh it off, saying that when you have something as good as her in your life it is difficult not to convince yourself that you are going to fuck it all up somehow. We approached the windmill and found them waiting. Phil had a twinkle in his eye, winking at Richard saying, 'All right, you know the drill,' ceremoniously handed over the envelope and told us they'd meet us at the other end. She kissed me before disappearing round the other side of the windmill after Phil, back into the common and out of sight.

The whole game was peppered with private jokes. Richard and I took the first clue: 'Look for what you know by the thirteenth hole.' Dutifully we trampled across the golf course, Richard urging me to follow before the signs got too disturbed, saying that we had to watch out for pesky kids interfering with Phil's master plan: sometimes his creations were too much to resist.

Richard laughed when he found what they had left us, but it made me go cold. They had created a crude scarecrow out of two pairs of tights stuffed with newspaper and sewn together, to form gangly arms and legs. They had dressed it in one of my old suits and stuck it in a tree. It wore a baseball cap of mine, one of the many garments she forbade me to wear in her presence. The face was a bright red balloon with no features. It was horrible, I didn't like it at all. I imagined her and Phil stitching this thing together, delighting in the caricature.

Richard said I should learn to laugh at myself a little. He took the newspaper that was wedged under its arm, and opened it to reveal a marker-pen scrawl, ordering us to head for Fishpond Wood, still looking for what we knew.

Then it was Richard's turn not to find things so funny. On the edge of the wood, aspiring shoots of silver-birch trees had been hacked off at an angle. She and Phil had given them great jaws and fierce eyes, which turned them into the monsters from Richard's computer games. They lurked, half hidden, under bushes and brambles. Phil's clever carvings created sharp teeth, and steely claws that reached out to swipe you; she had drawn black scales and broad wings, which gave them a devilish nature. Richard was solemn, shaking his head, saying that Phil should know better, that he knew where these creatures had come from. I said nothing; again, I imagined how she and Phil must have laughed together as they made these things.

We followed the trail of tree beasts into the wood. The further in we got, the more ridiculous they became, and Richard began to smile when he saw how she had parodied his fears. The creatures became cartoon monsters with buck teeth and huge glasses. We came to rest at a stump that had been transformed into a gurning beast, rearing up on its belly, with a gnarled knot for a nose, a natural split in the log forming a mouth that held a huge spliff. Down one side of the Rizla paper were our next instructions, telling us to follow the signs on the ground and to smoke if we dared.

Dare to smoke we did, as we followed a haphazard trail through the common, leading us round in circles. There was a fairytale element to it, undoubtedly her touch – a golden thread to guide us on, spun so finely through the trees it was almost impossible to see against the sunlight.

Richard knew this game of old: he said we had to be careful, we had to keep our eyes peeled. Phil liked to make his clues obscure, he liked to take the piss. Sure enough, we followed the thread for a good half hour, only to find that it led us right back to where we had started. I was worried that we had lost the trail, but Richard said no, this was vintage Phil: he liked to lead people round and round in circles.

There was an unpleasant moment when we lost our direction in the thick of the woods and Richard told me he thought that maybe the trees were closing in on us. The bright sun was reflected off the silver bark, dazzling me. The lines of silver birches multiplied as I squinted through, turning dark in the shadows, shapeshifting and gathering closer together. The sun blinded me for a second and all was darkness in front, and I was tripping on the stray growth of ferns and brambles that were creeping across the forest floor.

'We should be careful,' I said. 'I think we're getting lost.'

'We're not lost, just stoned,' replied Richard, laughing at me as I slipped and stumbled. 'Just keep looking, there's bound to be something . . .'

As he predicted, Richard found twigs placed to form arrows to keep us on the right track. Then there were chains of flowers hanging off trees and sticks bent over to make crude hearts to remind me that she loved me. One tree had a couple of her hair ribbons tied on it and they fluttered as markers in the breeze. White ribbons, marking the correct turning we should take. Then, finally, in the woods by Queen's Mere there was another procession of monsters, another carved ringleader with another spliff in its mouth, instructing us to take it up to Gravelly Hill and claim our prize.

Gravelly Hill, I should have known. It was her favourite spot. A surprisingly sharp, sudden hill in the middle of the land. You could stand on the top and see the expanse of the common rolling away in every direction. Editing out the distant buildings, you could almost believe there was no other land but this – just wide green fields and forests. When the boys had first taken us up there she had stood on the brow of the hill with me, and spread out our hands together, to blot out the intruding towers on the horizon. London Town was removed by that simple gesture, and there was nothing but the never-ending lines of trees. No streets forming rings around us at all.

Richard and I were like children again, racing each other to the top of the hill. They were both up there waiting, stretched out in the sun. She was lying with her head on Phil's belly, and sprang up when she saw us. She grabbed the spliff from Richard's hand and tackled me to the ground, smothering me with kisses through the smoke she exhaled.

'What's the prize, then?' I asked.

'We are the prize. I am the prize, do you like it?' She nuzzled up against me, making even the boys blush and turn away.

We went straight to the pub – what else was there to do with the day? Hand in hand to the Hand in Hand. A mischievous alignment. Her and me in the centre, flanked by Phil and Richard, respectively. On her command we formed a line and ran down the hill, concertina-ing and swinging each other round, till we were all dizzy and light-headed, stumbling across the road like kamikaze drunks. Looking back, that's exactly how it was: the boys, drawn into our relationship then flung out to the edges, giving us weight and ballast, keeping us centred and safe. We spent the rest of the afternoon drinking on the lawn. She insisted that we salvaged the scarecrow from the woods on our return. Phil was in his element again, tying knots in the misshapen creature's lanky legs to keep it secure on his shoulders. The balloon bobbed sickly from side to side as he ran across the common, waving the long, lumpen arms out beyond his, trying to catch us.

By the time we got back to the flats we were too tired to drink more and we parted at our respective doorways. She was negotiating ownership of the 'suitcrow', as they had christened my effigy. Richard winked and whispered, 'I told you so, nothing to worry about. Everything's all right, isn't it?'

And again I said, yes, of course, nothing had changed.

She won her argument with Phil and claimed the suitcrow as our own. That evening she sat it in my place at the table, saying that she would keep it there when I was out at work, to have something to remind her of me while I was away. When I told her how much I hated it, and how it spooked me, she told me I was superstitious and hypersensitive. But I insisted, so we made a game of it and ritually massacred the suitcrow: she popped his face with a cigarette while I sliced open his innards with a kitchen knife, until the floor was covered with a mass of shredded newspaper and laddered stockings. Then, satisfied with our day's work, we went to bed.

I should have slept soundly that night, but I didn't. I dreamt of the forest again. When I woke the next morning I blamed my paranoid dream on the anxiety I had carried with me all day, ever since I had woken to find her gone. I had relaxed into the game with Richard, and laughed along with the three of them in the pub all afternoon, but a quieter part of me had been watching her every move, watching her very closely as she had stood at the bar with Phil, teasing him for being a cheapskate as she wrestled his wallet out of his pocket. I kept my fears so closely hidden that it didn't surprise me when they came rushing out into my dreams.

I should have worked it out by then, seen that whatever happened in our daytime lives was somehow echoing through into the twilight, as if I had to live through everything twice in order to understand it.

However I chose to rationalise it, the facts of the matter are, I woke into a vivid dream, the same, and yet not the same, as the ones that had gone before. Again, the dream began with a heaviness, which only allowed me to watch her leaving, without the strength to move or the words to stop her.

Again, a strong light streamed into the room, but the moon had lost its silver sheen. This light was blue. The shadows the ivy cast were grey and ghostly. From my prone position, it was almost like being under water, drowning in a cold blue world. She was standing by the wardrobe. For a moment I thought the light had frozen her and the dreams were about to take an entirely different turn, that the nightmare would never leave our room, that I was paralysed and she was turned to stone. In accordance with her stories, I knew that all it would take were the most delicate of kisses and her enchantment would be broken. But I was bedbound and could not move an inch. Then, with a swift movement, she threw on one of my shirts, pulled on her jeans, leapt up on to the shelf, out of the window and was lost to the night.

I ran to the window and, sure enough, the moon was dappled by blue clouds that transformed the forest. The woods spread far and wide underneath the window, like a sea of blue tears, an ocean of sadness. Wind played with the leaves, making them rise and fall like the ebb and flow of the tide. Those blue leaves had siren qualities, beckoning me in.

I crouched in the window-seat, hesitating, the ivy shifting beneath my fingers. Everything in me wanted just to jump, to dive straight into that forest and lose myself in the maze of pathways. But my rational mind was fighting against the enchantments of my heart. Those woods were too beautiful to be trusted. I knew I needed an anchor to keep me safe; I needed to find a way through. There was something I could take with me, if only I could remember. My mind wrestled with itself, and an image from our daytime games came echoing through into the dream: a golden thread was spun through the trees, difficult to see against the sunlight. Just a fragile thread to lead me through the tangling woods.

I took some strong twine and a pair of sharp scissors and I leapt out of the window.

'It depends how you look at it,' she had once said to me.

I hesitated on the very edge of the woods. The change of light made the inside of the forest into a drowned world. The carpet of flowers was transformed, the darker blossoms blending into the undergrowth, the snowdrops and primroses catching the light and glistening like jewels, sunken treasure scattered beneath my feet. It was a beautiful transformation and I was full of wonder at the way my mind could refashion this place in every dreaming.

The forest had a silence about it that night, as if it was watching and waiting to see what my next move might be. But I was by no means afraid. Holding my ball of twine tight in my hand, I raced through the woods until I reached the clearing. It was as if I had Richard with me, running alongside me, telling me that this was just a game, the woods were there for our entertainment, just keep your eyes peeled and all shall be well. That courage gave me faith in my own command of the landscape. This time I was following the ivy path of my own free will: it was not tugging me along in its wake. I was free to make choices, and I was choosing to follow.

I ran down the left-hand path, into the more tightly packed lines of trees. As the blue light grew darker, I tied the end of the twine round a sturdy trunk and it unravelled behind me as I walked on. Although the echo in the forest was deceptive, I knew that I was close to her. Occasionally I would glimpse my shirt shifting between trees only a few metres ahead. It became a game of hide-and-seek. I would catch sight of her, sprint forward, trying not to get caught in my own tangles, then hide behind a tree-trunk, securing my string. And I became childlike once more, delighting in the game, trying to muffle my giggles by pressing my face against the soft black bark. I was determined not to be discovered. I wanted to creep closer and closer, ambush her from behind, grab her in a great bear-hug and carry her, laughing, through the forest, all the way home.

The deeper into the woods we went, the more the trees clustered. I was being very quiet, but she must have sensed she was being followed. She took the most winding routes through, twisting round and doubling back on herself. My twine caught on stray branches, weaving a net between the trees that threatened to catch me. The string would not stay steady in my hand: it snaked its way through my fingers, growing supple and insidious, as if the twisting forest was giving it life. It would not stay fixed upon the trees.

The further I crept, the more afraid I became of breaking the thread. So, step by step, we inched our separate ways onwards. Again and again I told myself that this was only a game, a game played out within a dream, a game I had already won in the waking world. I could catch her and claim my prize.

Except that my meagre ball of twine wouldn't stretch quite far enough. It ran out just as I could see that the trees were thinning, and I could feel a cool breeze rippling through the woods. I wouldn't let it hold me back. Not now that I was so close. But the minute the end of that thread had slipped through my fingers, a heaviness came upon me, the call of that old sleep within sleep. The ferns underfoot looked soft and welcoming.

But then buried deep in my pocket, digging into the side of my thigh, there was that heavy pair of scissors. I pulled them out, and they flashed keen and brightly in the moonlight. Through sheer force of will I walked forward, and started cutting every other tree with a swift slash of the scissors. The black trunks were surprisingly yielding. I cut the bark away, to reveal a line of lighter wood underneath, and sap streamed out like blood from an open vein. Marking my way, I moved right to the edge of the forest. I was shocked to see another land beyond the trees. It had never occurred to me that there might be more to this place than just the teeming forest. From our high bedroom window, the woods stretched far and wide and seemed to have no boundaries. But she was stepping away from the cover of the trees, out into another land.

There was a clear single path, which led out of the woods. No more ambiguity. No more alternative routes. Just a wide road, curving over a patch of grassland, a gently rolling hill, a path of sand or shingle; bathed in the blue light, it rippled like a stream, trickling away into the dark. She didn't hesitate.

She stepped boldly into the open, went down the slope and disappeared.

I hid behind a tree and looked out at the lie of the land. The wind was carving shifting spirals and whorls into the grass. I felt exposed. At the best of times, I was never comfortable in open spaces, and now the more I hesitated, the more my fear gathered. In this cold light that grassland looked unsafe, as if the minute I trod upon it the blue earth might open up beneath me. I stood at the edge of the forest, frightened and small, the trees rustling behind. The sway of the branches created whispers in the wind, echoing my thoughts: *Forward or back or forward or back?*

The longer I stood there, listening to the soft sighs of my own indecision, the more difficult it was to move. It was no longer a game. It would have been so different if Richard had been there. He would have been goading me on, running circles around me, asking me what I was waiting for, making me push forward. But I was there alone, stranded in strange blue dreams.

My fear grew too strong. It was like a physical barrier I could not push beyond. So I turned back, passed the cut trees and found the end of the thread to guide me home. From this side of the land, the forest looked more impenetrable than ever. The leaves and the branches were rustling in front of me and behind. A different whisper now, mocking echoes, murmuring, *Coward, a coward, a coward*, in long, drawn-out, disappointed sighs.

Angry now, I refused to be intimidated by the fears that I was pouring into the restless woods.

The twine still insisted on playing its tangling tricks against me, refusing to separate itself from the nestling branches. So I cut it. I cut straight through the stubborn thread, marking the bark underneath with the sharp point of my scissors.

I took to cutting a tall tree at every confusing turning. I told myself that this was right, that next time I would be able to follow the marks, run even closer behind her, catch her, claim her before she made it through, before the open sky overwhelmed me. Next time, I told myself, as I gashed almost every other tree I passed, next time I'd be quicker. With each savage slash, the whispering diminished. Strange how soon I had grown to accept that these dreams would come again, and stupid for me to think that I could shape them with such clumsy gestures. And, of course, I was not admitting to myself that this show of violence was born out of frustration. I was furious with the forest, which conspired to shield her from me. And in retrospect I was also angry with her, or this incarnation of her that I was dreaming up, where she was always one step ahead. I cut my way through the forest until I emerged on to the lawn. I clambered swiftly up the ivy and at last I was home, safely protected by the four walls that I knew.

And as dreams have their own momentum, sometimes taking you so far away from the character you play in the waking world, I was made bold by my violence. Perched up on the window-seat, I had a strong urge to cut the ivy. Just to hack it away so that the rope would fall from the window the minute she pulled on it. Then she would have to hammer on the door and call to me to let her in. Part of me wanted to make that happen, for her to need to call to me to come back. But she might also just turn tail and run into the clustering trees. Even in dreams that was something I couldn't bear to see.

So instead I got down off the ledge and undressed. I could hear the ivy on the side of the house, beating warning signals of her return. I pushed the string under the bed and was only just able to pull the covers over me before she came in through the window. Even before she came to lie beside me, I was dragged deeper and deeper into the sheets, down into that second sleep.

A few hours later, I woke briefly, just as it was starting to get light. She had managed to wrap herself up in all the bedclothes, tucking them over her head and under her body. I was shivering with cold. Not wanting to disturb her, I pulled out another blanket for myself, perched on the window-seat, and stared out as the world below revealed itself. Of course, it was only the common that emerged in the dawn, but I had to watch and wait to be absolutely sure before I could go back to bed and sleep. Catching the sunrise, the silver birches were small columns of fire drifting down from the sky.

# 10

I woke to find a huge gap in the bed between us. Half smothered by the blanket, I had pushed myself up against the wall in my sleep, and when I turned round she was right on the far side, about to fall off the edge, facing the window. She had thrown her covers back a little and I could see the collar of my shirt poking over the sheets. It disturbed me to see it: I thought I had dreamt that.

I thought even then that I might be still dreaming, that I was caught in one of those lucid dreams that mirror real life so closely that you think you are back in the waking world, until they turn against you and wake you suddenly with a surreal shock. As a child I was prone to such insidious nightmares. I would wake and get ready for school, wander down to breakfast to find my father sitting at the table smiling over the newspaper, and a golden sunlight streaming through the windows. My mother would be all softness and laughter and I would see the family I should have had. But no sooner glimpsed, my father would vanish and I would wake to find myself crying, crying for the loss of something I had never known I needed until then.

'Good morning, my love,' she said, rolling over the bed and pulling me under the covers.

'Am I dreaming?' I asked, my voice heavy with sleep.

'Well, if you are, it's a very nice dream.' She kissed me and began to unbutton the shirt, telling me how she got cold in the night and she liked wearing my clothes, would I warm her?

It was afterwards, as we lay dozing off in the early-morning sunlight, that I noticed there were marks on her skin. In the small of her back, and on the sides of her arms were shallow scratches. I couldn't bear to see her hurt. 'What's all this?' I asked. 'How did this happen?'

She laughed away my concern, saying that she had scratched herself to pieces out on the common with Phil, that he had been racing away ahead of her in his eagerness to lay the trail, that she had had to fight through brambles to keep up. I was angry with Phil for not taking better care of her, but she said I was being stupid; they were only a few little grazes, and wounds heal quickly.

I told her that it still hurt me to see it, that she was so precious to me, and I curled my body around her, like a protective shield against the world outside.

Stupidly, I fell asleep holding her to me, and had already switched off the alarm. I woke with a start as the sunlight hit my face and was already an hour late for work. She was still locked away from me in a deep sleep and didn't stir at all as I disentangled myself from her embrace, and began to gather my things and head away from her, out into my working day.

It was strange getting the tube that morning – there were places to sit in the carriage and a different selection of travellers. Tourists of various denominations, wrestling with oversized maps, trying to match underground and overland with little success. The London cartographers' own private joke. Deliberately public, a teenage couple were strap-hanging, playing into the rhythm of the train, kissing every time the uneven track jolted them together. I was incongruous, the only suited figure. I slumped against the window, resigned to my lateness.

The platform stretched itself out and shot back into the light as the train moved away. A depressing train journey. It begins with a civilised movement through the suburban streets of Wimbledon. In the winter months I had to hold my breath as it rattled between East Putney and Putney Bridge. Suspended above the water on a rickety iron bridge, every journey was an act of faith. In the winter dark it was terrifying: there was nothing but blackness on all sides, and a long way to fall. But that summer morning even the brown river was alive with the light. The dirty glass caught the sun and fractured it – even the grime of the city was made beautiful.

Then, abruptly, we were swallowed up underground. It felt like the land had caved in on itself and we were all plunged into darkness. No longer playing with the light like a kaleidoscope, the dusty windows reflected the bleakness of our trapped carriage back to me. I saw myself, hunched up and turned away from my fellow passengers, looking as if I was drowning in my unseasonal suit. The passage of the train pushed me from side to side, my legs jerking up in spite of themselves, and the carriage light flickered inconsistently, casting light and then shadow across my face. One moment I could see myself, the next I was plunged back into the dirt of the window-pane – faceless and formless, like a puppet whose strings had been cut. This revelation of myself brought back images of the suitcrow and his unhappy demise, and it felt like a warning. I ran up and down stairs and escalators as I changed trains, eager to be back in the warm world above.

But when I finally emerged from the tube station, the sunlight wasn't a relief. The blue smog hovered and poisoned the streets. This was not a place where I wanted to be. Inside the office wasn't any better.

James looked up at me as I took my place beside him. 'Where the fuck have you been?' he snapped. 'Do you know what time it is?'

'I overslept.'

'Well, thanks for that. We're shafted – we're already an hour behind.'

'I'm sorry.'

'You're sorry? Well, that's all right, then, isn't it?'

I'd never seen James so agitated.

Simon seemed to be enjoying the confrontation. 'After all, time is money,' he said.

'Too fucking right,' said James.

I told them both to calm down, took my place, and collated

the morning's figures at record speed. By lunchtime everything was under control again, and James was all brash apologies, offering to buy me a liquid lunch. But the last thing I wanted was to join the ranks of the desperate Monday drinkers at the pub across the road, inflicting a long, slow headache upon myself for the rest of the afternoon. So I stayed behind when the others left, to give the illusion of doing some work. Idly, I added up my figures. The sea of paper diminished. Order from chaos. I loved that simplicity of my work – the unshakeable logic and reliability of numbers. I mapped out the projected investments for the afternoon and, again, delighted in the wealth I could predict.

Suddenly, I felt a strong desire for the same authority over my own life. I wanted to be able to weigh up the odds, guarantee outcomes and create a secure future. In hindsight, I can see all too clearly that this was the start of something inside me shifting. Until then I had been living out our days in a constant present, with no need to stop and evaluate. I believed that every day would be the same, or better than the day before. But now, with the shock of the boys' departure, and my difficult blue dreams, I wanted to take stock of what I had. I needed to collate our history.

I began by drawing a map. A crude drawing of the land of my dreams. With our house, the trail of ivy and what I could remember of the meandering paths through the woods. I marked the various stages of my explorations, all the different turnings where I had lost her. In two dimensions, it looked very like the maps of unknown worlds that I used to create when I was a child, when other lands were found just behind the gateway of my mother's garden. It looked ridiculous to my adult eyes. I needed something more solid to remind me.

So I began to write: it was a difficult movement for me, from numbers to words. But I was determined to write down all the things I was sure of. It started with the briefest of notes, scribbled down during that snatched lunchtime. The story so far. And I was right, it did me good to fix the memories with dates and incidents. There were undeniable constants. We had a very strong starting point: *she had come to the city to be with me.*

But my sentimentality also frightened me.

What if James discovered these annotated confessions, my emotions and insecurities bleeding across the page, in such contrast to the bravado I was learning from him? I tried to think.

One of my tutors at college, a grey little man whose whole physical presence was an internal wrestling match of nervous twitches, had had a secret passion for cryptology. I had problems with the infinite spaces that could be opened up by matrices – grids of numbers that turned in on themselves, multiplying, compounding meaning. He showed me his textbooks on wartime decoding. Equations and key words wrapped tightly around each other. Nonsense strings of letters and numbers to the untrained eye, but once the code was cracked all the enemies' secrets were there on show. 'These are the real statistics of war,' he had said.

The obvious ironies didn't escape me as I drew up a matrix of my own, a tight net of numbers in which to hold my story. I encoded key words within my tentative narrative. To the untrained eye, the tale of our life together was just fragmented gibberish, punctuated by incongruous equations.

I still have them, the loose bunch of notes that grew a little more each week. They have been invaluable as I write. They are difficult to sort, and often I find myself with stubborn words that just don't fit. The paper is so creased and torn from the weeks when all I did was sit on our rooftop with these nonsensical pages, the strong wind almost blowing them out of my hand. And, even now, it isn't an easy process. I approach my codes with caution. Deciphering is a series of small explosions. Uncertain emotions, detonated at will. I undo the word hidden among the numbers, and strings of sentences tumble out by association, unravelling.

It was a difficult day. It was baking hot, but we couldn't open the windows because the polluted noise from the street below was too horrific. She intruded on my thoughts as I worked: a lunchtime of reminiscence had reminded me of what I had left behind, and what I was returning to. I wanted to call her up and tell her everything I had remembered. I wanted to tell her how I would never forget the way she smiled at me when I first carried her across our threshold. I wanted her to talk about that night we made angels in the snow and for her to turn it into a tall tale for me, for her to tell me that since that night we had been watched over by those angels of the winter, made in our own image, how they pour down soft blessings while we are sleeping. I wanted her memories of the first time we met the boys, I wanted her to fill in the gaps with lost conversations, patch together those long nights into some kind of order, regain those hours that we abandoned to bacchanalian rites. It seemed important.

I thought of phoning: it might just have been enough to hear her voice. But what could I have said to her in my crowded office, with everyone watching?

One of the secretaries brought me a coffee, steadying my hand, asking me if I'd had a good time last night and wasn't I a dark horse?

'Oh, you're in there, mate,' said James. 'It's that strong, silent thing you've got going.'

I didn't dignify his remark with a response. All I wanted was to get away from there, to run home. She smiled down at me from my screensaver, which made things worse.

But, of course, I didn't run. Feeling ashamed, I stayed until everyone else had gone, finishing my work, making up for lost time.

Mr Collins was walking out as I was packing away my notes and he insisted that I joined him in a swift whisky. I was treated to a lecture about my great potential; apparently it was all a matter of priorities and investing time accordingly. 'You're a bright lad,' he said, with avuncular concern. 'You could achieve anything you wanted, if you put your mind to it. It would be a great shame to let that all go to waste.'

I said all the right things and my errant morning seemed to be forgiven. Not until I got to the tube station did I realise how late I was. The year was unfurling to give us longer nights. It was easy to lose a couple of hours and not even notice.

The whisky made my journey home softer. The stations slid by quite easily. But changing at Earls Court I had an unexpected twinge of vertigo. Disoriented by alcohol, I swayed dangerously near to the platform edge – it would only have taken one more step. The announcements over the Tannoy were warped through the wrought-iron hull of the high roof. The train tracks stretched in trenches on either side of my packed platform. Above me, the old-fashioned announcement boards played their usual tantalising roulette – arrows and place names lit up in a variety of crowd-pleasing combinations. Each time, the next train failed to be the one that could take me home. I wondered if I would ever make it back, or whether I would be stranded on that platform peninsula for ever.

But, of course, the train did come eventually. Racing overland, tearing along the tracks, I could see patterns in the long shadows of the bridge. More grids and matrices. My panic quickly subsided. I comforted myself with my established absolutes: she had come to the city to be with me, we had built a home and met the boys. I was going back to company I loved. There was nothing for me to be so afraid of.

And the rest of the world seemed to agree with me. When I got out of the station the streets were holding the last of the heat of the day and everyone was smiling. I made my way up the hill and I got to the fork in the road. With the fence to one side of me and the street to the other I was tempted to take her old short-cut. After a couple of minutes, it was possible to pretend that the common was all there was – just the woods and the big sky. There were people still wandering around, couples sitting under the trees with bottles of wine. Families with their dogs and small children were out in droves. Glimpses of other lives.

I felt an affinity with the couples strolling hand in hand to the pub, lovers of all ages lying out on the lawn. None, of course, as rightly matched as she and I. No girl as beautiful as her. I doubted very much that any of these mundane lovers was as blessed as I was, with my house filled with laughter, and the secret paradise hidden away on the rooftop. How could anyone else have such magic in their life? How could she ever have an equal in this world?

'Oi, mate!'

Someone was shouting at me. There was a pair of feet, dangling in front of my face.

'Watch yourself, mate!' someone else shouted, as I skidded, nearly losing my footing.

'I think he's pissed,' said a girl's voice, and there was giggling coming from the treetop above.

There were three of them perched up there, young faces peeping out, almost hidden by the leaves. Two boys and a girl, they were about sixteen. She had short dark hair, cut close to her head, sticking up in tufts. She was wearing a pair of jeans that were too big for her, ripped at the knee and sagging off her hips. Her skin looked so brown against the white of her T-shirt. They had all caught the sun: the blond boy was glowing pink, wearing only a pair of shorts, his skin burnt raw. The owner of the sandals was also bare-chested, his jeans covered with paint and his long hair tied back in a ponytail. They had a carrier bag full of cans which they had tied to a branch.

'I think you're right,' said the blond one. 'Are you pissed, mate?'

I squinted up. They looked so young. 'No!' I belched, steadying myself against the tree, dazzled by the sunlight.

'Well, you should be, on a day like this.'

'Fancy a beer?'

Before I had a chance to reply, a can came hurtling through the branches. An accurate missile, it drenched me first, then caught me square between the shoulderblades. More laughter from above.

Suddenly Ponytail Boy was hanging right in front of me, puce-purple and grinning, with a spliff that looked more like a cigar clamped between his fingers. 'Smoke?' he grunted, his eyes bulging.

'You look like you need it in your fucking suit!' said a voice from above.

Intimidated by the hostility of youth, I walked quickly away.

In those long summer days our rooftop caught the sun and held it there for ever. When I got home they were still there, as I had imagined. There was music playing, of course, and she was lying on her stomach, propped up on cushions. Richard was earnestly scanning the paper and Phil was scuttling about with a dustpan and brush, sweeping up the mess from where he had cemented the steps down, just as he'd promised.

She leapt to her feet and threw her arms round my neck, asking me where I had been all this time. I stank of booze – what on earth had I been up to?

'Drinking with friends from work. Sorry.' I lurched again.

She pushed herself against me to see if I would topple. 'Don't be ridiculous, you haven't got any friends from work.'

'Ah, City Boy's got a secret double life,' said Phil. 'You want to watch him, love, he'll start going all corporate on you. Only a matter of time.'

She wouldn't be baited. She nestled up against me, in the last of the sun, wearing a T-shirt that day, I noticed, not her normal bikini, her scratches hidden from the boys.

'Where to go, what to do?' Richard was muttering as he pored over his paper.

'Stay here! Do nothing!' she said, with absolute conviction.

But the boys were restless. For some reason they wanted to take on the madness of a summer's night in London Town. They wanted to take us into Soho and stand drinking on pavements. They wanted to roam the streets in search of adventures. Phil was uncharacteristically active for that time of day, a man with a mission. Richard laughed at him and told us Phil got like this at times: when the nights were long and warm, he refused to sleep without company. 'He's an embarrassment,' Richard said. 'For God's sake, come out with us, he needs rescuing from himself.'

I was all ready to rise to the challenge. I liked the thought of the four of us fighting our way through the streets. I didn't doubt for a minute that it would be an adventure, a stupid, self-destructive Monday night. I thought of the person I could be if I had the boys as my allies, how crowds might part before us, and how we would come home drunken and laughing, retreating from the chaos they would no doubt create. And part of me thought it was important to have a night away from the confines of the rooftops and the flats, to spend some time in neutral territory with no fear of transgressing invisible boundaries.

Maybe she didn't notice but I was very aware that the boys were now a little more cautious around us and I didn't like it.

But her objections were predictable, and she would not compromise. She said she couldn't think of anything worse than being shut in a loud bar with strangers and no fresh air. Of course I could go if I really wanted, but she knew that I wouldn't leave her alone: our evenings together were still too precious.

Our refusal to accompany them created another moment of tension as we each separately digested the information and wondered if it made a difference. I broke the silence: 'Well, guess what I saw on my way home . . .' and told them about my encounter with the children in the tree. With obvious modifications – I had taken the beer they threw at me, accepted their offer of a smoke, but declined their invitation to climb up and join them. Phil and Richard were delighted – a new generation had discovered the tree. Their tree. Of course it was theirs. They'd found it when they moved into the flat, that first summer years ago.

When the boys had first arrived the house had been recently abandoned, with nothing left for them to unpack into. For years there had been a community of squatters there but the council had finally turfed them out and boarded up the derelict flats, selling off cheaply those that looked vaguely inhabitable. The communal stairs had been covered with graffiti and cartoon murals. The house had still smelt of all the previous occupants. They had the basic essentials: tools, and a small camping stove. They slept on the bare boards in sleeping bags, among the rubble, high on paint fumes and hopeful for the future.

They had set up the basics and then they'd just had to find a good tree, Richard explained; it had just been one of those days.

She knew exactly what he meant. 'Yes, you've got to climb a tree to survey your lands, haven't you?' she said.

Apparently that's true. And the boys had found a beauty, a good sturdy tree with parallel branches and thick leaves, bowing down close enough to the ground to pull yourself up. It invited you to climb it, like Nature's own ladder. The further upwards they had climbed the more the leaves closed in and you could barely be seen from below. They had made a nest up there and watched the sunset and the people walk by. A bag of beer hanging from the branches.

They had got into a progressively drunken state as it grew dark, and as the couples fled the common, they let out ghostly noises and made the girls scream.

The boys were eager to go and meet the new generation of tree-dwellers. She wanted them to take her along too, but I disagreed. It would be dark soon and I wanted to keep her close. I didn't want to be out on the common with the boys and the lairy teenagers. It would have made me nervous to watch her swinging off branches in the twilight. I felt responsible.

Richard tried to persuade us with tall tales of the best nights of their lives that had taken place there.

A sturdy old tree, it could support ten at most. Memorable times, but never memorable in their entirety, alcohol always creating confusing gaps in the narrative. Friendships were made, romances blossomed in the branches, and, occasionally, limbs were broken, but that was just par for the course. Nothing ventured, nothing gained.

Phil loved to climb right up to the top, away from the others. On a clear night you could see both the stars and the scattered street-lamps of the city on the far side of the common. Up there one night at the height of an acid summer, when Richard saw something nasty in the bushes, Phil watched the stars falling, fiery meteors coming at him from all sides before they hit the suburban streets like firecrackers and threw themselves back up into the sky. A shower of silver and gold, weaving together the land and the heavens, a dance that lasted until dawn. The most beautiful thing.

But one unfortunate night it all came to an end. They were in the Hand in Hand in the early evening, and it was packed with people celebrating the longest day of the year. Phil, inspired by the air of festivity, had announced that he and Richard were holding a gathering that night at the tree. Richard didn't have the heart to point out that the tree could not hold the entire clientele of the pub, however ample its branches. He never thought that they would all follow.

But, then, he hadn't really bargained for Phil standing on the bar, ringing the bell for last orders and leading the way.

So follow they did. They came in their droves: the pub just emptied and marched along behind Phil. It was like the Pied bloody Piper, Richard said. By the time they came to the fence, the gathering had swelled to more than forty as the houses at the edges of the common burst open, revealing more committed disciples, armed with torches, stereos and never-ending booze. Phil was at the helm, Richard bringing up the rear, and over the fence they went.

Once at the tree, the boys clambered straight to the top, and watched it all unfold beneath them. They were just about to go down and meet their followers when they saw the torches coming through the woods ahead. Of course, Wimbledon was still suburbia, a polite neighbourhood that clearly wasn't going to tolerate a group of drunken lunatics gathering round a tree and partying the night away just because it was midsummer. Curtains twitched and the police came running.

The boys in the treetop pressed themselves against the trunk, peeped out from among the leaves, trying not to laugh, trying not to make any sound at all that might give them away. The police were faced with a group of drunken louts who were not going to move. The people sitting on the lower branches mocked the men in uniform. With a cheeky 'Watch this, Officer!' one guy swung round, just the move I had witnessed earlier, so that his face was dangling right in front of the policeman, blowing smoke into his eyes and giggling.

The police were unimpressed and everyone was threatened with arrest. As sirens were heard in the distance, the revellers panicked and fled. Richard laughed as he described his and Phil's paranoia as they waited up there, freezing, bladders aching while policemen scouted around for stragglers, looking for people to blame. When they had eventually retreated empty-handed, the boys made their triumphant descent, dropping from branch to branch, trying not to slip for laughter. With a Tarzan yell they came crashing down to earth.

Fuelled by nostalgia, the boys quickly left, our stairwell echoing with their repartee: 'Come on, mate, no time to lose. Babes in the woods, like old times. Let's go and find us some branches to swing off. Why not?'

And they were gone.

We sat out and watched the last of the sunset. There were sounds of laughter coming over the rooftops, but we couldn't make out any distinct voices.

She looked thoughtful as we sat there, drinking our wine in silence, watching the borders of the common fade into the night. 'They have lived well, haven't they, those boys?' she said.

'They've had more time,' I said, not entirely convinced that that was all there was to it.

'We should go after them!' She leapt to her feet. 'Let's go into the woods and find them,' she said, tugging at my sleeve.

Perhaps I should have played along with her, but I wouldn't. It was a matter of principle. She had refused to brave the city so I would not hazard the darkening common and would not let her go ahead alone. In my own way, I was as wilful as her, or perhaps I was just learning tactics.

'You've no sense of adventure,' she said petulantly. 'You're getting boring in your old age.'

I asked her if she was bored with me, was that it?, and she laughed, but didn't give a straight answer. Instead she leant over and started to kiss me, to pull me down on to the fading Astroturf. 'Come on, live a little,' she was saying to me. 'The boys will be gone for hours, be daring!'

But when I reached up to her she held me down, so I was in no danger of touching her wounds.

She was lovely in the twilight, but there was a wildness in her movements, as if even when making love she was trying to race ahead of me. She fell asleep on the Astroturf and I carried her to bed, undressed her and wrapped her tightly in the sheets, as though I was trying to bind her to this world. I fell asleep soon afterwards, hearing laughter still coming through the window, laughter from across the common, calling through the night, like a reminder.

I might have been able to stop her running into the woods, but I could not prevent the woods coming to me. I woke into another dream, and was not so surprised to be there. This second waking, into a room that was and was not a room I knew, was simply becoming another part of our life together. I lay heavy and helpless in my own bed, as the room re-formed itself around me, waiting to see what shape the dream might take.

This time it was neither silver nor blue, but a yellow light that washed across the walls. A jaundiced light that took away depth and distance, made everything it touched seem fragile and ailing. She looked very vulnerable as she swung herself out of the window, the ivy rustling in her wake.

There was no doubt that in every dream she was growing more light-footed and agile. But I was gathering skills also, although mine were more abstract. I was trying to assimilate and assess, coaxing out my rational mind to untangle the landscape. This time I took the boys' tall tales into my dream. There had to be other ways to fight this forest than just blindly pushing my way through it. I had learnt from my previous dream that this was a place where I could act of my own free will. If I could muster the strength, maybe I could play the part of a different kind of man – someone with energy and impetus and strong resolve.

I devised a strategy: I would find a tall tree at the centre of the woods, at the edge of the clearing, before the paths split away from each other and forced me to make choices. The ivy would provide sure and sturdy handholds with which I could haul myself up. Instead of running after her I would climb. I would get myself a vantage-point, see the lie of the land, then decide which route to take. From an elevated point I would be able to see the pattern of all the pathways, map out the forest in my mind and find a way to sneak round her, get ahead and surprise her before we reached the open land.

But once I made it on to the window-ledge, I saw that it wasn't going to be quite that easy. The ivy was riddled with disease, very different from the ivy in our real room. That plant was thriving from the attention she lavished upon it. It was another ritual by now. Every morning she would throw open the curtains and turn the plant to the light, before getting back into bed and turning to me. But in my dream the ivy plant was dying. The leaves were crumbling. The rope wasn't strong enough to take my weight. Instinctively, in this dream, I knew that all would be lost if I broke it. If I did, something between us would also break, and the world I woke into would be for ever changed.

The moon had waned and looked sick and sorrowful outside the window. I could not see the forest below. As in the first dream, just a deep well of darkness confronted me, and I had the same flash of fear that had hit me the first time I saw it. I was suspended in the safety of my room, but she was gone into a world beyond it, a world of unknown shadows. But I pushed aside that fear and told myself that this was still just a game, nothing more than a puzzle to be solved or a code to be broken. There were other, safer ways of following than trusting that brittle rope.

So I went the long way round: I ran out of the flat and into our shared hallway. It was very dark, and the skylights over the communal stairs poured down the same ailing light that leached colour from all it touched. The entrance to the boys' flat was overgrown with blackness – it was difficult to see if the door was even there. I ran and ran down the steep flight of stairs, past the boarded-up, abandoned flats. Those sealed entrances loomed at me out of the dark. My heavy footsteps echoed all around; it sounded as if an army of men was in pursuit.

I stopped by the front door, suddenly uncertain. I wasn't sure what I wanted to find on the other side. Did I want the forest, bristling in that yellow light? And if not, would my doubts work against me, would I step out on to our normal suburban streets and be utterly lost? With my hand on the door-handle, I forced myself to believe that a dying forest would be a better thing to find than the manicured lawn, the quiet road, and the common beyond. I chose the unknown land, with her in it, rather than the everyday world without.

My fears were justified – the dream forest was only just there. There was a heavy rotten smell in the air. There was hardly any ivy growing down the walls. When I touched the leaves they broke apart in my hands. The trees were worse: they were shrunken and stunted, ugly black trunks. There was no canopy to shield her, no branches strong enough to obscure the paths. The whole wood was ravaged, and dissolving into a wasteland before my eyes. I had a clear view of her up ahead, sitting slumped over one stump, in the thick of the amputated landscape.

I wanted to run out to her, pull her away from this dying place and take her home. But those twisted tree-stumps terrified me. Huddled together in the yellow light they looked like rows and rows of crouching creatures, deformed and dangerous, waiting to pounce. My fear froze me. I stood hidden in the shadows by the side of the house, trying not to choke on the strong stench of decay. I wished with all my heart for it not to be like this. I shut my eyes and willed it, imagining a budding new forest, green and graceful, full of life. I pictured the diseased wood regrown into a tropical rainforest, with colourful parakeets calling from the branches. I saw her, dwarfed by over-arching trees, dancing in the centre of the forest, her clear blue eyes twinkling with laughter, her arms held out to me, and her laughing, calling me to come and dance with her, come and dance, it helps things grow.

I opened my eyes and, as she'd promised, things were changing.

She was crying, and stroking the nearest tree-stump. As she cried, her tears fell on to the wood. Where her tears fell, the bark turned green. When she stroked dead branches, they stirred, twitching in response to her touch. She got up and, wiping her eyes, moved hesitantly to another tree. Sure enough, as her tears wet the bark, the dead wood fell away, and there were patterns of new green growth forming underneath. She laughed and started to move more quickly, pushing aside the black bracken that was cluttering her path.

Wherever she walked, the forest flourished around her.

Flowers blossomed where she trod. I moved clumsily, trying to keep silent behind her.

She touched every tree she passed, stroking the bark with her hands – intimate gestures. She leant against the remains of a tree-stump and it rose up from her back. She looked up and smiled as branches sprouted above. She pulled one down so that it bent over, running her fingers along the twigs, laughing as buds burst forth under her fingers.

Whatever she touched lived again. Wherever she ran, beauty unfolded in front and behind. The whole landscape rippled around her. The carpet of flowers spread far and wide. Bluebells, crocuses, forget-me-nots flourishing. And they were even more beautiful than before, brighter and bolder. The forest floor was awash with colour, which seeped into the rest of the reawoken world. The trees grew back strong and majestic, shedding their black skins. The new forest was green and full, the canopy above now speckled with white and pink blossom. As the branches raced up to the sky, the light of the moon changed and all was silver again. She laughed to see it, and the forest, with its many echoes, laughed back to thank her.

I stood there, mesmerised, not noticing how quickly she was moving away. The forest kept up with her: it grew in her wake, with a pace of its own, wilder than ever before, ferns unfurling in front of me that reached my waist, obscuring the roots of the trees and making it easy for me to trip and fall. The forest rustled and spread its skirts all around. There was no question of climbing now: it was all I could do to maintain my momentum and not be overgrown. I ran blindly forward, but it was like trying to swim against the tide, running into those rippling woods.

Slowly but surely, as my breath failed me, I lost her. I stumbled and fell too many times. I didn't even make it to the clearing. Trees were rearing up all around, too quickly to count. But suddenly it didn't matter any more whether I caught her or not: what was really important was the sheer beauty of the place that she had created. I found myself standing there for a moment, in the warm air, just watching it all unfold. Even then, even while dreaming, I felt that this could only bode well.

But also, the force of all this new growth unnerved me. High up above, the green leaves were lacing together and threatened to block out the smiling moon. I didn't want to be trapped inside there with no light at all. This new-forming forest could drown me, I might never find my way through. I turned back towards home, confident that she would return. It wasn't so far, but the woods were thick and the brambles mischievous and wild, clinging to my clothes as I pushed past them, as if the forest itself was trying to embrace me.

When I stumbled out of it, the moonlight showed me a soft sea of ivy that had grown all over the lawn and out in other directions, as far as I could see. A silver-green reflective sea, covering the whole land, a fertile image from another age. The silhouette of the house was unrecognisable, bearded with ivy and haloed with stars. It took a leap of faith for me to think that this was my home. The ivy was no longer just a rope: it crept over most of that steep wall. It was easy to cling to as I scrabbled my way up. As always, I was careful not to look behind me.

When I tumbled in through the window I saw that, just as in the first dream, the bedroom was bathed in a sheen of silver. My dreams had gone full circle: we were back where we had started. Although I never managed to catch her, I felt that a puzzle had been solved. These dreams were there to show me what I already knew in my heart: that she was a charmed girl who could reawaken a dying world; that she was the source of everything I loved in my life; that the gentleness of her hands could banish my deepest fears.

I had been waiting for what seemed like hours, but might have been no time at all, when she came in through the window. She leant over the window-ledge and looked down on the world below that she had re-created. The moonlight poured itself down her back again, and her skin was beautiful, pale and unmarked. And I felt such relief to see that everything could be so easily healed. I was desperate to lift myself out of bed, walk across and touch her. All over again, I was in love with her soft skin. But I couldn't even keep my eyes open to watch her. I was falling, and for ever falling, back into a deeper sleep.

# 11

We were woken at an ungodly hour by a fierce, relentless hammering. The whole house was shaking, and it felt as if the walls would collapse around us.

'What the fuck is that?' I muttered, blinking myself awake.

It was the boys, shouting, 'RISE AND SHINE, RISE AND SHINE, WE'VE GOT YOUR BREAKFAST.'

She leapt out of bed, threw my trousers at me and said, 'It's all right to let them come in, isn't it?' Then the stereo was on and she was running to the door.

The next thing I knew, Phil and Richard came crashing into our bedroom. They had brought coffee and their bagels, and Phil bore a crate of beer proudly on his shoulder. They smelt and looked terrible. Their jeans were discoloured with grass stains, which rubbed off on our sheets. Phil was covered with scratches, he'd had a fall in the dark, but no harm done, nothing was broken. They had been on their way to bed, but then they'd noticed it was another fine day and it would be a shame to miss it.

'Beer for breakfast?' She took her can but I hid under the bedclothes in denial.

'We've decided to have a party,' Richard announced.

I poked my head over the sheets in disbelief. 'Not today, surely?'

So instead of our usual gentle morning together, we were bombarded by the drunken boys. They had been out in the park with the bright young things. 'Such energy,' said Phil, full of respect. 'It makes you remember what summer's all about.' They had run down to the tree and found the kids still there.

'The best thing about trees is that they grow,' Phil announced solemnly. 'Now there's room for five at the top. You missed a good sunrise.'

Over the next couple of hours we learnt all about the three kids. They were Kate, Tom and Jay, who had just finished their exams. They had the rest of the summer to celebrate. And as the night gathered force the boys had sworn a solemn oath to help them do it with style. An oath that inevitably led to nostalgic tales of their own freedom from school and the summer that had cemented their friendship.

Richard had told me all this before, how he and Phil had met each other at just the right time, when they were learning how to become different people, still hampered by adolescent awkwardness, but beginning to believe that things could be better. How they had developed a double act that had remained largely unchanged: how Phil would drink and Richard would smoke; Phil would be raucous and abusive and fight his corner, while Richard would see the funny side of things. Richard had always been the dreamer, for ever expecting romance on every corner, whereas Phil would dismiss it all, and the more he turned his back on love, the more the young girls came running. How at that early age Phil had not yet found his craft, and, while unchannelled, that energy could turn to violence – which had meant that Richard always felt well protected. They formed their reputations in one summer, by the end of which they could not, and would not, function apart.

But this time Richard was fuelled by a night of reminiscence, and insisted on telling us all about the summer that turned the tide, the summer that had in every way transformed them from boys into young men, a time of shedding skins. He said those months were filled with first experiences. First illicit parties, first nights staying up to see in the dawn. First sexual encounters in unknown houses, hiding in wardrobes to avoid discovery by prowling parents. First intoxications and learning, in so many ways, that strange contradiction that the very things that give pleasure to the heart and the mind can be poison to the body. First hangovers, but the sickness is outweighed by delight in the certain knowledge that the rest of your life is going to be just as exciting as the night just passed. First realisation that everything is ahead of you, and everything is possible. First loves and first heartbreaks. She encouraged them to go into every detail, but I didn't want to know. I saw exactly how the boys must have been when they were younger, all confidence and bravado. Exactly the kind of boys who had kept me in my corner when I was that age and made sure I never had the right to speak.

Then she was competing with them, a stream of childish anecdotes – telling them about her teenage countryside years, pulling photos down from the walls to show. And there she would be, with her gang, looking young and happy against a backdrop of sea or sky or mountain. Her hair cut shorter then, and pushed off her face, she looked beautiful, always smiling. Sometimes the photographs caught the child in her, as if her body still held memories of her toddler days when she would, as I had been told, race along the tidemarks and outscream the gulls. Then in some pictures she would look old beyond her years, while her peers would pout and pose; her younger self would look out from those photographs with an unflinching gaze, as if she could see into our flat, as if she could see what she had grown up into, and was holding it in the balance, judging whether this adult world met with her approval.

As the boys traded tales with her she teased them, saying they were showing their age now. Richard took great delight in the fact that he had smoked his first spliff before she was even born. Phil deduced that when she was a toddler he was busy getting arrested for under-age drinking and being a general menace to society. They told her she was still a novice, that she could learn a lot from them.

But she taunted them back, saying, 'It's always the quality not the quantity that matters.' Apparently every single one of her wasted nights had been magical: none had ever turned to violence or the psychosis the boys had known.

She told them how she and her friends used to build bonfires on the beach and refuse to give in to sleep. How one drug-fuelled dawn they had seen shoals of dolphins coming out of the waves at them, all the colours of the rainbow. She had talked to the dolphins for hours, as they told her tales of drowned sailors and all the treasures from sunken ships that lay scattered on the seabed. They had offered to carry her out to sea with them, to live a life of freedom among the waves, but if she went she would never be able to come back to dry land again. She had been tempted, but she declined, preferring the warmth of the firelight to the limitless ocean.

Phil didn't believe a word of it, but she was adamant, telling him that he hadn't been there, he hadn't seen the things that she had seen.

I kept silent: there was nothing I could have contributed to the conversation. I was quietly jealous of the bond she had with the boys, of the way all three of them seemed to have lived many other lives before their present incarnations. Yet again I felt so insubstantial with my compartmentalised life and my pretence of a job – a path so casually taken, with no sense of the sacrifices it might entail.

I left our smoke-filled bedroom, made my coffee as they opened more beers. I went back to kiss her goodbye. Phil was writing lists, saying they had the best part of a week to get ready and 'Let's do it properly for once, let's give those kids a night to remember. Let's show them how the old-timers can party with the best of them. Let's show them how to live.'

She was leaning over Phil's shoulder saying, 'Let me do it, I can make the words hit the page at least.' Their laughter. As always, I was the one turning away, setting out for a day apart from her.

I took my worries with me to work, and kept them close to my chest all day long. It unsettled me how the boys could reach back across the years and still find points of connection, building bridges with ease. I could see that she was exactly the same, that she had never really accepted she had to outgrow her younger self and was delighted to have an opportunity to re-create that time, with all-too-willing accomplices. For me, that difference was a huge gaping canyon of years I could never get across, the adolescent me stood on the far side, looking shrunken and nervous. And I was grateful for that distance, I welcomed it: I wanted to be utterly severed from my old self and all those years of awkwardness. I worried that if the three of them persisted in this regression, I would be forced back into that persona, and yet again become a self-conscious outsider, my voice drowned in the cacophony of the more confident, happier people.

In the short term I couldn't have been more mistaken.

The handful of days that followed were among our best. Our two households became one happy family. That night I returned to find a camp-bed set up in my study and a living room full of chaos. They had decided to do things in style and the boys had come to live with us for a week while they transformed their flat. She knew I wouldn't mind, we had plenty of space.

And so it was.

They moved in and prepared for the weekend while I worked through the long days. It was a golden week. The boys came to live with us and everything fell into place. We were balanced and centred again, and it was as if we had all just met. Our domestic routines became as one. Richard would be up, tidying the living room when I got out of bed. He would make me breakfast and, still both half asleep, we would share the papers. He set up his computer in my study and would often be working away before I left. All I would see of Phil was a comatose lump on the sofa. Any awkwardness that remained between our two households was swiftly dissipated: there were no more awkward silences, no more of those sidelong glances exchanged between the two boys, both anxious that they might again have overstepped the mark. She was in her element, she had her old ease about her. All of us were under her spell once more. She drew the boys into her schemes and they delighted in the secrecy: always when I came home I would find the rooms full of laughter. If the evenings held any surprises they were only ever pleasant. It was exactly as it should have been.

She thrived on the energy. Just like when we first moved in, every evening was an exercise in detective work, scouting the house for hints of what the weekend might have in store. It reminded me of the Christmases of my childhood when I would try to peep through the keyhole of my mother's suddenly locked wardrobe, straining my eyes and my imagination, willing uncertain shadows to transform themselves into colourful presents. When the day eventually came I was so over-excited that anything she gave me was bound to disappoint.

But they had a whole flat next door in which to hide the evidence, so there was pitifully little left for me to base my deductions on.

She resurrected her old sewing machine, a black iron affair with a huge handle. On the second day I came home to find the house filled with a fierce, determined buzz. Phil had motorised her machine and she was stitching cloth together at a rate of knots. On the third day the bath was streaked with dark stains from the dye. But I was never allowed next door to see. Our evenings were punctuated by enforced DIY programmes on TV. We saw neighbours transforming each other's rooms, in varying degrees of kitsch, and Richard would tease me saying, 'Yes, that's exactly what we've got in mind.' She and Phil would shout at the screen, insulting the mediocre colour schemes and shoddy workmanship. Richard was sworn to an oath of secrecy and wasn't going to give anything away. 'Wait and see,' he said, with a wink and a grin.

But I, too, had developed a routine that week. With the boys in our house, I broke my habit of lounging in bed with her until the last minute. I arrived at work early, sometimes even sharing the lift with Mr Collins who was impressed by my commitment to the firm and was more certain than ever that I had a bright future. I found myself in agreement, but was not about to define my terms.

I spent the extra hour scribbling my notes, but now that all the bad dreams of wild forests had been banished I recorded different things. What had been a defence mechanism now turned to a system of celebration. I wanted to keep hold of every part of these good days, and became slightly obsessive: I tabulated my nightly consumption of alcohol; I noted down almost every mouthful of fine food they made; I counted her kisses, and kept note of how many times a day she told me she loved me.

James was intrigued, asking me what I was up to. Was I planning some kind of private investment, did I have some insider knowledge I wasn't sharing? I laughed and told him, yes, I supposed I did, but not in the way he thought.

The week continued to be too warm for comfort. In the confines of my office, time hung heavy in the air, as close and claustrophobic as the hot weather. I felt I was living a false life, a static existence, unfairly separated from the energy and scheming in the flat. I walked back across the common every evening, stopping to stare and wonder at the clear blue sky above me, and the six o'clock sunshine warmed my skin, soothing away the difficult edges of the unnatural day. I would look out for the three of them, come running to meet me, linking arms. We'd stride out to the pub, sit on the lawn until the light began to fade, then chase each other down the dry paths that took us home.

The nights were long and we would go to bed exhausted. She slept soundly, weary but happy. She never stirred. They were calm nights. It didn't surprise me that I had no more difficult dreams. I had no need for them. That swift-green forest had been a hidden premonition, a blessing in disguise, showing me how she could heal anything. We were back where we had started, and everything about our shared life was stronger for being tested.

The fourth day was Friday, and their excitement was almost palpable as they pushed me out of the flat. I found work a real chore, my mood unbalanced by the anticipation of the weekend. I watched the three clocks ticking away too slowly in front of me and I thought of all the wasted time they made. My mind wasn't on my job. For the first time I accepted James's offer of a sneaky lunchtime drink. But the weather was too good to be stuck in the pub. We bought sandwiches and beer and James took me to one of his favourite haunts.

Bunhill Fields graveyard was a five-minute walk from the office, incongruous in the middle of the city, but even here there was no getting away from the world of business. Men in suits sat on the benches under the trees, plugged into their mobiles. Some worked their way around the graves, with that very British gait to show they were respectful of death: hands clasped behind the back, head slightly bowed, nodding sagely at every inscription. I didn't like it. The famous tombs were an unwanted glimpse of a wider picture.

But I was still grateful to James for the escape and made every effort to engage him in cheerful banter. We began talking about work, but after our second beer James was expounding his theories about the women in the office. I was astounded by the breadth of his knowledge – he knew all of the secretaries by name, and a fair number by taste and touch as well. I smiled as he rattled through their scores out of ten and other significant statistics. I told him I was sure he was more of a man than I would ever be. He laughed and told me that if indeed my 'virtual girl' – the name he had coined for my screensaver picture of her – was real then I was a very lucky boy. We got to the office late and the afternoon passed in a pleasant haze. I exchanged a few salacious emails with James, just to prove a point. I practically ran out of the office when five o'clock came.

I strode out at Wimbledon full of anticipation. Anything might happen this weekend. I knew I was lucky, in more ways than James would ever comprehend. I felt lucky like the lord of a land is lucky, like the proud rich princes of her fairytales. I even felt sorry for Phil, who would never see maybe that there is no greater power in this whole wide world than love, who would never understand what love could do.

I made my way across the common, following the paths and short-cuts home, which were now second nature. When the sun emerged from behind a cloud and shone brilliant, warm upon my face, it felt like a gift, as if even the hazy sunshine was there because I willed it so.

I walked straight past the boys' tree and heard a cacophony of jeers at my back. The kids were catcalling at me across the common. She was there too, along with the boys. They had been watching me for ages.

'You were in a world of your own,' she said, laughing at me. 'Grinning like a muppet. Are you pissed again?' She was perched up on a branch with Jay, plaiting his long hair into tiny braids. 'Come and join us,' she said, 'if you can still climb.'

Jay actually blushed when he saw me. 'Fuck me, no way it's you!' he muttered, and she just laughed.

The kids were quiet and incredulous as I climbed up to join them. They were obviously confused: with their limited experience and youthful assumptions, there was no way they could make sense of us as a couple. Later I learnt that, on the afternoon of our first encounter, they had been leading their own particular revolution against the squares and straights of Wimbledon village. Spooking a middle-class family scored ten points; heckling snogging couples earned twenty, but soiling a passing suit was worth a massive thirty points and clinched the game. Kate had been out to prove a point: the precision beer attack was nothing personal. But set boundaries had been drawn. At first sight, I had been identified as an enemy to be mocked and repelled, and I don't think they, or I, ever quite forgot it.

Richard helped me up on to the lowermost branch. From there, hugging the trunk, I climbed. There were Kate and Tom to my left, secure in the crook of one branch, with a bottle of vodka, staring out at the common. Then, a couple of metres up and to my right, there was Jay sitting beside her, her hands plaiting his hair. I could be stupidly jealous of the touch of her hands. I had no time to loiter – Richard was right behind me, shouting, 'Upwards and onwards!'

It was worth the climb. Right at the top there was the boys' bower. The leaves curled above our heads, shielding us from the sun and any hint of a wind. Between the three of us, we had a panoramic view. It was much higher than our rooftop: we were sitting in the centre of the sky. The boys insisted we stayed up there drinking until the sunset came. We were crowned by multicoloured clouds, and it was beautiful but I felt too exposed. The treetop creaked with our weight, and the soft sway of the leaves gave me an insidious sickness. I thought I could hear them whispering to me, repeating and reminding, *Far to fall, far, very far to fall.*

My vertigo caught me and pinned me tight to the trunk as if any slight movement might make the land below come rushing up to hit me in the face or, perhaps worse, the branches might pitch me forward, and the soft green grass of the common retreat as I fell down, and I would be trapped, for ever falling, tumbling towards land that wouldn't catch me.

'Time to make a move,' said Richard. 'It'll soon be too dark to see.'

But I couldn't. I was frozen, hugging the trunk to me for safety. In the end, Richard had to guide me down, step by step, standing patiently behind, placing my feet on safe branches. I felt clumsy and stupid, especially in front of the unknown kids. She laughed at my caution, and left her perch with Jay, mocking me with gymnastic tricks, catching branches, falling and turning. All with absolute precision. The others, waiting below, applauded when she hit the ground.

Despite their drunken state, the kids still had the unlimited energy of youth and were off into the village in pursuit of more adventure. And if the village was as dull as usual they would set off into Town, and of course we were welcome – why didn't we come too? But we resumed our old alignment, the four of us linking arms and ricocheting our way home.

Side by side we stumbled through the darkening common. She was full of mischief in the dying light, drawing Phil into her old games, running and hiding – they repeatedly ambushed Richard and me on our way back: with great warrior yelps they would come rushing out of the bushes and knock us over with the force of their attacks. Phil would jump Richard, swiping him with saplings broken from passing trees. She would push me on to the grass and, in the shadows, cover me with kisses, and I would feign death and injury, just screams and laughter in the twilight.

The boys left us at our door, moving back to their flat to set the mood, insisting on no visitors until closing time tomorrow.

The silence of our home was a shock after all the week's activities.

A different atmosphere. Still mischievous, she was saying, 'Let's make like the early days and christen every room.' A week of abstinence in the boys' presence had obviously taken its toll. We held each other down on the floorboards again and delighted in our space. Music played in every room and it was a long night. When, finally, we got to bed I discovered a few tell-tale sequins scattered on our sheets.

'Wait and see!' she said.

The next day was lazy. We dozed the hours away, woken occasionally by sounds of preparation next door as the boys tested the full capacity of their stereo. We ate takeaways in bed, a defiant gesture, setting the tone for the night. When we finally got up she made me wait in the living room while she changed – the first of many surprises.

She had made a party dress, especially to please me. It was made of rich dark blue silk, covered with silver sequins. It looked like she had coaxed the heavens themselves down from the sky, and wrapped them around her. The soft material flowed in a train, like a peacock's tail unfurling behind. Her hair was pinned up off her face, and interwoven with silver threads and jewelled slides. She was almost too beautiful to touch. Her clear blue eyes were twinkling with laughter as I came close to kiss her.

'Will I do, then?' she said.

I told her she was the most beautiful thing I had ever seen.

When she walked into the boys' room they were similarly struck. Phil said, 'I told you so, fits like a glove.'

'As pretty as a princess,' Richard said.

I had a fixed smile as Phil told me how he had taken all her measurements and drawn up a pattern for her with the accuracy of a blueprint, while Richard hadn't even been able to thread a needle. 'It's a beautiful dress,' I said. 'A proper work of art.'

She smiled and said it was all for my benefit.

That's what the boys said as they led me through their transformed house. 'All for you, mate,' Richard said, slapping me on the back. 'Just to show you we care. Just to let you know.'

The whole flat was evidence of a week well spent. The strips of muslin she had been sewing replaced their heavy curtains. They swept down one side of the living room, covering the windows. She had dyed them in varying shades, very light at the top, blending to a deep dark blue at the bottom.

I told her not to stand too close to them, I would never be able to find her.

The staircase was spectacular: she had bought every imitation flower you could imagine and wrapped them round the banisters. At first glance it looked as if a rainbow of fresh flowers was pouring itself into the middle of the room.

'It's a bastard to climb, though,' Richard warned me. 'Like a dark tunnel – you can't see where your feet are.'

Then there were stout bushes borrowed from our rooftop, with fairylights draped among the branches, shedding pools of light in the room and shadowing the walls with the patterns of the leaves. They had covered parts of the walls with tinfoil to cast light all around and warp the room, turning it into a cave of silver. She laughed at our distorted reflections, me transformed into a squat, pot-bellied, grinning thing, her stretched thin and towering above me, nothing more than a rippling, tenuous image. 'What a funny pair we make,' she said. 'Would you still love me if I looked like that?'

I told her of course I would: we would breed a freak show and travel the world together.

They had removed every bit of furniture and the floorboards stretched for ever in front of her. I think that everyone turned to look at her as she moved across the room. When she walked past the fairylights, they were reflected by her sequins. She shimmered with light.

The kids, of course, had ensconced themselves already. Jay tried to make amends the only way he knew how. 'Can I interest you at all, mate?' he asked, as he emptied the bottomless pockets of his combat trousers, revealing an array of pills and powders – something for everyone. I wasn't interested. I didn't want anything from him, no doubt confirming all his suspicions of me as a City-bound pseud.

She went over to argue with Kate about her choice of music, while Tom just stood there mouth open, staring at her, much as I must have been doing myself. Richard put a drink in my hand and told me yet again what a lucky man I was. 'She did it all for you,' he told me. 'Not many would.'

He gave me the grand tour, to show me exactly what had been done for my benefit. Their rooftop was worth the climb: the fairylights decorating their fence gave us a gentle beam of light to aim for as we felt our way upwards. On the patio there was a sea of multicoloured cushions she had made. I warned

Richard that people might get trapped up here, condemned to an entirely horizontal night. He grinned and said it had been Phil's best idea all week.

I could hear her laughing downstairs with Kate, the applause from what sounded like the beginning of a drinking competition, but Richard didn't want to join them just yet. He produced a couple of beers and made me sit down beside him as he rolled us both a spliff to start the evening off. 'So . . .' he said, with his first exhalation '. . . how are things?'

I repeated the usual platitudes about work, and told him that of course, tonight, I couldn't be happier.

'But really? Even after the other weekend? Come on, mate, tell it like it is.'

I took the spliff from him but would not let it loosen my tongue. I had no intention of giving anything away. Not even to Richard would I confess how she crept into my dreams when I was sleeping, that most private of places. Not even to Richard would I tell the tale of how she had made the forest live again, with her tears and the tender touch of her hands. Not even to Richard would I confess what I found hard to admit to myself: that although the nights were calmer without those visitations, a renegade part of me missed the dreams when they didn't come. That after a week of being caged in the office, and the comfortable familiarity of our evenings on the rooftop, part of me missed the wild beauty of the dream-forest and its unpredictable adventures.

So I adopted James's vocabulary instead, made light of our love, deflected Richard's suspicions with details I would be ashamed to write down now. In graphic terms, I told him how the last twenty-four hours had shown me that, beyond a doubt, things were better than ever.

An awkward silence followed. Then, 'Fair enough, only asking.'

'Why, what else do you want to know? Ask me anything.'

A good double bluff. We smoked in silence, and made our way back down.

I found her crouching in a corner with Phil, looking at the space where the bookcase had been. There on the wall, written in biro, in marker-pen, in differing degrees of legibility, was a multitude of names. There were pictures and messages, hearts and kisses left for the boys in ornate handwriting. Crude drawings and obscene jokes clustered in one corner. There were a few of Richard's doggerel odes to summer written in sloping lines that eventually collided with the skirting-board. It was testament to all the nights they'd had and evidence of a decade of redecoration. Phil told us to be sure to write something before the night was out. It was the only bit of the house they vowed they would never paint over. Write things down and they stay.

The room filled with folk as the night rolled on. Phil and Richard were in their element, rushing around filling glasses, shouting greetings as more and more people tumbled in through the door. I felt overwhelmed. This was supposed to be my party and I knew no one. The music was too loud.

And everyone looked the same to me: old friends were reunited in dark corners, and laughter echoed around me, but I couldn't even begin to make my presence felt in this sea of strangers. I had a lurch of memory, back to those painful teenage years, of how I had never learnt how to make my presence felt in a crowded room. How, at those awkward parties, I would try to approach pretty girls with nervous conversation, and how they would just look through me, as if I wasn't there. I could never find those magic words to make the girls laugh. And I would return home, stupidly drunk and lonely. Before I went to bed, I would stand in front of the mirror and have whispered conversations with my own sad reflection, desperately practising, kidding myself that next time I would get it right.

The force of those memories made me unexpectedly clumsy. I kept trying to push my way through the room to reach her but it meant breaking through circles of conversation, tripping over prone bodies. I upset drinks. A stray cigarette flailed in front of me and burnt my hand. Overwhelmed by the noise and the laughter, which yet again just made me feel invisible, I loitered by her curtains, which moved around me in the night breeze, half hidden. I decided that the easiest way to cope with this bombardment of unknown people, all casting admiring glances at her, was to get myself so inebriated that I couldn't see and didn't care. I drank whatever came to hand and retreated further into the curtains, hoping that she would come looking.

Actually it was Richard who found me, soon after midnight. His grinning face swam sickeningly into my vision and he pulled me out of my slump, shouting that I was looking green around the gills, the night was young, all I needed was a little fresh air and I'd find my second wind. He grabbed a bottle of whisky and helped me up the stairs, calling, 'Come on, time for Phase Two. If all else fails, drink yourself sober.' From the foot of the staircase I caught a glimpse of the dress as she shimmered through the crowds, Phil with his arm casually draped around her shoulder and Tom tripping hopefully behind.

We found ourselves a quiet corner on the rooftop and stayed there until our bottle was empty. Lost hours. I can only see snapshots – Richard nodding, frowning, looking too sincere, me trying to say something, grappling for meaning, my words spilling out in the wrong order, Richard laughing, telling me to spit it out, for God's sake, one of these days I was going to have to learn to say what I really meant. I wish I could remember what I told him. It was something important.

I do remember going back down to the party. Standing at the top of the stairs, I was overwhelmed by a wave of vertigo. The dark stairwell gave me a tunnel-vision glimpse of what lay below, a seething mass of people, a babel chorus of voices over music echoing upwards, with her among them somewhere. I tripped and tumbled my way down, an impressive somersault. There was a shocked silence as I hit the floor, then great applause as I stood up and gave a lurching theatrical bow. She came out of the crowds, laughing along with the rest of them. She put her arms around me and massaged my sore shoulders, giggling. 'No damage done, you pisshead.'

She gave me strong coffee and we sat in a quiet corner, trying not to subside into the cans and empty bottles that lay in banks along the edges of the room, washed-up detritus and washed-out people. The tinfoil was ripped to shreds and scattered about the room. That was Jay's fault. Standing with his face to the wall, attacking his own reflection, he was a man possessed if ever I saw one. At least I wasn't the only casualty of the evening.

Richard, obviously the good Samaritan that night, led him gently to our corner, sat down with him and began to roll a spliff. All part of his sympathetic ritual, a simple case of administering the right medicine. I didn't want to join them. Jay's inarticulacy and moody insolence irritated me: I recognised his kind.

We wandered over to the other side where a circle of people were playing cards with drunken concentration, cigarettes in place of money as the stakes. Tom was triumphant with a pile of fags in front of him. A gaggle of people had formed a pancake-making production line in the kitchen, and I could see Phil in clouds of steam, cursing at the espresso machine.

'Let's go and leave our mark,' she said, leading me over to the space where the bookcase had stood. Kate was already there, scribbling away. They worked well together, passing a bottle of tequila between them as I watched. Marking out their space, she drew a border of roses and hearts while Kate caricatured us all, not without skill.

She handed me the pen and I signed my name alongside hers. 'Now there's another bit they'll never paint over,' she said, clapping her hands, giving me her arm so that I could help her up. Kate grinned a slurred hello at me, grabbed my leg to pull herself to her feet. Both of them fell against me, their arms wrapped around me, her tripping over the folds of her dress. The hem was torn, and the front was covered with burns from her stray cigarettes. 'It doesn't matter,' she said. 'Good dresses should only last the night. The best things in this life are never built to last.'

It infuriated me, that carelessly destructive side of her. I hated it when things were broken: many times, on the rooftops with the boys, wineglasses had been shattered, our favourite old records scratched, plant pots knocked aside and smashed to pieces. She and Phil had once spent a whole week making a side table for the patio, beautifully painted and varnished. Then, two days later, she lurched against it in a drunken moment and it splintered beneath her. Both she and Phil had mocked the poor state of their workmanship, but I couldn't laugh about it. These things all held a little of her in them, and it hurt me when she broke them. Countless times I would tell her to watch out, slow down, be careful, and she would laugh at me and tell me to stop worrying, calm down, things don't last. 'Things never last,' she would say. 'It's people that matter.'

She fought her way through to the stereo and insisted on more volume and more rhythm. I finally got my promised second wind as she put on one of her favourite songs and spun me round. She kicked off her tall shoes and hitched her dress up around her waist, pulled me close and made me dance along the length of the room with her. Trying to keep up, I stumbled out of time and had to collapse on to the cushions when the song ended. I envied her energy.

Later I learnt that the wicked glint in her eye and her quick movement had been amphetamine fuelled – Jay's box of tricks. I was furious: it felt like he had polluted her. I trusted him even less but kept my anger close to my chest for a more appropriate occasion.

Tom could not believe his luck when she strode over to the card game and announced that she would dance with the winner. She pulled him up, and waltzed around the room with him, gently teaching him the steps. As I looked at his awestruck face as she guided him until he was confidently turning her so that her dress was flung out in shimmering folds, as I watched how she moved him, I loved her all the more.

Kate sat down beside me, offering me the dregs of her tequila with a lopsided hospitable grin, telling me what a great night it was. 'Well done!' she said, as if the party had been anything to do with me. She was watching the dancing as well. 'What an amazing dress!' she whispered. 'Amazing light show.' Then she clumsily put her hand on my knee for a second and, blushing, said she guessed there was no point in asking if I danced with anyone else.

I was embarrassed and stuttered, slurring, telling her no, no, there was no point at all. Then Phil came to my rescue with a cup of coffee, took Kate's hand and said he was a born dancer, would she do him the honour?

Card games were disrupted, conversations stopped as others took to the floor, and she was there, changing the records, moving among the crowd. I couldn't just sulk in a corner. Everyone was up on their feet, responding to the boys' demands. She wove her way through the malcoordinated bodies, pulling me to her, dancing closely then twisting away, catching other partners, a law unto herself.

Then Jay sprang to his feet with an energy that was demonic, shouted, 'SUNRISE!' and ran up to the roof. There the survivors of the party sat on her cushions, and toasted the summer sun as it streamed through the clouds.

The following day had a mania about it that can only be gained, Phil informed me, by dedicated intoxication. When we finally filed down from the rooftop, the extent of the damage to the flat was evident. As the sun hit the skylights, there was a rising smell of stale smoke and beer. The whole place looked as if it had been ripped apart. The last few guests slunk away, making arrangements to see us later, up in the tree, you never know, let's not underestimate our ability to cope with the vertical world. I went back home for a shower, but she was still restless, saying, 'We can't sleep now, not in the daylight. Not on a Sunday morning.'

So we went walking over the common. She was still wearing her dress, insisting that it wasn't the end of the night yet. She looked stunning, her sunglasses obscuring her bloodshot eyes as she strode out, sparkling in the morning light. And the boys, too, were as wired as she: every sentence had an edge of the surreal, every footstep forward was an experiment in balance and perspective. Richard decreed that we must press forward, as to turn back meant facing the stench of their flat and the epic task that lay ahead, and if we could only make it up Gravelly Hill then we could curl up into balls and roll our way across the common until we hit the pub. Phil was leading the way and consequently we went round in dizzying circles, trying to navigate by the sails of the windmill. Eventually I took control and led us all down to the Hand in Hand. We whiled away the rest of the day on the lawn and I lost several hours as we pieced together the events of the night, trying to put names to faces.

To begin with I felt proud to be with them. We were an incongruous sight; her glamorous attire attracted curious glances from sedate families and curious children. But I couldn't keep up with them as they challenged each other to drink on. They had no fear of the next day to stop their jubilation, whereas I had a working week just about to come rushing round the corner, and everything to worry about. None of them noticed as I grew quieter: they were too busy congratulating each other on the night just past. She told them how people would talk of it for years to come and mark it each year with an anniversary of hedonism, although they would never be able to capture the magic again.

And the boys, even Phil, indulged her as she told them how charmed they were, that when they were born they must have been blessed with the gifts of laughter and energy, that they were destined to carry these gifts across the world, drawing good people to them wherever they travelled. With her artful words, she re-created the raucous night into the stuff of legends, an initiation for us all. She declared that Bacchus would be envious and announced that the four of us should start our own religion of feasting and drinking. We were destined to become minor deities, and people across the ages would tell stories for ever more of our wild nights. The flat would become a shrine and folk would travel from far and wide to see the place where it had all begun. And we would welcome them in and get them pissed and they would become our followers, spread our teachings to every corner of the globe. The boys would be waited on by a hundred handmaidens, who would cater to their every need. Together, the four of us would never grow sad, and never get old.

'Too right,' said Phil. 'It's what the world needs.'

I smiled in agreement. I was pleased for them that the evening had been such a resounding success. But it had been their night, not mine.

The sun was setting as we dragged ourselves home across the common. I was so grateful to Phil and Richard when they declined our drunken offers to help them tidy everything up. Richard just grinned and said, 'Tomorrow mate, we'll sort it all out tomorrow, don't you worry. Get some sleep.'

We stumbled into our flat and she was pulling me through to the bedroom, giggling, saying, 'The party's not over, not just yet, my lovely man, not yet.' Then she lost her momentum and collapsed on the bed, and was asleep within seconds. I curled up beside her. No noise at all next door. I smiled to imagine Phil and Richard, also drained of sound and movement, passed out in the debris of the night before.

# 12

In retrospect, it's easy for me to form many theories about why the forest came racing back that night. The next morning I told myself that I had poisoned my body and mind so thoroughly that it had had to come seeping out somewhere, and by now I should have known that all the abuses and upsets of the daytime would filter through into my dreams.

But in truth the dreams returned because I willed them. Maybe it was in reaction to the isolation of the party, a night that should have been magical but wasn't. But for whatever reason, as I drifted off to sleep I was yearning for the beauty of those wild woods and all the enchantments they contained. Because although during the last week in many ways I had never been happier, when new dreams failed to come, the old ones gathered nostalgic detail in my memory. I thought of the beauty of the forest that had regrown at her touch. I thought about all the hidden treasures I might find there, if only I was given another chance to see it. I saw that those dreams had turned me into an explorer, after all. I had tackled savage landscapes and fought with the elements. I had been tested and I loved that sense of my possible potential as I struggled with the push and pull of courage versus caution. The forest at night was a challenge, allowing me to play at being a very different man.

As always, the dream began just as she was leaving the room. She was still wearing her dress and, silhouetted against the night sky, it was as though she was moving inside the constellations. She sang to the ivy and it curled around her with more intimacy than before, tendrils lingering on her arms and stroking her hair. This time the rope held a little more of her in it, a delicate weave of her golden hair.

I watched the train slither out of the window, a soft river of sequins spilling into the dark. More than ever, it didn't feel like a dream. We had cheated time that weekend, challenging the night to outlast us. And although I woke into a world of darkness, it had such clarity, as if, through upsetting our daytime patterns, I had gained more constancy in this shifting world. The sky was dark, and the air had a thickness about it, as though the night was trying to grow into a solid thing. The rustling of the leaves sounded as if the canopy of the woods was stroking the velvet edges of the sky, trying to coax the stars down to nestle in the treetops.

I was pulled towards that enchanted place, took tight hold of the ivy, and jumped. It was only a dream and the free-fall down the side of the house couldn't hurt me. This time I loved the sudden rush of controlled fear as I slid down the strong rope and the soft carpet of ivy came rushing up to greet me. I yelled with delight as I came whistling down the sky, and landed unharmed.

With the dream came freedom. I was not weighed down by the poisons of the previous night's revelry. I was as swift as a child and ran, laughing, into the forest. The new growth had flourished in the night and everything was fertile, and full of promise. The trees, now released from their black skins, were larger and stronger than ever. The landscape dwarfed me: these green serpentine trees had roots as thick as my arm. Yet again I was lighter than air as I ran across that carpet of flowers, which danced under my feet. In this new incarnation, the ocean of blossoms had no edges, an unfathomable, limitless beauty. And now, as they brushed together, they chimed in the night, with a soft music that sounded like laughter, or the gentle voice of a woman, calling from far, far away. A lesser man than I would have been captivated by that sound, and sent racing down false turnings, in search of the source.

But I was not so easily seduced by such tricks and kept running. Again, I had that feeling of running as fast as I could, but gaining no ground. I began to doubt this world again, wondering whether, if everything was so utterly changed, the clearing would still be there, or if the forest had re-formed itself completely and I would have to start all this exploration anew and learn other routes. I had not come this far to let my doubts undermine me. I forced myself to believe I would make it to the clearing and find the familiar paths.

And the minute I gained that resolve I saw it there, through an opening in the trees. But the woods still held some new tricks: now four paths stretched out before me instead of two.

But I recognised the shapes of the gateway trees that stood by the central left-hand path. Even though they were green and broader, the shadows they cast on the ground, that tight-knit interlock of branches, were still recognisable. This place was changed, but not utterly transformed.

If there were physical constants then I could pin down time and distance and I wasn't lost at all. I counted my footsteps as I ran down the path, and my fears were silenced. Even so, it was a difficult journey. Very little sound carried in the forest now. The thickness of the wood was conspiring to keep her undiscovered. There was no physical trail to follow. When I pushed myself through the ferns they sprang back quickly. The forest wiped out any trace of either of our passages through. I wished she had left me some kind of sign.

Even as the wish was forming in my mind, thin slices of moonlight broke through the leaves and I saw a river of tiny stars that had tumbled down on to the forest floor. I looked again and saw what it really was: sequins had come loose from her dress and had been caught by the tendrils of the ferns. There was a stream of silver that could only lead me to her, weaving through the trees. Still, it wasn't easy to follow. If I looked down it dazzled me: I had to squint into the middle distance and ignore any insidious suspicions that this might be a false trail, designed to keep me turning in circles, gaining her all the time she needed to run out to whatever was waiting in that open land beyond.

I kept my faith in that path of sequins and, sure enough, it led me to the edge of the woods. I was almost too late: she was on the point of being swallowed up by the darkness, blending into the night in that dark dress, but I could just make out the glimmer of her walking away. I was overjoyed to have come this far, and to be so close behind her. I only had to close a few feet of distance that lay between us, and I would catch her. I couldn't hang back, retaining my original caution. It might matter if she saw me, but it mattered much more that I should be able to see her, or what little of her the night would reveal – shifting silver specks of light, growing ever more distant, a column of stars drifting further away, a fluid constellation, plucked down from the sky and set on the earth to guide me.

So I scuttled after her, turned the corner, lost my footing and tumbled down on to sand. The grass verge had stopped abruptly, the path given way to a six foot drop. I stepped out into thin air, and fell into a completely different land – a dead and desolate world. There was a great expanse of desert that stretched in all directions. After the richness of the woods, I can only define this place in terms of absence. It was a barren wasteland. The sand swallowed up the moonlight, and it was like walking through a field of ashes. It had no beauty, and I could see no end to it. This was not a place I would have ventured into of my own free will.

Neither was it somewhere I thought she would linger, but there were sure signs of her movement. A long snaking line was scoured across the sand ahead, where her trailing dress had left its mark. Yet again, I shrugged away my doubts. I had willed this dream, and I had to accept the challenge I had dreamt for myself and overcome my habitual fears of open land. I had called this world into being: now it was up to me to push through it, to find her and bring her back. There was a slight wind and fine grains of sand were blowing into my eyes. I kept my head down, my breathing regular, trying not to swallow sand, careful not to scuff the line she had left as I stumbled after her. There were no landmarks to keep me secure, and I had no way of measuring my footsteps. The lie of the land was the same before me as behind – a dust-ridden world with no edges.

I lost my sense of time out there. It might have been minutes or hours later that I realised the wind was getting stronger. A storm was brewing. The line I was following was weaving about for no reason and, yet again, I wondered if she was leading me astray. But up ahead something caught my eye, waltzing, twisting silver lights. She had stopped in the middle of the desert, and was dancing with the wind. Maybe she was lost, maybe she had become suddenly overwhelmed by the desert. I ran and ran to catch up with her. I was desperate for her, and fought with myself to find the words that would persuade her to turn round, to hold my hand and have her walk beside me as we followed our double set of footprints home. I would tell her that there was something quietly dangerous about this lifeless place. Like a hero from her fairytales I would tell her that she had accidentally strayed into the land of the dead and I had come to lead her back safely to the land of the living where there was colour and laughter and life and love.

But the desert was playing strange tricks with perspective, and the more I ran towards her, the smaller she became, shrinking away from me, twisting round so as not to face me. When I eventually reached her, and tried to touch her, I found myself swiping out at air. She wasn't there at all: it was just a fragment of her dress, that long gracious train caught on a rock and ripped in passing, the wind imbuing it with an echo of her movement. Clutching it in my hand as a reminder, I bowed my head and forged forward. My doubt, gathering force, whispered all around me, telling me to turn, turn round, head home, before it was too late. I looked round at the lie of the land behind me. Still there were footprints I could follow. But the treeline of the edge of the forest had long since been swallowed by the night. Nothing but dust remained.

The further forward I went, the deeper the sand-drifts became. I was sinking up to my ankles with every step. I began to think that there might be dark spaces lurking just underneath the desert's skin, and that the land might open up at any moment. I saw the surface breaking beneath my feet, saw myself falling further and further below, sliding down skeins of sand. I watched as the desert floor re-formed above my head, leaving no more than the tips of my fingers poking through the white-ash sand, clawing at the night. The minute I began to think these things, the land ahead became restless; the dunes on the far horizon were undulating, re-forming themselves and creeping closer.

Then a wall of sand came flying at me like a fury. It rose up suddenly from the desert and wrapped itself about me, filling my eyes, my mouth, my nose. I shook it out of my hair and tried to press forward, but it forced me back, spinning me round and disorienting me. I fought with it, spitting out great lumps. I lashed out, trying to beat a way through, but it clung to my fingers. The weight of it was pounding me down, bending me double, beating the very breath out of my body.

I squinted through it and saw the cause: there she was, only a few metres ahead, swaying from side to side. She had her back to me, flicking her skirts behind her as she walked, stirring up the land, creating a sandstorm and a great wind that was not touching her.

That fear, which I had kept at bay throughout this dream and the ones that had come before it, finally caught me. It came rushing up behind me and I was paralysed in the middle of the dead land, watching this wall of sand streaming out behind her, and racing across the desert to smother me. I turned tail and ran, I ran for my life, back along the line of footprints. Only once did I turn and look behind, to see the storm whipping at my heels, erasing our double line of steps. I scrambled clumsily up the side of the grassy hill, terrified of slipping back and being buried.

The storm left me alone when I reached the forest but hovered a few metres away, like a warning. My fear pulled me along in its wake, and guided me through the trees. Every part of my body was seeping sand. I tried to remember the calculations I had made on my outward journey and count the trees. But my fear was stronger, and did not give me time to gather my wits. 'There is more to this world than facts and numbers,' she had once said, and for the first time I think I understood.

I ran through, pulling myself around the trees, terrified by the black gaping distances between. I was bruised and tired, I just wanted to sink on to the forest floor and crawl home. But my fear tugged at my hand, running circles around me, pushing at my back, whispering in my ears, telling me to run, run fast, run fast and run sure, that if I stopped the sand would come and it would catch me.

The fear would not even leave me when I reached the side of my house. *Don't fall, don't fall*, it whispered to me, as I tried to catch hold of the ivy and stop myself from shaking. But the sand coating my skin made it difficult to climb. I pulled myself up slowly but kept on slipping, and it didn't feel like I was out of danger – the drop down the side of the house was very far to fall. But I found my footing and managed to scrabble up those last few metres, finally launching myself into the safety of our room. I still had the scrap of her dress knotted around my fingers, like a lucky charm. I threw it under the bed, undressed quickly and brushed the sand off my skin. It ran off me in golden rivulets and disappeared between the cracks in the floorboards. I took up my position in our bed again and very soon afterwards heard her returning. When she undressed, none of the sand had stuck to her at all. She was clean and pale and beautiful.

I fell into another dream, but the desert still had its hold over me. And just as sleep reached out to claim me, I had another glimpse of that ghostly place, but as if from a great distance. I was looking down on the limitless land, and saw myself scurrying through it – not a brave explorer at all but a stumbling boy, lost in a foreign place and fearful of the force of nature.

I was woken suddenly by the harsh summons of my alarm clock. I sat bolt upright in bed, as if I was still fighting for air, and ran my hand through my hair, half expecting another shower of sand to fall down on to the sheets. But, of course, it didn't. I looked down at her and she seemed too peaceful, curled up inside her dreams, smiling. Her serenity felt like a betrayal. I shook myself awake, trying to shrug away the residue of the nightmare. 'Dreams are only dreams,' I muttered to myself. 'They can't hurt you.'

The child in me still wanted to believe it. But then there was another part of me, the part of me that was growing older and wiser and yet more lost. That part wasn't quite so sure. Before I left the room, I looked under the bed, just to check that the train hadn't slipped under there after all. Of course there was nothing, just skittering balls of dust, lost socks, discarded cigarette papers – all the obvious litter from a normal home.

A dull ache in my bones was calling me back to sleep. But I didn't trust it. I felt as if I could sleep for days, and knew I had to fight it. I wouldn't allow myself to fall back into bed beside her. I left the flat quickly and forced myself out into the real world. There were noises coming from Richard and Phil's flat as I walked past. The furniture was being shifted back into place and I could hear them shouting at each other. I could hear Richard cajoling Phil, laughing, saying, 'Nearly there, nearly done. Don't give up on me now!' and Phil swearing back at him, telling Richard he was a hard man to please. Thinking they might appear at any minute and catch me hovering on the landing, I was down the stairs in seconds.

I got into the office early, but Simon was already there.

'Morning, Simon,' I said, as I took my place beside him.

'You're early.'

'Thought I'd surprise you.'

He smiled and handed me some guidelines about his latest piece of programming.

'Nice one,' I said. 'Let's start making us some money, then.'

That was James's mantra at the start of every day. Let's make some money. It made everything seem so simple.

I dutifully got to work. My typing was so quick and accurate that there was no time for me to be haunted by my screensaver image of her. And then James came rolling in with his usual cheeky precision, making his arse hit the chair just as our clock hit 9:00. He made me smile as he launched into an account of his outrageous weekend. 'And how about yours, mate?' he asked. 'You're looking dog rough.'

'Well, actually, that's because I spent last night walking through a fucking desert looking for my girlfriend,' I said.

Of course I didn't say that. But I wanted to, just to see the expression on his face. And I was so strongly haunted by the horrors of the dream that I almost felt it could have been true, and that some part of me had still not yet made it back from that ashen land. But instead I told him tales of our party and turned it into the evening that it should have been. I took Phil's place in the proceedings, and told him about all the beautiful women I had danced with, and how I had been the life and soul: getting the young ones pissed, making new friends, outdrinking them all.

I notched up yet more points. At this rate I was in danger of really becoming one of the lads. James laughed at me, telling me I was talking a mile a minute. I'd better keep it down, I was clearly still pissed. He bet me a tenner that things would seem very different in a few hours. He was quite right. By eleven o'clock I was fading fast: my body was crying out for sleep. The columns of numbers hurt my eyes. James was trying his best to help but my computer was conspiring against me, juggling numbers with a mind of its own and crashing before I could reach any marketable conclusions.

And the numeric constants kept being jarred by upsetting flashbacks. Looking back on the weekend from a position of gathering sobriety, I experienced a rush of vertigo and nausea. What had I told Richard up on the rooftop when I pulled him close and said, 'Now, promise you won't say a word . . .'?

The afternoon stubbornly failed to pass as it should and I became increasingly sure that I had let something slip. What was it?

Glimpses of semi-formed sentences came to me. I had been frightened of something but I wasn't sure what it was. I had asked Richard for some sympathy and some guidance, but was it for her or for myself? The dark shadows and rustling ivy of the rooftop had felt like another world coming in, but had I shared my fears or only thought them? And, to my shame, I think Phil featured in there somewhere. In a drunken jealous rage I think I must have said something – about my love for her and how it hurt to see her and Phil always laughing and quietly conspiring, and my worry that if Phil didn't believe in love then how could he possibly see it when he held it in his hand? Had I confided how I worried for our love sometimes, and how I would hate Phil for ever if he accidentally broke it? I think I asked for Richard's help and he smiled and told me he couldn't help me, he couldn't even help himself.

And I believe that Richard told me that Phil was careless, but he was not cruel. Then Richard was laughing at me and saying that we were still so young, and if our love got lost or broken, we would have only ourselves to blame. I consoled myself that he must have been at least as drunk as I was, and he, too, probably wouldn't be able to remember – but I knew I couldn't depend on it.

And as I write this, now even more time has passed since those forgotten hours, it's harder still to be sure about that conversation. Even now I could be a victim of my own lost memory, trying to fill in the gaps with the most obvious words.

Trapped at work, my blood still thick with alcohol and weighed down by lack of settled sleep, I began to doubt everything. The only moment during the whole of the party when I had really been happy was when we danced together and I felt her close and was carried away by the force of her movement against me. I was proud that all eyes were upon her, that everyone saw that she was with me, but now I remembered how I had stumbled then too, couldn't catch her properly when she turned round and flung herself into my arms.

That was one thing Richard had pointed out: she could hold her liquor. As in all things she did, when she drank she did it with style. Elegant at the start of the evening, raucous by the end, she had carried the whole mood of the party. As she knocked back drink after drink that was brought to her she never once slurred or said the wrong thing and provoked an awkward silence. It all came easily to her. I didn't notice it at the time but now I could see that in many ways the night that should have been a celebration of the two of us had only made the differences between us embarrassingly public.

As the day went on my pessimism and self-awareness gathered force. Everything went wrong. I spilled coffee over my notes. By half-way through the afternoon I had given up completely, and James, for all his sarky comments, was on my side – he covered for me as I stared into space and played on the Internet. The characters who were wandering around the office seemed as unreal as the pictures on my screen, flickering and shifting before my eyes. Even time was conspiring against me. I swear the minutes started falling backwards during that last hour. I kept a constant eye on the clocks just in case.

By the time I made it back to Wimbledon, I was virtually running home, driven by my unquestioning need for her. I knew that when I got back she would care for me, understanding that I had had a difficult day. On a warm evening like tonight, I would find the three of them on the rooftop, spread out in the last patch of sunlight that gathered by the railings. I could see exactly how it would be: I would arrive and complain about my hard day, and Phil, or maybe Richard, would take the piss and say I wouldn't know a hard day's work if it came up and bit me on the arse, whereas they had had a punishing day of manual labour, reclaiming their flat from the chaos of the party. I would be told that I should count myself lucky: all I had had to cope with was a few sums. She would spring to my defence, tell them to leave me alone, I was exhausted and we all needed an easy night. And then maybe we would cook together, or maybe we would spend an evening apart, but either way I was going home to a haven of music, friendship, rest, and a whole wealth of love.

\*

I wasn't unduly worried by the quietness of the flat. After all, she had been exhausted when I left, although I did wonder whether she had just slept the whole day through, and part of me was angry that she had had that option.

But when I got into the bedroom she was wide awake, and I could see, just from the way that she was holding herself, that everything was wrong. I cursed Jay and his box of tricks, the pills or powders or God knows what that had clearly poisoned her. She had been crying. She was sitting against the wall again, hugging her knees. She was curled up inside her own black cloud, holding it close.

'What's wrong, love?' I said, reaching out to her. 'What is it? Tell me.'

It was difficult to touch her. I put my arm around her shoulders but she shrugged me away. I tried to take her hand and saw that her forearms were red from where she had been scratching away at them. She must have been like this for hours. I tried to coax some kind of explanation out of her, but she was saying nothing. As we sat there, frozen, the silence gathered around us. No sound reached us through the walls.

The silence, of course. That was what was upsetting her. She thought they had gone again.

I turned her towards me saying, 'It's all right, don't be silly, they haven't gone. I doubt they could even move today. They'll be resting. We'll see them tomorrow. Don't worry.'

She pulled away viciously and said, 'Why don't you take a look at the rooftop and then tell me?'

She pushed me forward and stamped up the stairs behind me.

The door caught against something as I shoved it open and one of her favourite plants crashed to the ground. There was barely room to stand in the corner of the patio: the whole space was filled with what at first I thought was rubbish thrown over from the party.

But no. This was a collection of all-too-familiar objects. The cushions she had made were stacked up against the fence. In front of them was a pile of books, dog-eared with familiar titles and cracked spines. There was a record case, full of the albums she had lent them. Our spare crockery was in another box, wrapped up in the day's papers. In the centre of the heap there was a big brown parcel bearing our names. I brought it back to her as she stood there, propping herself up in the doorway.

Cautiously, she put her arm around me. 'I couldn't open it without you,' she said.

Their last joke: it was like a party game. They had cut up the curtains she had dyed for them, and used the material for wrapping. This just made her cry.

We sat on the steps Phil had built and patiently undid it. Between layers they had left us little gifts. Chocolate coins dropped out into her lap. A little bag of grass tumbled on to the tiles and was lost in the shadows. There were candy necklaces for her to wear, and a packet of Love Hearts for me. In spite of myself, I was smiling, admiring their trademark ingenuity.

But she couldn't smile about it.

She was sobbing as she removed the last layer. It was a lovely gift, one of Phil's frames, wood twisted round to fit the shape of the photographs. There were four pictures from the night just past. The two of us, caught as we walked into the room, her with a smile breaking on her face and me holding her hand. Then Richard and me, reclined on the cushions, the glimmer of the lights in the ivy just visible behind us, with slightly startled expressions, surprised by the sudden flash. Then her caught dancing with Phil, my favourite picture. That evening Phil, concentrated, agile, had spun her round the room. I had forced my double vision to become single as they salsaed before me. And the camera had caught the moment perfectly, the arch of her bending away from him as his arm supported the small of her back.

Then there were the four of us, at the end of the night, the one image that reminds me most clearly of how it was. We were sitting in a line, propped against the curtains. Phil, barely visible in the left-hand corner, a dark shape among the beer cans. Richard was next to Phil, but turned away from him. He had one hand on my shoulder, the other brandishing a huge joint, raised with a flourish above his head as he made a particularly salient point. Probably 'No, absolutely, you're right. Why not?' There was me, half focusing on him, but really looking down at her, lying in my lap.

There was a message for us on the back: 'Until next time!' Their familiar signatures underneath. So she was right. It was not even the end of the summer, and they had left the city, casually casting the two of us aside.

\*

I don't know how long we sat there, staring at the wreckage. Their pile of presents became blurred by the night, forming sinister shapes, crouching in the shadows.

We were both in shock. I tried to comfort her, but what could I say? I was too unsteady. I didn't understand. Only a week before, we had all been living together: the four of us had made plans for the rest of the summer and yet all that time they'd had a bigger plan they had never told us. Or, even worse, the boys had meant what they had said, but my stupid confessions to Richard had thrown everything off balance and pushed them away. I asked her if she had guessed that they were preparing to go and she shook her head, whispering through her sobs, asking how could they do it, how could they leave her alone?

And I told her that she mustn't be silly, she had me, didn't she?, she'd never be alone.

But my voice was just a whisper, and although she smiled through her tears and said, 'Yes, of course, I know, of course, I'm just being stupid,' we both knew that something terrible had happened.

We were stranded on that rooftop, inches apart, but frozen and unable to touch. I felt the shock of a thousand promises breaking quietly in the air around us. Our shared week of cohabitation had been full of future projects. Phil had declared that next weekend we would camp out on the common, like the old times – he might even make a bivouac, and we would be children of nature. Richard and I had planned to have a night of old films, and reminisce about our teenage escapes in dark cinemas. We had discovered a mutual love of classic *film noir*, where the women were black and white puzzles to be solved. We laughed at our shared teenage aspiration to be private detectives, to talk the talk, to unravel every mystery and always to get the girl. There had even been discussion of removing the fence that stood between us, and turning the two gardens into one for the rest of the summer. She had been reluctant at first, until Phil had pointed out that her picture could be repositioned against the far wall of their patio, and with that amount of perspective, it might really look like the sea at night. She had agreed and she and Phil had spent an evening drawing up designs.

Abandoned on the darkening rooftop, it was difficult to see the good things that were left in our life. It was the brutal shock of a sudden separation. In a chilling instant I saw our future spread out before us, without the colour, energy and variation that the boys provided. I saw the two of us, brought back to ourselves, with so many days stretched out interminably in front of us, a cold grey wasteland of time. I wasn't sure that we could fill it alone.

I came to my senses and helped her down the stairs.

She had a bath first and I made us some food. I left her getting ready for bed as I eased myself into the warm water. Filled with exhaustion and that aching sense of loss, my sobs echoed off the tiles. The force of my grief was a shock. It was full of things I had never even realised were there. I had been so reluctant to let the boys in to begin with, but those feelings belonged to another version of me, a self I had outgrown, I hoped. Now their abrupt departure carried echoes of an older abandonment that I could barely remember. My grief was coloured by a child's sense of betrayal, by that deep-rooted mourning for a father who sailed away to foreign shores. To have that abandonment come so suddenly and so unfairly into a world that I thought I could control was an awful, unimaginable change. Part of me, somehow, somewhere, was certain that it was my fault.

I lay there, wallowing in my own guilt when there was a noise from the rooftop: a thud and crash as something clattered down the stairs. I raced up to see, hopeful that it was one big joke and they had come back.

Not at all. There she was, in just the slip of her nightdress, in the midst of all the clutter, records under her arm, books piled up to her chin, trying to navigate her way to the door. Not crying now, she moved with a purpose among all the junk. 'I just have to clear it all up,' she said. 'Always better to clear things up.'

Now, this was something I recognised, that destructive determination of hers that came out on very bad days. No good ever came of these attempts to fix things. And again we were divided by our differing points of view: for me these random objects were the only security we had. These things, with their ghosts of the boys' presence, were the only link between them and now. But to her they didn't matter, they were inadequate reminders, and in her present state of mind she would probably destroy them all. I didn't trust her. I put her to bed, promising that I would sort out the mess. I sat beside her until she went to sleep and then, true to my word, I set about gathering in the detritus from the roof.

It took me most of the night.

I had forgotten how much they had borrowed, and it was difficult to sort through; snapshot memories flooded in from all sides. There were wineglasses to replace those of ours they had broken when Phil insisted we should drink toasts then hurl the glasses into the fireplace. I couldn't do it: I hate the sound of glass breaking. She was squealing at my shoulder: 'You're such a wimp. What are you so afraid of?' Phil was goading me, was I man or mouse, mate, mouse or man, he said, until I lost it and threw the glass into the fireplace with the rest of them, delighting in the destruction. I forget what we were drinking to.

There were clothes of mine that they had borrowed, a jumper that Richard had loved so much it was pulled out of any recognisable shape. I had lent it to him on one of our rooftop nights early in the summer and he had stretched the heavy wool over his knees and huddled himself inside it, delighted to learn that it was one of Mother's own creations: wasn't I the lucky man to have a mother who still knitted me jumpers and a girl who cooked me dinner and loved me? Who said that the chauvinist's life was dead, these days? He had made light of my protests. 'Jesus mate, I was only joking. You're going to have to learn to laugh at yourself a little.' That had been at the very start of the summer.

There was a whole set of her little wire sculptures, made from summer's champagne casings. A box full of people and strange animals – a Noah's ark collection from a different time. I never realised that Phil liked to hoard them as well. I could list everything I found up there, but it would only hurt more. There were many, far too many things, all with a little of the boys in them.

By the time I finished the sky was turning light. And as the dawn came gently in I wished for another world, or another life, without this loss, and wondered, not for the first time, whether it wouldn't have been better in the long run if we had never met the boys. Our lives would have been simpler, for sure. As I locked the stairwell door I heard the sounds of her moving behind me. She was half asleep, clutching the bedcover around her. She took my hand and said, 'Thank you, bless you, you always make things better. Come to bed.'

She slept deeply beside me and I tried to sleep too, but the birdsong mocked my efforts. The subtle whispers of my own fears kept me awake, telling me that things weren't going to be easy now. I tossed and turned beside her, knowing that the voices were right. There were some black and difficult days ahead. It was inevitable.

She had told me, that first weekend we met, that the black days would come and get us in the end. I told her that was impossible: there was nothing but light and goodness about her when she moved.

'Don't be naïve,' she said. 'I will make you feel sadder than anything you have ever known and then you will leave.' She said it was a curse, something she had carried with her ever since she was a child, and she couldn't tell me where it came from or why it came. I hadn't believed a word of it. When I touched her in those early days, there was nothing but joy and laughter, and any blackness lurking in the corners was only my doubts and fears, and my own clumsiness.

Then one night, when I had only known her for a few months, I woke to the sound of her crying as if her heart was breaking. And it felt like something inside me was also breaking, out of sympathy. I held her and held her for hours on end, until the dawn came, and all through the rest of the day. Everything seemed bad to her: there was nothing that I could say to make things better, and nothing she could say to me. It was as if she was being eaten up inside by something terrible that she couldn't even put a name to. It took me a long time to learn how to help her when she was like this. I would rest her back against my chest and wrap my arms around her, trying to stop her shaking. I would hold her hands by her sides so that she could not scratch herself to pieces.

This time, I knew how to comfort her in theory, but was no longer so confident about the practice. Coward that I am, I left the flat early while she was still asleep. It hurt me to leave her but it would have hurt me more to stay. I needed my wider context, needed another role to play so I could then return with the strength to help her. All our boundaries were shifting: just as my work was no longer a prison, my home was not a haven any more.

# 13

I got to work early, even before Simon, sat at my desk and made a few more notes. I tried to put pen to paper, but my sleepless nights really were catching up with me. I only stated the facts, but this time at least I had the courage to state all of them. No more selective editing, there were things that had to be recorded. I wrote down what I was certain of: *I dreamt of a desert beyond a forest. The boys have left. I cleared the rooftop: painful gifts. Difficult days. She isn't talking.*

It's just as hard now to fill in the gaps.

Shortly afterwards Simon arrived. He handed me another memo, pointedly leant over my desk and switched on my computer.

'All right, Simon, howya doing?' Only a frowned response.

James came bounding in an hour later, yet again playing his precise tricks with time. He took one look at me and laughed, saying, 'Jesus, mate, you're cutting it a bit fine. Have you looked at yourself this morning?'

'Not my fault, mate,' I said. 'My girlfriend kept me up all night.'

He laughed, and I scored yet more points.

Not the case when Mr Collins arrived. He took one look at me and summoned me up to his office. He sat in a fat leather chair behind a broad desk, a sheer wall of glass behind him. From my perspective, it looked as if the whole London skyline was resting on his shoulders. He bombarded me with precise criticism, telling me I looked like shit and that a grey face like mine was not a good face for the firm.

I stammered something about insomnia. It took me a good ten minutes to convince him that, no, it wasn't drink or drugs or debt or any other of the pitfalls of our profession. After a while he relented, told me to take the day off and get a good night's sleep. He tried gentler tactics, telling me that I was an integral part of a great team and that it would be a shame to have to lose me. I acquiesced as best I could, saying that I really had no intention of being lost. Not in any way.

He gave me a bottle of tablets, personally tried and tested. He told me that they should come issued to us all nowadays, compliments of the company, along with our diaries and our Christmas bonuses. They weighed heavy in my pocket on the long journey home.

The streets of Wimbledon were full of midday sunshine when I emerged from the station, but it didn't make me any happier. Perhaps other people would have relished the gift of an unexpected day off, but for me it was just further proof that the structure of my life was not as secure as I liked to believe. I was in the wrong place at the wrong time. I dragged my feet all the way home, more than a little worried about what I might find there.

She was just getting out of bed. No kisses to greet me, she was silent and confused. I slipped out and brought us some coffee and food.

I came into the bedroom mimicking the boys: 'Morning! Yet another good morning!'

But she started crying. How stupid of me. How could I have hoped to fill their space by perpetuating their rituals? Phil would come striding through the door, shouting, 'Good morning! Another fucking great morning!' and it was a guarantee. When I tried, the words sounded flat and empty.

But she put a brave face on things and we tidied away the boys' stuff together. She wouldn't let us use any of it. The books were not allowed back on my shelf. The photos were wrapped up in their cloth, tied up in new brown paper and hidden. She explained that it would be a present for us all to open next year, on the very first night the boys returned.

'And they will come back,' she said, with a quiet determination. 'I know they will. Just when we least expect it, we'll hear them through the walls.' She thought they would probably come back at night, to try to surprise us. 'But we'll be waiting for them,' she told me. 'We'll be waiting and we'll jump over the fence and run down to find them and they will be so overjoyed to see us.' They wouldn't be able to stay away for too long, she was sure, they'd miss us too much. And she told me stupid stories about where and when they might surprise us. They might drop down from the treetops and jump me when I was walking home from work. They might creep into the flat early in the morning and wake her up with a fine breakfast – exotic fruits and gifts brought back from their adventures. 'I can't imagine life here without them,' she said. 'They've got to come back.'

I didn't want to argue with her. She was certain that somehow it must be her fault, that yet again she must have said or done something to push them away. I couldn't share my guilt with her, and tell her all my fears of what might or might not have been said. It was easier to let her sit and wallow in her own distress while I played my supportive role, quietly packing things away. Everything in its proper place. Soon all that was left were the gifts that had been caught up in the parcel. A collection of lucky charms she arranged in a line beside our bed.

By now the heat of the day had passed and I suggested we should take our traditional stroll across the common, go to the pub, have a drink for absent friends. She wasn't ready.

She just wanted to batten down the hatches. 'We should let no one and nothing in until the morning,' she said. 'They'll probably be back by then.'

After an early dinner, we went to bed and ate some sweets, smoked a little of the grass together. I wanted to talk to her but she put her fingers on my lips, reached across and put some music on.

One of the boys' favourite songs blasted out, far too loud. She was crying gently to herself and when I started to touch her she pushed me away, saying, 'Don't you see? The music should bring them back. They left us their music because they wanted to be called back.'

I was so tired. It was Tuesday night. I hadn't really slept for four days. My head hurt and she was shaking the walls with loud music that only made her worse. I thought about what the boys would say if they could see what they had done. I wondered if they'd be sorry.

I needed space to think and went up on to the rooftop alone, and watched as the sky grew dark. From that elevated perspective it was as if the world I knew was slowly being erased and eroded. But sleep deprivation also brings a strange clarity, and the little I could see had very clear edges. Certain facts were obvious: I couldn't go to sleep while she was like this. Her restlessness would keep me awake; and even if she slept, how could I trust her not to wake in the night? Would she race across the darkened common, calling for the boys? In the shadowed corners of our patio, was something moving among her plants, scrabbling among the greenery? Or were the plants growing taller, moving out towards me? I looked at it straight on. The leaves lay still. This was no good. I needed to rest. But I had to know that she was sleeping beside me, properly sleeping. It was for our own good; we both needed to be stronger.

I made her a hot drink, crumbled a couple of the pills into it, and watched her as she fell quickly asleep, gently moving her hair aside so that I could see her face. I loved watching her sleeping. Her expressions would change throughout the night; she would frown, mutter, then giggle to herself. I used to imagine her dreams as I learnt every movement.

But that night she looked like a stranger. A blank canvas, almost featureless. Her face was pale, and her lips a thin white line. I wondered what I had done, what I had turned her into.

Nevertheless, I too drugged myself, partly through fear that if I didn't I wouldn't sleep at all, my mind was racing so. I just wanted to be numb: I didn't want to have to think or feel anything any more. I swallowed a couple of tablets and hid the bottle under the bed. And a heaviness swiftly melted through my limbs. It scared me, it felt as if all the life was draining away from me. I was caught between waking and sleeping, and thought I could feel things pulling against the covers – something was scuttling over the end of the bed. But I could not open my eyes. I was falling and forever falling, down through the covers, through the soft cushions of the sheets, down and further down into an unfathomable darkness.

The next thing I remember, the alarm was ringing in my ears and she wasn't there. The sunlight was blinding me but it was difficult to move, difficult to fight my way out of this soft sleepiness. It felt like I was trapped in one of my dreams, and I wondered whether my mind was playing tricks on me, whether the forest was about to come rushing up to greet me again, but this time in broad daylight. I kicked the alarm silent and moved to the window, and there was the common, glorious in the early morning. I pushed aside the ivy plant and trapped my fingers against the window. The sharp pain told me that this was no dream, this was how things were. I hoped she wasn't far away. Then there was a crash in the bathroom and the sound of her cry as she hit the floor. I rushed in and found her pulling herself up on the basin so she could lean over and be sick again.

I had seen her ill before, but never looking as bad as this. Her skin was grey, dirty grey, and her hair was lank and sticking to her head. She was shaking and I had to hold her until she had emptied her stomach. This was all my fault. I wondered if she knew – she was so angry with me, pushing me away as I tried to help her. For all her sickness, she still had her wilful strength.

I couldn't leave her.

It was long past nine thirty when I rang work, and got put straight through to James. 'Where the fuck are you?' he shouted.

I told him she was ill, really ill, and I couldn't possibly come in today. Could they hold the fort without me?

'You'd better get your priorities straight,' he warned me. 'You're using up all your brownie points in one week.'

But I told him I did have my priorities straight, that was the problem. I promised I'd be back the next day. Without fail. Could he cover for me? Could he make an excuse, something good, something that would work? I was always crap at this kind of thing.

'All right.'

He wasn't pleased.

'All right, but she'd better be worth it.'

I switched on to autopilot. I stood her up in the shower and washed her as she leant against me. She was shaking and sobbing still, as if something was tearing away at the very heart of her. She wouldn't even look at me. 'Fuck off!' she shouted, as I wrapped her up in towels and dried her.

She wanted to go back to bed and pull the sheets over her head, shut out the day and tent in her grief. But I wouldn't let her.

'Why don't you just fuck off and leave me alone?' she screamed, as I forced her into her clothes and pushed her out of the door.

I told her that the light and air would do her good. I told her that we needed to get away from this isolated flat.

It was a difficult walk. She was stumbling and weak and still looked poisoned – we drew suspicious glances from the families we passed. I stared back, defiantly, wanting to shield her from all disapproval, holding her frail body close. She was pleading, saying couldn't we just go home, get away from the shitty people of this shitty world. But I knew full well that it was better for her to walk the black days out and, anyway, our house was too empty and hostile to return to.

But even the outside world posed problems. The crowded common was empty without the boys. Every bit of our landscape was so loaded with memories. It was hard not to be drawn back into old habits. Out of the corner of my eye, I was scouring the bushes for any treasure-hunt clues. Just in case it all was a game and Phil was already bivouac building, waiting for us to come looking.

'When the boys come back they will take us out into the common and we will find new hiding places. When the boys come back the common will grow twice as thick and twice as full just to welcome them home.'

That was what she had promised me last night. The child in me wanted it all to come true.

But there was no sign of them. I carefully steered her around the boys' tree and wouldn't let her look back.

I insisted that we stayed near people. I knew her – she

wouldn't cause a scene among strangers. I found an open patch strewn with couples just like us. I let her lie back with her head on my chest as we soaked up the sun together. She fell asleep, but I wouldn't let the sunshine lull me into a false sense of security. I didn't want to miss anything, especially not that moment when Phil and Richard would appear out of the undergrowth, run across to meet us, with Richard bending over and slapping me on the back, saying, 'Did you miss us, then, mate?'

They never came.

To delay the return to the flat, I took her out to dinner in Wimbledon village. She spent the evening picking at her food and once home went straight to bed, while I retreated for a while and made notes in my study under the pretext of work. There was very little to write, only, 'The boys have not come back.' I wrote it again and again, line after line, trying to make myself accept this sad truth. *The boys have not come back. It feels like the end of the summer. The boys have not come back.*

But there were other sorrows lurking at the edges of that version of events. I should have said: *The boys have not come back. I can't do anything to make it better. She talks in riddles and is living in stories. It feels like the end of summer. Our house is too quiet and empty without them. It is all my fault.*

When I got to the bedroom she was waiting. She was lying on one side, propped up on her elbow, but I couldn't see the expression on her face. Her hair fell in front of her eyes and cast shifting shadows on her skin. I climbed in beside her and moved across, but she was turning away. Reaching down, she said, 'Do you want a Love Heart, dear heart?' with a dry laugh. She dropped the bottle of pills into my hand.

Then I saw she was crying and I reached out to touch her. 'I just wanted to help,' I said. 'I wanted to help you rest so that you would feel better.'

She cut through all my empty words. 'If you ever do anything like that again, I will leave you. You're so fucking stupid.'

She turned off the light. That was the end of it. Her ultimatum rang in my ears long after she had gone to sleep. I wanted to reach out across the expanse between us and touch her side. I wanted to wake her up and say how sorry I was. I wanted to hear the boys hammering our walls down, telling us they were back already. I wanted to reach across the last three months and have the early days again, when the boys came tumbling over our fence and I couldn't tell them apart and everything was beginning.

# 14

As I lay there beside her, I was caught up in the ebb and flow of my own insecurities. I knew that the forest would be waiting for me the minute I fell asleep. In fact, as I drifted between sleep and waking I thought I could hear rustling outside the window, gathering force. Only a couple of nights before, I had wished for those woods to unfold again, and now it was the last thing I wanted. I thought of her warning from months and months ago: 'Be careful of what you wish for, it might come true.' As sleep caught me, I wished hard that whatever came into my dreams, the desert would not return. I tried to hold on to the beauty of the forest, fixing in my mind the delicate patterns of the moonlight, caught among the flowers, trying to choose how the dream might unravel.

In fact, it was her anger that dominated the dream that night, as if all the energy that had been sapped in the daytime had come back with a vengeance. Everything she did was an act of aggression. The dream began with her leaving our bed.

There was none of her earlier caution. She was laughing wildly to herself: she flung the covers back in my face, almost as a challenge. There was a feline grace in her movement as she stretched out of the window, throwing the ivy down. She was a changed girl that night. She leapt over the window ledge and was gone. There was something of the wildcat about her when she jumped.

And her words from my waking life came calling to me through my dreams, telling me I had really done it this time: I was very stupid, and now she was leaving.

I knew I had to prove myself to her, to run after and claim her. To show her that I was strong enough and cared enough to keep her. I had to prepare myself for all the wiles of the woods, and the dead world beyond. I took one of her dark scarves and wrapped it around my face to keep out the storm. The moon was a thin crescent, a small scar on a dark sky, a fingernail fragment. It wouldn't give me nearly enough light so I took a small torch to help me find my way and was out of the window in seconds.

The forest was beautiful, as always, but it had regrown full of new tricks. As I ran across the chiming carpet of flowers, they gave out sweet, seductive smells that drew me down to the forest floor. These soft fragrances held an edge of lotus danger. The sweet scent rippled around me, calling me to a calm sleep within sleep, promising me dreams where I was always the hero, always loved. I wouldn't be caught, but that smell . . . Like many things from that summer I wish I could have bottled it and kept it as a reminder.

I ran beyond the flowers, although my limbs were heavy and

my aching heart felt heavier still. I ran through the clearing and into the ever-thickening trees. The paths were overgrown and the pathetic beam of the torch only made things worse, picking out a narrow tunnel of light for me to follow. As if seeing things would make the journey easier, when all it showed me was how the reawoken forest was becoming still wilder in the dark. The tall trees had grown in all directions. The canopy blended into the black sky. It felt like the forest had caught the night in a net of leaves and branches and was holding it captive. The lower branches had now grown so close together that it was more like manoeuvring through a series of smooth green tunnels that crossed over each other, turning the forest into a labyrinth. The further in I went, the more tangling the trees. I caught branches that were growing towards each other to block my way and pushed them behind, not caring, by then, about how I might get back. This new forest had a will of its own, played out in supple movements that I recognised: borrowed gestures of hers.

Of course I could not catch her before I came to the edge. I reached the open land and switched off my torch, afraid to give myself away. The change in the light disoriented me. Everything was suddenly so dark. I could barely see the ground beneath my feet and I had only my instincts to guide me. I jumped down with a little more grace than last time and, sure enough, there was the desert spread out in front of me. I was not strong enough to will it away after all.

Instead I wished again for clues. There were her footprints. Unevenly spaced, it looked as if she was still having problems walking. That Morse-code message of her moonlit steps just served to spell out my guilt. I had poisoned her, and she had stumbled back to this ghostly world. It was up to me to find a cure and bring her back. This hesitant trail was all I had, so I raced after her, looking at the ground beneath my feet, rather than the limitless horizon, thinking that if I did not look out for it, this time the sandstorm would not come.

But it did. I walked into that same solid wall of ashes. I pulled the scarf tighter and squinted up into the oncoming storm. There she was. Again, only a few feet away, fighting her way through the clouds of sand. Strange that there should have been such a flurry of grit and dust flying up around her. She was only wearing her old jeans this time: there was no trailing gown to stir up the land.

But, if anything, this time the storm was stronger. It rose up like an impassable wall, clouds moved over the moon and all was darkness and dust. The wind was so great that I feared her footprints would be blown away. But this dream held more complicated traps than that. As I stopped to tie her scarf more tightly, the clouds moved and for a second I could see clearly.

The whirling sand caught in the light, and I saw how it was streaming out from behind her. She was swaying with a rhythm entirely her own. Her footprints were not the uneven tracks of a girl too ill to walk straight. They were precisely planted. She was dancing away from me, and it was the pattern of her dancing that whipped up the wild storm. She was a ghostly apparition, like something rearing up from the desert, a wanton spirit made of white sand, rather than the girl I knew and loved. She was a column of cloud, twisting its way towards the horizon.

Then the clarity was gone and I was lost again. But I had

seen what she was doing. There was method in this madness. Terrified, but determined, I placed my footprints on top of hers. It was difficult. I lurched, and kept smudging her trail. Tiptoeing through the night, my clumsy larger steps erased the marks she had made. But after a couple of minutes I picked up the pattern. Then suddenly everything was clear.

As I mimicked her steps, the sand fell down before me. The sandstorm simply parted and folded itself behind me. I glanced back once, and could only see a thick fog snaking along in my wake. I laughed out loud, a cold, heartless laugh that echoed for ever across the open land as I saw how I might turn this dream round. The boundless desert would exhaust her eventually; she would be caught by the storm she created. But I would dance through it and save her, catch her in my arms and claim her, and we could waltz our way out of this world of dust together.

But the more I mimicked her movements, turning round and round in circles against myself, the more I was drawn back into the night of the party. In double, triple vision I saw her and Phil circling each other and smiling and laughing, moving with the same rhythm, while I, helpless, could only watch as they brushed closer and closer and suddenly spun away, putting the whole length of the room between me and them. The desert warped and widened as I danced through it, creating an endless, ever-expanding distance between us.

I was looking down at my feet, not up ahead, so only noticed the change when shells and tiny pebbles tripped me up. The sand was finer now, and there was a cool breeze, which came as a relief. The night was clearing, the moon lower in the sky. The land was changing. Among the white ash desert there were golden grains mixed in with red. Pearly shells caught the light and glistened. I rubbed the sand away from my eyes and looked ahead. She had led me down to the sea.

Now this was the cruellest trick my mind could have played on me, pulling out my most deep-rooted fear of all. In the early days, when we had laughed about the differences between us, I had answered her tales of childhood freedom by the ocean with my stories of claustrophobia in swimming pools. How my patient mother had tried to teach me to swim, and how, as a child, I had screamed my lungs out whenever she tried to push me into the water. I clung to the porcelain edges of the pool as other kids dive-bombed me, showering me with piss and chlorine. My mother prised away my fingers, telling me just to kick my legs and I would be fine. I sank like a stone.

That fear has always stayed with me. I never got out of my depth again, and never had the courage to learn to swim.

The beach curved down ahead of me and I could see her sitting on the shoreline, with her back to me. In the half-light the water carried a sheen of silver and rippled away into the dark. I was terrified, exposed, and couldn't move any nearer. The wind changed and carried the sound of her singing to me, the same tune she used to hum when she first started plaiting the ivy, all those months ago. But it was stronger and clearer as it cut through the night air. It was a song that called to me; it was a wild song from a different age, a charm and curse wrapped around sweet music. I had to put my fingers in my ears to keep it at bay. It made me want to lie down on the seashore. To curl up and sleep among the clustering shells.

I could see the silhouette of her by the water's edge, combing the sand with her fingers as she sang. What little moonlight there was poured itself down from the sky to meet her and washed all over her transformed skin, and as she sang she stroked the sand with the tenderness of a lover's touch. I grew jealous of this strange land, and cautious of her siren beauty. All my explorer urges had done, in the end, was take me right to the heart of my own fears.

The longer I stayed there, the harder it was to step out and show myself. Part of me wanted that more than anything else in the world, but the water lapped behind her like a warning, murmuring, *Don't touch, don't touch, don't*. I gazed with wonder at my beautiful singing girl, and wondered more at this secret place where the sky and the sea and the land rippled in front of me as if they were flowing into each other, as if even the elements could be bent and shaped according to her will.

She looked so peaceful just sitting there, serenading the sea. She looked happy and well, and all the things I could have wished for in our daytime world. But her song sounded like a lover's lament, as if she was charming something or someone out of the ocean to greet her. I was suddenly more frightened of that incarnation of her than I was of anything that the desert or the forest might hold for me. I could not move forward to claim her – she was no longer the girl I knew.

So I turned and I ran, straight back into the storm. I tried to remember the moves. Sure enough, as my feet found their confidence, the sand parted in front of me, closed behind, and I was back at the edge of the woods. On a whim, I tried the same trick with the forest. I danced along the treeline. And, just the same, the trees opened and closed behind me in response to my movements. This only terrified me all the more. If the quick-growing forest was a sentient thing, a mischievous partner in a dance, then surely it could lead me astray, and close itself around me if it chose to. I concentrated on every step, and would not let my fear trip me and break the pattern of my footsteps. The forest pushed at my back, and eventually spilled me out on to the lawn of ivy. Finally I was home.

But when I scurried up the net of ivy that hung down the side of the house, the plant was pulling at my heels, footholds unknotting the minute I put my weight on them. I refused to be caught like this. I twisted the ivy against itself to form a rope and, inching up the brickwork, hauled myself back into our room. From the safe side of the window, I looked down upon the woods and saw the landscape expanding with my every quickened heartbeat, pulsing with the rhythm of my fear. Too terrified to watch, I hid under the covers and waited.

When finally she returned, everything about her was unfamiliar: the darting energy with which she moved around the room, and the briny smell of her skin. I lay there very quietly and prayed for a second sleep to come, a sleep that would draw me back to my real world with all its mundane complexities, a sleep that would take me back to the girl I loved.

I was woken by a howling gale and a shrapnel attack of heavy rain. It sounded like the sky was falling. The heavy summer weather had broken, and a strong storm rattled against the windows and shook the whole house. Suddenly it was a different season. She was already sitting bolt upright in bed when I woke, pulling the covers up to her chin, hiding herself from me. I could see the grey clouds gathering, framed by our window. When she realised I was awake she stood up, pulled the rest of the sheet around her and walked off into the bathroom, leaving me shivering.

We spoke through the closed door. Could I make her a coffee?

She didn't want anything from me. 'Is that coffee with or without sleeping potions?'

'I'm really sorry.'

'Are you now?'

'I've got to go. They'll string me up if I don't go in today. I'll make it up to you this evening.'

'I'm sure you will.'

There was nothing else for me to say. My bad dreams had drained any courage I might have had. So I ran away from her again. Away from her and away from all my stupid mistakes. I ran down the stairs, out of the door; I ran quickly through the warm rain all the way to the tube. It was another difficult journey, with awkward delays and a cramped, claustrophobic train, smelling of the rising damp of the day. The windows misted over as we raced across the bridge. Nothing but greyness on all sides, and then a dark plunge underground.

I didn't want to be any part of this drowned and drowning world.

Every race through the darkness that stretched between stations was a reminder. The curve of the tunnel walls seemed speckled with green light, and shifting shadows, like the forest pathways. The lurch of the train was a buckling of the land beneath my feet, and I braced myself for a rush of wind to come whistling down the tunnel to claim me. I wondered if now our life would be like this for ever, if her black mood would never lift but just follow us for the rest of our time together like a stealthy shadow, like a heavy cloud that we had somehow created between us and neither had the strength to shrug off. I lost myself in the labyrinth of my own bad dreams and fears, as the tube tunnelled its way underneath the City of London and delivered me to my working world.

# 15

B ut there was no welcome for me in the office. Another place that ought to have been a safe haven held only awkwardness and suspicion. Even the security guard at the front desk raised his eyebrows and, in the most sarcastic tones, asked me if I was feeling any better. A memo from Mr Collins was waiting for me, summoning me to his office at nine thirty. James had saved my job that day. Underneath the memo was a detailed description of my illness. I had acute food poisoning and hadn't been able to sleep for my stomach turning. In a moment of genius he had used his computer skills to mock up a fake doctor's note, complete with plausibly illegible signature. The man was a professional. Even so, it wasn't easy.

Up in the expansive office, I felt vulnerable. Mr Collins was frank and confrontational, saying this was the oldest trick in the book on the hottest day of the year – did I really expect him to believe that this was just coincidence?

I pleaded an allergic reaction to his pills: apparently they didn't mix too well with my 'other medication'. He didn't want to know. It must never happen again.

I tried to thank James but he just waved it away. 'You're cutting it fine, mate,' he said. 'What the fuck were you thinking of? Do you not need this job?'

Even Simon had his say: 'If they fire you, no one else will take you. You only get one chance in this game.'

Suitably chastised, I spent the whole morning working between them in silence. By lunchtime the backlog was cleared and money was flowing just as it should.

I worked through lunchtime on my notes, which wasn't easy. Writing it all down fixed things: *I fed her sleeping pills and she threatened to leave me. I dreamt of the sea.* I was angry with my stupid actions, and angrier with the naïve imagery of my dreams, which put an ocean between us, as if I needed to see it spelt out so crudely. As if I hadn't felt hints of it the minute I realised the boys had gone – the cold shiver that came creeping over my skin, like a sea wind, a sudden chill blown from foreign shores.

I sat pale and quiet for most of the day, which of course made my illness excuse seem more plausible. Even James was impressed by my powers of deception. I made it up with Simon also, staying an extra hour to help him test his programs. Not entirely an altruistic gesture – I didn't want to risk leaving. He had been quite right: without the job I would have nothing; if those glass towers shut their doors against me, I'd never be able to find my way back in. Without my place in the City we would lose the house, and without those strong stone walls to keep her safe, there was no knowing where she might run to.

On my way home I bought her some flowers as a peace-offering. I paid a ridiculous sum for an extravagant bouquet, concrete proof of my love, but still she sidestepped me when I tried to kiss her. I asked her how she had been and she said she had felt sleepy and sick and hadn't done much. I tried to apologise again, but it all seemed pointless. She said I should just forget it and that it didn't matter any more.

Of course it mattered. There was an ever-growing distance between us now, and I didn't know how to get back. I felt stupid. But she didn't make it easy for me. I felt as if we were playing a game of chess, second-guessing each other's moves. If I walked round the coffee table to sit next to her on the sofa she would leap up and change the record. When I stood behind her while she cooked, just about to slip my arms around her waist, she stumbled back and scowled at me, said that I was crowding her and could I please wash and change: I still smelt of the filth of the City and it was making her feel sick again. Then by the time I had scrubbed my skin red raw I went into the kitchen only to find that she was just finishing her meal: she had been so hungry that she hadn't been able to wait but mine was still warming for me on the stove. Whilst I was serving myself my back was turned and she slipped through into the bedroom leaving me to eat alone. Her spontaneity and warmth had given way to coldness and calculation – that foreign, defensive side of her that was so very difficult to love.

As I washed up there was no music coming from our room. When I went through I found her crouched on the window-ledge, squeezed up into the corner where the ivy plant left a little space. There was no room for me to sit beside her. She was staring out at the sky, and dark clouds were gathering on the other side of the window: the bad weather was returning. I hovered in the doorway and asked her if she was going to come to bed. She said that she would sit there for a while: she wanted to be able to see the thunderstorm when it came.

But then the moment was broken by a crash from next door. There were footsteps creaking the floorboards.

She jumped up and was at the boys' door in seconds.

This sudden return was, of course, what she had predicted the previous day. 'They're only trying to test us.' she had said. 'They'll be back soon enough.'

And she had told me how we would be curled up in bed, maybe touching, when we would hear a soft tap on the wall. At first we would think it was our imagination, that gentle tap-tap-tapping, and the low whispers. But then we would cautiously call back to them, and our whispers would turn to cheers and celebration as our suspicions were confirmed: the boys had returned. Phil and Richard would come tumbling over the fence again, begging our forgiveness for leaving so quickly – it had all been a joke, an elaborate practical joke, a test to see how much we cared, if we cared at all.

But I told her she didn't know what she was talking about: how could the boys ever be quiet? Had she ever known it to happen? No, they would wake us up at some godawful hour as they stormed back into their flat, shaking the floorboards, playing music to wake us, pounding on the walls, shouting, 'OI! NEIGHBOURS! DID YOU MISS US?' If we failed to reply straight away, they would vault the fence, and invade our home from the rooftops. She agreed, yes, I was quite right, when the boys came back, they would return with more noise and rioting than we had ever known.

Whatever time of day or night it was, they would demand a toast to their return, and we would drink with them all night long, and for all the days to follow, so that the time without them would be beaten back into a faded memory; we would never really know or believe that they had left us at all. These lonely days would be like a lost dream, an enchanted sleep from which you wake saddened and shaken but cannot remember why. 'You wake saddened and shaken,' she said, 'but the colour and the brightness of the world that welcomes you back soon washes away any bad dreams. And this is how it will be,' she said, 'when the boys return. We will wake up back into our old lives and these difficult days will fall away and be nothing but dust.'

But now she was hesitating outside their flat. Their door was ajar and that was a tell-tale sign. I had always felt it would be rude to leap the fence and wander down into their flat uninvited, and indeed they always kept their door locked and sometimes when their music was too loud it would take a good few minutes of hammering before they let us in. 'Sorry, mate,' Richard had said. 'Sorry, mate, you should scream and shout with all your might. Keep a locked door between you and the outside world, that's always been our motto.'

But their door was open. The latch had been roughly forced, an amateur job. 'The bastards,' she said. 'The boys have barely been gone and some robbing bastards have come in to take their place.'

I got my torch and we pushed the door open together, forcing our way in. There in the lamplight, their faces freckled by dancing dustmites, were Kate, Jay and Tom. She enveloped Kate in a huge bear-hug, with a strength of affection I hadn't seen for days. Before I had a chance to protest she was leading them back to our flat. I loitered for a moment in the dark shell of the boys' living room. The weak torch beam showed me nothing but empty shelves, bare walls and eerie shadows. It was as if they had never been there. As if we had imagined it all. And for a swift second, those shadows re-formed and refashioned themselves, into shadows of ivy, perhaps, creeping across the walls, black twisting tendrils stretching out. I shut the door fast behind me, and even when I got back to our flat, I locked our door to make a barrier between us and all that empty space.

I was angry with the three kids for their lack of respect, for breaking in where they had no right to go. Our flat was suddenly filled with laughter and music – all of which was a little too hollow for my liking. She dug out one of my best bottles of whisky and the four of them sat squeezed up on our sofa. Jay was perched on the armrest, endlessly rolling joints. I sat cross-legged at her feet and felt like an unwanted guest.

'Let's have a toast!' she declared to them, handing out overfilled glasses.

'What shall we drink to?' asked Kate.

'To us!' she replied. 'What else?'

And the kids laughed along with her and clinked glasses in agreement, for they had no idea of the private language they were violating. I wondered at her clumsiness, especially when she had been so upset by my stupid attempts to perpetuate rituals and routines that belonged to the boys alone. Yet again I hated the side of her that would so easily share her life with others. With a sudden rush of cold fear, I looked into the future time ahead and wondered whether there would come a moment when someone else inherited all those habits and intimacies we had built up together; whether one day she would lean over a different man, smile down at him, and laugh away his paranoias, saying, 'I don't want to be anywhere else apart from here, with you.'

'Drink with us, you miserable bastard!' she challenged me.

'To miserable bastards!' laughed Kate, and I was rechristened thus in my own living room.

But even though she was being clumsy with me I couldn't help but be moved by her kindness to Kate. She patiently dried Kate's tears and told her that she was beautiful and that Phil was a fool if he couldn't see it and when the boys did come back, as she knew they would, she wouldn't be surprised if the first thing Phil did was head out on to the common to see if Kate was waiting for him in the treetops.

She told Kate how they would build a home in the branches, with a fine vantage point so that she could spy for Phil's return. She promised to visit Kate there every day, take her baskets of food and fine wines, and they could hide out in the forest, like a couple of renegade princesses. Then when Phil came back, he would have to prove his love by climbing up to claim her. They would set him traps in the lower branches, snags and snares to send him tumbling to the ground. If Phil did love Kate, he would have to use all his cunning to bring her back down to earth. And if he did not love her enough to reach her, it was no great loss. Such was Kate's beauty that she would soon draw to her others, who would risk life and limb to scale the highest branches to woo her. Men would travel far and wide to brave the climb: the foot of the tree would soon be littered with the broken bones of failed suitors. But this much she knew – Kate would find love again, or it would find her, and there was nothing to be so sad about, nothing was really so broken.

She had a way with words, when she chose to use them, and could turn the tragedies of anyone's life into tales of redemption. Although she was being kind, I was infuriated. She should have been using these skills to try to heal things between the two of us, not giving out her gifts so indiscriminately. And, also, I felt more than a little foolish. Kate and Phil. Phil and Kate. Had this occurred in the lost hours of the party? Was this another subtle change I had failed to notice? Part of me was shocked at Phil – the girl was barely seventeen. But, then, she was beautiful, little Kate, with her wide green eyes and soft young skin.

She took Kate off into the kitchen to find more booze, and we could hear their private laughter.

Tom tried to make conversation: 'Sright bastard, y'man Phil.' I wasn't having that. 'You didn't know him,' I snapped.

'Yeah, but what a bastard.'

I recognised Tom's indignant tone. 'Jealous, are we?' I asked, and Jay sniggered at Tom's blushes.

This nastiness was cut short by a strong peal of thunder, rolling directly overhead. The rain came pounding down in sheets upon our roof and the room was suddenly lit by the strobe light flashes of the electric storm. She came running back into the room, grabbed the whisky bottle, Jay's joint in the other and sprinted up the stairs. We all had to follow.

The whole sky was gathering over our house. The clouds were huge and dark, hanging so low that it felt as if they could swoop down and smother us at any moment. She was standing in the middle of the patio, with the rain falling in sheets around her, slicing through the night. As we leant back to follow her gaze the sky roared and there was a great flash of lightning, which marked the whole hemisphere with electric lines, scarring the dark. Illuminated by the white light, her shirt clinging to her as she spread her arms out wide, she leant back and screamed up at the storm. Unrecognisable, still.

I walked up behind her and took hold of both her arms on the pretext of steadying her from falling. I held them down to her sides, then wrapped myself around her, trying to shield her from the weather, trying to draw her to me. 'You'll get cold and ill again,' I said. 'Come inside.'

But they wouldn't. They had to stand there and watch the storm roll over them. And on her cue they were all screaming up at the lightning, trying to outhowl the gale. In the dark of the night, their banshee cries carried across the rooftops, and I was frightened of them, these four rain-drenched figures, screaming like demons. Again and again, she howled out and the kids echoed. No one was laughing. It was as if she was invoking something, calling the dark night closer.

When the thunder had moved on she was talking in that low, conspiratorial tone she had always used with Phil. She was telling them that we should all go out and chase the storm. That's what she and her friends had done when she was their age, spending half the night catching lightning, daring each other to stand out in the open. 'Let's go and laugh in the face of the bad weather!' she said.

She told them that if they beat the bad weather, if they could live to see the dawn, then tomorrow they would have a whole new world at their feet, that the rain-ravaged common would be a land of treasure. She said that a storm was a challenge to our very natures and that what didn't kill us would only make us stronger. She said that if only they had the courage to brave the elements and outlasted the night, they would always carry some of that storm in their souls, and would go through life a little less afraid.

They believed every word she said and were eager to follow. I just stood there and wondered what natural disasters she must have run through, what strange quirks of weather had given her that steely determination and made her the girl she now was.

I caught her hand as she pushed past me. The other three were already below us, unaware that I had stopped her. 'Now, that's enough,' I told her. 'Don't be childish. Don't make yourself ill.'

I pulled her arm a little too roughly as we went downstairs. I wouldn't let go, and told them that it was getting late and we were both tired. With my other hand I turned the latch and awkwardly held open the door for them as they filed out.

'Come back tomorrow!' she called after.

Then she pulled free and ran to have a shower. I sat and shivered in the kitchen, not confident to suggest she should have company. She came out and went to make some tea, but by the time I emerged clean and warm again she was in bed, of course. She had most of the sheet drawn up around her and was pretending to sleep. Stalemate. There was nothing for me to do but retreat to my corner and hope for a better morning.

Late into the night the storm came back. The wind and the rain were winding their way around our house, pulling slates off the roof and sending them crashing down past our window. It was the sound of things falling that woke me. The ivy was shaking in the gale. The rain that had come in through the crack was running down the green ledge in a waterfall, as if the sea itself was trying to pour into our room. As she struggled to wrestle the window shut, she was lit up by the flashes of lightning that split the sky. I propped myself up in bed and watched her, incredulous – would she really let herself out of the window in such a night as this?

'What the hell are you staring at?' she snapped. 'Get up, help me!'

I was by her side, soaking up the deluge with our towels. For a moment we were laughing together – she was flicking water into my face. We made a dam of dirty laundry and kept our bed dry. She said that she always felt so much better when the weather broke, that heavy days made black clouds gather in her head until she couldn't think. She was sorry if she had been mean.

My relief got the better of me.

She curled up in the bed beside me, propped herself up on cushions so that she could watch the storm. She made me a hot drink with some whisky in it, to help me sleep and sat and held my hand. And that was all it took for me to believe that all was well between us. That tender touch of her hand on mine wiped away the previous days' estrangement. I drifted off to sleep soothed and settled, and I thought I had nothing to fear. In hindsight, such trust seems desperately naïve, after everything that had happened. But caught up as I was in her subtle enchantments, all I wanted was to believe in her. After all, I was still only twenty-three years old, and she was the only person I had ever loved who had loved me back. If I lost my faith in that love, what else would be left for me to believe in?

# 16

I thought that I slept, but it felt like I was waking. Her hand slipped away from mine, gently pulling away, and I was overcome by sadness, by that simple gesture. I wondered at how my dreams and my daytime life were all so tangled and turned in on themselves that it was hard to see where one part of my life ended and another began.

The lightning had followed her into my dreams, every flash illuminating events with a savage clarity. Her usual fluid movements seemed brisk and mechanical as the lightning afforded me only glimpses. Watching her departure was like watching an old silent movie, every expression exaggerated by the sudden exposure. She was by the door, getting dressed. Then perched on the ledge, pulling on her sturdy boots. Another flash and she was crouching by the window, about to pull it open, then hesitating. Water would have streamed back into our room, creating a second ocean.

When the next flash came the bedroom door was gently closing behind her.

I had been counting seconds to judge distances. The storm was hovering dangerously near. I was mistrustful of this dreamscape, a world I had once hoped to shape but had had to accept had a life of its own. I was beginning to understand that, instead of giving me control, the dreams seized on my deepest fears and re-formed them, projecting them on to an ever-changing landscape.

I couldn't predict how the storm might manifest itself in this place. Would it grow with unnatural force and uproot the trees? Would forest fight with desert and ocean to create a whirlwind of the elements? There was no way of knowing. But I knew I must follow. I still believed she needed rescuing, if not from this uncertain world then definitely from herself, and all the violence she could carry with her. It was my duty to save her from black clouds and bad weather that might destroy her and break my heart in two.

I dressed accordingly. Jeans and jumper, my strong boots, and a black raincoat to blend into the night. I was learning. I ran down the staircase after her. The whole house was echoing, and again it sounded as if an army of men was chasing me. The weather was hostile, yet it had not unleashed the full destructive force I had feared. No, the storm was biding its time, testing my strength. The wild wind flung itself at my door, trying to keep me in. When I pushed my way out, the rain slapped at my face and I was buffeted back against the brickwork. My earlier explorer ambitions seemed ironic now. Pinned to the side of the house by this dance of the hurricane, I was no more than a passive observer. Above me, the ivy flailed in the winds and whipped against the wall, beating a savage rhythm in the midst of the hurricane. The dark clouds clustered over the trees and the lightning made its crooked way across the sky. Those spidery lines of light were racing towards the forest, just as the ivy was running over the lawn and winding its way up the trees, reaching up to the electric storm. Everything was bristling.

I knew she was far ahead and that I didn't have much time to make my journey safely. Awkward in my heavy clothing, I pushed through the paths I knew. I was stumbling, disoriented by the harsh strobes of lightning, which lit up the whole forest for a second then plunged me back into darkness. I had to muster all my strength to dance against the wind, and it took me too long to get to the clearing. As I stood in front of those multiplied paths again, I made the mistake of looking up above.

The spidery lightning raked up the sky, like a shattered piece of black glass, the rain swirling in a vortex. I huddled by the trees, acutely aware of the danger. The fragile sky broke and re-formed in static charges, carving grids across the heavens.

My fears were screaming at me above the storm, telling me that this was not a safe place, that those tall trees would catch the lightning in their branches and I would be crushed or burnt or both. There seemed to be no way through and no way back and I was terrified that I would never make it home again.

But my rational mind fought against these fears. This vicious land of tricks and traps still had rules by which it must abide. Slip-sliding on the sodden ground, I began to dance. The wind-whipped trees had no choice but to part before me and even the lightning shrank away. It wasn't easy: my whispering fear was a distraction and I kept losing the rhythm. Every time I took a wrong step, the fierce weather came rushing up to grab me. And behind me I could hear the sound of wood cracking, and the ground shook: everything that was beautiful in that forest was being cut down and blasted. I will never forget the sound of all those trees falling: it beat through the whole forest like the war drum of a terrible army. Like a giant's footsteps, she would have said.

I fought my way to the edge. I got clear of the falling trees but the weight of the weather was levelling the land. The grassy hill was transformed into a quagmire, pock-marked with dangerous dark pools. I slithered over the drop in the land, tumbled down into the desert and ran through the cloying sand, which gathered around my ankles. If had stopped I would have become stuck fast, cemented to the spot and slowly drawn under.

I limped on until the pebbles gave me a surer footing and I found myself, breathless and beaten, falling down on to the beach. I looked at the vast ocean ahead and it was a mirror of every fear I had ever known, water so terrifying it was worse than water. The moon was full and fat, with stormclouds forever racing across it. From a distance, it looked as if the winds had pulled a second moon down from the sky and broken it across the length and breadth of the ocean. Fragments of silver light trickled down the high waves and fell onto the shore with the full rush and freefalling crash of a thousand shattered mirrors. The waves, as far as I could see, were gathering ranks across the ocean, forming tall impassable walls. Looking out at these ever-advancing waves, I could feel how, if I got too close, they would fall on me and pummel every last breath out of my body. I could taste the salt water in my mouth, just at the thought of it.

This wild landscape spelt out the differences between us. She was fearless, dancing along the very edge of the tidemarks. And as she danced with the savage sea it settled obediently in front of her. The towering waves receded into the dark, and the tide came lapping at her ankles, coaxing her in. The bad weather would not touch her.

At the shadowed edges of the shore, I found a convenient boulder to hide behind. I clung fast to the rock, my back to the hurricane. I told myself that, although I had come to save her, it was best just to watch and wait a little longer. A secret habit of mine, I always loved to watch her without her knowledge. I would feign sleep when she came to bed, and watch her as she danced round the room, undressing. I would watch her as she washed, half glimpsed behind the shower curtain, shrouded in steam.

She waited until the sky had cleared completely; until the clouds had gone from the moon, and she had the full light to work by. In front of her the water was still, and the second moon re-formed itself, watching up from the black sea, curious at her every movement.

She started to run back and forth across the beach, the lines of her footprints leaving sneaking patterns spiralling out into the night. She was moving with a purpose. As she got nearer to my hiding-place, I could hear her singing. She didn't see me. She was focusing on the ground in front, collecting treasures. She came very close as she scavenged the shore, but she was in another world, locked away in her own schemes. She probably wouldn't have noticed even if I had stood up and called out to her. I watched as she bundled pebbles and shells into her arms, couldn't stop myself smiling as she tried to carry too much back down to the sea. She was like a small child, full of energy and mischief, laughing at herself, echoes of Phil's magpie eagerness in her movements.

She went back to the shoreline and sat looking out to sea, her collection of finds scattered all around her. She began combing the sand with her fingers and arranging her shells and stones in patterns. The moon grew brighter still, giving her a generous light to work by. I lost track of time as she leant over and back again, her fingers tracing curling lines through the sand. Beautiful repetitions. Then suddenly she stood up, smiled at her handiwork and walked away.

It took me a moment to register what she was doing. I had almost been lulled to sleep – those hypnotic movements of hers had lost none of their charm. She had undressed and was wading waist-deep into the water before I was on my feet and racing up to the shore. I had to reach her before she swam too far away, before I was pulled out of my depth.

I ran straight into her sculptures. She had made a barrier along the very edge of the tidemarks. Curling lines in the sand wound themselves round polished pebbles and shells that sparkled like jewels in the moonlight. Like everything she had ever done, it was a work of art. I was drawn to touch it. But when I tried to lift one of the pebbles it burnt my palm. It was like trying to pluck coals out of the sand. In the moonlight I could see that even the pattern of the burning was repeating itself, small coiling lines running over my palm and up the inside of my wrist. I had to bite my lip and stop myself crying out.

She was still walking into the sea.

I needed to reach her.

I stepped on to the barrier, but the heat seeped through my shoes and I couldn't walk for the burning.

I took a few steps back to try to leap over it, but behind me the storm was getting nearer as she waded further out of sight. Now the shoreline itself was conspiring against me. The patterns she had made were unfurling in her wake. Lines unravelled towards the ocean; shells and pebbles came crawling up the beach to meet them.

Beyond the barrier, she was disappearing from sight.

There was joy in her movements: her long back was breaking the waves, curving up and disappearing under the surface as she duck-dived, then pushed herself up for air. The sea was calm and carried a sheen of silver. The stars shone with an intensity I had not seen before, their arrangement mirroring the patterns she had made in the sand – the very constellations were rearranging themselves for her. And why shouldn't they?

But I was held back and trapped in a different world, stuck in the hostile land. Behind me the rain came hammering down. I felt desperate: caught between wind, fire and water. I couldn't reach her. I couldn't get anywhere near. And those restless waves were surely not to be trusted. It took all my courage to turn back to the forest, to push my way back into that storm, and to make the forest re-form with my dancing.

The return to the woods was terrifying. Again, there was the strobe illumination of the lightning, giving only tentative glimpses of what lay ahead. The forest floor was scattered with fallen trunks and blackened branches barring the openings of pathways. The wind whipping through the treetops was a shrill shrieking, like that of a wounded animal. I hesitated at the edge of the forest, uncertain that I could dance my way through any of this.

But as I stood there, the forest began to open before me. The lightning retreated back across the sky, and again the moonlight picked out one path that was not buffeted by the wind, and held no obstructions. A wide river of silver, snaking through the chaos, calling me home. Gathering what little courage I could, I ran into the light. Glancing over my shoulder, I could see her moving quickly between the trees. This safe passage home was entirely of her making. It was she who was willing the weather away, not me.

I made it home barely in time. I sprinted across the ivy-covered green, slamming the door behind me, stripped off my clothes and threw them into the wardrobe. Seconds later, she came running into the bedroom. Her clothes were dry, but her hair was still wet through and there was a strong smell of the sea about her. There were scaly patches on her skin where the salt was beginning to dry and small white crystals, like cobwebs, forming on her face. Beneath the patterns of the salt her skin had an incandescent sheen, as if the water she had been swimming through had held in it some of the moonlight, and this was clinging to her, caressing her skin.

When she spoke it was as if she was calling me from somewhere far away, as if her voice was part of that silver light falling in the forest. 'Go back to bed and sleep, love,' she said. 'Sleep, love,' she crooned into my ear, and that second dark sleep came drifting in, gathering at the corners of my consciousness, like the shadows on the ceiling. I fought against it. I would not be a victim of my own dreams. I was beginning to realise, at last, that the battles we played out in these twilight hours, with all their impossible strategies, did have consequences.

With familiar dancing moves, she was leading me over to the bed. 'You should sleep,' she whispered again, but I found something to say.

'Where have you been?' I asked. My words fell heavy on my tongue.

'Out into the wild night,' she said, laughing quietly. 'Out into the woods and beyond.'

'Which woods?'

More laughter. 'Which woods do you think?'

She pulled me over to the window. But this time, when the two of us looked, all that spread out beneath us was the common, the silver-birch trees whipping against each other. Lightning danced across the leaves, severing trunks at will. There was nothing more I could say.

'Sleep now,' she said, as she led me over to the bed and wrapped me up tightly in the sheets. 'Sleep now, there will be a whole new world out there in the morning.'

She was singing to me and stroking my hair. I could resist no longer: that heavy second sleep came closing in. I pulled the sheets close, my hands balled up into fists that I hid under the pillows, wanting to hold her but ashamed of the burns and blisters on my skin.

*

Her predictions were correct. The next morning I drew back the curtain to see that the storm had washed the street clean and it basked below, slipstream gleaming in the August heat. The day was already warm, and the sunshine, playing over the green of the common, was projecting patterns across the grass. The reawoken common did indeed look like a new world, a gift from the outside in which I could trust.

But as I pushed open the window the catch caught on my fingers, and a searing pain shot right into my heart – it felt like my whole arm was burning. Looking down I saw the cause, the sores from my dreams had stayed with me. But they were no longer those delicate curling patterns: I now had a savage red burn running from the palm of my hand up to my wrist. My feet were likewise blistered. I took a shower and scrubbed myself clean. I had some stupid belief that, just through going about my normal morning routine, I could wash away the traces of the night. The hot water ran into those open sores, and my feet were on fire, my arm was burning. I felt as if I had molten metal running through my veins, and it was hard to stop myself screaming. Our towels felt as rough as sandpaper as I patted my damaged skin dry.

It's hard to say honestly what I thought when I saw I was wounded. Part of me believed that it might be psychosomatic, that I was so much in the grip of my dreams that I had willed it all to be true, that the pain and fear I was keeping private were forcing their way on to the surface of my skin, pulling my nightmares out into the open. Or could it be a stranger sickness still? Had my self-reproach sent me sleepwalking to cut and scald myself, do damage to my own body, telling me that this was what I deserved?

But stronger than my fear and my confusion was an overwhelming sense of illness. This gave me the most obvious explanation – I had been drunk and stoned by the time we lurched to bed. Was it possible that I had harmed myself by accident and not even noticed? That my dreams carried an echo of a trauma that I had been too wasted to remember? It seemed possible, so ill did I feel. It was as if I had pure whisky running through my veins and I was so tired of all this self-imposed sickness. In contrast to the 'mornings after' that inevitably followed late nights with the boys, there was no sense of time well spent. Realising that if I could not think straight I had no chance of maintaining control and stopping the violent collision of all these worlds I had to fight through, I made a secret resolution: this unfocused hedonism had to stop.

She was still in bed, no doubt also reeling from the night before, although she never let it show. It made it easy for me to slip away.

I told her I was feeling like shit and wouldn't survive at all if I got caught in the rush hour. Anyway, an early start would mean an early end to my day and we could spend a nice long evening together. It took a real effort of will to sound cheerful and inconsequential, but it was Friday, at last it was Friday, and we had the whole weekend in front of us. I asked her to think about how she might want to spend it: we'd had a rough old week and we should think of ways to be kind to each other.

'I'll have a good think, I promise,' she said, smiling. 'Good luck with your day.

'Hurry home,' she said.

I smiled at her, but I held my wounded hands behind my back so that I wouldn't reach out and touch her by mistake.

When I stepped out of the front door I walked straight into the light. I took off my jacket and set out towards the station. But I had only taken a few steps when something made me turn away from my normal route, and head towards the common. After the destructive visions of the night before, part of me needed this familiar green, open land. I needed to root myself back in a friendly landscape, where things stayed put. Before I knew what I was doing, I was slipping through the hole in the fence and wading through the long grass. Like a child, I took off my shoes and socks. The morning dew was cooling and it soothed my blistered feet.

Deserted at that early time, it felt as if the common had been made just for me. The landscape, too, was carrying wounds from the previous night and just waking up for a day of recovery. Even the birdsong sounded cautious. Plants had been uprooted by the strong winds and lay scattered across my path. In spite of the sun's best efforts, a sense of desolation still hung in the air. Even here, it was as if some echo of that nightmare had been carried through to the real world, to show me that nothing was quite as permanent as I believed.

Then I turned the corner to find Richard and Phil's tree blackened and charred beyond recognition. It lurched to one side, roots wrenched up from the ground. I could see where the lightning had come down – the trunk was split in two. Clearly it would no longer support the boys' weight. Only black, pockmarked wood was left. It crouched at the edge of the common like a diseased thing, a cancer on the landscape. And all the land around it was laid waste. As the morning breeze pushed spindrift pieces of foliage across my path, I was unsettled by the rustling of the bushes and the shadows in the under-growth. And just as in my dreams, where I ran away from anything and everything that I didn't want to see, I turned my back on that tree and ran up the slope of the common.

I came to rest by a buckled willow. It had been bent double by the force of the winds, and the branches bowed down to form a delicate curtain, swaying softly in the morning breeze. I sat down for a moment to catch my breath. The sunlight danced through the leaves above my head, a kaleidoscope of golden rain falling upon me. I closed my eyes against the fractured light and, before I knew it, I was asleep.

Through the curtain of leaves I saw her walking towards me. The sunlight on her hair was a halo, and her pale skin was marbled with the reflected green of the common. She was dressed in white and her blue eyes shone with laughter. She had woven the silver flowers from the forest into her hair, and wherever she walked, just as in the previous dreams, there was nothing but new growth, a pathway of flowers blossoming in her wake. The air was alive with birdsong as she approached, parted the curtain of leaves and gathered me to her. She was stroking my hands and feet, bathing my sores in the fresh morning dew. She was kissing my face and whispering in my ear, 'Wake up. Wake up, love, before it's too late.'

I woke with a start. The sun had shifted, and I had been

sleeping for over an hour. I pushed my way out from under the willow tree – of course, the common was just the common again, storm-drenched and untransformed. But the strangest thing was, as I hurried to get dressed, my hands and feet were no longer blistered.

Or, at least, that's how I think it happened. My memory plays tricks on me. I had still been drunk when I got up that morning, and even now I'm not sure whether I really was wounded when I woke, or if I was just carrying the confusions of those vivid dreams with me. I couldn't work it out.

Neither could I shake off my tiredness. The tube ride into work was fragmented by snatched moments of sleep. The sudden stop at each station jerked me awake every time. When I finally emerged at Liverpool Street the stern architecture seemed comforting, after all the previous inconsistencies. The lines of office blocks did not shapeshift as I walked between them. The grey towers were clearly rooted to the pavement and stretched up for ever above my head. The automatic doors of our office block opened swiftly for me as I walked up to them. This was a place where everything was easy, after all.

This was further proved when I got to my desk. I was still early, and was amazed to find that James had already taken up his position, a little too bright and breezy.

'Fuck, mate, the state of you,' he said, shaking his head and laughing, picking clumps of grass off my jacket. 'I take it you made your peace with the missus, then? An early-morning *al fresco* reconciliation, was it?'

I laughed back, as he told me his stories of the night before, how he had got lucky on the last tube but had had to creep away early in the morning. He hadn't been home, but had come in early to use his emergency supplies. Hidden away in the back of his desk drawer were new shirts and toiletries for just such occasions. I was to help myself. So when Simon came in we were both looking fresh and efficient. The three of us were working up to speed by the time Mr Collins arrived saying, 'That's what I like to see, lads, keep up the good work.' Little did he know.

# 17

I had an intense morning of number-juggling. Simon had
introduced a new piece of programming that was much
more efficient but took me a while to get used to. I kept
accidentally giving false commands. Numbers cross-multiplied
in the wrong ratios, I made fictional fortunes, and then my
computer crashed. James was laughing at my basic mistakes,
telling me I ought to watch out, that at this rate I was going to
turn the whole Stock Exchange on its head. I was infuriating
Simon with my basic errors. 'It's really very simple,' he said. 'It's
a logical extension of the old network.'

James couldn't resist taking the piss, mimicking Simon's tone,
saying, 'Do keep up, it's really very simple. Don't let the side
down.'

I wrestled with my disobedient numbers. Another wrong
entry, and our company's shares were skyrocketing. I had a
sudden glimpse of how the City would be if these figures were
true. I saw the office blocks outside cross-multiplying in all

directions, the entire skyline of London cluttered by replicas of our building, and through every window I could see cloned versions of me, James and Simon, hunched over our computers, predicting and projecting.

By lunchtime I had a sickening headache, and needed a break. I went to a nearby café and, sitting out on the over-crowded pavement, spent an hour making some more notes. I couldn't avoid the basic truths: *She made beautiful patterns in the sand but they burnt me. I'm finding it harder to distinguish when I am awake and when I am sleeping.* When I got back to the office, I encoded my keywords, and hid the notes under a pile of paperwork. But the pressure of those loaded sentences stayed with me. In the heat of the afternoon, the office block opposite rippled and twisted as the sun hit it, the edges of the building blurring into the hazy sky. It worried me. I felt as if everything I thought was secure was drifting away from me. I must have seemed withdrawn, because James assumed that I was suffering similar afflictions to his. He kept me amused all afternoon, his sleep deprivation giving rise to a series of ever more obscene and surreal emails. I recognised the signs all too well. In a strange way, this was exactly what I needed: a blunt, boorish dialogue in contrast to all the fairytale theories that echoed round my head.

And I realised that, in his own way, James was the nearest thing I had now to an ally. His recent behaviour had been proof of an unexpected friendship. He had helped me to keep my job, and supported my place in the firm. In his eyes, I had an instinctive knack of making money that made me worthy of everything good in the world. He talked about the future that would await us, how if we played our cards right we could retire by the time we were thirty. 'And then I'm going to fuck off and travel the world,' he said. James's dream was to settle on some undiscovered island, buy a bar and set himself up for life. 'I'm going to get my own piece of Paradise,' he said. 'You'd be more than welcome, bring the missus. I bet she'd love it.' I smiled privately at the impossible idea of her and James ever meeting.

By the time five o'clock came round, I had just about mastered Simon's new programming, and was secretly excited about how it could revolutionise our work. It doubled our productivity and, in a few weeks' time, with clever investments, those millions that James dreamt of might plausibly be rolling in. But that could wait for another day. James switched off our computers and demanded that we treat ourselves to some hair of the dog to congratulate each other on reaching the end of the week unscathed. I couldn't agree more. So I shrugged aside my morning's resolve. James was my friend – this was a worthwhile investment of time.

We pushed ourselves into the corner of a crowded pub opposite work, full of men just like us, rolled-up sweaty shirtsleeves and red faces. The progress of the conversation is best charted by the number of our pints. It's funny to think back on how vocal I was, airing all the grievances that seemed acceptable. Keeping very close and quiet all those fundamental fears that I couldn't begin to put into words.

1. Work – what a day it had been. James had really thought he was going to pass out at one point. But then again, everyone's a bit of a dark horse in that place. There were rumours about Mr Collins and his late-night indulgences up in that office.

No, James couldn't possibly say, but you know how it is – it's always the ones who seem most straight who are most fucked up. Anyway, could you imagine having that much money? It's bound to make you develop some odd habits. It's always the ones you least expect. So what about Simon then? I asked. What do you think he gets up to? A cross-dresser, for sure, James was certain. And that's probably just the start of it.

Had James seen Simon's face when he found the two of us were there before him? He looked like he was going to have a coronary. Poor bloke, he'll probably start coming in at six or something now.

I worried about Simon sometimes, he always seemed so wound up.

Yeah, James was sure he was fast on his way to burn-out.

2. So, James took it that all was well with me now, but I ought to watch myself: surely I must know that I had been sailing close to the wind recently.

Yeah, I know, I'd been being stupid. But I could guarantee that I wouldn't be going back down that road for a while. Just a temporary lapse, I reassured James. But inside I was laughing at myself, wondering how I possibly thought I could make such promises when, in a world beyond this one, there was a dark forest reaching out for me. I drank quickly, pushing it into the far corners of my mind.

James knew that it wasn't any of his business, but was she really worth it? Was I sure? London was a land of plenty, and there were women galore out there to be tried and tested, no offence, but . . . I tried very hard not to take any. Horses for courses, I said, and I just knew she was the right one for me.

Well, if she makes you happy . . .

3. Yes, she did. Very. But the company she kept, sometimes, Jesus . . .

And then, out of nowhere, came an unexpected vitriolic rant about the kids. Maybe it was easier for me to see it because I had to come and do this fucking job every day of the week, no offence, but—

None taken, James knew exactly what I meant, it wasn't like any of us wanted to be here. Well, exactly, then recently every night I'd been coming home to find these fucking children that she adopts, these waifs and strays, talking cocky rubbish about absolutely fuck all, and then she said they're so sweet and remind her so much of how she was at that age and all I could think is that thank Christ I didn't ever know her then because she must have been a right pretentious little cow. And although, granted, Kate was quite cute it was all a bit much really, as all I actually wanted was a little peace and quiet, in my own home, with the woman I love.

James agreed with me every step of the way, said that it was fair enough, she was taking the piss. It was my house, I was the one paying the rent, after all. And what did she do with her day? What did she contribute? I should have more than a little say in the matter. Perhaps I should go home and sort it out.

I stumbled out of the pub and got on to the tube, my sleep-deprivation from the night before accentuating the power of the alcohol. Keeping tight hold of the indignation that James had drawn out of me, I reeled my way home, determined to sort things out when I got back, determined to reassert myself as man of the house. I was desperate to take some kind of decisive action, to force a change – I felt so crippled by my own reticence. I thought that if I could at least have some time alone with her, without the kids' constant interruptions, I might have a chance of turning things round between us, of retracing our steps and getting back to the land we knew.

Walking into that house was like walking into a furnace. The windows had been left shut all day, and I was hit by a wave of solid heat as I opened the door. But the whole flat was shaking with music, again, the corridor amplifying the cacophony, and I could hear laughter cascading down from the rooftop – all a little too sharp and too loud. I made my way up to find the kids there, well ensconced. There was something provocative about the way they were sprawled over the cushions where the boys used to sit, as if they were daring me to react. I wanted Phil to be there, half hidden by the blossoming flowers, roaring insults up at me, I wanted Richard to be handing me beer and spliffs and saying, 'The man of the house is back, welcome home, mate, welcome home.'

'Welcome home,' Kate said, then slumped back down on the Astroturf.

I smiled a weak smile, and stepped across their horizontal bodies, over to her. She was leaning against the railings, with her back to me, surveying the damaged common. 'Look!' she said, pointing to the tops of the broken trees. 'Have you seen what last night has done?' She had gone for a walk and found the children sitting against the remains of the boys' burnt tree.

'Aren't you sad?' I asked.

She kissed me and told me not to be silly. Of course the tree had gone, but why worry? The storm had wiped the slate clean and the boys would be back when the new growth came.

It seemed that now she was almost happy the boys were gone. She was opening up her house to the kids without any grief for the chapter that had just closed. Her faith in new growth sounded like a convenient excuse. These phrases and habits that I had so loved about her seemed to me to be growing tired and overused. I was increasingly less eager to play along. So I made my excuses and told them I wasn't in the mood for visitors. I went downstairs and locked myself away in my study, with my notes again, desperate to place things in order.

Still tipsy from my beers with James, I faltered with my letters and numbers. I wanted to write something about the kids, to get to the crux of why I resented them so. They were so young, and so naïve. There was nothing we had in common, apart from her – and they took her away from me. They latched on to her wild schemes, and kept me on the outside. Her fairytale phrases only encouraged them: she told them that this would be a summer of enchantments, they would cheat time together and weave spells through the twilight and that by the end they would be wise beyond their years. I doubted that very much.

It was bad enough that they invaded my house, I would not let them dominate my thoughts as well. There were more important things to think of, more intimate parts of our story to unravel. I revisited the events of the day, and seized upon my half-waking dream, when she came drifting across the common and healed my wounds with the morning dew. It had to mean something. If it was a clue, it stood to reason that there must be more clues lying hidden in earlier dreams, lurking in other places within our story. I started flicking back through my notes, decoding the odd word here and there. I thought about how that forest had come to play out the ebb and flow of our relationship, that push and pull between fear and love; between jealousy and tenderness. I looked at my embellished map of this uncertain world – a confused map of dreams, with undefined edges.

And in my semi-drunken state, this lack of definition was too difficult to take. What use was a map, if I did not understand the world it represented? I had been fooling myself all this time, I was learning nothing. On a whim, I tried a different hypothesis: I entertained the theory that those burns I thought I had when I woke might possibly have been real. And if they were, if I really had brought back evidence in the cuts and abrasions on my own skin, there might be other evidence, hidden away in the house. With drunken resolve, I went on a discreet search, only to put my mind at rest. I wanted to be sure. I needed to know where I stood.

I could hear her laughing up on the rooftop with the kids as I crept into our bedroom. She'd been in one of her houseproud moods, and everything was clean and tidy. My suits hung like sentinels in the wardrobe, ready for duty the next morning. Her summer dresses and sarongs nestled beside them, with incongruous intimacy, flashes of bright colour among the grey material. I pushed them aside, looking further into the back of the wardrobe, hungry for clues. The wardrobe was deep and dark, and I had to prop open the heavy door to give me light. Sealed boxes and bin bags crowded the floor space. I stumbled, feeling stupid, I didn't even know what I was looking for.

I knew it when I saw it, though: just a sequin glint of something familiar, a piece of material from her dress, a constellation scrap, winking at me from a dark corner. It was that soft snaking train, which had been ripped on the rock out in the desert.

The darkness of the wardrobe widened around me in all directions, the door swayed and creaked, the light from our room dwindled away, and the floor began to shift and strain beneath my feet. I felt ashamed, and guilty, like a child caught stealing from his mother's purse. I stuffed the train back inside one of the bags, and pushed my way out of the wardrobe, slamming the door tight shut behind.

All around me, my safe assumptions were shattering. I had understood nothing, over all these strange, enchanted months. But the bold facts spoke for themselves: that other world was more than just a dream world, more than a figment of my imagination. And, logically, if things had made their way back from that world, maybe they came creeping in every night. I wondered what else I would find, if I dug deep enough.

As a child, I loved simple optical illusions, those pictures where, if you stared hard enough, you could see two faces and a vase, a duck or a rabbit – and whichever you saw was said to define your true nature. The ones I loved most were in a book of Victorian postcards that had belonged to my mother. They were a series of curious characters that somehow held two pictures at once. Depending on your perspective, you could be looking at the portrait of a nobleman or a pockmarked thief; a beautiful lady or a wizened old hag. As a child, it sometimes took me a long time to see it, but I always loved that pull in my stomach when the other character within the portrait revealed itself. I wondered if real people were like that, if we all had hidden faces that could only be glimpsed from a particular point of view.

But this time round there was no pleasure to be found in the moment of revelation. If those dreams were more than dreams, how did that redefine our waking world? Did it mean that in turn this everyday life was a mockery, an illusion? I felt suddenly weightless as I thought these things, as if the world I was moving in was just a negative, a shadow of a place that I couldn't even see.

Suddenly I needed to be beside her – not to challenge her, not to force her to look at the discovered evidence. I am a coward, after all, and I find confrontation impossible. No, I needed the comfort that she alone could bring. For her to wrap her arms around me and lead me to bed and for us to say nothing and think nothing but just to melt into each other, laughing at everything and anything, as we did in the early days. I needed her gentle touch. I wanted it to be just the two of us again, to build up our closed world together, a shelter from all harm. I realised, suddenly, that if that night-time forest was real, it held an obvious risk – she could run into it and never come back. That possibility in itself made every minute precious.

Up on the rooftop, the kids were struggling to stand. It looked like they were leaving. I helped them along. 'Yes, quite right,' I said, 'it probably is time to go.'

'We were going anyway,' scowled Jay.

'Well, don't let me stop you,' I replied, bright and breezy, holding open the door for them as they filed down off the rooftop.

She let them go, but turned on me in an instant. 'You don't like people very much, do you?' she said.

The space between us was suddenly charged, electric, like a storm waiting to break. Usually when I saw an argument gathering between us, I would step away, give her space, back down and tell her not to be cross, we should never be cross with each other, it was such a waste. But this time all the unspoken resentments that had been building up between us had a force of their own. Words came tumbling out before either of us could stop them.

And as those appalling arguments always are, it was about everything except what really mattered. I kept the important things, the other fears that were nesting in the wardrobe, safely out of sight.

She said I was mean and rude, and that it was good for her to have company: she needed a world outside these four walls.

I exploded at her: 'I'm mean and rude, am I? I'm mean because I spend all my week working so I can give you whatever you want? I'm rude because I think I should have a say in who comes into my house?'

'I didn't realise it was your house. I didn't realise I was being paid for my time.'

A stalemate silence, and then a change of tactics.

She asked me how I could be so insensitive – couldn't I see how unhappy they were? We were lucky, we'd had three months, but those kids had only had two nights. The boys had run off so quickly, left so many things unfinished, we had a responsibility to make amends. And, besides, the kids made her laugh, they made her feel young again. She hadn't realised how old and serious we had been at risk of becoming, before they had arrived on our doorstep.

I didn't trust myself in this argument. I just said that she shouldn't be so generous. I told her that I didn't like her opening our door to whoever came knocking. It was my house and I had rights.

'But you never give me a chance to speak!' she shouted back at me. 'If you'd just listen!' She thrust a postcard at me, concrete evidence.

A beautiful golden beach stretched out across the card. White sands were lined with palm trees and the sea was bright blue with a spectacular sunset that melted into the water. Richard had written: 'The city isn't big enough for all of us. We've gone back to Paradise. You'd be welcome to join us.'

It had a London postmark. So my worst suspicions had been true – they had planned it all along. They had gone back to one of their winter haunts, placing thousands of miles and unknown continents between us. I was certain, now, that I must have driven them away, and possibly let slip even more than I realised. Maybe I had said enough to make Richard stay up all night and watch. And if that land was real, he would have seen it unfold beneath the window – that infinite ivy, and those tall black trees reaching out for ever. Richard would not have been frightened, he would have loved the adventure. He would have found his own route through the woods and run after her. Richard was a natural navigator, and wouldn't have been held back by fear of unknown places. He would have delighted in the chase, and, back then, when I was still getting stuck in the desert, if Richard had followed he would surely have fought his way through every challenge and reached the ocean. I realised that the postcard could well be a hint from Richard, showing sympathy for our plight, but calling us back to the real world.

But then the phrasing of their message hinted at another reading of events: *The city isn't big enough for all of us.* Maybe it was my jealousy of Phil that had driven them away. Maybe my drunken anger had forced a divide between our two households. Rather than have the summer soured by my every paranoid suspicion, the boys had decided to leave on a high note, so that the only tales they could tell about our shared households would be happy ones, untainted by arguments, suspicions or infidelities. It would be very like them to make that choice.

I thought of the way James talked about the paradise he would buy one day. I wondered, not for the first time, if, under the pretext of falling in love, we had somehow trapped each other into living utterly the wrong life.

And now she was crying, her voice quiet between the sobs. 'I. Just. Miss. Them.'

She let me hold her. 'Darling, so do I. I really do.'

Drying each other's tears, we worked out a compromise: the kids were welcome, but not all the time. She would make sure we still had our own space, of course it mattered. Our happiness was the most important thing. And this weekend would be a special gift, from her to me. She would make everything just right, just like the early days. We'd lock the door against intruders, and remind ourselves of how lucky we were to have found each other. Just me and her, and the rest of the world could go to hell. It was exactly what I needed to hear.

Looking back on it, I think it's inevitable that when love comes rushing into your life, it brings self-delusion in its wake. When you fall in love, all the laws you previously lived by are so easily discarded. From the minute I met her, the rest of the world fell out of focus. She made my heart beat again, and she brought colour and movement into my life, which had been grey and soundless for as long as I could remember. She taught me intimate tricks and built up a world between our sheets; she taught me to laugh at my life and everything in it. In this context, it wasn't completely implausible to me that she might conjure up another land outside our window. I accepted it, and tried to love it, along with all the other parts of her that I did not really understand.

But in this instance it was hard for me to be comfortable with my lack of comprehension. Something deep inside told me that if we were to have any chance at all, if we were to be able to beat away future arguments and rediscover our simple love, then I had to find a way of understanding the world that she had brought with her. I told her that I had to work and I hid in my study while she got ready for bed. I made more notes, then found myself covering pages with doodles as I transferred my codes. As I sit and write now, with the sad benefit of hindsight, I decipher more than numbers on these pages. I see that the patterns I was drawing loop around the edges of my margins to mimic the coils of the ivy and the pebbles of the beach. There was no getting away from it.

And although those all-important hours of the party were for ever lost to me, I remembered an earlier piece of Richard's advice, weeks and weeks ago now. 'Look for clues,' he had once told me. And I had laughed him away, unwilling to listen.

'Some women leave clues strewn around all over the place and you're still too fucking stupid to see them,' he said.

I saw what needed to be done.

She was wrong when she said that things didn't matter. They mattered very much. They provided us with links and fastenings to memories and emotions we might rather shut away. Why else would she hide evidence in the back of the wardrobe?

It stood to reason that if she could bring back mementoes from that strange land, I could take belongings of ours out there that might help us. But I knew it wasn't a simple equation, no set and certain trades. I had to guess the logic of this other world, to communicate in a way that she would understand.

I knew that I didn't have the words, or didn't have the courage to speak them. Words might well be able to build cities and change lives, but at this stage in the game I was beyond knowing which to use. They weren't going to save me – I knew that if I had ever been going to find the right words, they would have come to me by then. I would have been able to catch her, I would have raced ahead and waited for her behind a tree, leapt out and said the right thing to break the spell. And the minute I had spoken, that enchanted world would have fractured around us, the tangling forest would have melted away. We would have been back on the front lawn, with another road opposite our house, and a high fence between us and the common. I am fully aware of the irony that it is only now that the words come.

But still I hoped that in that night-time forest there might be other ways of communicating. I saw that her sculpture in the sand might have been a message, rather than a barrier. Maybe it wasn't intended to hurt me, and was just another treasure hunt, an echo of our daytime life, a code, clues to decipher.

Well, two could play at that game.

She knocked on the study door. 'Come to bed,' she said, on the other side, in her kindest voice. 'Let's stop shutting ourselves away from each other. Come to bed.'

I agreed. If dreams were not just dreams, it was important to do all I could to make her happy in this world and to remind her of all the good things it had to offer. We had a gentle couple of hours together, falling back into old rhythms. That night neither of us had marked skin, and it seemed a long time since we had both been so free to touch.

In another attempt to keep her with me, I lulled her to sleep with stories of our future: one day soon we would get out of this grimy city where the stench of the cars rose up to meet the cloudy sky and there was no summer air. One day soon, after I had made my money, I would take her to the beach that the boys had sent us – can you imagine their surprise? – and the four of us would live in palm trees. Phil could build us treehouses, which she could furnish with all her many arts: she could make us curtains and cushions, she could cover the walls with her pictures and photographs, re-creating our happy home on foreign shores. Richard and I would catch bright fish in the coloured corals. The sea would feed us and every night we would hold a banquet under the stars, evoking old toasts to bring love and luck into our life. We would live out our years basking on the golden sand. I would never have to journey underground again, and she would never have to spend lonely days in an echoing flat, talking to strangers, trying to fill time until I returned. She was still smiling when she fell asleep.

As for me, I didn't even bother trying to sleep. I was nervous, definitely, as I lay there waiting for her to stir. I knew that if she did get up and go towards the window then nothing would ever be the same again: I would have to accept there was a world she could create in the dark. It frightened me, but what frightened me just as much was the thought that she might sleep the whole night through. Then all my theories would unravel around me. I would have to accept that the forest and the desert and the sea beyond were, indeed, just in my mind. That I had put that evidence into the wardrobe myself to support my wild theories and that, through the heady vertigo fall into love, I had broken myself in two and hadn't even noticed. That in complement to my persona as her perfect lover, the other side of me was a saboteur of everything that was good in my life, creating false stories and clever traps.

But stir she did. I don't even know whether she was actually asleep: it was only an hour after we had gone to bed that she began to mutter to herself, turn away from me, apparently still in the pretence of dreaming. I watched her through half-closed eyes as she slipped out of bed, crept up on to the window-sill and made her quick getaway. The window was already open and she had only to touch the plant with her hand. The green shoots plaited themselves together, coiled their own way out of the window, by now more of a ladder than a rope.

I was consumed by excitement as I raced to get dressed. As I looked down at the rippling woods, it felt like that whole world was re-forming itself just for me, offering me another chance. If we learnt how to communicate out in that wild land, who knew what pleasures it might bring us? She could teach me how to tame the forest and it could be our refuge that kept us safe when the city was too difficult. Out there we could hide from the kids, hide from my working world, build the bivouac that Phil had promised us, and never be found. Out there, we could have everything she wanted: we could really be true children of nature, never get sad, never grow old. I was as eager and nervous as I had been in our early days together, when I was learning how to be a worthy lover, every day finding new ways to please her. I was going to leave her a message on the shore, a reminder of our happiness. I would, for the first time, leave my own mark on this place. Every previous adventure now seemed to have been just practice, training me for this night where I would take control.

I took a black bag and filled it with treasures from our home. I took down the first photograph of the two of us. It was one of my favourite reminders, taken in early, early days, in her village the first weekend I went to see her.

Every part of that journey had been an adventure. The train had shunted its way out of the station, and I was counting the beats of the wheels on the tracks that would bring me closer and closer to her. The city was shrugged off behind me as we hurtled south. A wide world spread itself out all around. Hay was gathered into huge bales, which sat proudly in the middle of the levelled land. A canal curled up by the side of the tracks and ran parallel for a while. People were sunbathing on the flat roofs of the barges as the train tore past; then the water curved away and made its way out along the sunny fields. It was everything she had promised. I had never seen anything like it. Picture perfect.

She was waiting for me, perched up on the high fence of the station yard, smoking a cigarette, looking around nervously. When she saw me emerge from the train she ran the length of the platform and hugged me tight.

The relief overwhelmed me. This was our first meeting after our strange weekend when she rescued me in that bar. I was sure that when she returned home she would have realised it was all a mistake.

But apparently not.

And, indeed, it was the golden weekend that I had hoped for. We stayed in her parents' house while they were up in the town. We built a campfire, uprooting a windblown and broken fence that separated her parents' rolling garden from the woods. She reduced it to kindling with swift strokes of an axe. Firemaking was second nature to her; she stacked the logs together, doused them in petrol and delighted in the explosion. It kept us warm all night as we slept under the clear stars and made all the right wishes. A full moon watched over us. The next day the sun shone with all the warmth she had predicted and we walked through the fields and rolled in the hay. We sat in country pubs and embarrassed the locals because we couldn't help but touch. The photograph I chose was one we took in the long grass at the bottom of her garden. We perched the camera on a high bank and set the automatic timer to catch us peeping out of the foliage below; wild flowers almost obscure our faces, but you can just about see the two of us smiling through.

It was something to remind her.

I snatched that sparkling train of her dress out of the dark shadows of the wardrobe. From my desk drawer, I took out the very few love letters she had ever written to me (we were never apart long enough to need words to fill in the gaps). I bundled these pieces of our history into my bag, slung it on to my back, and followed her out of the window.

'It depends how you look at it,' she had once said.

And that night I was looking at the forest differently, not with the distance and dislocation of a dream-bound self but with absolute certainty. This was a place she had brought with her, it was part of her, and I loved her so much that I could neither hate nor fear it. She could be careless but, despite all her self-berating, she was not mean by nature. When she did anger me, it was almost always my fault in the end, a case of me reading things wrongly and misinterpreting her good intentions. That was what I told myself as I rushed down the ivy rope, and it worked. I ran through the forest laughing, seeing nothing but her beauty, reflected and played out in this wonderful world.

Now that I had realised how to read this place, everything was magical and the moonlight was a blessing as I picked out my path. The ivy tangled between the branches like nets of finely spun silver, and as I danced through it the forest was dancing with me, holding up branches, gentle leaves stroking my skin with a lover's touch. I allowed myself to be pulled through the wood again, drawn out of myself by the beckoning ivy. And for the first time I recognised that gentle calling for what it was: it was the same irresistible force that had lured me out of the bar that night we first met: it was the sure and certain call of her love, drawing me out of shadows. That lotus smell of the flowers was the fragrance of her. There was her laughter echoing in the woods again, as if the very forest and everything in it were laughing along with me, and were happy for me because I was at last seeing things as they really were.

When I reached the edge of the forest, there was just a fragment of a moon in the sky, and the open space was a real contrast to the light dappled among the trees, but I was undaunted by the darkness. I had the clear sight of a carto-grapher who had spent months making detailed maps of his land and, despite the blurred boundaries, at last could see how continents combined to make a world he could navigate. This confidence gave me unexpected night-vision. For the first time, the darkness had depth and distance for me. I could see further and wider than ever before. And although I could see the tails of the sandstorm waiting for me on the far horizon, I was not intimidated. All the way through the desert, it waltzed around me like a cautious partner, watching from a distance and never coming close enough to touch.

So I made my way, fearless, down to the sea. There she was, just as the night before, gathering treasure to adorn the landscape. As I watched against this star-dancing backdrop I really saw for the first time how she must have been when she was younger. I saw her playing with the tide, skipping over the waves and back again, and I fell in love with the water-baby in her. I saw echoes of the very young girl she had once been, a wild, mischievous little thing, delighting in the never-ending treasures that nature bestowed upon her. She threw off her clothes as she danced, and ran out into the sea.

And even the water didn't frighten me so much: it wasn't the wild white ocean of the night before, no, the sea was settled and the lapping waves were calling to me again. But this time they were welcoming whispers, saying, *Closer, closer, come closer*. These soft sighs of the ocean soothed away any habitual fears. Pulled out of my hiding-place I ran down to the shore. And there, just where the tide stroked the edges of the beach, was her sea sculpture, reproducing in every direction.

It was like nothing I had ever seen in my own world. It was as if she had breathed life into the lifeless sand, and all around me patterns were unfurling, in front and behind, shoots of curling intersecting circles, spiralling out into the dark. Beautiful to behold. I thought of the mathematical Mandlebrot set patterns that had entranced me as a child – the nearest analogy I could find. I had learnt that those never-ending patterns had a meaning beyond their beauty, which if decoded might contain a key to the universe. That night I knew I was in the presence of something similar. *Closer, still closer*, the waves whispered, but I kept hold of my original intention and stepped away from the beckoning waters.

Instead I took a few steps back towards the forest. I knelt

down and, with my hand, drew a line in the shore. That night the sand was cool, soft and easy to touch. I undid my bag and laid out the objects in front of me, wondering how I might make a sculpture equal to hers. As the water rippled, so did her designs, lines breaking up and re-forming, shells shifting, pebbles turning over to catch the moonlight, inching towards the relics I had brought. The sands themselves were embracing all these tokens from our shared life, weaving hypnotic patterns around them, drawing our mementoes into the larger pattern.

I was resolute and pulled my treasure out of the grasp of the moving land.

I took up a stick and drew a clear line in the sand, forming a boundary between her work and mine. Then, on my side of that line, I drew geometric patterns, parallel lines, which divided up the space. I raked up banks of sand, and punctuated them with more supple twigs. I pinned the letters she had written on to their tips. They fluttered and rattled against each other in the breeze. On a second row of twigs I pinned that salvaged fragment of her dress. The sequins caught the moonlight and spun in the breeze, the soft material floating through the dark, echoing her dancing.

In front of this, I weighted down our photograph with pebbles. Side by side, we smiled up from the sand, as if we could see this wild world, and were happy to be there. I arranged coral along the edges, making a border between her work and mine, and nothing burnt my hands.

Peeping through the mesh of twigs and tatters I saw her rising from the water, drying herself on her abandoned clothes. I hid behind my boulder, ready to leap out and surprise her. I wanted to watch her as she discovered my sculpture. I wanted to hear her delighted laughter. At last, I had found a way to call out to her, and was ready for us to dance home together. But as I knelt on the sand, it was shifting beneath me; it felt unstable, and I found myself sinking into unseen hollows in the shore. I was wriggling uncomfortably, unable to stay seated: the sand was growing warmer and came creeping in between the folds of my clothing, abrasive and uncouth. I couldn't stay.

So, reluctantly, I began to go back. The desert, like the seashore, gathered heat to it if I stayed still. The restless sand urged me back towards the forest. And, coming at it from this direction, the dark forest was harder to venture into. It took all my self-discipline not to turn round and run back, to watch her from a distance as she read the message I had left for her, see her smile as she picked up her old love letters, hear her laugh at those pages full of golden promises. But I understood this land well enough by now to know that once a course of action was taken it was best to stick to it. I didn't have the confidence to turn round: I didn't know what I might end up running into.

So I danced through the uncertain woods, squinting into the middle distance to see the changes in the shades of the light. Putting all my faith in grey-shadowed pathways, playing with the dappled dark. I took a few wrong turnings, but eventually the forest set me free, delivering me home.

As I ran across the lawn and scampered up the side of the house I could hear the wind moving through the branches; the whole forest was heaving a great sigh in the middle of the night. As if even the landscape itself was now relaxing, now that at last we had found a common language. Not that I had found it so easy. I was unused to labour of any kind, and my hands were scratched to pieces. I went into the bathroom and filled the basin with hot water and antiseptic. I took her tweezers and a needle from her sewing-basket and picked the tiny splinters out of my skin, watching my blood cloud the water. I was careless and impatient: I wanted to be clean by the time she returned. Standing in front of the mirror, I was rehearsing all the questions I might ask her: what was her history with this place? When had these adventures begun? What did she find out there and what was she doing when she went into the ocean? Were there other places beyond the water that she was trying to reach? I wondered how she would play it. Would she have brought my sculptured treasures back? Would I find her lying across the bed reading aloud from her love letters, smiling and saying, 'I will love you until the end of time, until the mountains of this world have been weathered down to pebbles, until the seven seas run dry'?

But when I got back she was already in bed. There was something wrong. She was lying on my side of the bed, huddled into the very corner, covers over her head, breathing deeply, almost certainly asleep. Her fists were clenched under the sheets. She was still wearing the clothes she had gone out in, and hanging over the bed was a salty briny smell, rotten and ripening. I moved aside her hair to see her expression. I could only see one side of her face, but it was bruised; there was a graze along her cheekbones, and fine little cuts running down her neck. I hated to see her injured. I thought that she must have done it to herself when she was out at sea; perhaps a strong wave had flung her against the rocks and she had been cut to shreds. I was furious with this contrary landscape, which changed its shape and mood as often as the wild winds changed direction. I was furious with the damage it did to both of us, and the intrusion of the wounds that it could inflict.

And that wasn't the only intrusion that night. Up on the window-sill the ivy plant would not lie still. It was snaking around the pot and rearing up. It slithered towards us, hissing as it twisted again and darted back at the window, tapping on the glass. It was calling the outside in. I shut my eyes and pulled the covers over my head, hoping that, come the morning, none of it would be there.

# 18

The Saturday sun came streaming in like a false promise, the sharp light making our room into a golden haven. I rolled over to wake her, thinking that now something would have to be said. But she wasn't there, just the stains on the bedding where she had been sleeping, tiny spots and speckles of blood scattered across the sheets.

She had locked the bathroom door against me but I forced it. Shrouded in a towel, she was standing in front of the mirror, cleaning herself. She was furious at my sudden entry and flailed out, trying to push me away, shouting at me, 'Fuck off! Leave me alone! I don't want you to see this.'

It took all my energy to hold her down.

We went back into the bedroom after I had washed her. She was very quiet. 'It's OK,' I whispered, 'I love you. Just tell me what I can do.'

She traced the stains on the sheets with her fingers, joining the dots into an unseeen pattern, as she explained. She was sorry. She had done it to herself. She didn't mean to frighten me, and she assured me that none of it was my fault; this was nothing to do with our argument, she'd just had a very black and unhappy night. It happened sometimes and when it did she couldn't help herself. It was much better now. When the pressure of blackness inside got too much she would just cut it loose, let it all go. She'd never needed to do it since she met me, but there were some things that even I couldn't make any better.

'What things?' I asked. 'What are these terrible things?'

'Just thoughts.'

'Of the boys?'

'Partly. I don't know.'

I didn't press her. I just told her over and over again that I loved her and I couldn't bear to see her hurt. She told me she was so stupid, she was surprised I had put up with her for so long, that I had enough to deal with, I didn't deserve all this. I said there was nothing to put up with. I could never leave her.

And I didn't, not for the entire weekend. I stayed by her side, and told her over and over again how much I loved her. I told her that she might not be able to see it herself but she should trust me: she had a golden light that she carried with her wherever she went, that she illuminated the rooms she walked through, that everyone who had ever met her could only love her. I told her she was the most beautiful girl I had ever known, and that with her and me against the world, there wasn't anything we couldn't do. I held back the other voices that whispered to me, ignored the creeping fear that told me it was lies, all lies, that no matter what I said I could never be strong enough for her.

I remember that weekend as a stretch of dead time. She became as small and vulnerable as a frightened child, swaddling herself in blankets and hardly speaking. The air in our bedroom became cloying and claustrophobic but I insisted that we kept the window closed, especially at night.

The kids, of course, came knocking at our door on Saturday morning, but I wouldn't let them in.

'The sun's shining!' shouted Jay, pounding the door down. 'Get up, you lazy bastards!'

I kept the door on the chain, and whispered to them through the gap. 'It's not a good time,' I said sternly. 'She doesn't want to come out.'

Tom and Jay frowned back at me, as if I might be keeping her against her will.

I snapped at them, saying that she really wasn't very well at all – these things happened sometimes; she needed her sleep. They should go, they would only disturb her and make things worse. I don't think they believed me. And why would they?

She didn't even acknowledge them. She slept fitfully day and night and I watched over her. She wasn't smiling in her sleep any more. She wasn't smiling at all. I stroked her skin while she dozed, and her cuts and gashes healed a little, but only up to a point. And as the light died, and the night gathered outside the window, everything seemed dangerous and unknown. The ivy was still tap-tap-tapping against the glass. I spent hours pacing from our bed to the window and back again. I kept on thinking that the minute my back was turned, the forest would come creeping in. So long as I stayed vigilant, it was only the common out there. So long as I stayed alert, we could keep these fragile walls secure.

And as the hours passed so slowly I thought back to our last Saturday with the boys, and remembered then how time had run rings around us, how in our drunken state we had lost hours and dismissed sleep.

Lying out on the lawn outside the pub that afternoon the four of us had drunk toasts to all the time we had cheated and wasted between us that summer. Phil was making us all laugh with his determined boasts that he would never need sleep again, never ever, he'd gone beyond it. He'd conquered sleep so easily, and now the only hurdle left was to cheat death itself. He was play-fighting with Richard, attempting to commit hara-kiri with a penknife, just to claim his right to immortality. We were laughing along and she was goading him, saying, 'Go on, Phil, no guts no glory,' but the penknife was rusted and stuck so in the end Phil lived to tell the tale but never knew if he would have made it as a deity. We were free to laugh at everything then, so sure were we of our place in the world.

When Monday finally came her skin was healing, but something deep inside her seemed broken. It felt like I had failed her. I had tried everything I could to make her better, but she was still damaged and distant. I didn't know what I could do to charm laughter out of her, to bring her back to life. We were talking to each other again, but only in broken whispers.

'How are you feeling?'

'A little better.'

'Is there anything I can do?'

'Not really.'

'I love you.'

'I know you do.'

And so on, and so on. Cautious steps.

I didn't want to leave her alone, it would have felt like I was abandoning her when she needed me the most. I rang work to plead for more time off, but it wasn't an option. I was put straight through to Mr Collins who told me that the systems were playing up, and it was absolutely vital for me to be there. I really shouldn't push my bloody luck and if it was too difficult for me to arrive on time then I might as well not come in at all.

I felt torn between too many worlds. It was too difficult, this split focus that was required of me – as if I was being asked to live a whole series of lives, all in parallel. It was like trying to juggle a number of open equations: nothing could be concluded. Part of me was still stuck in that night-time forest, trapped somewhere in the puzzles of those shifting trees. Then another part of me was pouring all its energy into caring for her and trying to bring her back to me; another part still was trapped between Simon and James, a faithful cog in a machine.

Then the saddest part of me was lost for ever in the alcoves of the Hand in Hand, or abandoned on the rooftop, haunted by the knowledge that I had been happy then, grounded by the boys and certain of my role in relation to her. And I missed my more naïve self, that simple young man who had thought that nothing around him would ever change. I was suddenly furious with the boys for leaving, as if it was only their departure that had fractured my world so irreparably, as if I could blame them alone for all this fragmentation.

But then, right on cue, there was a knocking on our door again. A stupidly optimistic part of me thought it might just be the boys, come back to turn everything round, bringing a second summer and new hope. Of course it wasn't. Looking through the peephole I saw, distorted and gurning in the curve of the glass, the cartoon-grotesque faces of Kate, Jay and Tom, staring right back at me. Desperate times called yet again for desperate measures. I let them in with a false show of enthusiasm: 'Great to see you! It'll make her day!'

They hovered at the doorway, not quite sure how to take my words. But I drew Kate to one side and told her that there had been an accident over the weekend – not entirely untrue. I said that she had gone out climbing trees in the night and taken a fall. I really needed them to look out for her. Could they manage that, just for one day? I'd pay them.

Kate patted my arm, a patronising gesture borrowed, I noticed, from Phil. She said there was no need for bribes, they'd do it for love, it was the least they could do.

I found it hard not to laugh in her face: teenage arrogance, that fervent monopoly on love. And, despite all my concern for her, a callous part of me was glad that things had played out like this. I was sure that, in her vulnerable state, she would see the limitations of the kids. She would see that they were selfish, and did not care for her as I could.

She came out at the sound of voices, her first time on her feet for two days. She had done remarkable repair work: that familiar ability of hers to transform herself completely when the occasion demanded it. Her makeup was immaculate, her spontaneous hugs a perfect piece of deception. She was wearing some baggy jeans and one of my long shirts, which covered her cuts completely. Her cheek was still bruised but her facepaint was so good that you had to know it was there to see it properly. She gave me a brief kiss and pushed me out of the door, saying there was no point in being late and getting myself into trouble.

Suddenly a very different person again. She never ceased to surprise me.

That journey to work was hell. Every tube stop marking my movement away from her was a sickening tug in my gut. And when I finally made it into work, there was another series of problems ready to confront me. One of Simon's programs had crashed, the last thing that any of us had ever expected. A virus had got into the system and eaten away chunks of memory. James had a horrific hangover and, though he empathised with the state of mind of the ailing networks, could do little to help. 'Mate, I'm sorry, but I can't even look at the screen without getting seasick.'

Simon was no better, just frozen, like his programs. Outside influences had invaded his meticulous work, and he didn't know how to put it right.

I booted up my computer. It was a virus with a sense of humour at least. My spreadsheets looked fine to begin with, but then the totals started falling down from the bottoms of the columns and gathered momentum until the screen was a black mess of raining figures.

Outside the office, the weather echoed our predicament. It was that strange time of year when the elements develop split personalities of their own – as if the summer and impending autumn are locked in a tight battle. The sunshine was slowly pushed aside by ever-advancing banks of grey cloud. Monsoon downpours made it impossible to see the office opposite: we were an ark adrift, shrouded by mist and deafening rain. It felt like the whole city could be drowned. Not an entirely unattractive prospect.

James's plight was compounded by the fact that this structural collapse was all his fault. He confided in me that on Friday evening he had been accessing dodgy porn sites in a moment of boredom, and must have infected everything. Or, as he put it, 'Fuck me, mate, we've all got VD off the VDU.'

It was my turn to save his skin. Simon was sent home at lunchtime – he couldn't take the strain. James dutifully found old printouts and read strings of numbers to me as I typed in the finer details that the computers couldn't re-create. Caught up in the safety-net of my numbers, I didn't have to say anything. I didn't have to do anything apart from reconstruct my columns and totals, and the money soon started flowing the way it should, we reversed the tide, and now everything was salvageable. The relief was extraordinary – I knew who I was again, and what good I could do if I set my mind to it. I almost believed James when he told me that I was a prince among men; or, indeed, Mr Collins when he told me that I had saved the world.

But it took time. We worked late, late into the night, fuelled by coffee and takeaways. I watched the clocks and called her at regular intervals, just to be sure she was okay. She sounded too cheerful.

'Jesus, I told you I'm fine!' she said, the third time I rang. 'We're having a great time. Take as long as you need.'

I could hear the kids laughing in the background. It felt like I was intruding.

It was past eleven o'clock when we finished. Mr Collins was delighted – I was the saviour of the company. He slapped me on the back and asked me if there was anything I couldn't fix. Together, James and I had retrieved millions, we should be very pleased with ourselves. We should take tomorrow off. We ran out of the office, laughing. James couldn't believe he had got away with it and couldn't thank me enough. 'I owe you one,' he said. 'I'd have been fucked without you.'

But the journey back to Wimbledon was a nightmare, cramped in carriages with the drunks of London, careering their hopeful ways back home, so loud and brutal after the silence and concentration of the office. Every tube change was a test of courage. I had to push my way through surly crowds, racing up and down escalators, the iron steps shifting and tilting me forward. I was running on to platforms, leaping on to trains, squeezing myself through the quick-closing doors, which sprang shut, like sharp-snapping jaws, behind me.

The minute I got back to familiar streets, I couldn't race home quickly enough. I vaulted the wall and took our short-cut, to save a few precious minutes. It was a warm evening with a clear sky, and the moon showed me the way home across the common. In my state, it was a foolish route to take. After the first few minutes I lost my confidence: the snapping of twigs beneath my feet and the dark shadows dancing behind the trees were all too familiar. After the sudden rains, the ground underneath was sodden and uncertain. I tripped over hidden roots and couldn't look back, in case these trees were also shifting in my wake.

I quickened my pace. I felt something black at my shoulder.

The silver birches swayed slightly in the breeze, creaking and whispering to me, *What if? What if? What if?*

What if I was too late, if the kids had left and she had taken this golden opportunity to slip away? What if I came home to find an open window and an empty room?

What if she could charm these woods too, and the white branches closed together as I tried to push beyond them, if I was caught, caged until morning?

I could hear laughter somewhere in the dark ahead. Harsh, cackling laughter as if there was something out in the woods waiting, as if someone out there was laying traps. It was only a couple of drunks, cursing at the moon. Slumped against some windblown tree, in the half-light, they looked as though they were growing out of the trunk itself. I ran and ran the rest of the way home, terrified of everything and anything. My boundaries were dissolving. I couldn't see where one world might end and another begin.

In the most immediate sense, there was nothing to worry about. They were all still up on the rooftop, the patio was a bombsite of beer cans and shredded cigarettes. They were lying back on the cushions and she was teaching Kate to stargaze: 'That's Orion. He's a hunter. He was the best hunter in the whole world and he was loved by the goddess of the moon. But her husband Apollo was a jealous tyrant and tricked her into killing Orion with her silver arrows. When she realised the terrible mistake she had made, she placed her hunter-lover in the sky, to keep her company in the heavens. She sees him every night as she rides past in her chariot, but she can never come close enough to touch. And whenever her sun-god husband appears, Orion has learnt to vanish quickly from the sky.'

'Fucking . . . cool.' Jay's predictable wide-eyed response.

Kate tried to include me, asking me if I knew that shooting stars were really fallen angels, saying they'd seen two already that night, two falling angels plummeting through the sky after each other, and they had landed on the common. I had heard it all before and, besides, in Kate's words such notions just seemed childish, indulgent. I had little time for it. They were all in a stoned coma, and in every way the kids had brought her down to their level.

'I've got a day off tomorrow!' I said, all bright and breezy, leaning over to kiss her. But I was pushed aside. I was blocking the view.

I felt crowded out, a stranger in my own home.

And our flat was very overcrowded by that stage: the air was thick with words unsaid; I had now discovered that even the wardrobe at the end of our bed was bursting with poorly kept secrets that grew in the dark. Every morning, no matter which room I sat in, I was hemmed in by ghosts. As I made my coffee, out of the corner of my eye I would catch a glimpse of the boys, sprawled across the sofa, Richard grinning at me, raising one eyebrow as if to say, 'Have you worked it out yet, mate?'

The kids' invasion only made these ghosts all the more powerful. And she colluded with them, turning all the differences between us into public property. Part of what had been hard about that first night they came into the flat, the night when we had discovered them next door, was the larger public betrayal. They had told her all about what really happened the first time I met them out on the common, when they had hurled insults and beer cans down at me from the treetops. Kate was apologetic about it, saying they'd just thought I was a boring old banker who needed teaching a lesson. They had been drunk and stupid and hadn't meant any harm. She had laughed to hear Kate's version of the story, so much more plausible than mine. Then she'd turned on me, saying that she knew it, she could never imagine me being friendly to strangers, I was such a boring old bastard, and that the kids had done me a favour, putting me in my place. I felt exposed, as though for the first time she was seeing me as I really was. And I hated the kids for making it so plain.

This night was no exception: Jay and Tom had my old atlas spread out in front of them and were scribbling all over it, circling foreign cities, drawing up an inventory, spilling candle-wax on the pages. One of the few gifts that my father had ever given me, it was now soiled and marked by their plans of adventure, instead of mine.

'I told them you wouldn't mind,' she said. 'It's not as if you ever open the bloody thing.'

Inspired by the boys' departure, they were devising their own escape route across continents. Kate had drawn cartoon-strip caricatures of the three of them scaling mountains or riding camels through the desert and coming to rest in a tropical paradise.

With all this talk of travel I was suddenly terrified that I would suffer the ultimate humiliation, that in the end these children would be the ones to tempt her away.

I tried to be polite about it.

'I'm sorry, I'm very tired,' I said. 'Maybe see you tomorrow?' They left like a shot.

There was a momentary stand-off as I waited to see which side of her would emerge now that we had no public to perform to. But she was back in her mode of mischievous child. When I asked her how she was feeling she could only giggle in my face, and tell me she felt drunk and stoned, drunk and stoned, and that was the best feeling because it meant she didn't really have to feel anything at all. I told her that it wasn't very wise after her bad black moods, and that maybe she just needed to be herself for a while; shouldn't she just stop all this for a few days? But she laughed at me; I was being a boring bastard yet again, apparently, and that was no good to anyone.

And although I was irritated with her, I was also relieved to see that she had her old brightness back. She was wasted, but trying so hard to be kind. She had missed me, and made me a lovely dinner, and had tried to wait, but had already eaten hers due to a chronic attack of the munchies, leaving pasta sauce smeared all around her mouth and down her shirt. She smothered me with sticky kisses and her laughter became infectious and I couldn't be angry. It felt like I had spent far too much of our time together locked away in my own bitterness. I had wished so hard for her to get better, and now that she was well again, full of energy, it was petulant of me to resent where it had come from, that it had been the kids, not me who had brought her back to herself. I matched her kisses and told her to have a shower to make herself clean and sober.

I dutifully did the washing-up afterwards, and it was only when I was putting things away that I realised something was wrong. There were spaces in our cupboards where our best wineglasses should have been. I had given them to her on our first anniversary, two long champagne flutes made from pale blue glass that caught the light when we held them up and drank toasts to each other. And that was just the start. All through the flat, things were missing.

Our home was suddenly filled with gaps and gaping distances. The books on the shelves in the living room leant sickly against each other, sliding down. There were dark spaces where there had once been volumes of poetry, borrowed words of more eloquent lovers I had given her, to try to communicate how I really felt. In her wardrobe, dresses I had bought for her to wear for me had disappeared, the metal hangers chiming lifeless in the dark. And she had even removed her beautiful picture from my study, so I was faced with a wide white wall, warping the perspective.

I knew that I should try to be calm, that her seeming recovery was fragile, but really I was just too furious to reason.

When I went through to the bedroom to challenge her, she was sitting up on the ledge again, outstaring the dark.

'What have you done with our things?'

'What things?' she replied, giggling.

'You know full well. All our things.'

She was still very stoned, and seemed intent on playing games.

'Oh, those things. Wait and see.'

I wasn't prepared to. I let rip, accusing her of all sorts: had she thrown them out just to spite me? Was she really so petty? Or had she given them away to Kate, Tom and fucking Jay, just in case they didn't have enough from us already? Didn't she care? Didn't my gifts mean anything?

She wouldn't even look at me. She curled herself into a tight ball, pressing herself against the window. She said that I was frightening her.

'Just tell me what you've done with them,' I pleaded. 'Just tell me and that'll be the end of it.'

She still shrank away and asked me, please, not to be so angry with her all the time and couldn't I say something nice? I never had anything nice to say any more.

I told her that there was nothing nice to say. The facts spoke for themselves.

'What facts?' she said, laughing, and admonishing me yet again. 'People are more important than things.'

No, they weren't. Not in this instance.

I went on a mad rampage around the flat, looking for hiding-places but finding nothing. I threw everything out of the wardrobe, spilled boxes and bags across the floor.

'Is this a hint?' I cried. 'Do you want me to go?'

Finally, she was as upset as me. 'Of course I don't. Trust me.'

Richard's advice came rushing back to me. I didn't trust her at all.

'Have a little faith,' she said.

But how could I when I didn't know what to believe any more?

'Come to bed,' she said.

I did, reluctantly, but kept my distance.

If she really was trying to remove me so completely from her life, I certainly wasn't going to reach over and make everything all right.

I had so little patience. Her mood swings were as dangerous as the weather.

I turned away from her and pretended to sleep. Here was an interesting role reversal. She tried to stroke my back and soothe me, saying, 'It's all right, love. You'll see. It's all going to be all right.'

But I didn't believe a word.

I pulled the sheets tighter around me and wouldn't let her touch. I fell asleep to the sound of her crying, but I thought that she deserved that, at least.

It was the sound of her crying that woke me again, but the pitch was changed. She was up on the window-sill, howling out into the night, like a wounded animal. Her shrill keening terrified me. I hadn't meant to hurt her that much. But she wasn't crying because of me.

No. It was because of her ivy plant. For the first time, she could not control it. The tendrils twisted inwards against each other, and the ivy was not a rope but a serpent creature that wrapped itself around her arms, caressing her broken skin, scratching open old wounds. It was pinning her back to the window-seat, keeping her in. But she fought against it, stamping it down, and forcing it outside. The minute she pushed the plant out of the window it was just an obedient rope again, docile and there to help her escape.

Staring out of the window, I was terrified. The forest was seething. It held the shape of a savage animal, rearing up and raking the stars with its green, arching back. I was sickened by the speed with which my perspective could change: my mood swings had become as bad as hers. Last night this land had been full of beauty and possibility, now I could only see the terrors that lurked beneath those beckoning branches. There was no logic to this land, or to what I saw within it.

At the heart of all these inconsistencies, there was only one hard-earned truth: these two worlds were woven together, as intricately intertwined as the knots and plaits of her ivy. But what frustrated me was that I still couldn't see how – I still hadn't managed to crack the code of correspondences. I wrestled with an insidious fear that told me I was stupid to risk life and limb out there again and again. My fear whispered that it would be much safer not to chase after her at all, but to stay at home, with the four solid walls I could trust. But as soon as she landed on the lawn, the ivy drew itself up and began crawling back through the window. A new danger. If I stayed, the whole forest might come rushing in through the window, binding me to my bed for good.

And behind my fear lurked a cold, steely anger, not quite subdued after the evening's argument. I was furious with her for being so careless about her own safety. I couldn't forget the blood on the sheets. Something out there had done her a lot of damage, yet there she was, running across the lawn, running back out to meet it again, whatever it was. But also, in my heart of hearts, I knew that this anger was only displacement – I could be infuriated with her, but really I was angry with myself, and my own stupid failings. Another part of me was very, very ashamed at my reluctance to follow. I still knew that I should be there to stand strong and tall against the horizon, to be there to protect her. No matter what had passed between us in the daytime, I didn't wish her any harm.

So I pushed away my fear and wrestled with the ivy. I held the plant back, the way I had seen her do it, and forced it out of the window. The rope still tried to tangle itself around me as I slid down on to the lawn, but I was too quick to be caught. I weighted it down with a rock, to be sure our room would be safe until our return. Then I followed her into the forest.

It was almost too late. The forest was growing into something darker than ever before, a maze of false turnings. All beauty was gone, and the wood was re-forming itself into a very different thing – ugly and angry. The branches were weaving together at a frenetic pace, sealing away entrances, blocking pathways. I crawled through one of the last openings and found myself in almost total darkness. I had no night-vision, I had only the projections cast out by my fear, and insubstantial shadows grew into creatures with eyes made of moonlight, loose ivy tendrils into cunning claws that swiped out to cut me. They grew out of the tree-trunks and were skittering and scampering across the carpet of flowers, these step-dragging remnants of the forest, turning vicious, like the creatures of my childhood nightmares. But I stamped and shouted and they lay down, lifeless, before me. Through sheer force of will, I danced my way through. I didn't look back, but I could hear the trees snapping together like sprung traps, or the jaws of something closing behind me.

The desert was similarly hostile, full of wasteland wiles. It had no choice but to part at my dancing, but the land was restless under my feet, as if waiting for me to take just one wrong step so that it could suck me under. The night was very dark, no stars, and just a splinter-sickle of a moon, which gave me no light. Even the moon itself looked like a deep wound, cut into the black-skinned sky. The loud rumble of the waves guided me forwards, but with every step the light was dwindling, contrary to all the laws of nature. I ran forward, still trying to outrace my fear, and fell headlong into a mass of thorns and dead wood.

My barrier had grown in the night. The twigs had risen up far above my head cross-hatching the clouds. The dead wood was a tight-meshed net, spanning the sky. The letters I had so carefully secured had been pulled apart by the wind and scattered down on the sand like confetti. The scrap of her dress had grown wider, and whipped around like a sail in the wind far above. It was still shedding sequins, and they came tumbling down, cutting into my skin like shards of glass. I stumbled back from the wreckage and, seen from a little distance, that mesh of twigs and tatters was like a broken skeleton, a fractured carcass of some ancient sea beast, washed up on to the shore and left to rot. The wind whistling through the holes in its side was an eerie wailing, for ever echoing across the shore.

This was all so wrong. This was not what I meant at all.

I stood there, with a barrier of my own making keeping me from the sea. I leant my back against the blackened bark and looked down at the shreds of her love letters, lying at my feet. Soiled by the salt spray, the words I had read over and over, full of wonder, were now just a stain on the page. The sand that I had arranged into ridges and patterns for her was no longer gold and gleaming; it had turned into ash overnight, and blew up into my face to choke me. And that precious photograph, the first ever image of the two of us, was utterly destroyed. The frame had cracked, and the picture was buckled by the force of the elements. The water had seeped through, distorting our faces, washing out any colour.

My message of love had died and turned in on itself, becoming instead a wailing wall, a barrier of terror and violence. Now I understood what she had done. She had left me nothing in the flat that had any meaning, nothing that I could have brought out to the seashore to call her back. Nothing that could grow too great and do any more damage.

There was a gap where she must have forced her way through on her return. The water came trickling in from the sea, creating a quagmire. This explained the marks on her skin. She must have fought with all her might to push through. She had wanted to come back. That was something. The least I could do was make her return easier this time. My earlier anger with her turned against myself: I was furious that nothing I did here could come out right. I hated that bastard landscape, which turned good intentions into bad, and never held the same shape twice.

So I set to work. I thought that it would have been harder, but the structure yielded to me straight away. I kicked away the sand and pebbles, bringing everything tumbling down on top of me, a hailstorm of sticks and stones that beat at my back. As I put my hands on the brittle branches, they undid themselves for me, and came crashing down on to the shore. I sidestepped the hail of detritus as it all fell apart under my touch. And then I stamped it down, and snapped the twigs to pieces, and strained against them, twisting until I was left with only kindling splinters scattered on the shore.

But as the twigs fell down, they brought the remains of her dress with them. It came swooping out of the sky, and for a moment I thought it would smother me. But as it tumbled down, it shrank back to its original size. I grabbed at the tattered rag as it flew past, wrestling it away from the wind. It was the only piece of her I had left. It was sodden, disintegrating under my touch, but I stuffed it into my pocket. A ridiculous reminder.

The destruction of the barrier left only a wasteland before me. Her sculpture had shrunk away from my alien creation. Lines of those rippling patterns had been cut off mid-flow, and dissolved into nothing on the sand. The remainder of her sculpture had turned back towards the sea, and was softly rippling, beckoning to her, calling her back to the land. And sure enough, with the shoreline exposed, I could see movement on the waves just a few metres ahead. In a few minutes, she would have emerged out of the gloom and found me standing there, nervously shifting from one foot to the other, like a guilty child, unable to meet her gaze.

So I ran instead.

Now, looking back, of all the painful repetitions of time and place and incident, this is the hardest to face. I ran away from her all the time. Even when I had learnt that this world was more than a simple dream landscape, that it could be a place of savage consequences, I still ran far from her. I ran away rather than towards her. I listened to the tug of my fear rather than waited and tested the strength of my love.

As I ran, the trees parted as I knew they would. Oh, I was agile by then, I could hop, skip and jump my way home in a matter of minutes. I whispered to the woods, as if they could carry my words back to her. 'I'm sorry, I'm sorry,' I said. 'My love, I love you, I'm so, so sorry.'

But the forest was still angry. When I made it through to the clearing, the path home was closed to me. Brambles rose up and branches reached down to catch them, pulling up a towering wall of thorns to keep me at bay. I took a strong stick and beat a passage through, still trying to keep a rhythm of dancing in my steps. I was fuelled by my desperation to get home, and by my savage hatred. I hated this forest, which coaxed me in only to attack me. And I hated whatever it was that drew her through it, leaving me abandoned and betrayed.

I reached the wall of the house, and could see the light of the window above me. Behind me, as yet, there was no sign of her emerging.

Cautiously, I lifted up one of the pebbles that was holding the ivy down.

That was a mistake.

A tendril sprang up and curled itself around my leg in a second. It made its way up my thigh, snaking inside my pocket and pulling out the scrap of her dress, then it withdrew and pulled that final piece of evidence away from me. I lunged for it, but in one fluid movement the plant reared up and flung the cloth into the sky. I watched as the sequins spiralled their way up into the wind, catching the light from our open window as they flew past and made their way back out towards the forest.

Thwarted, furious, I stamped down the ivy. I found some heavier rocks, just to be sure, and scampered up the side of the house.

When she returned, the ivy obediently drew itself up for her. She sat on the window-sill and sang for hours, but I would not let her draw me into sleep. Her song had changed again, and it sounded like a lovers' ballad, a song without words, but full of yearning. I would have found it beautiful, if I could have believed that she was singing to me. She climbed into bed just before dawn, the new light shining on her soft skin. Of course, all the wounds were gone. I expected nothing less. But although I should have been glad that she had recovered, and hopeful for the morning, the serenity of her smile and her quick healing served as bitter reminders of all the differences, and distances, that had grown between us.

# 19

The next morning brought yet another change of tactics. Although it was my day off, she woke me with loud music at the usual hour and was jumping on the bed, saying, 'Rise and shine, love, rise and shine,' as if our previous estrangement had never happened. When I did try to get up she was kneeling close above me, holding the sheets down all around, so that I could barely move, coaxing and caressing me, but always keeping the bedclothes between us, no matter how much I struggled.

She kissed me between every twist of the sheets, saying, 'Am I forgiven? Do you forgive me now?'

I tried to remain stern and detached, but resistance was useless. The force of her. We made love in the sunlight, but it felt as if we were still fighting. She would lean forward to smother me, then move away when it mattered, her hair stroking my skin, yet also a screen between us. I put my hands on her waist, but she would turn away from me so that I couldn't see her face. I was torn between my grief at these games – which she knew I hated – and my love of her wildness. I was dislocated and insecure again, and for the first time did not even feel able to trust this, our most private world.

We were interrupted by a knock on the door, and she leapt away from me in an instant, laughing at my frustration, telling me that patience was a virtue.

Of course it was the kids intruding. I couldn't maintain my hospitable pretence of the day before. I didn't want to have to speak to them, I didn't trust myself. I disentangled myself from the winding sheets and pulled them tight around me, and lay there drifting between sleep and waking. I could hear her laughter from next door. That wild laugh of hers that used to belong to me alone.

There was a gentle knocking coming from the wardrobe, that wardrobe full of secrets. The door inched its way open and there was Richard, peeping out at me. He grinned his familiar grin and whispered, 'Pssst! Listen!' gesturing towards the open bedroom door. 'Listen!' he said, winked at me and was gone.

I crept along the corridor – familiar, stealthy moves. I hovered outside the lounge, opened the door an inch to squint through.

She was lying across the sofa, with the kids at her feet.

Kate had a sketchbook on her lap and was scribbling away. A pretty little domestic scene. From her sofa perch she was holding forth with an energy and humour I had not seen for a while. She was telling them a story, including them in another intimate ritual. I stood very still behind the door, calmed my breathing and strained to hear.

In the beginning there was a wise king who lived in a castle in a land somewhere over the way beyond the hills. He had a young wife whom he loved very much. She was all beauty and elegance in the daytime, all grace and laughter in the night. They lived and loved together well. Soon the queen was to have a child, and the king was overjoyed. He was sure that with a little one for her to dote over and for him to teach all the wisdom of his years, their life would be complete.

He was a wise man, and he was right, but he was wrong. The night came when the queen was to give birth. But bad luck came for her that night. It was the time of the year when the moon grows thin, and the summer night was filled with darkness.

In the forest beyond the castle walls all the slithery slimy things, the black creatures and the boggarts of the night came crawling out of their holes and sniffed the air. The summer wind carried the sound of the queen's cries as her child pushed its way out. The air that came down from the tall castle was filled with the smell of her sweat and tears. Now these were old and clever creatures, and they knew what these things meant. So they stirred the waters of the dark ponds with their scaly hands, and called up a great curse from the depths, hissing and spitting into the sky, cackling with glee at the thought of what terrible things they might make.

Their curse grew out of the dark lake and flew at full speed across the forest. Like a screeching black thing, it came down and gathered above the roof of the castle. Now, the king was wise and saw it coming at them from beyond the walls. He ran round his castle, barking orders at the servants, saying, 'Stand firm and stand fast. Lock all the windows and the doors and let no one and nothing in until the morning.'

The servants knew that their king was wise and they did what he said. Ten men guarded every doorway. Brave servants pulled all the windows shut and wedged them closed with their swords and daggers.

Outside the black thing hovered and waited—

'What was it?' asked Jay, clearly spooked.

'A black thing from the forest. That's all you need to know.'

'But what did it look like?' asked Kate.

'Like nothing you've ever seen, I hope,' she said, with a sudden solemnity. And she didn't stop to give any more information . . .

Now, it was a muggy, sweltering night and the castle grew hotter and mustier with all those closed windows and doors, and the black thing wrapping itself around the rooftops. The queen was wailing and cursing her husband for his strange orders. She called for him from her high tower, but he was busy in the room below, giving his commands, checking every room for intruders, comforting his frightened servants. There was only the queen and her old midwife at the top of their castle.

As her child kicked inside her, the queen was gasping for air and she called out to the midwife, saying, 'Open the window just a tiny crack, or I will never breathe again and the child will die in my belly.'

Well, it was a dilemma, and what was the old woman to do?

She had her master's orders, but the queen was pale and breathless, looking like she was being eaten up by some great sickness.

So the old woman opened the window, just a tiny crack, not seeing what was waiting outside.

The black thing came rushing in and covered the queen's bed. It wrapped itself around her and squeezed tight, until there were no more screams. Then, as swiftly as it had come in, it rose up and returned to the forest.

The boggarts saw it come racing back to them and they cackled, clapping their scaly hands and shrieking with glee.

But although a terrible thing had happened that night, there was also a miracle and the king found he was both cursed and blessed. For when the black thing left the bed, and the king beat the door down to find out why the midwife was wailing so, there lying beside the broken body of his queen was a beautiful newborn baby girl, smiling calmly up at her father, not aware of the horror that had come with her birth.

So the king had his daughter to comfort him through his grieving, and she grew to have her father's wise and solemn eyes, her mother's fine features, slender limbs and light laughter.

When the boggarts heard of this they were more furious than ever. They bided their time until the girl was ten years old. Then, on the night of her birthday they set off across the forest to find out what they might see and do inside the castle walls.

Now, his daughter's birthday was hard for the king: every

year it was a day that began in laughter and ended in grieving. After his daughter had gone to bed, he would walk around the rooms of his lonely home and remember his dead queen.

The boggarts formed a circle outside the castle and listened through the walls to the sounds of his sobbing. Then with their great scaly hands, fingernails like knitting needles, they began to scrape away at the walls. They carried on late into the night and throughout the castle there was the terrible sound of steel scraping against stone, as if a thousand scythes were being sharpened.

More things came from the forest to help them, great winged dark things with little red eyes and beaks like razors, which nestled on the battlements and tapped at the slates on the roofs, trying to peck their way through.

As these things worked away they cackled and sang a song in time with their scraping and pecking. They cried out:

> 'Best build strong walls, tall and wide,
> Lest the boggarts come inside.
> They'll take the little one far from home,
> Leaving you nothing but sticks and stones.'

When the servants heard this noise outside they were driven mad with fear. Some tried to open the doors and get away from the terrible place, but the guards stood fast and slaughtered any that came near.

As the blood seeped from under the strong door, the creatures fought with each other to lap it up. They were pleased with their work.

The king ran from the madness, all the way up to the tall tower where his precious daughter was sleeping. She was sound asleep, wrapped up in her warm blankets and her dreams. The things with beaks that were pecking at the windows could not disturb her. The king stood there all night, his back to his daughter's bedroom door, watching for signs of anything breaking through. When the dawn came, he could hear the boggarts outside howling in frustration and they raced back to their dark pools, fleeing the light. As they ran he could still hear them singing:

'Best build strong walls, tall and wide,
Lest the boggarts come inside.
They'll take the little one far from home,
Leaving you nothing but sticks and stones.'

The little princess woke in the morning light from a long sleep, and she had never looked fairer, never sweeter or more innocent to her father than she did that morning. He held her in his arms and was happy because she was safe.

But the other people in the castle were not so lucky. Without their wise king to tell them what was right to do, they had panicked and fallen foul of the boggarts' terrible cries. The king and his daughter came down to a ruined castle scattered with corpses. Here was a man who had run himself through with his sword, so frightened was he by the howling outside. There was a servant who had been driven mad by the dark night, cut the throats of his family then hanged himself with his own wife's headscarf. As they stumbled through the rooms, opening windows to let in the light and fresh summer air, the king realised that he and his daughter were all alone.

And that wasn't the worst of it. The boggarts had been hard at work all night with their scraping and scratching and pecking, and the castle was a ruin of what it had been before. All of the queen's rich tapestries, which merchants had brought back to her from lands across the sea, were soiled with the blood of the household. All the fine wineglasses were shattered, remnants of the night's feasting scattered over the floor and mixed in with the blood and other remains. The king wouldn't let his daughter walk through it. He lifted her up on to his shoulders so that she would not cut her feet or stain her pretty clothes.

The sturdy doors had been shaken and splintered in the night by the creatures trying to make their way in. The strong bricks and mortar had been scraped away by their steely claws. The proud castle collapsed behind the king as he walked through it, carrying his daughter through the wreckage, out into the sunshine and the clean air that wasn't so filled with the smell of blood freshly spilt.

Now, I told you that the king was a wise man, and his wisdom remained with him after his servants, his fine clothes, his food, wine and water and his tall house had all been torn apart. He still remembered the boggarts' howling song:

> 'Best build strong walls, tall and wide,
> Lest the boggarts come inside.
> They'll carry the little one far from home,
> Leaving you nothing but sticks and stones.'

So he set to work rebuilding his castle. He took a strong axe and went out into the woods, chopped down trees and made one room safe and secure. It had no windows for the boggarts to peep in through, just firm stout logs driven into the ground. His daughter spent the first night there, safe from harm, while he stood watch.

To cut this long story a little shorter I shall leave you a few years to fill with your own tales of their time together. The king worked by day and stood guard at night until he had secured his home and fortress. Logs and thatched roofs replaced the crumbling bricks and mortar. His daughter learnt how to chew the pithy stalks that grew by the pools in the forest. Her father would go down and gather handfuls by day, and she would sit and chew them while he rebuilt their home. Then she would beat out the pith with a stone and spin it into long threads. Her father built her a loom and she would sit singing and weaving in the sunshine, making shirts for their backs, cloths for their tables and sheets for their beds.

So the years passed, and the time came for the princess's sixteenth birthday. It was a poor shadow of what it should have been. She should have had musicians and jugglers, a fine carnival in her honour. But the king had grown as cautious as he was wise. Although the things from the forest had left him alone since that bloody night, he had never forgotten their terrible song. It ran through his mind every night when he lay down in his lonely bed to sleep. Out of love for his daughter, who was growing more beautiful and graceful every day, and every day more like her lost mother, the king never stopped building his walls of wood and briars. No one would venture near that place now: travellers told legends of the mad king who lived there, a fierce man with a tortured soul who had killed all his family and servants in one night of bloody madness. No merchants stopped there with fine dresses and birthday gifts for the princess. The king's realm dwindled to the confines of his dark, echoing wooden castle.

The princess's bedroom was his finest piece of handiwork. Each tree had been set in place with his love and hard determination. On the walls of her room he had carved strange laughing fairy figures to keep her company at night, he etched roses and forget-me-nots on the smooth wood of her bedposts. In the corner of the room, where a window should have been, he placed an old mirror that had belonged to her mother, one of the only objects he had saved from the night when the boggarts tore down their walls. Where she should have had a fine view of her father's land, a wide window to throw open during those hot summer nights, she had only the tarnished mirror, only ever saw her own fair face reflected.

This had been all very well for her when she was a little girl and was happy running after her father, cooking his food and making the clothes that kept them warm through the cold winters. But as she grew older, the air in the castle seemed to grow colder around her, causing her to shiver in the daytime, almost smothering her to death at night. As the girl grew older, she need the sunlight to warm her pale skin, she needed to know the speech of other living things apart from her father. As she grew older, she began to pay more attention to her father's handiwork. She watched how he put the strong wood together, digging far down into the earth and setting it firm and tall, building walls that circled each other, running round the castle in rings.

Then by night, when her father was sleeping, she would go down to the darkest corner of the courtyard, the edge nearest to the creeping forest, and twig by twig, stick by stick, she pulled at the first wall.

The boggarts sent things flying up from the woods, things with broad black wings and big grey eyes to watch in the night-time, and they cackled with anticipation when they heard what had come to pass. They came creeping out of their holes and left little gifts by the walls for the princess. There was her mother's headscarf beyond the second wall. Beyond the sixth wall they left one of her mother's diamond necklaces. Beyond the ninth wall there was a pair of silver slippers.

Well, the princess didn't know what to make of this. All her little life her father had told her about the danger of the forest, the dark things that watched and waited there, but now it seemed to her that it was only her fair mother out there, leaving her pretty presents, calling her to come and play.

She began to look at her father in different ways.

She began to wonder about this strong, silent man, who spent his days always building walls, and every day had fewer words to say to her, gave shorter answers to her questions. She began to see him as a mean, sullen man, who had pushed her mother away beyond the boundaries of his kingdom, and spent the rest of his life building walls between them. She gathered her gifts to her chest, hid them under her bed so that he might never find them, and she carried on digging.

I couldn't stay hidden and listen to this. Every word hurt. I didn't want to know how it might end.

I forced the door open and stepped into the bright morning light.

There was a sudden silence, as if I had stepped into a world where I was not welcome.

Jay fixed me with that surly glare of his. 'For fuck's sake,' he said, 'we're in the middle of a story.'

'Oh, I know, I've been listening.' I sat down beside her and, with a false smile, said, 'So go on. I'm curious. So the princess was sixteen . . .'

She picked up the story despite my presence. And as she continued, her subtle voice wove the tale around me, despite my stubborn determination to resist . . .

So it was that on her sixteenth birthday the princess crept out at night as she always did, thinking her father was safely sound asleep. She pushed aside the ivy she had planted by the fences, to conceal the holes she had made, and began to wriggle her way through the barricades.

But the old king wasn't asleep. He was still walking his rounds of the castle, weeping for his lost wife, as was his sad solitary ritual. He heard the scurrying, scraping noise outside and ran out full of fear, thinking that the boggarts had come back for his daughter.

He was right and he was wrong.

The boggarts had come back, but they were waiting beyond the last wall. They formed a circle all around the firm structure he had built, waiting for the girl to push her way out. And as they waited they sang, not with shrieks and cries this time, but with their other voices – the soothing, hypnotic chants they always carry with them. The songs of old that make men go mad with love and longing, the songs they know to draw travellers down into their dark pools in the woods, songs as sweet as the night air and as dangerous as the black water.

The princess heard these sounds calling her through the night air, and thought it was the song of her own lost mother. She pushed forward all the faster, breaking through the last few walls.

When the king walked out into the dark night, he could hear, in the distance, the sound of the walls falling. He ran round the courtyard, calling his daughter's name, but she was too far away, and the boggarts' song too strong, for her to hear him and turn back.

But in the gleam of the moonlight, something caught his eye: there, by the first hole in the fence, was a little piece of rough cloth. In her haste, the princess had caught her nightdress on it as she had squeezed her way through.

Fighting back his tears, the king tried to follow his daughter. But, oh, the difference between a young girl and her old, weeping father. The holes she had made were far too small for him to squeeze through. He had to stop and pull at the walls to fight his way through, bringing down his own handiwork in a hailstorm of sticks and stones, which beat at his back.

As he got further away from the castle, and nearer to the forest, the sound of the boggarts' singing began to come at him through the night. Being a wise man, he ripped his shirt and stuffed the material into his ears so that he, too, wouldn't be caught by their tricks.

If he hadn't then, as he reached the last wall, he would have heard their singing change to shrieking and cackling. The princess came struggling out of the last hole in the wall, only to be greeted by swarms of the dark things that had waited for her all this long while. They rushed at her, their long scaly fingers grabbing at her pretty skin, pulling her hair, ripping her little nightdress. And they carried her up on their shoulders, out into the forest singing,

'You built strong walls tall and wide,
But the little one crawled outside.
Pity the king of sticks and stones,
Left in the forest to live alone.'

So when the king finally fought his way through his own walls, there was nothing left of his daughter to greet him, only marks in the earth where the boggarts had scampered away with her.

As the dawn broke, the king was still standing there, frozen to the spot. His house in ruins and his heart broken, he could not move another step. As the years passed and the seasons changed, the king grew roots that held him fast in the ground, his face unchanged, looking out to the forest. Long after the tall timbers that formed his house had rotted into the ground, moss and ivy came creeping over his skin, covering his face, finally stopping his breathing.

And even today, travellers who walk the forest at night

always look out for the tall tree that stands like a sentinel in the middle of the woods. If you pass the tree you must always bow and leave a gift, and the king will watch over you, making certain that you do not wander close to the dark pools where the boggarts took his wife and daughter.

'That's. Very. Cool,' said Jay, nodding sagely and passing yet another spliff up to her.

What the fuck did he know? I fought back my tears – I wasn't going to let them see me cry.

She kissed me briefly, falsely. I couldn't stand it.

Then Kate held up her sketchbook, showed us the drawings she'd been making: pictures of black creatures and broken homes. I intercepted the sketchbook as Kate passed it over. Before those fairytale pictures ran page upon page of private images: her and the three kids, up on the rooftop. An outline sketch of Richard, high among the treetops. A rough charcoal drawing of Phil, lying back on the sofa, laughing out of the page at me. I was nowhere among them. It was too much. In a swift, angry movement, I pulled the pages out of Kate's book and ripped them apart. The sharp, tearing noise cut their conversation dead.

'Fuck off out of it,' I said, borrowing words from James. 'You're not welcome.'

Kate was crying quietly as Tom and Jay collected their things. She hugged Kate, and led all three of them downstairs whilst I ran away from them, up to the rooftop. She could read me well enough to know that this was something she shouldn't challenge. I gathered all the pieces of Kate's pictures and threw the scraps over the railings. The wind caught them and scattered them over the common, like dirty bits of confetti.

I would do exactly the same thing now if strangers appeared on my doorstep masquerading as friends. No matter how far they had travelled to find me here, I would turn them away if they were not welcome. That was one of the things I have learnt. Whoever you choose to let in through your door, choose carefully and choose well.

When I went back downstairs she was making as if to follow them out, but I pulled her back, holding her against the wall for a moment, uncomfortably close. Still I wanted her.

She was furious and fought back, slapping my face.

We sprang apart, the whole distance of the living room suddenly between us. I kept my back to the door, just in case. 'Love,' I said, 'what's going on? This isn't like us.'

She crumbled, as if strings had been cut inside her. The tears came, and instantly she was a different girl again, very small and stranded at the far end of the room. Suddenly she did need me and I could walk across to hold her. 'I hate this,' she said, as she pressed her fists half-heartedly against my chest.

'Oh, me too,' I said. 'I really hate this.' I told her to hit me if it made her feel better, that was fine, I could absorb any shocks she wanted to give me, but she had to let me in.

She said I had to learn to let other people in also. 'Spread yourself around a little,' she said, spitting through her tears. 'Learn how to be nice to people other than me.'

'But not them,' I replied, with an insistent passion. 'But really not them. I just can't stand it.'

'If you'd just let me speak,' she said, 'then I could have told you they were going anyway. There was no need.'

It seemed I had underestimated those kids. They had turned their two-dimensional atlas plan into a real journey, packed their bags and made plans to travel the whole world in two months. They had only come to say goodbye.

'They brought me presents,' she said. 'Look, one from each!'

There were three necklaces twisted tight around her neck, but after one look at the workmanship I knew immediately that they weren't from the kids.

The first was made of a supple green bracken, knotted together and plaited into sections, slippery to touch. The second was a single polished stone hanging from a piece of leather. A heavy black rock. It made my skin crawl when I touched it. I was surprised it didn't burn me. The third confirmed my fears: tiny shells were threaded together on to a long loop of cord. Their silvery surface caught the light. They were beautiful, but every shell was cut to a sharp point, vicious, serrated edges. It was brutally clear to me what these things were: she had brought back treasure from the beach.

'Very nice,' I said with another false smile.

'They didn't get you anything because they knew you wouldn't accept it. So don't sulk. You bring these things on yourself.'

Well, I knew she was lying, but what could I say?

She had hidden all our shared possessions, and now she was replacing them with mementoes of an entirely different place, riddled with obscure meanings. And, in my heart of hearts, I knew that this was a clear shift of loyalties. She said that things didn't matter, it was only people who mattered, but that was just another lie. It was a convenient excuse so that I didn't realise what she was really doing. She was calling that dark outside world into our house, she was wearing reminders to challenge me, pushing me out to the very edges of even our everyday life, keeping me at a distance with things I couldn't touch.

But she was too clever for me: she had given me an explanation that shamed me, and I had no way of arguing without seeming petulant and possessed. There was nothing to be said. The day off, which should have been a gift, was proving to be a very bad day indeed. I looked to an old game of ours for security, a tried and tested method for wiping the slate clean. Now that even the present was insecure the only safe space left was a retreat into the past.

'Can we start the day again?' I whispered, holding her close. 'Please, love, let's start again.'

Bless her, she agreed. I went out to get our breakfast and came back to find her lying across the bed, feigning sleep. I tickled her till she woke. We ate croissants in bed and rubbed the crumbs into the sheets. We used old terms of affection for each other and pretended we had only just met, talking in character.

'What will you do when you finish your degree?' she asked me. 'How can your mathematics save the world?'

I told her how I would calculate the best way for a man to spend his twenty-four-hour day, turning minimum effort into maximum pleasure. I would use my mathematics to break the most complex banking codes: armed with my laptop we could conduct a heist from the privacy of our bedroom and then the world would be our oyster. But in the meantime, I had to move to London to execute the first part of the master plan. Would she do me the honour of joining me?

'Let me take you to London,' I said. 'Come and live with me properly . . . and be my love?'

This time she didn't reply.

We dozed for a while and woke in slightly better moods. It was late afternoon, and we went out on to the common and walked ourselves awake. She let me hold her hand. I was reluctant to break this fragile peace and determined not to return to our argument of the previous night. But there was something else I had to ask . . .

'I wasn't supposed to hear that story, was I?'

'Oh, it's just a story,' she replied, laughing.

Her grandmother had told it to her when she was a child. She must have been very young, because she could remember how tall the garden fence seemed when she pulled herself up over it and ran out into the forest to play. The forest, of course, just at the bottom of her parents' sumptuous lawn. The whole village had been up in arms, searching the woods for her. But she never heard them, she was too busy looking for fairies. When she came back at nightfall she was put across her father's knee and soundly spanked. Then her grandmother smuggled her dinner upstairs and told her the cautionary tale. 'It's a warning for travellers and over-curious children,' she said. 'They need to be told what's out there.'

'So you're not tempted to follow them?'

I couldn't look at her but she just laughed at me again and

said, not without conviction, 'Why would I want to be anywhere else apart from here, with you?'

Round the corner we came across one of the weeping willow trees, still buckled and broken by the force of the storm.

'Are you brave?' she said to me. 'Do you dare?' she whispered, with a wicked laugh, as she pulled me behind the curtain of leaves and wrapped herself around me.

And I did dare, but I took little pleasure in these stolen favours. I dared to make love to her hidden in the tree only because I didn't dare not to, because I was prepared to use any tactic necessary to keep her grounded in this world with me.

We hid there for hours and watched the sunset gather. But, yet again, the darkening common made me feel unsafe. 'We should make it out before night-time,' I said, 'or we might never make it out at all.' I took her hand again, and she let me lead her home. Once inside she demanded that we should get absolutely hammered; she said it had been too long since we had celebrated, just the two of us.

I tried to explain my new resolution to stay sober but she laughed in my face and told me that resistance was useless. Every time I drained my glass, she was by my side, filling it again, saying, 'It's your day off, my good man. Relax, forget your worries, drown your sorrows.' Against my will she made me smoke spliff after spliff with her, trying to soothe away my rough edges, saying, 'Remember this? You used to love this. Don't be scared.' By the end of the night she had to help me to bed, steering me through the living room as I swayed into the coffee table, laughing at me, putting her fingers on my lips to stop my slurring words.

With the naïveté and need of a child I was repeating and repeating: 'I love you. My love, I love you. Are you a princess?'

She helped me undress, smoothed the bedcovers down around me, gave me water to drink and stroked my forehead, saying, 'Be quiet, you're wasted, sleep now.'

# 20

She must have kicked the glass of water as she slipped out of bed. The sound of it shattering woke me. I felt nauseous and I couldn't move. Now the whole day seemed to have been a minutely planned exercise in deception and distance, beginning with aggression and a cautionary tale to warn me, ending with nostalgia and a false security. My blood was thick with cannabis and alcohol. A nasty mixture. Cannabis always opens up holes in my thread of reasoning, huge, gaping pitfalls in the middle of my sentence structure. I get swallowed up by my own convoluted arguments. Grand statements circle unsaid, desperate for the right noun. And alcohol makes me lose my footing, both physically and mentally. The combination afflicts me with the efficiency of a computer virus. I heard her moving around the room, but couldn't open my eyes. Caught between sleep and waking, all I could see were those columns of falling numbers. Falling all the more rapidly to the rhythm of the ivy beating against the wall.

My anger forced me awake and pushed me out of bed. I cursed her as I dressed, shouting loudly enough to wake the neighbours, if only we had any. If she was really going, I wouldn't allow her to leave like this, with me drunken and unaware, abandoned at the top of our tall house while she swam away across the ocean. After her story, which she must have known would speak to me too, it felt like I was being given an ultimatum. She was chasing her freedom, with no thought of the danger. She was running away, far from home, and I had to take action. I had to bring her back, or she might be led astray and lost for ever. As I slid down the ivy and the land came rushing up to greet me, something in me knew that this was the last time, a final test.

Everything in the night played with my perceptions. From the far side of the lawn, the forest was a solid green wall, trees packed together so closely that there was no obvious entrance point. But as I ran nearer, the wall shifted, and individual branches beckoned and pointed, offering me openings, then twisting back on themselves before I could run through. I mimicked her dancing steps, and the trees began to shift, bowing before me and parting to reveal a multitude of pathways inside. *Come dance with me, dance*, the forest whispered, as I made my way forward. *Dance with me, make things grow*.

That night the forest held all the possible seasons within its arms, like a reminder of the time we'd had together, all the varied months we spun out between us. First came the spring-time wood, which now had no edges, just a sea of moon-dappled blossoms, chiming away into the night. Then at the clearing I was greeted by a sad, cold wind, and fading leaves were scattering down the sky, as if a sudden autumn had come. But these falling leaves were not that beautiful burnished golden brown: when I tried to catch them they were grey and brittle and fell through my fingers like dust. When I took the left-hand path the trees clustered closely on both sides, as if the forest knew this was my last visitation, and was trying to keep me. The canopy of leaves tented in the warm air. It was like a monsoon summer in there. I struggled to breathe as I forced my way further and further inwards.

When eventually I emerged on the other side, the green hill was a welcome resting point. I sat down for a second to catch my breath, and the sky above was full of stars, shifting around each other in a whirlpool dance. It was too beautiful and frightening to watch for long: it felt like the heavens themselves were reaching down to claim me. I ran down the shingled path and jumped on to the shifting sand. The desert was white with unnatural light, the ash-ridden world looked like a carpet of fresh-fallen snow. It made me wistful for the night we had made angels, when the only unknown land was the darkening common, and that, in itself, had been enough for us both.

I had an unsettling moon to thank for the pallor cast upon the desert. Against all natural laws it was full and bright, hanging just over the horizon. It drenched the whole land in an eerie light, which warped the perspective of the plane so it was hard to see this world in three dimensions. Everything was flat and faded. The land I had to navigate seemed as artificial as a painted backdrop, an old stage print hung down from the heavens. But I forced myself to believe in it, to give that place a depth and distance. There, hanging over me, was the man in the moon, now looking pale and sorrowful rather than surprised. I wondered at this strange world where even the moon was forced to fatten according to her whims.

As was to be expected, the desert was no longer the desert I knew. Without my barrier to keep them at bay, those curling patterns of hers had made their way across the sands, right up to the edge of the forest. The moonlight was caught in the curves and curls, which re-formed and settled themselves again, beckoning me forward, as subtle and shifting as the uncertain stars. I took courage and I danced, and those mischievous patterns played with my footprints. They raced back behind me, and bedecked the trail I had left with shells and jewelled pebbles. I laughed to see it: it was as if the land was bestowing gifts upon me, showing me the kind of sculpture I should have made to call her home. I kept on turning to look at my transformed steps, and did not pay enough attention to the lie of the land ahead.

I caught up with her too quickly. Suddenly, only a couple of metres ahead of me, I could see her silhouette. I skidded to a stop and made myself completely still and silent. She was standing in the middle of the desert, arms stretched wide as if to pull the whole sky to her. She seemed as proud and removed and unrecognisable as she was that night she screamed at the storm from our rooftop. I held my breath, frightened to make any sound that might make her turn round. But I was not safe – I had broken the dance and the land was quick to respond. The patterns reared up and threw sand in my face. I fell down in a fit of coughing.

She turned sharply, and in quick defence I ducked down,

hoping to blend quietly into the night, as still as stone.

'Intruder!' she shouted into the night. 'Intruder! Show yourself.'

She stood with her hand on her hip, waiting. She looked wild and defensive, and I was terrified. I slid on to my belly, as if to bury myself alive in the sand rather than have her see me.

'Coward!' she shouted. 'Come no further!'

She ran away into the darkness. I should have listened. But I had still learnt nothing. Too frightened to step forward and claim her but still needing to watch, I went on.

She was wise and she was waiting. She was determined not to be followed. So a few metres on she stopped again. This time she didn't even turn. She just reached up and put her hands behind her neck and undid one of her necklaces.

A lump of stone dropped in the desert.

Its impact threw up the sand in front and behind. She walked calmly ahead. The earth moved around me as the stone buried itself deeper. Sand flew up and stung my eyes – a sudden kaleidoscope explosion of stars filling my vision. When I could open my eyes, there was no light to guide me: all the quicksilver patterns had shrunk away and something had blotted out the moon.

A dark shadow stretched across the sand towards me, and the sky was black above, and I was afraid.

A mountain had grown where the pebble had fallen.

A great impassable black thing grew out of the desert. It had smooth sides, was icy cold to the touch and as tall as the sky itself. It seemed to swallow up rather than reflect any of the moonlight that hit it. There was no way over it so I had to try to find a way round. She had left me no clues, no help at all – I was an intruder, after all. All I had for guidance was her footprints, which led straight into the slab.

The stone was so cold it hurt my hands, but it was the only thing I had. I felt my way round, with shaky footsteps, hugging it to me, always reaching blindly ahead. My patience was rewarded when I felt the rock curve under my touch. I followed it round, to the other side, confident that when I got out of the shadows I would be able to see my way ahead, and dance through the desert, down to the ocean. I thought that I had made it when I saw a line of prints perpendicular to mine cross my path. But the rustling of the trees behind made my heart sink. I had crept round to meet my own footsteps. The stone led me back to where I had come from. The trees were whispering at my back, *Go home, home, intruder, go home*. But my house was not a home without her in it.

I was furious, not wanting to believe I could be defeated so easily. I flailed out with my fists and kicked at the rock. 'Bastard necklace!' I shouted into the night.

I stood in the footprints she had left behind, my feet firmly planted in front of the immovable mountain. 'Bastard pebbly piece of shite!' I yelled, and the rock muffled my cries.

The rock muffled my cries, but it shuddered when I finished, as if it was alive and as if my words had wounded it. I waited for another movement, but nothing happened. What words had I said?

Feeling foolish, I called, 'Bastard?' into the wind. My voice was so feeble that the sound barely carried and of course nothing changed.

'Pebbly piece . . .'

My courage failed me and I couldn't even finish my sentence. I felt small and ridiculous in the dark shadow of the rock. But it moved. It shuddered again, shrank into itself, like a frightened animal. Another few footprints were revealed in the sand in front of me where the stone had shifted. I stepped forward and spoke a little more boldly. 'Pebble. Piece of stone. Small rock.'

It moved again, dwindling with every word, giving me back the line of her footsteps. I became stronger, naming it for what it was. 'Tiny pebble from the shore. Necklace.'

And there it was, lying small and unassuming on the sand where she had dropped it. Just a tiny pebble that would have fitted into the palm of my hand.

Suddenly everything was clear to me. I could use words well, if I used them simply. I laughed as I thought how my practical words could shape this place, the enchantments not as complex as I might have thought. All I had to do was stand sure and fast and face my fears, naming things for what they really were. (In fact it was the nagging memory of that night that made me start all this decoding. It was the one night that always remained with me, even in the early days, when I was unsure what was the truth and what was the distortion of grief. But I was always sure of this one. I stood on her beach and I made the landscape change around me with my words. I called the mountain a pebble and so it was. When I began writing this it was out of the same desire. Name things and they stay fixed. Find the right words and stop the landscapes shifting.)

But even when reduced back to a simple stone, that black rock frightened me and I would not touch it. I turned my back to it and carried on following the trail she had left, snaking off into the night.

The moonlight showed her on the far horizon. She looked as if she was sleepwalking, so slow and lazy, but still graceful in her dance. I tried to keep my distance, but she was hypnotic, drawing me closer out of the darkness despite myself. I couldn't take my eyes off her.

Perhaps she thought the sandstorm gathering at my heels was the sound of an encroaching intruder but, anyhow, she wasn't taking any chances. Again, that arch of her back as she lifted up her arms and undid the clasp of the second necklace and ran further down towards the sea.

It was the necklace of shells this time. They fell off the cord and tumbled down into the sand where they stuck fast. And then they grew, razor-sharp, slicing through the black night: a wall of monstrous shells rose out of the desert, a dragon's-teeth barrier. They formed a line that stretched out in both directions as far as I could see, and was swallowed by the night. I placed my footsteps in hers and waited for the land to settle. The shells were reflecting too much light. The heavy moon seemed to be sunken in every surface, as if she had pulled all the stars out of the sky and scattered them on the sand to keep me at bay. Moving closer, I saw the cause. The shells had changed when they hit the sand: they had a silver sheen now. Her barrier flashed like a challenge, a sparkling line of light running for ever across the dark land.

She had been very clever.

The shells were as smooth as mirrors, and on every surface there was a warped reflection of myself, crude and cruel. On one I had a bulbous nose, which dominated my face, my eyes squinting and pushed up into my forehead. On another my mouth was a wide, gaping gash that cut my oval face in two – that face grinned back at me, and winked, as if in recognition. And however I inched around that barrier, those things watched me, their many eyes following my every move. The worst was the one that lodged in the centre of the sculpture. That domed shell held a pale face with two tiny dark eyes peering out of the centre, no mouth or nose at all, just a deformed white mask, too ugly and cruel. But it was difficult to look away from those fractured faces, all of which had a little of myself in them. I tried to open my mouth to speak, but the reflections twisted, every movement exaggerated a thousand times, every gesture crooked and mean.

Like a child, I put my hands over my eyes to keep out the fear and stood firm and fast in her footprints. Not daring to look, I shouted out into the night, 'Seashells! Only seashells!'

Sure enough, the trick worked. The mirrored surfaces began to tarnish.

'Tiny shells. Necklace of fragments.'

The barrier fell forward, the surfaces clouded over, and every version of myself was quickly corroded. The shells smashed together, and in that open, echoing land it sounded as if the sky was falling. I put my hands over my ears to shut out the cacophony, and the chaos subsided, leaving behind the simple necklace, shrunken back into the sand and easy to step over again. I ran quickly beyond it. I ran on and on through the darkness, wanting to put as much distance as possible between me and the memory of those warped reflections. She had made me look grotesque, fragmented into a line of deformed creatures that crouched and waited in the sand. I didn't like it at all.

I hadn't realised how near I was to the beach – but how could I have when the land never lay in the same place twice? Maybe it was the momentum of my fears, but it felt as if the sand was warping beneath my feet still. It reared up, and pushed me into the shallows. I crashed into the icy water and salt seeped into old wounds. Waves pushed themselves back at me and I was suddenly reduced to a child again, overwhelmed by the vast sea. There was nothing for me to cling to, no edges to be seen, but again, there was the shape of her ahead, just on the border before the sky swallowed up the ocean.

The water was lapping at the small of her back, her hair was sodden and ran in a straight line down between her shoulder-blades, like a dark scar. I could see that she was beginning to turn round. From this distance, in this light, I knew she would not recognise me. She would see just the vague shape of an unknown stranger, lurking in the shallows. I was terrified as to what she might unleash against me. Desperate, fighting all my fears of past and present, I ducked down under the waves. I tried to open my eyes to see if I could detect her movement under water, but the salt stung my eyes. I had no choice but to crouch there, blind, pressure roaring in my ears. The weight of the ocean threatened to press the life out of me. It felt as if my very body was disintegrating, being pushed further and further down into the sea bed.

I stayed still as long as I could, but my lungs ached for air and I had to push my way up to the surface. She was nowhere to be seen. She had dropped the third necklace into the water and swum on. It hadn't been bracken at all: it was a strange sea plant that grew up to meet the sky and burrowed roots down to the ocean floor to hold it secure. The green thing came racing along the surface to meet me, and as it gathered speed it grew, forming a net across the waves. Before I could utter the words, it caught me. Tendrils from below ensnared my ankles, ensnaring me. Vicious green sapling shoots from above beat at my back and forced me under.

I was stuck fast, with one foot on the land, and one in the water.

'Seaweed!' I shouted, in desperation, the cold spray lashing at my face as the waves came after me. It made no difference. Without her footprints to hold me in place, I had no hope. I couldn't even finish the word. I was forced face down into the shallows.

I felt the icy cold come rushing into my lungs. I couldn't see and I couldn't breathe. Sand rained down on top of me. The sea and shore were working together. I thought I would be buried or drowned.

I tried to fight to the surface, but there was an ever-growing expanse of water above me. I kicked and flailed, and the bubbles of my last breath were racing above my head, seaweed was coming at me from all sides, and I was held timeless in a cold blue world, beneath the ocean. Bright colours danced through the water, and a clear column of light came racing towards me. I pushed and kicked one last time, and broke through the surface of the sea. But I was still unsafe. The black, starless sky was crouching on top of the water. That blackness was something more than the night, something heavier than the summer sky, and was pushing me back down. I tried to turn, but I was stuck fast. Now the sea was rising up into walls of waves that towered over and above me and flung themselves out on to the shore. The salt water was caught by her patterns. The sculptures were flooded: the concentric circles shifted themselves round again and became irrigation channels, creating a bottomless ocean ahead of me as well as behind.

I knew that I was lost.

Perhaps it is true that your whole life flashes before you when you are about to die. Certainly when the plant held my head above water just one last time, giving me a final glimpse of the shifting land before it swallowed me, I had a few seconds of clarity. Images not of my life but of her filled my mind, stronger and clearer than the twisting landscape. My life with her, that was what I saw.

The first time I set eyes on her, when I was huddled in a dark corner of a bar, and she strode over and asked me for a light. When I said that I didn't smoke she said that it was only an excuse, really she wanted me to buy her a drink. Her hand touching mine half-way through the evening and my awareness that something was beginning.

Her first bold intrusions into my life, when I took her to my grey little room with peeling wallpaper and bad heating. She didn't mind. She came for one night but stayed for the weekend and then nothing could go wrong.

Walking across the common to the pub with her, hand in hand, laughing at our new beginning. No one could come near us, we wore our joy in each other like a bright banner wrapped around our shoulders, proclaiming it to the world.

Her among the flowers, our house in springtime, dancing, always dancing, dancing at the boys' party, dancing across the lawn on her way back from the forest and all the things that followed.

All of this flashed before me and made my heart ache for her and, in desperation, I called her name into the night before the plant pulled me under for good.

I called her name and suddenly everything was quiet.

The sea lay still. The water retreated silently up the static lines and the shore revealed itself again. The sand fell down and lay there, motionless. The twisting green thing shrank back to a piece of seaweed, caught up around my ankles, easy to kick free from and to crawl to safety.

I fell down on to the beach, and sucked air into my lungs until I could breathe again, rubbed the salt out of my eyes so I could see. Still the black sky hovered above, and I was afraid. All the stars had disappeared, and it looked like the moon itself was being forced down into the ocean. I was in the eye of the storm. Nothing was safe. As soon as I could muster the strength to move, I crawled up the slope of the beach, still fearful of the water. How stupid I had been to think she needed me to rescue her when all this time her name was a word that could charm the elements. Of course there was nothing here to harm her. The landscape unfurled itself to please her, was full of gems for her to play with, gathered around her to keep her safe. I was only going to damage myself by trying to break through.

It was her place, not mine.

And it showed me, clearly and coldly, exactly what I was: an intruder and a coward.

I didn't even want to wait for her. I knew that if I stopped moving the shock would begin to take hold and she would find me curled up in some corner of the forest, sobbing and paralysed, too frightened to move. I couldn't bear for her to see me like that, weak and wounded, reduced to a shadow of the man she had loved.

Or, worse still, I feared that if I lost the dance again, even for one moment, then the forest, acting under her instruction, would catch me. The beckoning branches would sweep down and, working with the swift-tangling briars, they would bind me to the trunk of a tall tree, and ivy and wild flowers would wrap themselves all round my face so that I could not speak and hardly breathe. And I would stand there, caged, and watch, helpless, as she danced past me, following a safe path of moonlight home. And that would be the final irony – she would be the one who woke to find an empty bed, and I would be lost for ever in the forest, never to be found.

I just wanted to get home, to four solid walls. I pulled myself up off the beach and limped my way back into the desert.

I barely had the energy to dance. My clothes were soggy and saturated, weighing me down. I set myself goals. Past the three necklaces and I'd be half-way home. Then up to the clearing and it was only a matter of minutes. Across the lawn, then pulling myself in through the window I fell down on the floor in a shower of sand and sea water.

It must have been the shock. Once safely inside I found it hard to move. I huddled against the wall, by the window, the ivy pressing into my back. I wanted to stay and watch for her – there was nothing I needed to see more than her emerging from the thick of the trees, but my fingers and feet were numb with the cold. I knew I had to get warm.

I ran a bath and lay in it with all my clothes on. The sand and salt and bits of seaweed formed a dirty ring on the white porcelain and the water turned green around me. I lay there until I could feel the warmth come back to my limbs. Then I stripped off my clothes and had a shower. The smell of the sea rose up off me and I was sick. I scrubbed until my skin was raw and bloody. I put my sodden, stained clothes in a bin-bag and hid them under the kitchen sink.

When I made my way back to the bedroom she was already there, curled up on one side, sheets pulled down, sound asleep, or faking it well. All the puddles of water and sand I had left on the window-ledge were gone. There was no evidence at all, only the ivy, gleaming in the moonlight.

I was surprised by my reaction to her reappearance. Again, various voices conflicted within me. There was the old me, the naïve self who loved her always, no matter what she said or did, and was only thankful for her return. That part of me held nothing but joy, and told me that this was yet another new beginning, a second chance. She had come back, and that in itself was enough. She might love that wild land, but she loved me more.

But there were many other voices, some angry and shouting, demanding to know who the hell she thought she was, this selfish girl who thought she could slip between worlds with ease and always be welcomed home.

There was a very quiet voice that asked me what did I really know about her? Who was this girl who could charm another world into being just outside our window? Did I know her at all, or was she a changeling child who had come along one night and replaced the girl I loved?

Still other voices were afraid, wondering whether she had really meant to harm me out there, wondering whether, even now, she was safe to touch.

One thing was sure: something in me had been broken by that night. I could no longer see our love clearly. Every time I looked at her I was assaulted by this cacophony of voices from within, so loud and so powerful it felt like they were coming from outside. A debating chamber of rabble-rousers inside my mind, shifting position, telling me that she did and did not love me, how safe we might or might not be.

Exhausted by all these dramas, I tumbled into bed beside her. I moved her hair from the nape of her neck, thinking to curl up secure against her back. But she was wearing the three necklaces, reclaimed from the seashore. I thought it best not to touch and turned over, huddling a safe distance away from her in my little corner. It felt as if the black clouds had followed her in through the window that night and were hovering over the bed. I wanted to sleep, but couldn't risk it. I just propped myself up on pillows and waited for the hours to pass. When I saw the light come creeping in through the windows and heard people in the street below I finally closed my eyes, safe in the knowledge that someone would see her and stop her if she went.

# 21

The birdsong woke me a few hours later, and I turned round to touch her, but yet again, she wasn't there. No, instead she had left our bed, curled up on the window-ledge and was sleeping soundly among the ivy. The morning light was reflected all around her, bathing her skin in chameleon green. It broke my heart. Nothing had made any difference, none of the compromises and confidences of the day before. I had wanted a new start but that defiant gesture wiped away the tenderness of our history together. She must have waited until she was very sure that I was sound asleep, then gone back to the window. Only a few feet separated us, but I could no more reach through the air between us than I could have pushed my way through the black rock. She was wedded to a different world from mine.

I turned my face to the wall and cried myself to sleep, only to be woken yet again by the sound of something shattering and then her laughter, coming from up above. It sounded as if the sky was falling down in a hailstorm of pottery and glass. I ran up to the roof with a heavy heart.

It was a crisp, bright morning and she should have looked beautiful in that light. She was wearing an old shirt of mine buttoned carelessly together, gaping over her jeans. Her hair was pulled back from her face with an elastic band, all knotted and matted with clay and dust. She was surrounded by all the things she had removed from the flat that previous night, many of them already smashed to pieces. Her reckless side was out in full force, indiscriminate in its eradicating passion. The beautiful picture she had given me had been stamped on and shattered, a cracked cobweb of glass obscuring the tall tree. She was laughing as she danced across the terrace, pulling out old records and flinging them like frisbees from the roof, throwing night-lights to the wall. True dervish dancing. Our patio was now a graveyard of all our missing things.

She wouldn't stop. I called out to her but I don't think she could hear me above the sound of all that shattering. I strode over to her and grabbed her by the arm, terrified that she was going to hurt herself. She turned around and grinned a grin I had never seen before. She looked wily and strange. 'You never thought to look next door, did you, silly boy?' she said, rattling the boys' spare keys in her hand. She handed me one of our glasses, goading me on, saying, 'A quick flick of the wrist, that's all it takes: show me what you're made of.'

I couldn't do it. I wasn't going to collude with her in destroying everything we had. I wasn't going to make it quite that easy.

'Come on,' she said, one arm around my waist, whispering in my ear. 'Come on, trust me.'

I couldn't do it.

'Come on,' she said, impatient. 'It's tradition. Smash up the old ghosts.'

It was a parody of that night with the boys, when we had drunk toasts to our bright future and hurled the glasses into the fireplace. It felt like she was even asking me to break up memories now, turning old rituals into acts of cruelty.

'Come on,' she said, echoing Richard's intonation. 'Come on, it's a celebration.'

When she nestled up to me, all I could smell was the overpowering stench of the sea on her skin, mixed up now with the clay and wreckage from our home. I couldn't stand it. I clenched my fist too tightly and the glass shattered in my hand. She laughed at me again, but she took me downstairs, and washed me clean. More role reversals.

Then she took me through into the living room. There was a pile of cardboard boxes for my inspection. 'What's all this?' I asked, not able to look at her. 'Are these my things?'

It looked like this was the final part of her destructive mission: she had packed up all my possessions and it was time for me to go.

The whole room swam and tilted. The floorboards started to move apart under my feet, straining and splintering, about to reveal the huge chasm waiting for me, teeming with all my worst fears.

'No, they're mine,' she said. 'But I wanted to give them to you.'

'I don't understand.'

'The seasons are changing, and we must change with them.'

'I don't understand.'

'Love, a house is not a home if you don't change it with the seasons.'

'So you don't want me to leave?'

'Don't be so stupid,' she said, laughing at my fears and kissing me. 'Go to work,' she said. 'I'll make it nice for you when you come home. It'll be just like the old days.'

I wasn't completely convinced. I had a slow breakfast, but she wouldn't unpack a thing while I was watching.

'Trust me,' she said. 'Let me surprise you.'

Well, at least she was rebuilding things, and this, at last, was something about her that I recognised. Something I had almost forgotten.

Of course I was late into work again, but it seemed I was still in favour. James was teasing me with his wunderkind references.

Simon was more snipy, though, maybe threatened by my new saviour status. 'Don't push it,' he said, as James and I frittered away the day, playing computer games and talking shite.

Simon's terse comments upset me more than he could have realised: 'You're not irreplaceable, you know,' he said.

I phoned her every hour, just to check. Every hour she told me that she loved me and I should hurry home.

I picked up a lavish bouquet of flowers on the way back, my contribution to our new home. I came back to transformed rooms, a den of treasure, echoes of the boys' flat in her clever designs. She had set ornate oil lamps burning in the corners of the living room. The softer light changed the shape of the room, gave it curves and dark corners. All the photographs had been replaced and I was treated to views of her home village in winter when the snow covered the land, the nearest we could come to a change of scenery.

'It's a room we will never need to leave,' she said.

A warm blue rug spilled across the floorboards and faded drapes hung on the walls, tenting us in.

She said that the flowers were perfect, beautiful and really, I was too kind. She placed just the right arrangements in her elegant vases. 'Don't you just love it?' she said, laughing up at me like she used to.

And I did. I loved this soft, warm room with its rich colours and dappled light. Every part of me wanted to believe it would last. I ignored the whisperings at the back of my mind, as insidious as the wind in the trees, warning me over and over again: an illusion, a box of tricks, all an illusion.

'I thought we needed a new start, love,' she whispered in my ear. 'I thought it was time for a change.'

She took my hand and said she wanted to take me up to the roof one last time this year: she didn't want me to remember it as I had seen it this morning.

The patio was scrubbed clean and the battered Astroturf rolled up into one corner, giving us much more space. She had placed a row of night-lights by the railings. They cast light on the sorry remains of our fence. The paint had blistered in the sun of the long summer, and the bits of mirror had fallen off, leaving dirty patches. 'I couldn't bear to paint over it,' she said. 'I thought it might be better to let it fade.'

Our steps looked ridiculous next to it – firm and unweathered, cemented down to stay. As if anything could stay that fixed.

'It's the sea by night, you know,' she said.

I laughed at her. 'No, it isn't. It's exactly what Richard said it was. Minimalist landscape of kitsch.'

'No. It's the sea by night. I made it to remind me.'

'To remind you of what?' I asked. 'Is this going to be yet another cautionary tale?'

'Maybe.'

So then came the story of the place she had tried to paint. Of course, a story from her youth.


'You remember my summer photographs?' she said. 'Well, it was when I was about that age. In my seventeenth summer the good weather lasted for months on end. My parents prayed for rain to save their garden, but the rain never came. I prayed for the heat to last and for the nights to be clear, and they were. Every evening was spent by the sea with friends from the village. There were eight of us and we didn't need to know any others. We were a faithful gang and the rest of the world didn't matter.'

'We found a secret part of the beach that no one else knew. The sea stretched up to meet the sky. We would be sure to get there for the sunset, our first hour spent in silence as we watched the colours moving over the horizon, bleeding into the water. It was almost too beautiful. Then the moon came and watched over us, a large, yellow, brooding summer moon. But I loved it best when it was like that,' she said, pointing to the pathetic piece of board. 'When everything was clear and the stars shone like fairylights in the sky.'

'You could only get down there through a thick, thick forest,' she said. 'Tall trees and winding paths to lead you astray. I always thought that no one else in the world knew it was there and that was why it was all deserted. But one night when we were all sitting there drinking and chatting someone said, "It feels like tonight might be the night."

' "What night?"

' "Oh, this place is enchanted, did you not know?"

' "One night a year, and no one knows when, a figure comes out of the sea. The women say it is a beautiful man who rises out of the water like a god but the men say, 'No, not at all, it is a gentle mermaid who swims through the waves and sings sweet songs from the edge of the ocean. It has to be a mermaid,' the men argue. 'Only women can sing enchantments sweet enough to make all kinds of folk walk out into the water."

'So let us say that it is a mermaid,' she said. 'A slender woman who swims across the sea at night until she reaches land. She stands at the edge of the water, scanning the shoreline for visitors.

'Yes, of course she can stand,' she said, when I protested. 'Don't be so naïve and believe the fairytales. Mermaids are not those strange animals, half woman half fish – how could such a creature ever really charm a man? No, they are women who are made of water, who come out of the sea only to draw their men into it. They have long, lean limbs and large, dark eyes and they glide across the land with a beauty and grace equal to their strength and wickedness in the water.

'So, in the beginning, a woman made of water came walking out of the waves and stood waiting on the shore. A man was out walking one night and saw her there, naked and dappled with the moonlight. She saw him at the far side of the beach, almost hidden in the shadows of the forest. She knew that he was watching her and she started to dance.

'Very slowly she danced along the tidemarks, following patterns left by the ebb and flow of the sea, her legs kicking up the spray, her arms reaching up into the night sky as if to pull down the heavens themselves and wrap them like a blanket over her slender shoulders. The man from the forest came nearer, needing to see more, hoping in his heavy heart that she was not just a trick of the light. He wanted to reach her, to put his hand on her smooth white skin and draw her to him.

'The water-girl knew he was watching.

'When he crept closer he could hear her singing. You remember the boggarts' sweet songs that they made to call the princess away? Well, her songs were even sweeter than those. This was an old song, a song of love and new life, a softly-hummed song full of magic and wonder, like the echo that reaches a child in the womb when his mother sings to him. A song full of sweet promises and laughter. So what chance did the poor man have? The water-girl had no scaly hands or sharp shiny claws to frighten him away. All smooth skin and gentle music, there was nothing to warn him of the danger.

'When he was so close to her that she could feel his warm breath on her back, she looked over her shoulder at him and smiled. He had one glimpse of her clear blue eyes, full of longing and as deep as the water and he knew that he was in love.

'She saw the way he looked at her and it tore her heart in

two. Another misunderstanding: the mermaids are not cruel creatures, not wanton, evil, lurking creatures, like the boggarts of the forest. All they want is love. That is the deep sorrow that the man saw behind the water-girl's eyes. She wanted to be loved but she was only water. If he touched her she would shatter, and he would have been left trying to catch the salt water that would fall like tears into his hands.

'The water-girl saw love in his eyes and had to walk away. Still singing, she drifted out into the sea. The man followed. He walked until he was up to his waist in water and she was always just that little bit too far ahead, he could only touch the air that she passed through with his fingertips, but she could still feel his warm breath on her back.

'She could not bear it any more. She needed the touch of the strange man. She needed him to stay with her for ever in the dark waves, to hold her through the nights and to protect her in the days. The water-girl, half mad with love and longing, changed her song.

'She stopped moving and her lament became a charm, a terrifying screeching that startled her follower and made him put his hands to his ears to block out the shrill cries. The water-girl turned to face him, all wild laughter and shining eyes, and she stirred up the sea with her hands. He had never seen anything so terrible and yet so beautiful.

'It was the last thing he ever saw. For as she stirred up the water into a whirlpool the seaweed rose up and wrapped itself around the poor man's legs and held him fast. Then the sand and the silt and the clay and small rocks from the sea bed made their way up, following the water plants, until he was encased in stone up to his chin. He looked up at her, trying to breathe as the waves swept over his head, sand and silt cloying in his hair, his eyes full of fear and wonder.

'Then the beautiful water-girl leant over and kissed him. A lingering, long kiss like a sigh, as her body melted when she touched his lips, and all he knew was there was water rushing in through his mouth and nose with no room to breathe. The water-girl poured herself into the man she loved and stopped his heart beating. His eyes closed and by the morning all that was left of him was a pillar of rock standing tall and proud far out to sea, gleaming in the golden sunlight, crowned by the racing clouds.

'Sometimes at night she would come to him in a storm, all wild water with no female form at all, throwing herself up in white waves against the hard stone, as if she was trying to beat the tall pillar of rock into a man again, as if it could open its eyes and turn to look at her with love. But mostly she was happy just coming to him in the clear blue rippling waves that stroked down the edges of the rough rock until it gleamed in the moonlight, like a jewel set in the centre of the ocean.

'Only once a year, on the anniversary of his death, would she be a girl again. They say that on those nights she comes swimming over the water, back to the shore. She will catch you unaware one evening when you are walking with companions down to the secret beach to swim in the warm water. You will be lying back on the sand and you will see a movement on the waves and catch the faint sound of singing.

'It may be beautiful, but listen and you will be lost. You will be drawn out to sea and never set foot on the land again. You will spend the rest of your years as a rock in the ocean, weathered down by the water, your name and face forgotten to all but the water-girl who sang for you.

'And that was why we always found the beautiful beach desolate. Day or night, the sand was unmarked by strangers' footprints.'

'Except for yours,' I said. 'You were very brave.'

'No,' she said. 'No, I wasn't. I stopped going there after I knew. It didn't feel safe.'

'And the others?'

'One night they went off to the beach as usual but they never came back. The girls' bodies were washed up on the shore a couple of days later. Just a couple of young girls, the same age as me, battered by the waves, cut to pieces on the rocks, their bodies bloated with the water. But the boys were never found.

'Five mothers wept for weeks on end when they realised that their beautiful boys were never coming back. They were never going to come bounding up the front steps again, trailing mud through the house, smelling of beer and cigarettes and long nights out. Never again would their fathers shout at them from the doorway, demanding an explanation but receiving only sullen glances. The five sons were lost at sea.

'I went there one last time. I wanted to say farewell to my best friends with whom I had ruled the village that summer. I wanted to see the place that had taken them away, to stand alone on the shore and to cry for the friends who had left me behind. At the time my grief was so strong I thought it would have been better if I had drowned with them.

'And there, far out at sea, I could see a new line of boulders, black dots on the waves. There were five of them, huddled together, stranded and solid in the centre of the ocean.'

A cold wind blew suddenly across the rooftop, and I was startled, and jumped up, half expecting a sandstorm to come racing up to catch me. She laughed at my nervousness, and pulled me back down beside her. 'Oh, you fool,' she said. 'It's just a story.'

'Not a true story?'

No, I was just gullible. They told tales like that to frighten each other. They would build fires on the beach and sit up all night, scare each other so much they were obliged to make a pact to wait until sunrise before they disbanded.

I just didn't know which of her words to believe in any more.

She then declared it was time for us to go back to our new room downstairs. She pulled me down on to the living room floor. I fought back tears as, yet again, we quietly made love. She was all softness and compliments, but she would not open her eyes and look at me. Her slow movements were like sleepwalking. Afterwards, she pulled me to my feet and led me to the bedroom. Our discarded clothes lay abandoned on the rug, like remnants of a shipwreck. She tucked me into bed and put her arms round me, stroking my hair and whispering words of love. She was soon asleep, but I could not be so lucky. Those debating voices kept me awake all night, telling me not to be so paranoid, that it was just a story, and I should stop pulling our love apart with stupid suspicions. But louder voices told me that no, no, I should listen to her stories, I should be afraid, I should run, run out of the house, run back to my mother, or run and run out of London and never stop running, never for the rest of my life.

I lay very still beside her and watched until dawn.

# 22

Despite everything that had gone before, this is still the hardest part of the story for me to admit to. I am still weighed down by my own superstition: if I write things down, they will stay. And this will be the final truth of the matter, spelt out in black and white for all the world to read. The words hang heavy over me as I wrestle them on to the page. I wish I could fool myself with a different ending, write that all those dreams within dreams folded in on themselves and left me where I started. That like the simpletons of her stories, I had been subject to a cruel enchantment by the fairy folk, and had been living a waking dream, that I had been taken into another world, and seen how my life could have played out, only to be awoken suddenly with lessons learnt, and pride vanquished. I wish I could say that I woke to find that we were surrounded by the chaos of a new house, full of opportunities. That all the previous drama had only been in my mind and that we woke to find ourselves easily happy again.

But that would be a lie. In fact, the more distance I have the more I see the stark facts of the matter. As the year rolls round, it gives me perspective and makes me realise that, by this late stage, things were beyond my control. She was as good as gone. Worlds were colliding and there was nothing I could do to stop them.

I think I knew it at the time, but by then I had grown as adept as her at refusing to engage with all those things about our life that I didn't want to see. That morning, I crept out of bed, not even daring to kiss her goodbye. I stood above her for a while and watched the sheets move with the rise and fall of her breath. Old habits. Then I walked over to the window and locked it. I tried to move the ivy plant off the shelf, but by now it had flourished in the sunlight and grown all the way down into the floorboards. I tugged at the tendrils, but it was rooted fast. I got dressed quickly and locked the bedroom door behind me. I couldn't think of any other way to make her stay for sure, apart from to lock her in. Four strong walls to keep her safe for the day. That's all I ever wanted – just to keep her safe and well. I put the keys in the breast pocket of my shirt. They hung there, heavy, all morning long.

Work was an utterly different world. I made my way into the office with false confidence. The air-conditioning moved over me like a wave, cooling my skin and calming my head. I took my place at my desk. James was right behind me. We both did comedy double-takes as we saw each other's haggard faces.

'Good night last night?'

'Don't ask, mate, a bit of a weird one. Yours?'

'Yeah, a bit fucking weird.'

It was probably just as well that neither of us cared to elaborate.

We shared coffee and worked through our emails. Simon was conspicuous by his absence. He came rushing in at just past nine, looking unusually scrubbed clean and nervous. 'You're cutting it fine, Si!' laughed James. 'Looking good, though.'

Simon just scowled and pointedly pulled out a memo, which was hidden underneath the chaos of notes and maps and numbers piled high upon my desk. It was from Mr Collins reminding us that he had decided to give us our annual assessment a couple of months early, and we were to meet with him at eleven thirty.

James couldn't hide his enthusiasm. As the hours ticked away he was coming up with more ridiculous demands than ever, saying that we should band together and play Mr Collins at his own game, call his bluff, say we had been approached by rival firms and demand a pay rise equal to our merits. 'It's like anything,' said James, with authority. 'It's all about survival of the fittest.'

By the time eleven thirty came, Simon was frozen again. We had to prise him out of his chair and prop him up in the lift.

It should have been a good meeting.

We were seated across from Mr Collins's desk in deep leather chairs that dwarfed us. He was telling us that we had done him proud, and he was looking at a three-man promotion. That we had cracked the code, the three of us together, and shifted more wealth in the last year than any other junior team. We were a model to be replicated throughout the company, and had exceeded his expectations. We should go far.

Simon just nodded feverishly, a rictus grin fixed on his face. James was talking the talk, negotiating our next price.

So they didn't notice the disturbance in the corner of the room. The top drawer of the filing cabinet was open ever so slightly, and a trickle of sand was leaking out on to the carpet, snaking its way towards me. When Mr Collins opened the drawer to get our new contracts a wall of sand fell down behind him, followed by a huge typhoon wave of water, which knocked me to the ground.

Then James was holding me down on the floor of the office, the long strip of neon light hurting my eyes, swinging from the ceiling above me. Mr Collins was slapping my face and calling my name, and then a doctor was standing above me and telling me how everything was absolutely fine.

Then I was asleep.

It was such a relief to sleep. To have dreams that I was sure could only have been dreams. I was in the flat, and yet I wasn't there.

I wandered through our new living room and wondered at the beauty of it all. The glass stems of the oil lamps caught the light of the morning sun, which was streaming through the window, and the walls were awash with the reflections, streaks of blue green and yellow dappled light running down the wall, rainbows weaving around me on all sides. I was drawn to the lamps, wanting to turn them and watch how the light danced and the colours changed. But I couldn't touch them. They stayed solid while my hand passed through as if it was made of air.

I went into the bedroom and lay down on our soft new mattress. Again, I just sank through the sheets, passing through objects like a ghost, but I could feel the bed firm and warm under my back and I relaxed slowly, unconcerned about the insubstantial nature of my own body. I was comfortable, and it was only when I was about to drift off to sleep that I realised something was missing.

She wasn't there.

I didn't have the strength to get up and look for her. I was just so tired. When I held my hand up to my face to shield my eyes from the sunlight I realised how thin and insubstantial I had become. I could still see the shape of the window and the bright light shone through my transparent fingers.

But the banging at the window made me sit up and force myself to focus. She was thumping on the pane with the palm of her hand, calling my name. Her face was dirty and her hair was wet, and she was pressing herself up against the glass, her eyes wide and frightened.

'Let me in, let me in,' she shouted.

I reached for the keys, but they weren't there. I was only wearing a bathrobe they had given me at hospital, rather than my work shirt, and had no idea what had happened to my keys. I ran over to the window and tried to force it – there was only the glass between us and I could see the tears welling up in her eyes. The ivy had grown through a crack beneath the window-frame, she was hanging on very tightly, but the window was locked fast. She watched as I hammered on the pane, trying to make it break, but of course it was too solid or I was too weak. I shouted at her to wait but she smiled and I could hear her say,

'Locks and bolts, locks and bolts are never good.' She shook her head and began to climb down. I couldn't open the window. I couldn't follow.

# 23

I used to believe that when someone leaves you they must always leave for better things. I comforted myself with that thought as I grew older, as I left behind childhood friends, or as they left me. Everyone moves on and everyone learns and we all have happy lives among the company that suits us best. Now I find myself hoping that's not true.

So she went.

It must have been eleven thirty in the morning. All the clocks in the flat had stopped at that hour. I got back from the hospital at four o'clock, groggy and hoping to be comforted. I stepped into a silent home, still scattered with the remains of the night before. The sundress she had been wearing lay forlorn and formless, abandoned on the rug. I called for her as I wandered through the flat, but the only reply I got was my voice, echoing off the walls. I ran up the steps to the rooftop garden, and there, hidden among the overflowing blossoms, were the bottles and the wineglasses, remnants of our last night's revelry. The champagne corks lay strewn across the patio, a reminder of all the toasts she had enforced upon me.

'Here's to us!' she had cried. 'And only us!' and I had laughed along with her.

'I love you,' I had said. 'My love, I love you more than you could ever know.'

'Here's to love!' she had cried, refilling my glass. 'Here's to love, and long may it last.'

I ran back downstairs, having locked the door behind me. I looked in all her usual hiding-places, double-checked behind doors, behind curtains, even inside the wardrobe. But there were just her clothes, abandoned on the hangers, still holding some of the shape of her. There was no sign of her departure, just the clocks, frozen.

I'd like to think that that's how it really is. She has stepped out of the flat and time has frozen. A stasis. The world has stopped turning until she returns.

But it wasn't like that at all. When I dropped plates, or threw her photographs across the room, they broke into tiny pieces. They did not stop in mid-air, suspended in flight. Things break. They break all the time now.

So she has left me for better things. I couldn't catch her. I couldn't ever really keep her in my sight.

I look to the stories I remember, trying to find answers that might fit. In the end, it comes down to two possible interpretations:

1. She was always too good for this world. She was so perfect, so graceful and gentle on her good days, yet she was more

fragile than I ever knew, more so than I ever realised. She deserved a better place than that dirty city: she needed a landscape that blossomed with joy as she ran through it. If I had been able to, I would have made it for her. I would have pulled up that carpet of flowers and carried it home. I would have brought back saplings of those wild ferns and replanted them on the rooftop. I would have let the ivy creep over the whole house and shut us away from everything. Nothing else mattered.

But I couldn't give her the life she merited, so instead she ran back to her proper place, back out to sea. I can see her now, dancing along the tidemarks, singing up at the fast-racing clouds. I imagine her as a child again, transformed back to a little girl charming strange sea creatures out to the shore, climbing high up on their backs, then being carried back across the waves, off in search of the adventures that I could never give her.

If this is the case, I do try to understand, but her absence is hard.

Even now, on these crisp February mornings, as I wash, shave and prepare myself for another empty day, I am still not used to seeing only myself reflected. I hate it, standing alone at the bathroom basin, squinting back at myself in the morning light, my pale face as unrecognisable as those fractured reflections she used to mock me on the seashore. Some mornings I forget and expect to wake up, turn round and watch the smile break across her face as I stroke her awake, her hair falling across her shoulders, tumbling into the sunlight on the pillow. It still hurts when I remember.

But if this is true, if she really has just strayed across to that other land for a while, perhaps one day she may tire of her freedom: one day, she may return. Maybe she will still have some faint memory of our city-bound days and come back one night, out of curiosity. I imagine her face pressed up against the window, hidden in shadows, as she watches me preparing for bed. I see her carrying bunches of flowers, which she holds balanced in the crook of her arm, the other hand gently pushing open the window, inch by inch, biting her lip so that her laughter doesn't give her away. It may happen, she may care enough to come back, one last time, to lie beside me and soothe me to sleep.

I keep my window open always.

I imagine that I will wake in the middle of the night as she climbs back in, moonlight on her skin, her hair weighed down with water, carrying the smell of the sea back into my house, sand in my sheets again as she comes to lie beside me. I will wake to find her smiling down at me, her eyes as wild as the night sky. I will reach out to her and hold her close again. We will curl up in bed together and I will stroke her hair as she tells me tales of her adventures in strange lands, and I will tell her how hard the days have been without her, days and nights that I dragged myself through, and she will know she was right to come back.

'My poor troubled man,' she will say. 'I'll never leave you again.'

If it could happen like that, all would be well.

Those first few weeks, I really could see no other ending for us. There was no other option but for her to return, to realise that her place was with me. As the days passed, I grew more impatient. I would find myself roaming the common at dusk. I ran into the woods calling for her. I would hide behind trees and watch silently as other couples walked hand in hand down our pathways home. I would wait until the night grew dark, and then stumble back, blind, always straining for the sound of lighter footsteps behind me. I could almost hear her calling, 'Catch me if you can! If you can!' but I could never see her. Those nights I wouldn't let myself sleep. I sat perched on her window-ledge, outstaring the night, willing the common to re-form itself. I played with the ivy, plaiting it and unplaiting it between my fingers. The plant still carried traces of her hair, woven now into the very roots. But it never moved for me, and every night, the land outside the window was only ever the daytime woods.

When I went back to work, two weeks later, wrecked and with no explanations, I was told to take a holiday. Then there were the difficult visits by the police. They looked suspiciously at the blank spaces on our walls and the cuts on my hands.

They found it strange that I had no photographs of her. 'You have nothing, sir? Nothing at all?'

I think they suspected me of concealing evidence. I sat very still and answered their questions. Wisely, I only told them about our daytimes. I said she was restless. A good word – it eventually inspired sympathy and they left me alone.

But by then I had been away from work for too long. I got a large cheque and a two-line letter. They had found someone more stable to take my place and I never saw James or Simon again. It was just as well. I realised that the only reason I had loved the city for so long was because she shielded me from it. Without her it was all loud noise and sharp edges. The underground was a grey labyrinth with hostile people at every turning. There was nothing good to come home to, no bright rooms full of music and flowers to greet me. Nothing worthwhile left to greet me at all.

The flat I had once loved became unbearable. I felt haunted in every room, so I methodically pulled our home apart, packing our life away. All those hours and that laughter and warmth reduced to a series of bags and boxes. I took all her clothes out of the wardrobe, and scattered them across our bed. There was the long white dress she had been wearing the first night I met her; here her favourite old dungarees, still muddied from her time among the flowers. Here was her soft silk evening dress, which she used to wear to please me. She had worn it on the first warm night, the night before the boys arrived. That evening I had come home to find the house in darkness, and a trail of night-lights leading me up on to the roof. She had reconstructed an old picnic table up on the newly finished patio. I had to tiptoe through a maze of night-lights to reach her, and she was perched on the table, laughing, surrounded by bowls of oysters, champagne, asparagus, every aphrodisiac you could imagine.

'Are you hungry?' she said.

She had scattered rose petals all over the Astroturf and we made love among the blossoms. No one could see and no one could find us.

I allowed myself one night sleeping buried among her clothes, then the next morning I took them up on to the rooftop and burnt them all. The smoke danced out over the common, still carrying something of her in even that movement. The bright blossom of the plants was also too much of a difficult reminder. So I simply stopped watering them and let them die a natural death.

Apart from the ivy. I set to that with hammer and scissors, smashing the pot, cutting through the roots. After the initial fury it took half a day of snipping away between the floorboards to remove it completely, the Anglepoise above giving me a surgeon's clarity. Then I pulled our window tight shut for the last time and felt something inside me also closing.

So I left the city behind. I sold the flat and I moved south, it seemed to make sense. I didn't go and live in her village – that was hers and I had no right to be there. Instead I went looking for somewhere I thought she might like to settle, with more space for her. I was so sure she would come back and I wanted it to be perfect. Inevitably, I was drawn to the sea and I found a cove, a quiet little place that might have been the very beach where she had set her legend, except there wasn't a forest, only thick ferns, and a few more houses like mine, perched near the shore. I hope it doesn't get too busy when the summer finally comes. If it does come. I still can't imagine how summer might be without her.

So I moved to the sea, still tired and drawn out and waiting for her return. Those first weeks, I didn't sleep much. I remembered Richard and Phil's conversation, heard through the wall all those months ago, and I stayed up through the nights making a home she would have been proud of.

I put flowers around the room and I waited. But one night I

went to sleep by mistake and woke up and realised that she hadn't come and I hadn't missed anything. I am sleeping through more and more nights now – it's rare for me to watch until the dawn. I'm still frightened of the many moods of the ocean but, even so, when I cannot sleep I go down to the water's edge and watch the patterns of the waves, rippling through the darkness. I look up at a sky that is blistering with stars. Some nights I see shooting stars streaming through the firmament and think of her, and her love of fallen angels, and strain my eyes to try to see where they might land.

I have done everything I can think of. I have played her music. I have walked by the sea. I have learnt to cook the meals she once cooked for me. Nothing happens. And the more time that passes, the more what little I had left of her slips away from me. I can no longer see her face clearly. I am losing snippets of our earliest conversations. Even her favourite stories are beginning to fall apart. It is hard, without those love letters, or even any photographs. I have precious little to remind me of better days.

So I returned to my notebooks, their margins crowded with illustrations, revisited my encoded maps, and tried to tell our tale. As I said, I began writing this to pin it all down, fix the memories with words before they, also, became shattered or lost, eroded by the passing seasons. This is the last thing I could think of that might bring her back. She once told me that words could do anything – build cities and change lives. Her words, maybe. Mine stumble over each other on the page and create a poor, one-sided shadow of the life we shared: fragments of days stitched together with my clumsy phrasing, not at all like she would have told it. But she still does not come and the words are running out. So I have to face the other alternative:

2. I should have been more careful and kept her safe. She gave me plenty of signs. Her need for protection, the way she held my hand. Her mood swings that shook her so, those bad days when she was nervous and restless, with black clouds gathering all around. She tried to tell me what she needed, and I didn't really listen. I didn't use my time as well as I could have.

I should have been bolder and wiser, should never have been daunted by that creeping forest. No, from the ivy's first visitation I should have run hollering through the woods, run faster and caught her at the clearing. I should have held her in that pool of moonlight and kissed her, broken the enchantment. Perhaps any words might have worked, all she needed to hear was my voice, calling out my love to her though the night, and pleading with her to come home. It was through lack of courage that I lost her. I couldn't be the man she needed, the man who stood strong and tall and proud against the horizon.

So, like the princess, she wandered too far away, lost for ever in a world of overgrown trees and dark water, a world that was always lurking closer than I thought, just the other side of the wall, a strange black place that grew over the months, every night getting that bit nearer.

The shame at my own shortcomings still comes creeping over my bed at night, and I find myself waking, crying out for her, screaming that it should have been me, not her, who was lost, and then other voices tell me that no, no, my punishment is far worse and far more fitting, as I will wait alone, with false hope. Even now a world without her is unimaginable, and as I write, I catch myself looking out of the window – just in case anything is moving across the waves. As always, only the moonlight on the water.

So that's what it comes down to. My two endings. Now it is done, I still can't see which one to trust in. Two endings, like two paths that stretch before you in the middle of the forest. Not sure which will lead me to her I stand undecided, looking for clues.

# MAGGIE O'FARRELL

# My Lover's Lover

'A gripping exploration of the ambivalence at the heart of intimate relationships . . . keenly observed, superbly imagined' *Mail on Sunday*

When Lily moves into Marcus's flat, she is intrigued by signs of his recently departed ex-lover. A single dress left hanging in the wardrobe, a mysterious mark on the wall, the lingering odour of jasmine.

Who was this woman? And what exactly were the circumstances of her sudden disappearance? It doesn't take long for Lily's curiosity to grow into an all-pervading obsession.

'As soon as I'd finished *My Lover's Lover* . . . I rushed to my local bookshop to acquire her first [novel] – that is the drug-like strength of O'Farrell's storytelling' *Literary Review*

'Written so beautifully, with such startling, delicate and original images . . . a triumph' Barbara Trapido

'An unusual, suspenseful tale . . . her writing is exquisite, skilfully laying a trail of half-truths and mystery to ensnare and enthral' *Time Out*

'Brilliantly describes how old relationships can haunt new lovers' *Elle*

'A psychological drama with, at its core, the timeless theme of love betrayed . . . shock, grief and loss spring from the page as intensely as they did in O'Farrell's first book' *Sunday Telegraph*

0 7472 6817 7

**review**

SUSIE BOYT

# The Last Hope of Girls

'Sometimes Martha wishes that her experience of family life was more like that of other people. Luckily for us, it's not, for the heroine of Boyt's third novel is a wonderful creation' *Marie Claire*

Newly installed as live-in caretaker of four Oxford Street flats, Martha Brazil can scarcely believe her luck. After years of stuffy bedsits and seedy suburban flatshares, the future seems electric with the promise of renovation and repair. Cruising her local department store by day, and thrilling to the sounds of revelry that float through her window at night, it strikes her that surely an independent young person with flair and a surplus of willpower ought to shine in such a setting.

But when out of the blue a copy of her father's latest novel falls into her hands, it offers Martha a view of her world, and of her wayward family, that she can only ignore at her peril.

Praise for *The Last Hope of Girls*:

'Unconventional, unsettling and beautifully written... Witty, laser-assisted vignettes suffuse *The Last Hope of Girls*' Lynne Truss, *Sunday Times*

'Boyt has a painter's eye for colour and detail... her text is as alive with symbolism as a Holbein painting... Very likeable' *Independent on Sunday*

'[A] touching, romantic tale of a young woman adrift amid the bright lights of London' *Mirror*

'A very sensitively observed novel, as though the central character has one less layer of skin than other people... Written with a very visual, almost painterly eye for detail' *Daily Mail*

'Thoughtful and emotional... A really meaty read' *Company*

0 7472 6515 1

review

You can buy any of these other **Review** titles from your bookshop or *direct from the publisher*.

FREE P&P AND UK DELIVERY
(Overseas and Ireland £3.50 per book)

| | | |
|---|---|---|
| A History of Forgetting | Caroline Adderson | £6.99 |
| The Catastrophist | Ronan Bennett | £6.99 |
| The Mariner's Star | Candida Clark | £6.99 |
| Hallam Foe | Peter Jinks | £6.99 |
| This is Not a Novel | Jennifer Johnston | £6.99 |
| The Song of Names | Norman Lebrecht | £6.99 |
| In Cuba I was a German Shepherd | Ana Menéndez | £6.99 |
| The Secret Life of Bees | Sue Monk Kidd | £6.99 |
| My Lover's Lover | Maggie O'Farrell | £6.99 |
| Early One Morning | Robert Ryan | £6.99 |
| Missing | Mary Stanley | £6.99 |
| The Hound in the Left-Hand Corner | Giles Waterfield | £6.99 |
| God Breathes His Dreams Through Nathaniel Cadwallader | Charlotte Fairbairn | £6.99 |

TO ORDER SIMPLY CALL THIS NUMBER

**01235 400 414**

or visit our website: www.madaboutbooks.com

Prices and availability subject to change without notice.